I0664940

On Paradise Row

Also by Sharon L. Jansen

Margaret Cavendish: The Female Academy. Saltar's Point Press, 2017.

Margaret Cavendish: The Convent of Pleasure. Saltar's Point Press, 2016.

Mary Astell: Some Reflections upon Marriage. Saltar's Point Press, 2014.

Mary Astell: A Serious Proposal to the Ladies. Saltar's Point Press, 2014.

Anne of France: "Lessons for My Daughter." The Library of Medieval Women. Boydell & Brewer, 2012.

Reading Women's Worlds from Christine de Pizan to Doris Lessing: A Guide to Six Centuries of Women Writers Imagining Rooms of Their Own. Palgrave Macmillan, 2011.

The Monstrous Regiment of Women: Female Rule in Early Modern Europe. Queenship and Power, ed. Carole Levin and Charles Beem. Palgrave Macmillan, 2010.

Debating Women, Politics, and Power in Early Modern Europe. Palgrave Macmillan, 2008.

Sharon L. Jansen

On Paradise Row

Saltar's
Point
Press

First published 2020 by
Saltar's Point Press
14300 32nd Ave. NE, #401, Seattle WA 98125

ISBN-13: 978-0-578-65506-2

Cover design by Kristian Jansen Jaech.

Cover detail from G. Munson's "water-colour drawing" of Paradise Row, reproduced
in Reginald Blunt's *Paradise Row; or, a Broken Piece of Old Chelsea* . . . (London,
1906).

Your glass will not do you half so much service as a serious reflection on your own minds.

Mary Astell
A Serious Proposal to the Ladies
1694

Contents

Author's Note

On Paradise Row is a work of fiction. Mostly.

The novel imagines a few weeks in the life of the seventeenth-century English philosopher and writer Mary Astell, who has been called the first English feminist. A quiet woman who spends her day in meditation and study, Astell is surprised by the sudden arrival of a young woman whose unwelcome presence interrupts her peaceful routine and challenges her calm certitudes. To solve the problems created by this uninvited guest, Astell must negotiate not only the vast city of London but also the obstacles women face there. As she makes her way through the dirt and dangers of the crowded streets, she must also find a way through the social, political, and religious institutions designed by those who have little interest in, much less sympathy for, anyone who is not rich or powerful—and male.

While the story is entirely the product of my imagination, the novel's plot incorporates many details and events drawn from the lives of real women who lived in late seventeenth-century England.

Mary Astell was well known in literary London, her person and her work both celebrated and satirized by her contemporaries. Today her most frequently read works are *A Serious Proposal to the Ladies* (1694) and *Some Reflections upon Marriage* (1700). In late 1696, when the events of this novel unfold, she had just come to live in a newly constructed terraced house on Paradise Row in the village of Chelsea.

Several of the other characters in the novel are also based on real women, Astell's friends and acquaintances in Chelsea: Lady Catherine Jones, daughter of the earl of Ranelagh; Elizabeth King, the wife of the rector of All Saints Church; and Mary Methuen, whose sweet-smelling honeysuckle was admired and commented on by several of her neighbors, including Mary Astell.

Other characters include historical women whom Astell might have encountered as she went about her business in the city: the scandalous Hortense Mancini, duchess of Mazarin, who also resided on Paradise Row; Anne Tenison, wife of the archbishop of Canterbury, and her "faithful" attendant, Ann Stubbs; Mary Kettilby, author of *A Collection of above Three Hundred Receipts in Cookery, Physic, and Surgery*, printed by Richard Wilkin, the bookseller who published many of Astell's works.

Still others who make an appearance in *On Paradise Row* are women who were known in seventeenth-century London, but who were probably not the kind of women with whom Mary Astell would have had an acquaintance—outside the pages of a novel, that is. Among them are Gertrude Rolles, a successful milliner with a shop in the Royal Exchange; Mrs. Ball, the proprietor of a marriage house in the Fleet; and Elizabeth Wisebourne, a notorious brothel-keeper whose premises were on Drury Lane.

All of these women—Mary Astell, her friends, her neighbors, and her contemporaries—have left at least some evidence of their lives in London, and I have tried to make real characters out of the tantalizing bits of information that have survived.

For the lives of the other women whose stories are told here—disgruntled maidservants, working women, impoverished widows, and runaway apprentices—I have turned to a variety of sources, including witness depositions, criminal examinations, trial records, settlement and poor relief appeals, livery company records, wills, and other kinds of archival material. These female characters may be fictional, but the circumstances of their lives are real enough.

For the reader who would like to know more about the history behind the fiction, I encourage you to visit the novel's companion website, *On Paradise Row* (https://onparadiserow.com). There you will find maps, portraits, a timeline of historical events, biographical details, and a variety of contextual materials. There are also links to copies of newspapers, like the *London Gazette*, to diaries and summaries of parliamentary debate, to legal proceedings and court reports, and to information about Chelsea in the late seventeenth-century.

I have spent years thinking and writing about Mary Astell. I've read her work with scores of students. I've walked the length of Paradise Row (now Royal Hospital Road), visited the Chelsea Physic Garden, and had my picture snapped while I was standing next to a sign reading "The Royal Borough of Kensington and Chelsea, Astell Street, SW3"—in the photo, I am grinning like a madwoman. You might well conclude that I am little obsessed.

And so I have a confession to make. Mary Astell hated "idle novels" and thought that reading them was not only a waste of time but would also lead "to the practice of the greatest follies." I am sure she would despise *On Paradise Row*. I can only offer my apologies and, in my defense, say that it is a product of much love and admiration.

Friday, October 16, 1696

She was not beautiful. Nor was she charming, a word so often used to describe a woman who was not beautiful but who was, nevertheless, appealing in some ineffable way to her many admirers. There were no admirers.

Her hair was not silky and abundant, nor did it curl loosely around her face in soft tendrils. Her eyes were neither sparkling nor full of mischief, her nose neither slender nor pert. Her laughter did not tinkle merrily, nor did she giggle delightfully. On the rare occasion when she might be persuaded to smile, no captivating dimples appeared on rosy cheeks. There was nothing at all soft or sweet or yielding about her. And she was no longer young.

Nor could she be described as elegant or graceful. She dressed plainly and modestly, with no regard for what might be considered flattering, much less fashionable. Although she carried herself with dignity, she was awkward, holding herself stiffly, her back rigid with a kind of stubborn pride.

She had no interest whatsoever in cultivating the dainty arts for which women were so widely admired and praised—she did not sing or play or draw or embroider. Neither did she involve herself in the pastimes with which women of her class filled the otherwise empty hours of their days: she did not pay afternoon visits or amuse herself at cards or attend balls or go to the theater. She did not exchange pleasantries, encourage gossip, or engage in tittle-tattle.

And, then, she was not at all deferential, nor was she soft-spoken. In her conversation, she was straightforward, her words few and to the point. This habit of directness might be admirable, but it could prove troublesome: she was at times impatient, even abrupt, and she could also be a little condescending. She was frequently curt, her tone sharp, her criticism unsparing if honest.

While she was acknowledged as that most unlikely of creatures, a woman of reason, she could on occasion be so certain of the truth of her own views that it was difficult to persuade her that she might be mistaken. She was also possessed of a fierce intelligence, although many who encountered her considered this to be among her most lamentable attributes.

On that bitterly cold October evening, as she made her way across London in the rain, home to Chelsea, she was troubled. She may even have muttered to herself as she walked, a deep furrow creasing her brow.

Still, while she was not beautiful or graceful or delightful in any way, while there was nothing about her that would appeal to any young admirers, much less inspire them to flattery or to acts of gallantry, there was something about her. More than one man was struck by her figure as she passed by him that evening. And once he had observed her, no man could ignore her or forget her.

But she paid none of these curious observers any mind as she walked on, through the evening and the rain, intent as she was on reaching Paradise Row.

One

The narrow entry hall of the house on Paradise Row was crowded as she pushed open the door, three shadowy figures pressing toward her in the dim light.

"Oh, Mary, just as I feared—you are wet through," murmured Lady Catherine, "and not even a link-boy to light you on such a night . . . " She paused and shook her head in exasperation, but she saw no point in any further reproof.

Nor would she remind her friend that the Ranelagh coach stood at her disposal or that a hackney might also have been hired, an expense that Lady Catherine would gladly have borne herself. To remonstrate would be useless. Mary Astell would hear of neither, judging either mode of more comfortable transport to be unnecessary, even considering the day's unusual circumstances. To be altogether fair, however, neither would Astell complain about the rain or the darkness of the hour or fatigue, so Lady Catherine rightly judged that nothing more should be said on the matter.

A young housemaid, animated by the series of events that had disrupted the usual dull routine of her usually dull day, pushed forward from behind Lady Catherine, nearly toppling that most dignified of personages in her excitement. In her careless way and in disregard of all decorum, the girl compounded her error by treading on the skirts of Lady Ranelagh. Although these improprieties were duly noted by Lady Catherine, who missed nothing, she thought it best not to draw attention to Sarah's indiscretions and failings.

Lady Catherine was responsible for having inserted the untrained girl into Astell's household, a maneuver that had required persistence and not a little subtlety on her part. So, at least for the moment, Lady Catherine thought it best to overlook the minor transgressions of her protégé, who had, so far at least, proved to be utterly resistant to discipline and of no real use whatsoever in the small house on Paradise Row. Whether Sarah's rash behavior might yet be subdued and turned to good account was still to be determined. As for Lady Ranelagh, she was far too interested in what Mary Astell might have to report than to pay any mind to her skirts.

"Please, ma'am, may I have your cloak?" Sarah asked. "I will hang it by the fire so it will dry." The girl was indolent and undisciplined, an unfortunate combination, but on this occasion, she was determined to play a role, however minor, in the drama that was unfolding in the house.

"As long as you can avoid putting it *in* the fire, Sarah," Astell replied, her tone a little sharper than she intended. Although she would scarcely admit it (even to herself), she was very tired and almost overcome by the drama that had interrupted her otherwise ordered life. On another day, she would have been the first to acknowledge that further damage would hardly render the garment any less unattractive than it already was.

"Not so close to the flames this time," she added, as the girl snatched the shapeless lump of wet wool from her mistress.

Nearly upsetting Lady Catherine once more in her haste to be about her task, Sarah retreated to the kitchen without another word, trailing the cloak behind her and leaving the three women to themselves in the shadowy and somewhat cramped entryway.

"Will you take some refreshment? Have you had any nourishment at all today, my dear Mary?"

"How is she faring? Has there been any change in her condition since I left?"

"Were you able to find anything out, Mary?"

The three women spoke at once, their anxious questions left hanging in the chill air.

•

The Lady Catherine Jones, daughter of Richard Jones, first earl of Ranelagh, was Mary Astell's oldest and dearest friend. The two were among the growing number of unmarried women then residing in the village of Chelsea, and like so many of those single women, they had long ago decided to continue their pleasant way of life without the unpleasant encumbrance of a husband—although, in truth, there was little likelihood now of a prospective suitor emerging for either woman.

Having determinedly pursued a life of independence, Mary Astell was quite willing to concede the value of marriage for others. The institution was, as she readily acknowledged, the only *honorable* way of continuing mankind. But if marriage were indeed such a blessed state, why then, she had been known to ask, were there so few happy marriages? This was a question upon which she had reflected for some time. As for herself, as she once wrote to a friend, "I cannot be sufficiently thankful that I have been so very fortunate as to escape a state attended so generally with so many mishaps."

Like Mary Astell, Lady Catherine was not interested in a husband—or, to be more accurate, she was not interested in acquiring one of her own. Some years earlier, after a brief turn as one of the king's many mistresses, her elder sister had married John Fitzgerald, the eighteenth earl of Kildare, while her younger sister was soon expected to marry Thomas Coningsby, recently appointed to the privy council. (Unfortunately, Sir Thomas was already in possession of a wife, an entanglement that was most inconvenient for Lady Frances Jones.) The successful resolution of her family's campaign to acquire two such excellent husbands had done nothing to inspire in Lady Catherine a desire for one of her own. Now approaching her thirtieth birthday, she was still a very handsome woman, but neither her person nor her father's connections had attracted the interest of would-be suitors in quite some time, a state of affairs with which she was well satisfied.

Lady Catherine had first made the acquaintance of Mary Astell almost a decade earlier. Newly arrived in London, the young Astell had found herself disappointed by friends on whom she thought she could rely. When they proved themselves to be less than reliable, the penniless Mary Astell was reduced to a miserable state, forced to pawn her clothing for subsistence. When Lady Catherine learned of this desperate situation, she had considered it her Christian duty to offer alms to the friendless young woman in her time of distress.

But the prickly Mary Astell had rejected Lady Catherine's charity. She did not look for pity, nor could she abide condescension. And to the amazement of those who thought to find her a "suitable" position, Mary Astell refused a place as a lady's companion and declined the opportunity of becoming a governess—she insisted that she had come to the capital to become a writer. Those whose assistance she rejected shook their heads and whispered among themselves that the poor young woman's wits had been turned. But Lady Catherine Jones thought otherwise.

Instead of charitable relief, she offered Mary Astell her patronage. Thus supported, Astell took up her pen and threw herself into the political and religious battles then commanding all the energies and ambitions of the city's philosophers and fools. Astell rather quickly proved that she was not to be numbered among the fools. Now, some ten years on, Lady Catherine was Mary Astell's most intimate friend as well as her most loyal patron. And at long last, after their many years of devoted friendship, Lady Catherine had persuaded her friend to allow herself to be installed in the terraced house on Paradise Row.

The countess of Ranelagh, by contrast, was an altogether different kind of woman. Although Lady Ranelagh was much the same age as Lady Catherine, she had come into her life only recently and in a most disagreeable way: Lady Margaret Cecil had married the earl of Ranelagh five months after the death of his long-suffering wife, Lady Catherine's mother.

While a man of his birth, breeding, and rash nature might be expected to remarry, and that quite quickly, the earl of Ranelagh's chosen bride was some thirty years younger than he was and not at all inclined to be a faithful wife to him. Lord Ranelagh was nonetheless exceedingly pleased with the bargain he had struck and considered himself most fortunate in the match—his wife was a rare beauty and, not concerned with marital fidelity himself, he did not require it of her, trusting in the discretion, if not the constancy, of his new countess.

Lady Catherine Jones had looked askance at her father's choice for a second wife, judging his swift remarriage to be a more intemperate act than was his usual intemperate wont. But to have offered an opinion on the matter would have been futile even if the reckless old earl had solicited it, and since he had not, there was nothing to be done but for her to accept the new countess with grace and forbearance.

And yet Lady Margaret Cecil had proven to be irresistible, whatever Lady Catherine's initial hesitations may have been. The second Lady Ranelagh was undeniably very beautiful—indeed, she was lauded as one of the great beauties of the day, her portrait commissioned by Queen Mary, painted by the renowned Sir Godfrey Kneller, presented to King William for his pleasure, and even now hanging in the Water Gallery at Hampton Court. She appeared also to be flighty and frivolous.

But her superficiality was a convenient mask, a guise allowing Lady Ranelagh to avoid burdensome duties she did not wish to bear and disagreeable acquaintances she did not wish to encounter. "Only a fool will suffer the intolerable waste of her time," she asserted, a judgment with which neither Lady Catherine nor Mary Astell could disagree. Lady Ranelagh's vanity, however, was undeniable, and her love of fashionable display accounted for the volume of the silk skirts upon which the unfortunate young Sarah had so carelessly trod.

Still, what had begun as a relationship of necessity between Lady Catherine and Lady Ranelagh soon became one of affection, and even the serious-minded Mary Astell could not resist a growing fondness for her new acquaintance. Thus the presence of the Lady Ranelagh in the house on Paradise Row that evening.

"I suppose you came through Five Fields, Mary, and of course you have traveled alone, but you really should not have done—if you persist in refusing to hire a coach, you might certainly have remained in town with Mr. Wilkin and his family. It would have been much safer for you to return home in daylight. We could have managed here until your return, as you well know."

Although she meant to mind her tongue, Lady Catherine found that, after all, she could not keep silent. Her relief at her friend's safe return overwhelmed her discretion for the moment. But even to herself she sounded somewhat peevish.

To travel home to Chelsea from the city, Mary Astell would have come not on the king's private road but by means of a well-worn track through open fields, and, as she approached the village, she would have had to cross the little Westbourne as it flowed south to the Thames. The small stone bridge over the river at the boundary between Westminster and Chelsea was a favorite spot for the footpads, rogues, and robbers who lurked nearby, lying in wait for the solitary or unwary traveler.

This path had a notorious reputation, and to travel its length at night was a risk that many men would not have taken without companions to accompany them on their way. Indeed, even those entitled to travel on the king's own road faced ever-present dangers. Just a week earlier, all Chelsea had been consumed by the report of a gentleman and two ladies traveling to town from the village during broad daylight—their coach had been waylaid by three highwaymen who thrust their drawn swords into the coach, relieving the occupants of their valuables.

"I would have liked to consult with Mr. Wilkin, my lady, but I did not dare to stop on the way to Lambeth, and then, since I had to wait such a long time to see His Grace, I thought I had best make my way home directly," said Astell. "There was really nothing more for me to do in town."

She was aware of Lady Catherine's concern for her safety and irritation at her frugality—it was a well-worn source of disagreement between them, and usually the two women could smile even as they went through the motions of the familiar argument. For now, though, Astell attempted to address her friend's fears, if only indirectly. "By the time I left His Grace, it was so late that I got a sculler to cross from Lambeth rather than walking all the way to the Bridge."

Astell carefully removed her hat as she spoke. Her skirt and petticoats were wet and muddy, but she was otherwise reasonably dry—her wool cloak was no thing of beauty, but it was thick and warm, despite its age and wear. And though she might have grudged the penny she paid the waterman for her passage across the Thames, she had spared no expense when she purchased her wide-brimmed beaver hat, her finely knitted boot-hose, and her sturdy leather boots. They were not in the least bit fashionable—Lady Ranelagh would never have worn them under any circumstances—but they were of excellent quality, and Astell had taken great care with her purchases to ensure their comfort and durability. "Perhaps we should go through," she added.

Suddenly aware of the chill in the hall and of the coal fire burning in the parlor, the three women turned from the dark entry into its warmth and light.

Lady Ranelagh wrinkled her nose. Although the room was undeniably warm, she did not at all care for the smell of the coal that was burning in the grate—at Ranelagh, they used only wood for their fires, despite its soaring cost. But Mary Astell, whose father and grandfather had been coal merchants, did not mind the fumes, a bittersweet reminder of her childhood home.

Moreover, a distant cousin, recently arrived in London, had proved himself eager to keep Astell furnished with a plentiful quantity of coal and of fine wax candles—a small enough expense for the canny young man of business, who regarded it as a sound investment. A generous supply of both was now regularly delivered to the house on Paradise Row. In return, Mr. John Astell could happily dine out on his tales of "the ingenious Mrs. Astell," the woman whose writing was the talk of the town, from the fashionable residents of Pall Mall to the impoverished hack writers of Grub Street. At the same time, the enterprising young man made no secret that he hoped Astell's connection to the earl of Ranelagh, member of the Privy Council, Paymaster-General of His

Majesty's Forces, and treasurer of the new royal hospital in Chelsea, might prove to be the source of profitable business for him at some point in the near future. Since Astell had no fear that the shrewd and unscrupulous old earl would allow himself to be used by an ambitious young merchant, she was content that her exchange with her cousin was a fair one.

The terraced house on Paradise Row was part of the wave of new development that had followed the construction of Chelsea Hospital, founded some years earlier for destitute and disabled military veterans. As soon as the hospital project was underway, canny aristocrats like Lord Ranelagh acquired leases from the crown (on excellent terms, of course) in order to build grand houses on land surrounding the massive complex. At the same time, ambitious speculators, eager for quick returns on their investments, had begun to develop desirable properties on what had once been open fields. Work on Paradise Row began just as the Hospital was nearing completion; constructed of warm brick with a continuous red-tiled roof, the two-story terrace was the first of many developments undertaken in the rapidly expanding village.

The house Mary Astell occupied was small, but the rooms inside were surprisingly well proportioned. The ceilings were high, and the rows of double-sashed windows across the front ensured that the rooms on both the ground and first floors were filled with natural light.

The front room, just off the entry, was carefully though sparsely furnished. While Astell's own needs were few, she was concerned for the comfort of her guests, so the parlor was furnished with four padded armchairs upholstered with Turkey-work. Placed handily to the side of each of the chairs was a small walnut table, free of unnecessary ornaments.

Rather than the dark colors favored by her Chelsea neighbors, Astell had whitewashed the ceilings of the parlor and the small dining room just behind it; likewise, she had not covered the wainscot with textile hangings or panels of figured wall paper (a densely foliaged "forest-work" pattern being especially popular with her neighbors). Instead, the highly polished oak panels gleamed in the light of the coal fire, the endless task of smoothing and rubbing them until they glowed being one of the routine tasks that young Sarah found particularly disagreeable.

No carpets lay over the wide floorboards, which were always cleanly swept and polished. Rather than the velvet and damask favored by her neighbors, the curtains at each window were plain linen, not edged in lace or held back by tassels and ribbons or topped by an ornamented valance. They were simple, like the other furnishings in the room, but the overall effect of this simplicity was harmonious and restful.

Aside from the colorful woolen embroidery on the upholstered chairs, the decorative elements in the parlor were few: a border of blue and white Delft tiles surrounding the brick fireplace, and, on the mantle, a pendulum clock in a simple wooden case (quite unlike the ornate Boulle clock that so delighted the earl of Ranelagh—covered in gilt bronze and inlaid with bone and tortoise-shell, the earl's clock was pleasing to the eye but failed altogether in the keeping of time). A rather large mirror in a kingwood frame was hung to the side of the fireplace. Lady Ranelagh found the glass irresistible, and even on this occasion, she could not avoid casting an appreciative glance into it as she caught her reflection; she was still looking particularly fine, even as the long day was drawing to a close.

Astell bent to warm her chilled hands at the grate. Lady Catherine saw how tired her friend looked. "Now where is that troublesome girl?" she asked, a note of irritation creeping in her voice. "And why is she never to be found when she is wanted?"

At that very moment, Sarah burst through the door and into the parlor. She was gripping a tray with both hands, her arms trembling with the effort. She placed her burden on the small table next to the chair where Astell usually sat and then sighed with relief, the task having been completed with no accidents or upsets. A flush of pride appeared on her cheeks.

"Thank you, Sarah," said Astell, "that is just what was wanted." The fare Sarah had thought to provide was simple but reflected her mistress's preferred refreshment, a bit of cheese, some bread, and a flask of small beer.

"I think we must also have the brandy, Sarah," said Lady Catherine to the girl. And then, to Astell, "We sent to Ranelagh for it, and just a drop will do you much good."

Having finished her quiet self-examination in the glass and being quite content with what she had discovered there, Lady Ranelagh sank gracefully into one of the comfortable padded chairs, taking care to arrange her skirts artfully around her. Since Astell scoffed at the notion of a fire screen, Lady Ranelagh always chose the armchair farthest from the blaze—she would take no chances when it came to her complexion.

"At last," she breathed, her skirts now displayed to her satisfaction, "now we may begin."

Two

The day had begun quietly in Mary Astell's small house on Paradise Row. Indeed, the quiet sameness of the daily routine was what most chafed young Sarah, provoking the outbreaks of temper and small acts of rebellion that punctuated her usual carelessness.

As was her custom, Mary Astell had risen very early in the morning, well before dawn. She was content to dispense with Sarah's presence for the first hours of the day. If she had been questioned about this unusual arrangement, Astell would undoubtedly have answered that she believed the girl's health was much improved by the restorative effects of the additional hours of rest she had been granted since her arrival in the house on Paradise Row. But, in truth, Mary Astell dedicated the early hours of her day to solitary reading and reflection. If Sarah were expected to rise at the same time as her mistress, the wayward girl would have required constant supervision to keep her from mischief. (As for rising even before her mistress had wakened in order to clean the grates and prepare the fires, well, that was entirely out of the question.)

Since Astell required no assistance in dressing, took no food or drink before midday, and could manage the coal fires quite well herself, she found it expedient, if not altogether laudable, to let Sarah continue in her bed. Lady Catherine might object, suggesting that such leniency served only to reward the girl's indolence and would not, in the end, lend itself to her training in service, but Mary Astell considered the arrangement, however unconventional, convenient for both mistress and maid.

Her period of meditation complete, Astell had left the house in order to attend the morning service at All Saints Church, where the Reverend Mr. John King had succeeded as rector just as she had taken up residence on Paradise Row. The Oxford-educated churchman had made many changes in the parish after his arrival and had proven to be a great sermonizer, although he had become somewhat distracted of late by his researches into the exact location of Sir Thomas More's manor house in Chelsea. This scholarly preoccupation now consumed a great deal of his time.

It must also be said that the rector had become somewhat remiss in the performance of his more mundane duties because of his determined effort to reform Sir Willoughby Chamberlain, a wealthy colonial planter who had recently taken up residence in the village. Sir Willoughby had been implicated in a conspiracy to turn the English colony of Barbados into "an absolute popish, if not a French, island," in the words of one witness in the case that had been brought against him. Further damning testimony had revealed Sir Willoughby to be a "quarrelsome" man who was "drunk almost every night" and who "beat the ordinary sort of people within danger of their lives."

But the lengthy inquiry into the planter's misdeeds in the colony had gone nowhere, and in the end neither the scandal nor the subsequent investigation had prevented his safe retreat to England, nor had the well-publicized evidence of his notorious behavior precluded his acquisition of a knighthood—although Sir Willoughby's reputation did account for Mr. King's reforming zeal. While he freely acknowledged that the planter's life had demonstrated "little prudence" and even less "self-government," the rector of All Saints was nevertheless confident of his ability to effect a reformation in the reprobate. "I begin to observe in him a visible change and desire for repentance," the Reverend Mr. King assured anyone interested—or not—in hearing about the spiritual progress of Sir Willoughby Chamberlain.

For her part, Mary Astell was firm in her belief that a portion of every day should be devoted to observing the rites and rituals of the church.

Despite her reservations about some of Mr. King's hobbyhorses, she was scrupulous in her attendance at worship services. The weakness and folly that even those who serve God might on occasion display were no excuse for neglecting one's spiritual obligations.

The parish church stood in the center of Great Chelsea, just a short walk from Paradise Row. Before leaving home, Astell had made sure that Sarah was awake. Despite the girl's extra hours of sleep, she had tripped clumsily down the stairs from her room under the eaves, mumbling crossly all the while as she descended, though Astell declined to hear Sarah's complaints, intended either to elicit sympathy or to annoy her mistress or, more likely, both. Astell had reminded the girl about the duties that would need her immediate attention. Even so, Astell was uneasy in her mind, worrying about what Sarah might get up to if she were left alone too long without guidance—and a vigilant eye.

"The grace of our Lord Jesus Christ and the love of God and the fellowship of the Holy Ghost be with us all evermore. Amen."

Mary Astell's lips had tightened into a straight line as morning prayers ended. Her misgivings about Sarah had distracted her throughout much of the worship service, much to her annoyance.

A vague sense of unease had also prevented her from stopping at the rectory to check on Elizabeth King, who had missed the morning service. Mrs. King had recently given birth to her fourth child, a boy. Although she was an efficient and capable manager, and the baby, named John after his father, was a thriving child, Elizabeth King remained ill at ease and cautious—her first infant, a girl, had died within a few weeks of her birth, a loss that the rector's wife still felt. The household was also chaotic, and Mr. King, what with one important thing or another to occupy his time and attention, was rarely to be found there.

But instead of spending a few moments with her fellow worshippers after the service or making a quick visit to the rectory to check on Mrs. King, Mary Astell had left All Saints just after the service was over, walking east along the riverside highway, passing the Feathers Inn and its garden, the old Tudor brick wall of Shrewsbury House (once belonging to the redoubtable Bess of Hardwick but now a boarding school for girls), and then the Magpie tavern, where Mrs. Herne was known for her charity to the poor of the parish.

After reaching the Great Garden, Astell had turned onto Paradise Row, which ran diagonally from the Thames to the courtyard of Chelsea Hospital. The morning was bright, though it was exceedingly cold. The heavy rain that would fall later in the day had not yet begun. Astell had briefly considered a visit to consult with Mr. Doody, the curator at the Apothecary Garden on the south side of the street, just across from the rambling old house belonging to the countess of Radnor. Despite the cold and wet summer, Astell's sprouts and leeks had settled well into her garden; she was thinking about planting some corn salad as a winter vegetable and perhaps even autumn-sowing a few rows of beans if there were ever a long enough period of dry fall weather to make planting possible. But, still uneasy, she had not stopped.

Astell's residence was the last but one in the row, just next to the end-of-terrace house occupied by Mary Methuen. As Astell had approached the corner of Mrs. Methuen's garden, she was startled to see a tangle of old clothing lying in front of her own gate, what looked to be a pile of rags abandoned just outside the brick and ironwork fence that separated her front garden from the road.

Mary Astell at first supposed it be a bundle dropped by the old fripperer lately seen (and heard) throughout the village, with his cries of "old satin, old taffeta, or old velvet, old cloaks, old suits, or old coats!" But then, what she had assumed to be a heap of old garments suddenly stirred. Startled, she had stopped, taking a step back before cautiously moving closer. She could see that she was looking not at a jumble of clothing but at a young woman, her slight body overwhelmed by a mess of tatty finery. What might once have been a costly—albeit showy—garment was now dirty and disheveled.

Despite her slight movement, the woman lying on the ground seemed hardly alive, and when Astell had bent over her to look more closely, she saw that "woman" did not quite seem like the right word to describe the senseless figure. The unknown woman seemed to be a girl, hardly older than Sarah.

As if summoned by mere thought, Sarah had chosen that very moment come bounding out of the house and across the garden, throwing open the gate. "Oh, Lord, oh, Lord, oh, Lord," she had yowled, "Who can she be? Oh, Lord, mistress, why is she here? Where is she from? What could the matter be?" She was shrieking loudly enough to be heard all the way to the church.

Mary Astell was a composed and capable woman, quick to respond decisively in every situation. Life had taught her to be steady and resourceful: when she was still a girl, younger then than Sarah was now, her sheltered, comfortable childhood in Newcastle had come to a sudden and abrupt end after her father's early death. Mary Astell had learned from her mother, a widow dogged by worry and debt, that she could face any difficulty she might encounter with dignity, never forgetting that she was a gentlewoman.

"Hush, Sarah," Astell had said, "stop that noise at once. What a commotion! It is neither necessary nor helpful. Come here and help me to raise this poor soul."

But that was not to be. Astell could not raise the stranger by herself—indeed, she was not altogether sure the girl was still alive, although she thought she could detect a few shallow breaths—and Sarah, as usual, had proved to be less help than was needed. Astell looked quickly at Mrs. Methuen's house, to her left, and at Mrs. Smith's to her right, realizing that neither woman kept a manservant who might be called upon for assistance.

"Please allow me to assist, *madame*." The voice was deep and resonant, the accent unfamiliar.

Startled, Astell had turned and recognized the man addressing her as an intimate of the duchess of Mazarin, who resided in one of the large apartments at the opposite end of the terrace. Before Astell could reply, the man had reached down, carefully raising the body of the girl.

He was not tall; indeed, he was not as tall as Astell herself, but he had no trouble in cradling the stranger in his arms as he looked at Astell expectantly. "Shall I take her inside for you?"

Looking back, Astell was startled at how quickly events had unfolded after that moment, and more than a little bothered at her own indecision. Astell had shaken her head to clear her mind and then nodded to the man before striding briskly through the gate and into the entry of her home, gesturing for him to follow her. With no time to consider, she had pointed up to the first floor, where there were two bedchambers, one of which she used as her study. The man carried the still-unconscious young woman up the narrow staircase with little difficulty, then waited for Astell to direct him.

"There I think," she said, pointing into the room where she usually slept, watching as he entered and lowered his burden gently onto her narrow couch-bed. As in the parlor below, the furniture in the room was simple, the bed fitted with no canopy or hangings.

"I am most grateful . . . ," she began before pausing. She was uncertain how properly to address the dark-skinned man who had appeared so unexpectedly to assist her. She had seen him often enough since she had taken up residence on Paradise Row, but she was not sure whether the man was a privileged guest in the Mazarin household or whether he was an attendant who served the duchess. It was altogether impossible to be sure: an unending parade of strangers made their way from the city to Hortense Mancini's residence in Chelsea, the rendezvous of anyone who was—or who hoped to be—the talk of the town. Actors and aristocrats mixed with lawyers and idlers, all of them partaking of the food, drink, and diversions on constant offer. Indeed, the earl of Ranelagh was at times to be found there, consuming great quantities of fine claret while losing great sums at the basset-table with great good humor.

The African's distinctive clothing provided no clear indication of his place within the Mazarin household although, whoever and whatever he was, he was beautifully turned out. He wore a long dark coat, made of fine wool and fitted quite closely, with extravagantly large upturned cuffs. Underneath his coat was a black velvet waistcoat embroidered with gold thread. His shirt was white silk, but instead of a lace-edged cravat, he bore a thick band of silver about his neck. Rather than knee-length, close-fitting breeches, he was wearing long Turkish trousers. His red velvet slippers were entirely unsuitable for the weather.

"Mustapha, *madame*," he had said quietly, introducing himself and gesturing toward the bedroom's window. "Her Grace would like to know whether she might send for your friends to assist you. She would be most happy to let them know at Ranelagh that you need their aid. Or perhaps not, Madam Astell—we are entirely at your service." He inclined his head slightly, waiting for her response.

Astell remained silent at his words, still considering the man before her. *Is he a member of her household, I wonder, a manservant of some sort? Or is he a guest of the duchess? But "we"? Not a servant, then, surely?*

Still perplexed, Astell followed the man's gaze down to the street below. She had not noticed the duchess of Mazarin's coach as she had approached the terrace. In fact, Astell was fairly certain that it had not been in view, although her attention had been focused on the bundle lying on the ground in front, so perhaps she had just failed to observe it. But now she could see it standing just outside her gate, the glossy black horses and the liveried footmen making a brave show on the otherwise sleepy street. Although Astell assumed that Hortense Mancini herself was inside, behind the glazed windows, the duchess remained hidden from view.

"Thank you," Mary Astell had said at last, "that would be most kind." While she was still uncertain about the correct form of address for the man, she thought Lady Catherine's advice would be welcome and was grateful for his sensible suggestion. While Sarah was perfectly capable of taking a message to Ranelagh, which was just short walk from Paradise Row, the girl would be a quite unreliable messenger on this occasion.

His burden deposited on Astell's bed, the man had nodded in farewell and descended the staircase without bustle or fuss. Astell stepped to the window to watch him emerge from the doorway and enter the coach.

As usual, when her services were wanted, Sarah was not at hand. Still looking down, Astell saw that she was hanging on the iron railing below, gawping at the African as he passed her by. Sarah was perhaps hoping to catch a glimpse of the scandalous duchess as the door of the coach opened.

Rather than waiting for Sarah to make her way back up the stairs, Astell had turned her attention to the figure lying on the narrow bed. The young stranger was desperately ill, that much was clear, and Astell decided to consult with Mrs. Methuen as quickly as possible. Sarah could not be relied upon to carry a message to Ranelagh, but she was surely capable of summoning Mrs. Methuen from next door. After checking the still figure once more, Astell made her way down the stairs and out to Sarah as quickly as she could. *There is something to be said for the manner of that man, whomever he might be. No commotion or bother, just a calm deportment and an economy of action.*

Mindful herself about avoiding any public display, Astell had waited until she was upon Sarah before speaking. "Close your mouth," she said sharply to the girl, who was still staring down Paradise Row, though the Mazarin carriage had long disappeared. "Go and ask Mrs. Methuen to come to us as soon as she is able."

Some twenty years Mary Astell's senior, Mary Methuen was regarded as a widow by almost all of her Chelsea neighbors, but in truth she had not lost her husband—or, rather, she had not lost him to death. After a decade of marriage and the birth of five children, John Methuen had decided to abandon his wife. Despite both his neglect of his family and his reputation as a notorious libertine, he had somehow managed to get himself appointed as the English envoy to Portugal. Widely recognized as "a profligate rogue," a man "without religion or morals," and a man who was, in the plainest of terms, "without abilities of any kind," he had taken up his post in Lisbon, where he promptly seduced the young wife of the consul general.

Now, some years later, Mary Methuen lived quietly with her daughters in Chelsea, content to be thought a widow by her neighbors. She was appreciated throughout the village for her medical knowledge, her skilled nursing, and the drops and powders that she prepared herself for those who might summon her during a time of need.

Having sent Sarah on her way, Astell had climbed back up the stairs to her bedchamber. The girl lay still, hardly breathing. Turning to the basin of water that Sarah had neglected to empty and replenish that morning (although this was one of the duties she was expected to perform), Astell moistened a linen towel and began to wipe the grime off the unknown woman's face. Like Mrs. Methuen, she was a great believer that cleanliness helped to ward off malady.

It had taken only a moment of careful bathing to see that the stranger was indeed very young—as Astell had thought, she seemed more a girl than a woman. Sarah was only thirteen, and the figure on the bed seemed to be not much older, if she were older at all. It was hard to be certain, though.

Her face was thin, her features drawn and wasted with cold, hunger, pain, or a mix of all of these. She was also very pale, but there were hectic spots of red on her cheeks. Her hair was matted and dull. It was also damp and stuck to her head. Astell patted the girl's face dry after she cleansed it, but a sweat began to break out again almost immediately. In a moment of unusual tenderness, Astell stroked the girl's cheek and lifted her lank hair off her forehead. She turned as she heard the door open below and her neighbor's brisk step on the stair.

With Mrs. Methuen's arrival on the scene, events had moved swiftly. A few low words delivered under her breath to Sarah had caused the girl's eyebrows to shoot up and her mouth to open in a wide O. Whatever Mrs. Methuen had said to her prompted Sarah to hurry down the stairs—noisily, as was usual, but quickly and with no complaints, as was altogether unusual.

"I do not dare send her for my apothecary chest," said Mrs. Methuen. She had not stopped to greet Astell but had gone straight to the girl lying on the bed, feeling for her pulse, counting her shallow breaths, checking her fever, and appraising the heightened color of her cheeks. "Her cheeks are flushed, but she is sweating," Mrs. Methuen murmured. "Not hot and dry, then, and she seems to have no cough, so likely not a consumption of the lungs . . . "

While her neighbor continued her examination of the girl with her accustomed efficiency, Astell could hear Sarah returning. She had charged into the room, carrying a large flask of cool water gripped in both hands and yet more cloths, a bundle shoved under her each of her elbows and pressed tightly to her sides. It had occurred then to Mary Astell that perhaps her own methods of dealing with Sarah might not be the best. The maidservant might be capable of more than her mistress assumed.

Just then Astell had heard a coach below, this one carrying Lady Catherine to her door. She had arrived much more quickly than Astell anticipated—while it was only a short walk from Paradise Row to Ranelagh House, Lady Catherine was not much inclined to walking, either for exercise or for transportation. In truth, it would take longer for a coach to be readied for the brief journey than simply to cover the distance by foot, so Astell had been surprised at her friend's quick appearance.

"We were on our way to town just as we were waylaid by the duchess of Mazarin, and what a shock that was, seeing her coach draw up to Ranelagh," Lady Catherine had hurriedly begun, as if reading her friend's mind. The two met on the stairs, Astell heading down as Lady Catherine had begun her way up. As they climbed the stairs together—carefully avoiding the trail of cloths Sarah had dropped—Lady Catherine asked, "That man of hers relayed the news. Now, I wonder, what is there to be done?"

A vexed question, but one that Mary Astell had answered promptly. "I think I must go up to town, my lady."

"Oh, no, my dear, no," said Lady Catherine, shaking her head. "Not to Lambeth. You will find no answers there, Mary. He will have nothing useful to offer—it is an exercise in futility, and you will have made the journey for nothing. You know that I am in the right."

"I really must go, my lady." Contrary to her dear friend's assertion, Mary Astell was certain that *she* was in the right—though she was not, perhaps, altogether reasonable.

When she had first arrived in London, so many years earlier, Mary Astell had found a friend in William Sancroft, archbishop of Canterbury. After months of disappointment and in a desperate state, she sought his assistance. "I come to you, Your Grace, as a humble petitioner," she wrote in an appeal addressed to him. "My Lord, I am a gentlewoman and not able to get a livelihood—I can find no work, and to beg I am ashamed, but necessity forces me to trouble you, Your Grace. I hope for your pity upon my unhappy state."

Although the archbishop had his own troubles—he had just been released from the Tower, where he had been imprisoned for his public objections to King James's Catholic sympathies—the cleric had taken pity on the "poor unknown" who sought his help. He had opened his doors to her at once, and it was he who had contacted Lady Catherine Jones on behalf of his desperate petitioner.

But Archbishop Sancroft was no longer at Lambeth. Shortly after he introduced Mary Astell to Lady Catherine, he had run into trouble once more, this time with the new monarchs, William and Mary, and he had found himself suspended and deprived of his see. He had cheerfully packed up and sent his books and papers off to his family home in Suffolk, but he had refused to budge from the archbishop's seat until he was forcibly removed from the premises. Mary Astell had continued to correspond with her old friend and advisor during the years of his retirement.

In the meantime, John Tillotson had been elected to succeed William Sancroft as archbishop of Canterbury. Tillotson was known to be a man of great generosity and sweetness of disposition, but Astell had never felt confident of his judgment—he was, after all, the son of a Puritan, a fault he had compounded by marrying the niece of Oliver Cromwell. And he had brought his wife with him to London, installing her in a large apartment in Lambeth House. No wife of an archbishop had been seen there for more than a hundred years. Not long after Tillotson's election, William Sancroft died and then, just a year later, John Tillotson himself suffered a fatal stroke.

And so another new archbishop, Thomas Tenison, had been installed just the previous year. He was generally regarded as modest, pious, and prudent—but dull. He was "His old solid Grace," in the lethal words of an anonymous satire that appeared shortly after his appointment. Although he too had brought a wife into Lambeth, Astell had a degree of sympathy with Tenison's views—he had a horror of all frivolous pastimes, but most especially of card games. And he also expressed misgivings about the treatment that had been meted out to Archbishop Sancroft, thus earning him some measure of Astell's respect. While she rarely found Mr. Tenison's recommendations to be of much practical use, Astell found that advice offered by Mrs. Tenison was very sound.

"But, Mary," Lady Catherine said, exasperated by Astell's obstinance. "I remind you again that your old friend is no longer there—and I am certain you will be sorely disappointed with whatever advice you might receive, if you are even able to see His Grace at all. The journey will take you away just when you are needed here. Besides, the coach has already gone—Lady Ranelagh could not stop, and she has traveled on to town. You will have to go to Lambeth by foot, and, mark my words, it will all be for naught. If you must go, it can wait, surely." She reached out for Astell's hand, as if the gesture would convince her friend not to undertake a fruitless journey.

Astell was not to be gainsaid, however. Lady Catherine was probably correct—the archbishop would not offer many practical suggestions for her in this situation—but, as she would be the first to acknowledge, her habit of looking to Lambeth for advice was difficult to break. Although Astell had a sense that Archbishop Tenison regarded her as something of a burden that must be borne and did not welcome her when she appeared at his door, she believed that to seek spiritual direction in such a situation should be her first order of business. Mrs. Methuen would attend to the physical, Lady Catherine to the practical—she herself would make sure that they were acting in accordance with their duties as Christians.

But there was something else as well, though Astell had not wanted to alarm Lady Catherine. If it were only a matter of spiritual guidance, Astell could consult with the rector of All Saints. But in consulting the archbishop, she was seeking more than spiritual advice: she wanted assurance that they were acting according to the law, and that is where His Grace, for all his dullness, could be of immediate assistance.

As Mary Astell knew only too well from her own experience so many years earlier, the girl who had wandered into Chelsea that day was in legal peril. While the law made it clear that each parish had a duty to provide care and support for the poor, the aged, and the infirm within its boundaries, parish churchwardens (and ratepayers) were only too eager to rid themselves of "the great and exceeding burden" of destitute strangers.

The law might proclaim its purpose to be the "relief of the poor of this kingdom," but it also condemned the "foolish pity and mercy" of those who offered alms to the transient poor: vagrants, itinerant laborers, and beggars. The wandering poor were to be apprehended and, in accordance with the terms of the legislation, removed from a parish. Unfortunately, where they were to be removed *to* was not always clear. The law stipulated that they were to be returned to their place of legal settlement, but those who were eager to expel the unwanted from their parish were little concerned with where they should properly be sent.

Astell was equally aware that those who sheltered the poor were also suspect. The act of concealing a vagrant might lead to any number of legal difficulties. Whatever advice Archbishop Tenison might have to offer her on these weighty matters would be invaluable. And Mrs. Tenison could be relied upon for sympathy and benevolence. And so, leaving the mysterious young wanderer in the capable hands of Mrs. Methuen and despite the skepticism of Lady Catherine, Astell had hurriedly taken up her cloak and left Paradise Row for the city.

A cold rain began to fall just as she reached Stone Bridge.

Three

A t last," said Lady Ranelagh. "Now we may begin." She made one final adjustment to the silk of her skirts and glanced expectantly at Mary Astell, who was lost in thought, remembering the events of earlier that day.

Recalled once again to the present, Astell suppressed a sigh. While Astell found the day's events distressing, Lady Ranelagh was enjoying herself a very great deal and made no show of assuming a grave demeanor or furrowing her brow. Quite the contrary, the countess of Ranelagh's pleasure was evident in her countenance. While she was a compassionate woman, willing to support a worthy cause intended to relieve the misery of the poor and unfortunate, she was also a woman who had little personal experience with the reality of suffering.

Then, too, she was more easily bored than even Sarah and spent much of her time in pursuit of novelty. Sheltered and indulged as she had been for most of her life, she clearly regarded the sudden appearance of the stranger as a welcome diversion, if not an entertainment arranged solely for her amusement. Her only real regret seemed to be that the girl had not wandered onto the grounds of Ranelagh instead of down Paradise Row. Thus Lady Ranelagh's swift arrival at Astell's lodgings after she had completed her business in town. But she had grown weary during the long wait for Astell to return home; now, however, Lady Ranelagh's high spirits had been restored.

"Alas, I am afraid there is not much for me to say," admitted Astell. "Lady Catherine's prediction was, as usual, correct—my trip to Lambeth proved fruitless. But before anything of that, I had rather hear about the girl. How is she? What more has Mrs. Methuen to say about her state?"

"Just so," said Lady Catherine. She narrowed her eyes and frowned at Lady Ranelagh. Lady Catherine was a pious woman, full of rectitude, and she thought there was nothing enjoyable or amusing in the plight of the young stranger lying ill and insensible upstairs.

For her part, Lady Ranelagh refused to acknowledge having said or done anything amiss, much less having committed any impropriety. Even though she took no pleasure in the young girl's suffering, she could still be delighted with the day's carryings-on. She saw no reason for dissimulation or pretense, and she was not inclined to let Lady Catherine shame her.

"The girl? How is she?" Astell reminded her two companions that she was still waiting to hear about what had transpired while she was gone. Lady Catherine and Lady Ranelagh could resolve their differences later.

"Mrs. Methuen left just a short while ago," Lady Catherine began. "There was nothing more to be done tonight. As for the girl, the unfortunate creature has not spoken a clear word all the while you have been gone—nor has she come to herself. Her condition has shown no improvement, but at least she seems no worse. Mrs. Methuen made her as comfortable as possible, though the poor girl's fever is still very high." Lady Catherine paused before adding, "I thought I might well send for Old Bridget to watch over her through the night."

"Old" Bridget had a member of the Ranelagh household for all of Lady Catherine's life. Early in his political career, when the Anglo-Irish peer was still quite a young man, Richard Jones had held several lucrative posts in Ireland, and when he had sought further preferment in England, he brought with him a select few of his servants, including Bridget, who would eventually act as nursemaid to all three of daughters. (It is perhaps best not to speculate about what interest the rakish earl of Ranelagh might have had in the comely *young* Bridget before the birth of his children.)

Now the Irishwoman was indeed well into old age, though she was not as old as the earl himself. While there had been no children in his household for many years, Bridget remained, beloved by Lady Catherine and her two sisters. The former nurse was generally left to herself to enjoy the quiet her many years of service had won for her, yet she was happy enough to be of use whenever Lady Catherine or one of her sisters might have need of her.

"And, Sarah, please take yourself upstairs to watch over the girl until Bridget arrives," Lady Catherine said, her tone rather sharp. Although Sarah thought she had hidden herself from view, Lady Catherine knew the girl was lurking outside the parlor door, all ears. "Mrs. Methuen has given you your instructions, so you know what you are to do."

Astell was surprised to hear no complaint from the wayward Sarah— instead, she heard the girl's heavy footfall on the stair. The maidservant stumped loudly on each tread as she climbed to the bedroom, her disgruntlement clearly conveyed with each slow step. Even so, Sarah was doing as Lady Catherine had bidden without answering back, her compliance representing something of an improvement over her usual reaction to being assigned an unwelcome task.

As Mary Astell expected, Lady Catherine had taken matters on Paradise Row into her own capable hands. Astell valued her dear friend's ability to plan, organize, and command. Lady Catherine managed the household at Ranelagh as if she were a great general, marshalling her troops, deploying them with assiduity, and marching them briskly into action. The old earl would rather absent himself from the field than do battle with his formidable daughter and, as for the countess, she was neither interested in challenging Lady Catherine for command nor prepared to refuse the general's orders. Lady Ranelagh chose a wiser course and just declined to hear them.

By contrast, Astell preferred to concentrate on her work, pouring all of her energy into her writing. She was not interested in overseeing the operations of her household. On the whole, she was grateful to Lady Catherine for arranging many of the mundane aspects of her daily life and appreciated all that her friend did to make it possible for her to spend her day in her study. On some occasions, it must be said, Mary Astell had her own ideas about what was best to be done, and when she found herself in conflict with Lady Catherine, she proved to be every bit as stubborn as her friend was determined. There had been many clashes of will in the early years of their friendship, but with the passage of time, each had come to know the limits of the other.

And so, when Mary Astell asked Lady Catherine *not* to send for Bridget, indicating that she would prefer watch by the stranger's bedside herself, Lady Catherine paused. She studied Astell's face carefully for a moment and then, calculating the state of things, nodded in agreement. There was no further mention of sending for the old nurse.

"But surely there is more, my lady," Astell said. "What else did Mrs. Methuen have to say about the cause of the illness?"

"It is clearly a challenging case," Lady Catherine began slowly. "Mrs. Methuen examined the girl carefully, but since she has been incapable of answering questions put to her, Mrs. Methuen can say no more. There is no swelling in the girl's throat and no cough, nor is she spitting up blood, so it is not likely to be a consumption."

Astell nodded—all this confirmed Mrs. Methuen's initial impressions.

Lady Catherine continued. "The fever is acute but intermittent, and it alternates with terrible chills. Mrs. Methuen believes it to be a violent ague—we can hope it is not a tertian or a quartan, but that remains to be seen. She will be back in the morning to see how the night has gone and, of course, to check on you as well. In the meantime, we must pray for the girl's swift recovery."

"Pray!" scoffed Lady Ranelagh. "Is there nothing else to be done? Prayers are all fine and good, but surely more might be done to make the poor creature comfortable."

"There is nothing more to be done tonight," said Lady Catherine sternly. "The unfortunate girl has been murmuring and sighing, but she is still unaware of *where* she is and has been unable to say anything at all about *who* she is. Mrs. Methuen offered her some sips of boiled and cooled water, but I am afraid the girl did not swallow much. As for any further treatment . . . Well, that will need to wait until her symptoms can be ascertained—as I said, Mrs. Methuen has done all that can be done for now."

Lady Ranelagh knew all this already—she had spent the last few hours getting regular reports from Sarah, who was thrilled to be of use to the countess. Lady Ranelagh had climbed the stairs only once, shortly after her arrival, to take a brief look at the girl lying in her sickbed before returning to the comforts of the parlor below. But she did not like the idea that she could offer nothing more than prayers.

Seeing that Lady Catherine had no more to add, Lady Ranelagh was ready to hear about Astell's meeting with the archbishop—he might not have had anything at all useful to say, but he was so unaware of his inadequacies that he was a source of great delight.

"And now for the wisdom of the Most Reverend and Right Honorable Archbishop of Canterbury, Primate of all England," Lady Ranelagh said, turning her attention to Mary Astell. As she spoke, the countess shot a quick sidelong glance toward Lady Catherine, who was not amused by Lady Ranelagh's flippant tone but who chose to say nothing. For her part, the countess of Ranelagh was satisfied with her wit and sure that Lady Catherine was at least mildly annoyed. "What words of wisdom did the noted doctor of divinity have to contribute today? Surely he has weighed in with some great insight."

"It was unfortunate," Astell began, "but His Grace could not spare much time to see me." Astell knew she needed to be somewhat careful here—her journey to Lambeth had taken her much longer than usual, and she wanted to avoid raising the somewhat tricky subject of her mode of travel.

The distance from Paradise Row to the archbishop's residence was not great—once Astell crossed Stone Bridge and entered Westminster, it would have been an easy enough matter to turn onto St. James's Street, continuing toward the river until she reached Parliament stairs, where she could have taken a sculler directly across the Thames to the Stangate stairs and wharf, just a short walk from Lambeth House, the archbishop's residence. It would have taken her an hour, or perhaps a little more, to cover the distance of some three miles.

But there was that matter of paying a waterman. "I have more time than money," Astell would frequently remind Lady Catherine when disputes about her mode of transportation arose, and even on this unusual day, Astell had decided to take her usual route to Lambeth, although it made her journey much longer: once she left St. James's Street, she had skirted the abbey, walked along King Street to Charing Cross, then down the Strand to Fleet Street, and on toward St. Paul's.

She had planned to stop briefly at Mr. Wilkin's bookshop in St. Paul's Churchyard at the sign of the King's Head. Astell was midway through her next project, and some details remained to be settled. But the rain had slowed her as she traveled into the city, and so, instead of seeing Mr. Wilkin as she intended, she had hurried on, wending her way through a tangle of smaller streets, making her way to London Bridge.

Once she crossed the Thames, she had considered following the river until she reached Lambeth, but she thought she could save some time if she traveled more directly. And so, instead of turning west, Astell had followed the Borough road through Southwark to St. Margaret's Hill and then to Blackman Street, eventually turning toward the river and finally arriving at Lambeth House. On most occasions, Astell could cover the six miles in a little over two hours—she did not mind the walk, and she saved her penny. On that day, however, as the rain grew heavier and her pace slower, she had come to regret her choice.

It had been well past midday before she finally reached Lambeth, thoroughly chilled, her skirt and petticoats damp and muddy. She had been politely, if coolly, greeted upon her arrival. The great hall was abuzz with its usual activity. The archbishop's clerical staff—his deacons and his archdeacons, his priests and his prebendaries, his chaplains and his canons—bustled from here to there, dodging and weaving through the waiting crowd of supplicants and suitors. The smug religious avoided making eye contact with those who waited patiently for favors—or for simple kindness. The low hum of the visitors' quiet prayers filled the air.

Astell had taken her place among the hopeful supplicants until she was finally summoned by an officious secretary who was unable—or unwilling—to offer her any information at all about when His Grace would return to Lambeth or whether he would have time to see her when he did.

The archbishop's secretary had stowed Astell in a cold passageway, and while she might have resented his treatment, she could not really blame him. She had arrived without arranging an appointment ahead of time, and the archbishop was a very busy man, working diligently at all his day-to-day duties. He kept a detailed record of his many activities in a ledger book—little more than a year had passed since his installation, and he had already filled more than two hundred and fifty pages, as he had informed Mary Astell on the occasion of their last meeting.

But the archbishop was scrupulous on the subject of the law, and that is why Astell was determined to wait, no matter how long that wait might be. Though he might be dull and consumed by his record-keeping, and although he would never be the warm friend and unfailing advocate that William Sancroft had been, the new archbishop of Canterbury could be relied upon for the accuracy of his knowledge of legal matters.

Astell doubted that Lady Ranelagh had any idea of the difficulties the situation presented, but she knew that Lady Catherine was aware of the unfortunate state of things—after all, it was much the predicament Astell herself had faced after arriving in London so many years earlier. Astell had traveled to the capital with the necessary certificate of her settlement, but when she had found herself alone and unable to earn a living, she had faced the daunting prospect of a removal order: if she needed poor relief, she would be compelled to return home to Newcastle. Only Archbishop Sancroft's intervention on her behalf had enabled her continued residence in London.

Although Astell could not be sure, she suspected that the young girl who had turned up that morning outside her gate did not have the proper settlement document. Indeed, the stranger had nothing at all on her person, nothing aside from her bedraggled finery—she had carried no money, that was certain, and had no papers of any kind. She was not a member of the parish of Chelsea, that Mary Astell knew, and there was no telling, at least for the moment, where the girl had come from or where she intended to go. If she were without friends and, more important, without support or work, the parish would be expected to provide for her—or, more probably, would expel her.

Of course, as Mary Astell sat waiting, weary and chilled, in a drafty corridor of Lambeth House, she acknowledged to herself that she might be anticipating problems that would never arise. The girl might have relatives in the parish, she might have found a position in the area and fallen ill on her way to take up her post, she might have been traveling toward another destination altogether, she might—

"Mrs. Astell, is that you?"

The quiet of the passageway had been broken by a booming voice. Astell had looked up to see Thomas Lloyd, one of the archbishop's footmen, looking down at her. He seemed happy enough to see her. She had risen slowly to greet him, her joints stiff with cold, and as he directed her to follow, she had done her best to keep up as he jetted back down the passage where she had been deposited; the well-fed footman dodged clerics and visitors as he led her back through the hall and along a wainscoted gallery, around the chapel, and down a warren of passageways to the archbishop's private lodgings. There she had been announced to Mrs. Tenison, snug in her apartment with Mrs. Stubbs, her faithful woman, keeping her company—

"Mary?" asked Lady Catherine softly, her voice full of concern.

Astell realized, to her dismay, that she had not yet answered Lady Ranelagh's question. Instead, her thoughts had drifted away again, back to Lambeth and her memories of the long day—the rain, the journey, which had been more tiring than she would admit, the wait, and the worry. Such inattention was not like her at all.

"Oh, Mary." The fun had slipped away from Lady Ranelagh, and she was her warmer and truer self, no longer interested in needling Lady Catherine with her barbs. "I am so sorry, but what has happened?"

"I was only in the archbishop's presence for a few minutes when he stopped by briefly to announce his return to Mrs. Tenison, who was gracious enough to have received me. Parliament just opened its session on Tuesday, and His Grace was really only interested in recounting what His Majesty had said about the current want of coin and the progress of the great recoinage—and then, when I had just begun to inform him about the state of the young girl found outside my gate, he launched into one of his unfortunate tirades against the 'notorious sins and vices of this nation' and the need for moral reform. It was quite unsettling and beside the point."

"Perhaps," said Lady Catherine, who had her own suspicions about the girl lying in Astell's bed.

"How ridiculous," scoffed Lady Ranelagh, "when all the world knows that it was the Reverend Tenison himself who attended Nell Gwyn on her deathbed—why, he even delivered her funeral sermon. And then he distributed money in her name among poor *papists*."

"Ah, yes, but then she was a *fair* penitent," said Lady Catherine. The irony was unusual for her. "And in any case, she was thoughtful enough to have died quickly, without any fuss, and his preaching drew an enormous audience, as he knew it would—why, there were copies of his sermon for sale on the streets within hours! But perhaps he learned his lesson about sinners, even penitent ones, because his praise of Nell Gwyn cost him dearly, and if Queen Mary had not been a generous and forgiving monarch, that act might have cost the Reverend Tenison any further advancement."

"I do not charge the archbishop with hypocrisy," said Astell, "I believe him to be an honest man of faith. But my reason for seeing him was not to hear warnings about public immorality and certainly not to hear about clipped coins. What he had to say was not *à propos*—we know nothing about the girl's character. Rather than listening to my concerns, he pulled a fist full of papers from his bag and began reading from His Majesty's letter to clergymen recommending 'a general reformation of the lives and manners of all our subjects.' And there were drafts of various bills aimed at punishing the sins of adultery and fornication: death for adultery, imprisonment for fornication. The old Puritan laws reborn."

"And, you may be quite sure that there will be no member of Parliament or member of the clergy, much less a member of the court, subject to such laws," said Lady Ranelagh, "—they are cobweb laws, in which the small fly will be caught while the great will break through."

At that pronouncement Lady Catherine's eyebrows shot up, but she could not disagree. She knew her father only too well, and in a few short months, she had also come to know something of Lady Ranelagh.

Astell had her own doubts about the efficacy of such laws—and, perhaps, of the character of their authors. "Those who will not take the Old and New Testaments for a rule of life will never be reformed by an act of Parliament," she said. She rose to add a bit more coal to the grate. "It was Mrs. Tenison, of course, who was most helpful. Whether such legislation will ever be ever enacted, the campaign of those moral associations is growing more intense throughout the city—she says that they have begun publishing a 'black roll' with the names and crimes of every offender they have identified and that they are posting these lists throughout the city as a warning to sinners and an inspiration to those 'godly men' who pursue them. They are even proposing that every parish should appoint 'secret inspectors' to spy on those who are suspected of offending."

"But surely all this is beside the point," objected Lady Ranelagh.

"Indeed," said Astell. "As I say, we know nothing of the girl, neither who she is or what she is, much less whether she is a sinner. I may have been too hasty in my concern." And then, looking across at Lady Catherine, she added, "Well, *may* is not altogether right, is it, my lady? Doubtless I *have* been too hasty. We must wait until tomorrow, when we can hope that much of this uncertainty will be gone. Our efforts now must be directed to caring for the girl, as the Lord has commanded: 'For I was hungered, and ye gave me meat; I was thirsty, and ye gave me drink; I was a stranger, and ye took me in.'"

As Astell spoke, Lady Ranelagh and Lady Catherine looked at one another, their faces impassive. Mary Astell was undoubtedly right about their duties as Christians. But Astell also knew better, as did they. Although the parish of Chelsea was not the city of London, it had its share of believers who were not quite as full of Christian charity as they might be. There were also a fair number of men and not a few women who were only too eager to search out the weaknesses and failings of others while ignoring or excusing their own.

Four

There would be no sun that day—so much, at least, seemed certain. Mary Astell stretched wearily as she rose from the low chair she had drawn up to the bed, alongside which she had watched throughout the night. The girl was sleeping fitfully. After a sigh, Astell crossed the room to the window, peering out into the empty street. It was growing light or, more accurately, the deepest night seemed to be retreating, but the day promised to be dark and gloomy, and the chill rain continued to fall.

The winters of late had been exceptionally cold, and although the previous year had seen some small break in the pattern, it had been bad enough—the first frosts had appeared in early August. A miserable fall had been followed by a bitterly cold winter, an all-too-brief spring by a rainy, cool summer. In July, as Mrs. Methuen commiserated with Mary Astell about the lamentable state of their gardens, the older woman had ruefully observed that the cool days and "continual and impetuous rain" had turned the summer into "a perfect winter."

And now autumn had returned. Although she still had some hopes for her winter vegetables and had not entirely given up the idea of sowing seed for early spring crops, Astell was not alone in her anticipation of another hard winter. The weather continued unseasonable, and it was widely rumored that a poor harvest would mean food shortages and rising prices.

Those who were old enough to have experienced the Great Frost knew that it could all be worse—during that awful winter, the Thames had frozen solid for more than two months. Of course, the frost fair had been memorable that year—stalls selling roast beef and gingerbread, booths for puppet shows and magic tricks, gambling dens, horse racing, bull-baiting, sledding, bowling, ice-skating, and even, reportedly, an elephant crossing the ice—the whole glorious carnival played out on a stretch of the frozen river from Blackfriars to the Bridge.

But the fair had offered revelers only a momentary respite from the desperate cold. Fuel became so costly that those unable to afford it perished, while those who managed to stay warm found the air so filled with a dense layer of smoke and fumes that they could hardly breathe. Although Mary Astell was still been living with her widowed mother in Newcastle during that dreadful winter, she remembered finding a bottle of ink that she had left by the fire one night frozen solid the next morning.

God willing, the winter soon to come would not be nearly as bad— although, like everyone else, Astell was fearful that the cold, ice, and snow would return with a vengeance. *Well, that's as may be. As for now, "take therefore no thought for the morrow; for the morrow shall take thought for the things of itself. Sufficient unto the day is the evil thereof."*

The verse came to mind as Astell turned away from the window to look at the young stranger lying before her. The problems of the day were indeed sufficient—and the weather, no matter her worry, was not an evil she could solve.

"Here, ma'am," Sarah said quietly. She had entered the sickroom without calling attention to her presence. It was much earlier than she was used to rise—and she had already been busy, as she carried with her a basin of water, still warm. "I will put it in your closet for you."

"Thank you, Sarah. I will be there directly."

By the time Astell crossed the hall to the room she used for her private devotions, reflection, reading, and writing, Sarah had gone back down the stairs. Quietly.

Astell sighed as she looked at the manuscript pages spread out across her desk. Beneath them lay a few proofs from her printer, Mr. Wilkin, still awaiting her corrections. She longed for nothing more than to sit down, pick up her pen, and return to them, but she was resigned to yet another day of departure from her usual routine, and she felt the loss with a pang. As soon as that moment of disappointment crossed her mind, she regretted it. *What kind of Christian love is this?*

Since coming to the city, and, more specifically, to Chelsea, she had devoted herself to the betterment of womankind. "I am determined to rescue my sex from the meanness of spirit into which the generality of them are sunk," she had explained to a female correspondent who had questions about her plans. In these efforts, Astell had been supported by the serious-minded women she now numbered among her friends. She wrote to and for women readers, and she had offered a defiant challenge on the title page of *A Serious Proposal to the Ladies*, the first work she published after her arrival in London: she addressed herself exclusively to women, her sole aim "the advancement of *their* true and greatest interest." The book had of course been read by men as well as women, men who proved to be not a little put out that the author failed to consider *them* within her pages, that, in point of truth, she had quite ignored them.

For some of her readers, she was the "sublime" Mrs. Astell, the "eloquent" Mrs. Astell, the "divine" Mrs. Astell. But for others, she was a figure of fun—she had dared to address herself exclusively to women, as if men were of no account whatsoever! She was ridiculed for her presumption. One wit dismissed her as "Mrs. Comma, the great scholar," and another satirized her as "Madonella," a woman who argued for "quiet and solitude" even while she herself made "more noise in the world" than any woman ought rightly to do. She was lampooned in the press as the founder of "an order of Platonic ladies" and pilloried on stage as a "she-philosopher."

Astell acknowledged these "little persecutions" even as she waved them away as "unjust censures": "I am too steady and well resolved to be shamed from my duty by the empty laughter of such as have nothing but airy noise and confidence to recommend them," she wrote to a sympathetic correspondent. In any case, the public controversy had quickly sent her "serious proposal" into a second and then a third printing, and Richard Wilkin was well pleased with the success of his celebrated author.

Now, two years after her *Proposal* first appeared, he was delighted that Astell was continuing her argument, adding a second part to her initial work. She had advocated the establishment of a college for women, but since no eager subscribers had pledged funds for the creation of such an institution, Astell planned to renew her appeal. She was well along in her project, and Mr. Wilkin hoped to bring out a new volume before the year's end.

But as she looked at her desk that morning, Astell knew that there would be no time for writing. Nor was it likely she would be able to attend services at All Saints. She could not ignore one young and needful woman, no matter how inconvenient her arrival. Accepting her burden, Astell sighed and began to wash, rubbing herself vigorously with the cloths Sarah had also remembered to bring, and then she quickly changed into a clean linen shift. As she finished, she could hear a querulous voice beginning to call out.

"Where am I? Where *am* I?" The girl sounded distraught, as well she might, waking up alone and in an unfamiliar room.

Astell hurried across the small hallway. "Hush, hush, do not worry yourself—you are not alone," she began as she entered her bedchamber. "It is quite all right, do not trouble yourself. We are here for you, and we are ready to offer you every assistance. You are very ill, my dear, but we are doing all within our power to make you comfortable. Here, a sip."

Astell offered the girl a small vessel of the cinnamon water Mrs. Methuen had sent over the evening before, the preparation accompanied by instructions that the feverish patient should be allowed to swallow as much as she pleased.

The girl pushed the cup away. "I do not want *that*," she said. And then, crossly, "Who are you?" And again, in some indignation, "Where am I? Why am I here?"

"And who are you?" Astell could only think to reply.

Although the girl was so weak she could hardly raise her head, she was able to lift at least her chin and reply haughtily, "I am Lettice de Beauclerk, and I have come to find my husband. He is Charles de Beauclerk, a very great lord. He told me his home is in paradise, and so I have come here to him." She frowned, looked with disdain at the woman in front of her, then added, "And when you speak to me, you must address me properly: 'my lady,' you must say."

"Indeed," said Mary Astell. "Indeed," she repeated. The girl's whole response was so improbable that Astell felt inclined to laugh heartily, something she rarely felt inclined to do. But, then, it was also so improbable that she felt inclined to cry—another thing she rarely did. Instead, she repeated for a third time the only thing she could think to say: "Indeed."

The young stranger's head fell back onto the pillow, her eyes burning with fever and rage. "Please do me the courtesy of sending for my lord immediately and telling him that I am arrived," she said. "My lord will be most grateful to you, for I am sure he has been filled with worry and near to despair. He is a great lord, truly."

"Indeed, my dear. And where might I send for him?"

Instead of answer the question, the girl burst into tears, turning her face away and burrowing into the pillow.

"Have a few sips, please," Astell said. "This will help reduce the fever. I will see about getting something for you to eat in case you have an appetite. And then we will speak further."

Astell heard what she thought might be a scoff as she left the room. She had just reached the bottom of the stairway when she heard a coach outside and then Lady Catherine's voice as she directed the coachman to remain. A few quick steps and she was inside the house.

"Thank the Lord, my lady," said Astell, "you really could not have arrived at a better moment, though I did not expect you so early."

"Why, Mary, she has not *died*, has she?"

"Oh, no, no, not that, my lady. All was quiet through the night, and she has just now begun to speak—"

"Well, that is surely reason to be thankful, is it not?"

"Yes, yes, of course." Astell paused briefly before continuing. "But she has only spoken a few words, and those of a most preposterous sort."

"Whatever did she say? Has she told you who she is? What is her name? Why was she wandering here?"

"That is just the problem, my lady. The girl claims that her name is 'Lettice de Beauclerk.' *Lettice*, I am sure! And *Beauclerk*—although she has mangled it most dreadfully. The name came out as 'Beeayooclarck' or some such nonsense, and never mind the absurd 'de.' She also says she has come to Chelsea to find her husband, 'a very great lord,' if you please, a man by the name of Charles de Beauclerk, though of course that cannot possibly be correct. Moreover, the girl believes this her great lord lives here, on this very street—or at least that is what she has decided, since she claims he told her his home was a 'paradise' of some sort, or that he lived in a 'paradise', or some such foolery. And this, it seems, is what has brought her to my door."

Astell paused again before adding, "And she says that I must address her as 'my lady.'"

Lady Catherine was no more inclined to laughter or tears than her friend was, so she neither laughed nor cried. Instead, the women looked at one another in consternation.

"Whatever can it mean?" wondered Lady Catherine.

"Indeed," said Astell, once again. "Indeed."

After this exchange, the two women grew silent, settling themselves once more in front of the coal fire in Mary Astell's parlor.

"Surely she is under some grave misapprehension," Lady Catherine began calmly, breaking the quiet. "She *cannot* mean Charles Beauclerk—that is quite impossible. Completely out of the question. He may have begun life as the bastard son of Nell Gwyn and the old king, but Charles Beauclerk is now the *duke of St. Albans*." As the daughter of an earl, Lady Catherine greatly respected a title. "Moreover," she continued, "the duke is a very gallant soldier, highly esteemed by His Majesty. And he could not possibly be married to this young unknown, whatever she might claim—if you recall, Mary, the duke of St. Albans was married not two years ago to Lady Diana de Vere, the daughter of the earl of Oxford. And she has just given birth to their first child, a son and heir." Lady Catherine may have begun calmly, but she was becoming most indignant.

"Yes, yes, of course," said Astell. "But there was another boy of that name . . . "

"A brother, James, yes, James Beauclerk—but he died years ago when he was still just a boy." Lady Catherine was incensed at what she regarded as the effrontery of the young stranger. "And in any case, the duke of St. Albans has only just returned from Flanders with the king's army—he arrived less than a week ago, in time for the opening of Parliament. He most assuredly has *not* been sending for any young woman to join him 'in paradise,' or anywhere else, for that matter. There is simply no excusing such a calumny."

"A slander only if it were intentional, my lady. Perhaps it is a misapprehension or perhaps she has misspoken. It was so ill spoken, indeed, that I may be mistaken and only assumed what she did not say."

"But she *dared* to tell you to address her as 'my lady'! Such impudence. That she should have the front to address you in such a fashion."

Astell had rarely seen Lady Catherine so indignant. "Well, whatever the case, I fear she has been horribly abused," Astell said. "There are no Beauclerks in this parish, or at least none that I am aware of—nor can I think of anyone whose name might be thus confused."

"Humph" was all Lady Catherine had to say in reply.

"And the duke of St. Albans has no association with Chelsea, or none that I know of, though you will know better than I."

"His mother did, of course, but that was long before *our* time, Mary. According to some, it was she who gave King Charles the idea to establish the hospital for old soldiers here in Chelsea—or, at least, that is the founding narrative my father prefers to recount." And then, after a pause, Lady Catherine added, "He knew her, you know."

"Your father knew the old king's mistress?"

"Yes—he saw her triumphant return to the stage in one of Mr. Dryden's plays . . . now what was it? *The Conquest of Granada*, I believe. She had quite given it all up."

Lady Catherine was watching the coal burn in the grate, but she seemed lost in thought. "The stage, I mean, Mrs. Gwyn had given up the stage, not the king. But she went back to it. Unheard of, it was—she had just given birth to the king's son! But my father—you know him well, Mary, you know his nature—he had just come from Ireland, and he must see her, 'pretty, witty Nell.' He was quite entranced."

She paused briefly, then began again. "He still talks of it—and of her, he came to know her well—though he speaks of it not so often these days, or of her so fondly. Now that Lady Margaret has become countess of Ranelagh, that is to say. Lady Ranelagh will hear none of it, though my mother cared very little one way or another—as you well know, my father has always been most indiscreet."

"But did Nell Gwyn have a house here in Chelsea?"

"She is said to have had a little house not far from here, where she would entertain the king, but that is nonsense. She is also said to have lived in Ship House, in Sandford Manor, and in any one of the other fine mansions in Chelsea, though none of that is true either. Nell Gwyn has more houses pointed out as places where she once lived than hunting lodges where Queen Elizabeth was to have stayed! But as far as I know, Nell Gwyn never lived in Chelsea, no, nor did her son."

"I thought not," said Astell.

"Though her mother did—the 'Old Madam,' as she was known. She lived in one of the Neat-Houses, down by the river. She drank too much brandy and fell into a ditch one day, and there she drowned."

Mary Astell made no response. She hardly knew what to think, much less to say, and yet the day had only begun.

"I never met her—Nell Gwyn, that is, not her mother—but of course I did see her on occasion before she died. And, then, my sister knew her—they were frequently together at court and grew quite intimate for a time." Lady Catherine rarely alluded to Lady Elizabeth's *liaison* with the king, of which she had strongly disapproved. "She died quite young—Mrs. Gwyn, I mean—not that long after King Charles, in fact."

"We will certainly have to look into this further," said Astell, "though I fear it will not be pleasant. The girl is clearly under the influence of some fanciful delusion, and the reality she may have to face will not be quite so agreeable."

"You may be right, Mary. If she has come to Chelsea in order to find some lost husband, a husband who is a great lord and who has somehow misplaced her, his dearly beloved wife, well . . . "

"It all sounds like the kind of froth and nonsense that comes from plays and romances," sniffed Astell, returning to one of her favorite topics. The esteemed rector of Chelsea was not the only one who had hobbyhorses. "You know how I feel, my lady. A woman may study plays and romances all her life and be never the wiser—from them she learns only the greatest follies."

"You are quite right, my dear," said Lady Catherine quickly, hoping to avoid any further steps down this well-worn path. She was not averse to attending a play nor even to picking up a romance on occasion. "But it is just too bad that Lady Ranelagh is not with us here now. She would quite enjoy this."

Their conversation was at that moment interrupted by a loud racket from upstairs—the sudden smashing of crockery, a petulant voice, and the unmistakable footsteps of Sarah.

"Now what?" sighed Astell.

"We will just have to see," said Lady Catherine, rising quickly from her comfortable chair by the fire, a great general preparing herself for battle.

It was clear at once that something was dreadfully amiss.

The outraged "Lettice de Beauclerk," hectic spots of scarlet on her cheeks, sat upright in Mary Astell's bed. The flask of Mrs. Methuen's remedy for fever lay on the floor, along with the cup of cinnamon water, now shattered, its contents seeping into the floorboards.

Sarah stood by, hands on hips, equally outraged. The housemaid turned to Astell while gesturing widely toward the stranger. "It is all this Lettuce person, mistress—" She got no further before she was interrupted by a screech from the girl in the bed, whose strength, if not her senses, seemed to be somewhat restored.

"*Lettice, Lettice*—I have told you, you stupid thing. And you must not address me as *Lettice* but as 'Lady de Beauclerk' or 'my lady'—"

"Lettuce," Sarah repeated, a mulish expression on her face. "That is just what I said."

Sarah's reply set off a fit of coughing in the patient. Before she could regain her composure and her voice, Astell dismissed Sarah, though it was clear the little maidservant felt she was being treated most unjustly.

"I have been trying my best, ma'am," she insisted loudly even as she flounced out of the room. "It was all that Lettuce person's doing, Mrs. Astell, it was all that Lettuce, indeed it was," she could be heard repeating as she stamped her way down the stairs.

"What is this nonsense?" demanded Lady Catherine, her imposing figure drawn up to its full height. In addition to her commanding presence, she had her grandmother's piercing brown eyes, now trained on the patient in the bed. Lady Catherine intended to stare the young stranger into silence. Whatever the girl might have made of Mary Astell, she could be in no doubt that Lady Catherine Jones was a very great lady.

With a toss of her head, "Lettice de Beauclerk" was indeed reduced to silence—a most obstinate silence. If Lady Catherine's intention was to restore the girl to her senses, it seemed that her senses were not meek and subdued. She might, for the moment, be quiet, but she met Lady Catherine's eyes with a stubborn glare.

"Now," began that formidable lady sternly. "Let us have no more such behavior. I hear you are the wife of a very great lord—if that is so, then surely you must begin to act like such a wife. Before we can be of any assistance to you, you must help yourself. We must know who you are, where you have come from, where you are going, and whom you seek."

The girl said nothing. She continued to stare at Lady Catherine as if she too were preparing for battle and taking the measure of her opponent before she engaged. And then, suddenly, she sank back down onto the bed, though it was not clear whether she had exhausted what strength remained to her with her emotional outburst or whether it was a calculated retreat. It occurred to Mary Astell that Lady Catherine might for once have been matched with a worthy foil.

But Lady Catherine had no doubts about her entire command of the situation. She stood silently, watching the girl, assured of her own superior force and ultimate victory. "What is your name, and whom do you seek," she repeated. "We must know who you are. Only then will we know best how to help you—and only then may we be assured that we have reason to do so."

Finally, the young patient roused herself. "I told *her*," she said, pointing at Mary Astell, who was standing at the foot of the bed. "I have told her once, and I should not have to repeat myself. I have asked her to send for my husband."

"Yes," said Lady Catherine. "But who might that be? Let us have no more nonsense. What is your name?"

"I have told you. I am Lettice de Beauclerk, the wife of a very—"

"A lord, yes, a very great lord, so you have said." Lady Catherine had heretofore remained calm, but Astell could tell her friend was becoming roused by the direction the girl was heading. It was also beginning to dawn on Astell that making such a claim against so powerful a man as the duke of St. Albans was not at all wise.

"But *your* name, my dear young lady, *your* name, before you became 'Lady Beauclerk.'" Lettice, if so she was, looked a bit confused, as Lady Catherine had pronounced the name as it should be pronounced.

The girl narrowed her eyes suspiciously. "What does that matter?" she asked at last. "My lord has raised me up to great heights. He is inordinate fond of me. I am Lettice. I have always been Lettice. And now I am become Lady Beauclerk." Although she stumbled over the name, she had learned from Lady Catherine's example and had amended her own pronunciation accordingly. The girl might be obstinate, but she was not stupid.

"How old are you, Lettice?" asked Astell as gently as she could.

The girl looked at first as if she would pretend not to hear her—she clearly thought Mary Astell was not worthy of her attention—but she changed her mind. "I am fifteen years of age," she said with as much dignity as a queen. With that, she sank into the bed, turning her face to the wall. She would say no more. Facing her opponent's unexpected retreat, Lady Catherine turned and left the room. After a moment's hesitation, Astell followed.

Back in the parlor, neither woman spoke. It was still quite early, and Astell was eager to do something, though she was not sure just what she should do. She might not be able to pick up her pen, but she had encountered a new challenge, a problem to be solved, and whether or not she had sought it out, it would require her attention.

A quick rap at the front door brought Sarah running. She had disappeared after her encounter with "Lettice," but she was eager to keep abreast of any new doings in the house. A hushed exchange was followed by Mrs. Methuen's entrance into the parlor.

"Thank you, Sarah," said Astell. The girl smiled and seemed to have forgotten her recent ill temper. She bobbed something of a curtesy, then left the room, though Astell suspected she was once more just outside the door, well within earshot.

"I know it is still quite early," began Mrs. Methuen, but her modest diffidence was quickly dismissed by both Lady Catherine and Mary Astell, who were relieved to see her. Within a few minutes, Astell had reported on the patient's health to her neighbor, while Lady Catherine had related something of the girl's preposterous claims.

"Most strange," Mrs. Methuen responded politely. Given her own experience, nothing much about men—and certainly not husbands—would surprise her. That is as may be," she said, uninterested in involving herself in another woman's marital peculiarities, "but I should like to see her again in order to adjudge her condition."

And that is what she proceeded to do with her usual calm efficiency. As Lady Catherine and Mary Astell remained below in the parlor, they could hear little of what transpired above, but it was not long before they heard Mrs. Methuen making her way slowly down the stairs.

"I am not entirely at ease in my mind," she said slowly. "I fear this may be something of a difficult case, Mrs. Astell. I think our best course is to consult with Mrs. Kettilby at once."

Five

Mary Astell was at last ready to depart. She had been in some difficulty in dissuading Lady Catherine from accompanying her on her way to fetch Mrs. Kettilby—Lady Catherine had insisted that they should make the journey together, warm and dry in the Ranelagh coach, which had been kept waiting on Paradise Row for just such a purpose. But she was at last convinced that, while the king's private road might be open to her, the rest of the way into Little Chelsea by coach would be difficult, if not impossible, given the poor state of the road in the best of circumstances. And circumstances were not the best—the persistent rain and the resulting mud had complicated all manner of travel.

For her part, Mrs. Methuen remained silent while all this was being debated. Once it was decided that Lady Catherine was to stay behind, Astell had hoped to persuade Mrs. Methuen to accompany her to Little Chelsea—Mrs. Methuen and Mary Kettilby had worked together many times, frequently on the most difficult of cases, and Astell thought that on their walk to Little Chelsea, Mrs. Methuen might reveal something of her fears—something that she had not yet felt herself able to tell Astell. But Mrs. Methuen made it clear that she thought it best for her to stay behind and keep a careful watch on the patient. Her abundance of caution convinced Astell to hurry on her way.

And so she was finally ready to take her leave. Her woolen cloak was still not quite dry from the previous day's soaking, but Sarah stood at the ready with it and with her mistress's wide-brimmed hat and sturdy boots.

Thus protected as much as she could be from the rain and chill, Astell set off.

Little Chelsea lay to the north and west of the village proper, about half an hour's walk from Paradise Row. Making her way toward the Thames at a quick pace, Astell followed the riverside highway, passing the church and the houses clustering around it. Reaching Lindsey House, she turned north. She soon reached Gorges House, the great hall built by a Tudor courtier who had captained one of the ships that helped defeat the "Invincible Armada"—now, however, the once-magnificent house had become yet another boarding school for "young ladies," this one under the direction of Josias Priest, who advertised for pupils in the *London Gazette*, where he styled himself as the school's "dancing master."

Crossing the king's private road, Astell took the track between Lord Wharton's park, on her right, and Lord Hungerford's farm, to her left. Reaching the road to Fulham, she turned west, arriving at the group of tiny cottages that had sprung up on both the Kensington and Chelsea sides of the highway in the midst of a patchwork of farms, parks, gardens, and fields. There, in the smallest of the small dwellings, lived Mary Kettilby.

Astell had been acquainted with Mrs. Kettilby for some time, and she had recently introduced her to Mr. Wilkin. The printer was intrigued by Mary Kettilby's "most useful" undertaking: a collection of recipes prepared for the many needs of "the fair sex." As she explained to Mr. Wilkin on the occasion of their first meeting, "Whether it be from the great tenderness of their natures" or from their "greater opportunities of acquiring experience," women were always "active and industrious" in their care of others. Her collection of recipes for cookery, physic, and surgery was intended for women as they undertook their many such tasks.

In describing women's acts of generosity and charity to the printer, Mrs. Kettilby had grown quite animated. "How often have I seen the rich in waiting upon the poor, and mistresses in nursing who become handmaids to their own servants? Women of tender constitutions walking through midnight frosts to the assistance of a poor neighboring woman in her painful and perilous hour?"

And then, seeing Mr. Wilkin nodding thoughtfully in agreement, she had gone further, adding, "Nor could I forbear recommending such generous and beneficial practice of charity to the gentlemen of the clergy—how greatly would the exercise of such useful arts endear them to their people? What opportunities of doing good would *this* procure them?"

That, perhaps, had been taking the matter a bit too far even for Mr. Wilkin, but he had nevertheless agreed to the printing and selling of Mary Kettilby's *Collection of Receipts in Cookery, Physic, and Surgery for the Use of All Good Wives, Tender Mothers, and Careful Nurses* (no further mention, thankfully, of gentlemen of the clergy). She was still hard at work on this project—her collection growing from fifty recipes to a hundred recipes and then to more than two hundred recipes for producing wholesome and tasty dishes and for preparing syrups, ointments, waters, and powders for the treatment of various illnesses. There seemed no end in sight to her expanding collection.

Nor did Mrs. Kettilby claim sole credit for herself as she labored on her ambitious project—although she spared herself no time or expense in compiling the material, she claimed no ownership. The collection was, she said, authored by "many hands," the product of all the women she met as she traveled far from her small cottage in Little Chelsea: poor women who labored in fields, hard-working wives of small farmers whose chores never ended, dedicated craftswomen who plied their trades in town, and great ladies who managed vast estates. Mrs. Kettilby gathered useful materials from all of them, great and small, rich and poor. (Astell herself had contributed to the collection, her mother's recipe for potted salmon, which Kettilby had headed "To Pot Salmon, as at Newcastle.")

Still, while she compiled material for her collection, Mary Kettilby needed to earn her living, and that she did by practicing midwifery, as her mother had done before her. Indeed, Mrs. Kettilby's services were so much in demand that she traveled nearly as far in that endeavor as she did in assembling her recipes and prescriptions. So frequently was she called away that Astell feared she might not find Mary Kettilby at home in Little Chelsea—though she also knew that, if such were the case, Mrs. Kettilby would have left word about where and how she might be found.

But home she was and delighted to see Astell, whom she welcomed warmly, drawing her into the tiny cottage's single room, which served as parlor, dining room, library, study, and laboratory all in one.

"Mrs. Astell, how good it is to see you," she exclaimed, helping Astell with her cloak. Mary Kettilby paid no mind to the garment's disreputable state as she placed it by the fire to dry. "And in this weather, too!"

"I am afraid this is to be no quiet visit," Astell began, "nor a long one, I am sorry to say, and I fear I have come to call you out into the cold and rain." As Mrs. Kettilby bustled about adding coal to the small fire, Astell was reminded to ask Lady Catherine whether she could spare one of the strong young men who worked in the garden at Ranelagh to carry a few bushels of coal from Paradise Row to Little Chelsea.

The battered desk on one side of the room was covered with bits and pieces of paper, all of them filled with writing in Mrs. Kettilby's strong hand, some of them blotted, others curling or folded, still others tattered and worn, as if they had been kept for some time in a pocket. Still more recipes, it would seem.

Wherever she went, Mary Kettilby carried about her person an array of pouches, sacks, and purses. At least one of these would be filled with powders wrapped in twists of paper, salves and ointment preserved in small clay pots, and medicinal concoctions carefully sealed into tiny vials. If she were on her way to a woman in labor, she carried the necessaries in a separate bag: clean linens, oils, scissors, needle, and thread. In still another purse were ink, pens, a pen knife, and paper. She tried to keep the receipts she copied out in a pocket kept just for that purpose, but sometimes, when she returned home, she found them shoved into the strangest of places.

"Have you a new book?" Astell asked, immediately distracted upon seeing a heavy volume on a low table beside the desk. Mrs. Kettilby often spent the little money she scraped together on expanding her library rather than on replenishing her coal box. Astell picked the book up and opened to its title page. She could make no sense of the lines of black type. There were letters she did not recognize, nor could she identify the language of the text.

"Yes," Mrs. Kettilby replied, "I am almost afraid to admit the lengths to which I was forced to go in order to acquire it, but it was a volume I simply had to have. It is by 'Justinen Siegemundin,' as she is called here. As a midwife, she began her career by providing her services—for free, mind you—to peasant women, and so great was her success as a practitioner that she soon was in demand everywhere, first called to attend them by city wives and then by noblewomen. But she never turned away from poor women. Now she is midwife at the court of the elector of Brandenburg. She writes that since she gained knowledge from books as well as from experience, she decided to write one herself. It is of special interest to me, as it is a manual on how to treat difficult and unnatural births."

Mary Kettilby's sizable collection of books about women's health was impressive—Astell knew of no medical man who would bother to amass a library of texts on midwifery, much less to search out those written by women. Although Mrs. Kettilby took pains to acquire the latest treatises written by physicians, she was deeply suspicious of men who wrote about women and their bodies, about pregnancy, labor, and delivery, and about women's diseases. What did men know about such things?

If it were possible, she was even more disdainful of those medical men who presumed to steal (or, as they preferred to call it, "borrow") from the manuals written by experienced midwives. Thus, although she had a copy of *The Complete Midwife's Practice* in her library, she did not put much faith in the four London doctors who claimed that the subject of the "conception, bearing, and nursing of children" was "so plain" that "the weakest capacity may easily attain the knowledge of the whole art."

"They are all most desperately deficient," she had concluded after carefully assessing their manual. Their assurances that they had published with the "approbation and good liking of the most knowing professors of midwifery now living in the city of London" meant less than nothing to her. In her view, the only reliable information conveyed by these men was the material they had taken directly from a manual written by Louise Bourgeois, the French midwife whose portrait had been used as the frontispiece for their book.

Not only did Mary Kettilby hold their translation suspect, but she was incensed by their claim that most midwives were "unskilled" and ignorant, "resting too boldly upon the common way of delivering women" and neglectful of "all the wholesome and profitable rules of art"—which they alone presumed to have.

Mrs. Kettilby had also been quick to point out their utter failure when it came to anatomy. They wrote in great detail about the structure of the male member, its glory and strength, and about the male seed, its vitality and its wondrous power of generation—but they had very little to say about women's bodies or, indeed, about women's role in procreation. In Mary Kettilby's opinion, it was better to consult *Observations diverses* in the original French than to rely on such an unreliable source as *The Complete Midwife's Practice*, even if the physicians claimed to be translating the work of Bourgeois into English.

Better still was Jane Sharpe's *Whole Art of Midwifery Discovered*, a good English book written by a good Englishwoman, a practitioner of the right sort, one who had been a midwife for more than thirty years. And, moreover, a midwife who understood women's anatomy rather than ignoring it: "in the clitoris lies the chief pleasure of love's delight in copulation," the source of "the pleasure transcendently ravishing us." Since men had so much to say about the power and glory of their own members, Sharpe needed to say very little about them.

Although Mary Astell was always interested in the new additions to Mrs. Kettilby's library, she looked doubtfully at the new volume she held in her hand.

"It is German," said Mrs. Kettilby cautiously, not wanting to press too hard Mary Astell's very tender spot. "And, mind you, like me this Justine Siegemund is a midwife who has not given birth to children of her own, although, unlike me, she is a married woman." And then, "Look here, Mrs. Astell, where the midwife has included a dedication to Her Majesty, God rest her soul."

Mary Kettilby hoped Siegemund's dedication of her book to the late Queen Mary might distract Astell at least somewhat—Astell was deeply sensitive about her own lack of languages. She felt disadvantaged by her inability to read French philosophers in the original and crippled by what she called her "ignorance in the sacred languages." Her "deficiencies" were frequently pointed out to her by men who may have been able to *read* French and Latin but who could *understand* very little of what they read.

Although Astell's education had been no more limited than that of most women—indeed, she had been taught to read and write, which the vast majority of women, even members of her own class, had not—she had received no formal instruction. What little money had been left after her father's death was invested in her younger brother's education at the Royal Grammar School.

While Peter Astell went to school, Mary Astell was taught to bake and brew and wash and mend, skills she did not regret having learned. But for history and philosophy and religion and mathematics, the young Astell had cobbled together what education she could. Her uncle Ralph Astell, a rather disreputable clergyman who had been suspended from his curacy for drunkenness, instructed her while he was alive, but he had died just a year after Astell's father. From that point on, her education was her own doing.

For Mary Kettilby, the story began much the same way, but it ended quite differently. As in Astell's case, her family's modest resources had been dedicated to the education of her brother, but he, in turn, had shared what he learned with his sister. Each day when he returned home from school, he had taught her what he had learned that day—and she so impressed him with her quick intelligence and aptitude that he had continued the practice even after he left for Oxford, sending her notes and books and taking the time to respond to her questions in a lengthy exchange of letters. His early death had devastated Mary Kettilby, who lost not only the dearest of brothers but the best of teachers.

And now, at least in part in remembrance of him, she was helping Mary Astell in her efforts to learn French. Both women were so busy, however, that the going was slow.

"Well, now," Mrs. Kettilby said, as Astell reluctantly closed the book she could not read, "no more of that. What is it that has brought you here?"

"It all began yesterday," Astell said.

While Mary Astell recounted the events of the past day, Mrs. Kettilby prepared to leave her home and work. She was a tiny woman, as modest and unprepossessing as Lady Catherine was tall and imposing, but she was quick and energetic. She moved rapidly and with great efficiency as she gathered together her many bags and pouches. She was so often called—and so often had to leave the cottage in Little Chelsea on short notice—that it took only a few minutes for her to collect all that she might need.

In that time, Astell told Mary Kettilby about finding the insensible girl lying outside her gate, about the long night's watch by the stranger's bedside, about Mrs. Methuen's opinion that Mrs. Kettilby should be consulted. Astell also relayed the details of her trip to Lambeth House, spurred by her fears about the girl's sudden appearance in Chelsea. She did not have to explain the reason for her fears to Mary Kettilby.

In her profession, the midwife had seen the way it went all too often for women. She had frequently been directed to withhold her services from poor women in an effort to force them from the parish. She had been compelled to question unmarried women in the throes of labor in order to extract from them the name of the father of their child. She had been pressed to give evidence against women who were suspected of killing their newborn babies and discouraged from giving evidence on their behalf in cases of rape. She was well aware of the pressures the young stranger who had appeared at Astell's door might face, should she be judged by parish officials to be a poor and friendless vagrant.

Having collected her things, Mrs. Kettilby put her hands on her hips for a moment and looked around them room before opening her door and leaning out. "Georgie, Georgie," she called into the cold and rain, startling Astell.

How can such a small person produce such a great racket? Astell tried not to looked shocked at Mary Kettilby's behavior. Astell thought it was most unseemly, but, then, it was the speediest way to summon the boy who had become a surprisingly capable deputy for the midwife. Unable to afford to keep any kind of servant, Mrs. Kettilby had come to rely on the services of the boy whose family who lived in one of the tiny cottages nearby. He was still young, younger even than Sarah, but he had proven to be singularly able.

George performed an invaluable service for Mary Kettilby—and, it must also be said, for the many women who relied on her. Although the midwife was frequently called out at all hours of the day and night, she was well aware that at any time another woman in her travail might have need of her services. The isolation of Little Chelsea had been a source of many difficulties for her after she had settled there. But in the past year and with the assistance of young George, she had devised an ingenious method of ensuring that her whereabouts were always known. Whenever she left her cottage in Little Chelsea, whether it was day or night, she now left the boy there in her stead. George kept track of where Mrs. Kettilby was going, how long she expected to be away, and how she might be reached if she were needed. She could send a messenger back to George if she were detained or if she were moving on or if she required something from her stock of preparations. George, with an ample supply of brothers at his disposal, could relay messages to Mrs. Kettilby and send her anything she might need but did not have on hand.

Since the two had worked out this reliable system of communication, Mary Kettilby was never out of touch, never missing when she was wanted. The boy was a wonder of organization and common sense, as quick and efficient as the woman herself, and although he could not write very well—a deficiency Mary Kettilby aimed to remedy, in recompense for his services—his memory was capacious.

The dark-haired George, lean as a rake, appeared out of the cold and rain, smiling at both women as he popped into the little cottage.

"Now sit down by the fire," Mary Kettilby fussed, giving the grate a poke and drawing a chair closer to the warmth. Young George was quite happy to be in the little cottage—it was much quieter than the home he had left, and he knew he would be offered something delectable to eat.

"And here is something for you to try," Mrs. Kettilby continued. On the opposite side of the room from her desk and books was her cook table, where she prepared variations on her recipes, always searching for just the right combination of flavors. She appeared to have been hard at work on perfecting her receipt for potato pie—a bowl of boiled, peeled potatoes sat on the table, along with the floury remnants of pastry dough and, luckily for young George, a baked pie, still warm.

"I am off to Mrs. Astell's, Georgie—you know the place," she explained. The boy was already digging into the pie, and although he did not look up, Mrs. Kettilby knew from the nod of his head that he had heard her. As she watched him eat, she smiled.

"This is a good one," he said, his mouth shoved full of potatoes, thick, buttery sauce, and rich pastry crust.

"Well, let us go," Mrs. Kettilby said to Mary Astell. And then the midwife offered a few parting words to her assistant. "I do not know how long I will be, Georgie, but you can send for me if I am needed." Without waiting for the boy to respond or to see whether Astell was following, she was out the door. Once Astell joined her, Mrs. Kettilby shut up the little cottage, confident that all would be well with her assistant in charge.

The midwife turned to address Mary Astell as they started on their journey. "I fear there is something more to it all, Mrs. Astell. Mrs. Methuen would not need me, not for a simple fever, not even if it were a violent ague. Mind you, she knows better than I how to treat a fever, and she has provided me with many of her own receipts. Indeed, there is no remedy I could supply that she does not already have. No, there is something more to it."

"That is my fear as well," Astell replied.

"And I do think," continued Mrs. Kettilby, warming to her subject as they walked, "that it is just as well for you stop to see Mr. King while I go on directly to Paradise Row. Not that he will have anything more helpful to suggest than the poor archbishop, I dare well say. But it is best to let him know all that has transpired—such news will undoubtedly have made its way to the church and the rectory already."

She was silent for a moment as she stepped around a large puddle. "Mind you," she continued, "even if he knows full well all that has happened, he will most certainly expect you to inform him all the same, though his head will be just as full of Sir Willoughby Chamberlain as ever it was. Pish! It is all nonsense, a great waste of time."

Mrs. Kettilby was so incensed at the great shame of "it" all, by which she meant the reformation of Sir Willoughby, that Mary Astell found it hard to match her pace. The little woman took three quick steps for every one of Astell's longer strides, but she was moving almost too fast for Astell to keep up with her.

Mrs. Kettilby stopped suddenly, turning to face Astell. "And she calls herself *Lettice de Beauclerk?* What nonsense. Mind you, there will be some story behind it all, you can be sure of that."

Six

The two women headed back to Great Chelsea, retracing the route Astell had taken on her journey to fetch the midwife. Although the rain had stopped, it was still difficult going: the track through the fields as they approached the king's road was impossibly muddy where it was not covered by deep pools of standing water.

Unlike Mary Astell, Mrs. Kettilby did not own a fine pair of leather boots; she wore simple wood pattens over her shoes. She picked her way carefully through the muck, but she nevertheless proceeded briskly. The two spoke little as they walked—there was nothing more to be said, really, so each woman kept her thoughts to herself and her eyes on the path they followed.

As they crossed the king's private road, their way became somewhat easier, though the track was so narrow that they did not walk abreast. Moving ahead of Astell, Mrs. Kettilby increased her pace, turning east when she reached the riverside highway. When the two women approached Church Lane, they parted ways, Mrs. Kettilby continuing on to Paradise Row. Heading up the lane, Astell soon arrived at the rectory. At that hour on a Saturday—it was just before midday—Astell was not sure whether the Reverend Mr. King would be found at home, but she would certainly call on him before returning home.

The rectory stood at the north end of the street, the oldest in Chelsea. Mr. King's predecessor in the parish, the Reverend Dr. Adam Littleton, had served All Saints for some twenty-five years, a worthy man who had cared little about the state of his dwelling. The genial clergyman had been a noted classical scholar and a distinguished linguist—he was hard at work on a Greek lexicon at the time of his death, his Latin dictionary having just been published in a fifth edition. During the many years that he served his parishioners and pursued his studies, Mr. Littleton had amassed an enormous library—to the very great impoverishment of his estate and the rectory.

When Mr. King succeeded to the living, he was dismayed to find the house, walls, and garden of the rectory all miserably out of repair, and he carefully catalogued the costs of the many "dilapidations" that could be imputed to his predecessor's neglect. But since Reverend Littleton was found to be insolvent at the time of his death—leaving his young widow, who had brought a fortune into the marriage, with nothing upon which to live—the Reverend Mr. John King soon realized that he would be unable to recover the costs of repair from his predecessor's estate. Although he generously agreed to oversee the sale of her husband's library for Susan Littleton, it was clear that the proceeds would not be enough to alter the widow's distressed circumstances, much less to restore the rectory.

And so, not long after his arrival in Chelsea, Mr. King had set about improving the sad state of financial affairs in the parish. He quickly concluded that it would be "inconvenient" to continue Mr. Littleton's practice of collecting tithes in kind—turnips, carrots, beans, and peas were all very well, but they would not put the rectory back into a state of repair.

In order to increase his income, Mr. King also looked to the property that was the chief source of the Chelsea living. He raised the rents of tenants and, taking advantage of the many speculators eager to build close to the new hospital, the new rector leased out the parish's glebe land to them. He also claimed the rights to common pasture that had been transferred from the old parsonage to the new more than a hundred years earlier—although his right to let that pasturing was hotly debated, let it he did.

He then negotiated with parishioners to secure a new Easter tithe from every person in the parish over the age of sixteen, and he made sure that *all* tithes, old and new, were received—he even sued the widowed duchess of Beaufort for full payment of all of the taxes that the duke, in a feud with the Reverend Littleton, had refused to pay. The new rector also decided to let a few choice pews within the chancel, the rents generating both a handsome addition to his income as well a simmering resentment among his parishioners. And, of course, he was diligent in collecting all fees due him for marriages, baptisms, and burials.

In short order after the arrival of the Reverend Mr. King in Chelsea, it is fair to say, the living of the parish had not only been restored, it had been quite nicely amended and augmented. And while his parishioners might have grumbled at the new rector's financial reformations, the increase in his income had made it possible for Mr. King to restore his residence to a state he deemed livable. Over the course of the last year, there had been much activity around the place as workmen set about the necessary renovations.

As she approached the rectory after having parted from Mrs. Kettilby, Mary Astell could see that the old brick wall surrounding the courtyard had been newly repaired. Turning through the gate and entering into the garden, long overgrown, she could see that it was also in the process of being restored to order. She was only halfway down the walk when the front door opened and the rector himself burst out, his curled and powdered wig slightly askew.

"Mrs. Astell, Mrs. Astell, you have come at just the right moment," John King began as he hurtled toward her. Although he was not elderly, the rector was a man somewhat past his prime, and after only a few steps, he stopped short, breathing heavily, his plump face an alarming shade of red. Astell was immediately reminded of her encounter just the day before—like the archbishop on his return to Lambeth, the Reverend Mr. King had a fistful of papers and was eagerly waving them at her.

Drawing a deep breath and wiping his brow, Mr. King thrust the papers right into her face, exclaiming as he did, "Such utter nonsense on the subject of Sir Thomas More's house is not to be countenanced—he dares to write, and I will read it to you, 'It is the same house where Sir John Danvers's lately stood, where two pyramids are at the gate'! He is most certainly ill-informed, and I should be glad to know what authority he has for saying so!"

As the rector paused to take a breath, Astell tried to stop the flow of his high indignation. Although she had no idea about the identity of the man to whom the rector was referring, she thought it best not to ask for clarification. At least not at the moment. "Perhaps you will be able to inform him the better—"

"—I have no end in sight but the truth, as you well know, Mrs. Astell," the rector continued, increasing the volume of his speech in order to talk over her the more effectively. "And, while it must sadly be acknowledged that time is the great devourer of all things in this world, it is my opinion that Beaufort House bids fairest to be the place where Sir Thomas More's stood. My reasons—"

Having been interrupted herself and believing that the problem she faced was more immediate than identifying where Sir Thomas More's house may once have stood, Astell was less concerned about cutting off the rector's flow of words than she might otherwise have been. "I am most sorry, Mr. King, but I have a pressing reason for seeing you. May I speak with you, sir?"

The Reverend Mr. King looked aghast at Astell's temerity—whatever could be more important than correcting the misapprehensions of his current antagonist?—but he graciously withdrew his sheaf of papers from under Astell's nose and drew himself up to his full height (which, alas, was not great, much to the rector's everlasting regret). He adjusted his peruke, and spoke with as much dignity as he could muster: "Perhaps you will be so kind as to look over my pages when we are through. There are no fewer than four houses in this parish that lay claim to being Sir Thomas More's residence, but the evidence for Beaufort House is clear."

"Yes, yes, I am certain that you are in the right, Mr. King. Shall we go in now? Perhaps we will be able to speak more freely in your study?"

Astell would have preferred the comfortable sitting room of Elizabeth King to the rector's library, but she could hear the angry cries of the youngest King child just then being met and matched by the howls of his two elder sisters.

"Come this way, then, if you please," said the rector primly, only at that moment noting the mud that caked her boots and the dreadful state of her skirts. His nose wrinkled with some measure of distaste, but he made no move to relieve her of wet cloak, nor did he offer to summon a servant to assist her. He did, however, overcome his displeasure sufficiently to lead her inside and up the stairs away from the noise, the source of which was somewhere below, toward the back of the large house.

Unlike the few sputtering flames in the grate at Mary Kettilby's cottage, the fire in the rector's study burned hot, the logs sending up a fountain of sparks as Mr. King poked them, rather viciously, upon entering the room. He gestured toward a hard, wooden chair that sat to the side of his large writing-desk. Astell obediently seated herself there, eyeing with trepidation the open books, heaps of papers, and scattered drawings spread out on the desk's vast surface, all of them related in some way to the various houses that had been suggested as belonging to Sir Thomas More.

On top of one stack of papers lay a rough sketch of the floorplan and elevation of Sir John Danvers's old house, about which the rector was so incensed—it had just recently been demolished although most of the beautiful gardens had been preserved.

"Danvers House is most certainly *not* the house, nor is Shrewsbury House, and nor is Lady Powell's. Humph." With that contemptuous snort, Mr. King settled into his own comfortable chair, pulling it up closely to his side of the desk. "The evidence for Beaufort House is quite clear," he repeated, adding, "First, his grandson, who wrote his life—" He stopped himself. "Humph." Having uttered a second snort, even more contemptuous than the first, he poked at the various papers and books on his desk, clearing a small space in front of him and then folding his hands. His puffy face had returned to a more normal color. And with that, Mary Astell felt she could at last begin.

"Well, Mr. King," she said slowly, considering how best to put the situation to the rector. "Although it was only early yesterday morning, you may already have received some word about the poor young girl who fell ill while traveling through Chelsea." That seemed as good a way as any to acknowledge what they both knew—that the rector had surely heard gossip about the stranger's arrival—as well as to avoid what he probably knew but that Astell would like to avoid saying—that she had provided shelter and care.

"Yes, of course, Mrs. Astell, most troubling, most troubling, a most troubling event," he acknowledged, unable to resist poking at the stacks of papers in front of him. He jabbed at them almost as violently as he had stabbed at the logs in his fireplace.

"Indeed," she replied, wondering what, if anything more, she ought to say.

"And I am concerned, Mrs. Astell," Mr. King continued, furrowing his ample brow. His luxuriant eyebrows met as he demonstrated the degree of his concernment.

"As am I, Mr. King. As are Lady Ranelagh and Lady Catherine, I might add. Indeed, Lady Catherine is with the unfortunate creature now, even as we speak. We are all of us much concerned." That, perhaps, might end the discussion before it could go further—Mr. King was mindful of the influence of the earl of Ranelagh.

But it was not to be as she hoped. "Humph," he snorted yet again, still eyeing the papers in front of him. "Am I to understand, then, that you have taken this young girl in? And that she is properly a resident of this parish? I take it you ascertained as much before deciding to harbor her? Her name, if you please? And her family?"

"She is very ill, Mr. King, but she assures me that her husband is a resident of this parish." It was the truth, if not, perhaps, the whole truth. Astell wished to avoid the question of the girl's name if she could. "She was traveling to meet him when she was overcome by her illness."

"And where is this husband of hers? Why is she not with him? And who is he? *His* name, Mrs. Astell? And I am curious about just how he came to be separated from his wife in the first place. You are certain that he has his settlement in this parish? A house, perhaps, or work? Has he paid his parish taxes?"

So many questions. And none of them about the young stranger's well-being. Not even one. Perhaps Mrs. Kettilby is right about the need for clergymen to receive instruction in the "generous and beneficial practice of charity." The exercise of such a useful art might indeed mean well for his parishioners.

As Mary Astell reflected on the clergyman's notion of the most urgent questions to be asked at this moment, Mr. King added, with an entirely unwarranted degree of pomposity, "As you know doubt know, Mrs. Astell, we must always be concerned lest a stranger be found to be chargeable to the parish. The continual increase in the number of the poor is most worrisome, their needs exceedingly burdensome. And we altogether fail in our duties if we do not undertake the faithful execution of the laws and statues that have been made solely for their betterment."

Now it was Astell's turn to utter a snort of contempt, though she dare not. It was better not to alarm the rector, better, in fact, not to say too much of anything. He was a busy man with many important matters on his mind.

"As you may know, Mrs. Astell," he continued, in a tone that implied that she did not know much at all, and certainly nothing of what he saw fit to tell her at this moment, "the poor are restrained by statute from gadding about wherever their fancy leads them. They simply cannot be allowed to settle themselves wherever they will—should that be the case, we would all find ourselves *devoured* by strangers!" As he warmed to his topic, Mr. King was growing as agitated as he was apt to become when the topic of Sir Thomas More's house arose.

"As you may also know," he added, poking among the papers on his desk, as if searching for a document to prove his point, "it is the duty of the churchwardens, the constables, and the headborough of every parish to be vigilant. If a destitute stranger enters into a parish and seeks help, he is to be interviewed and sent home to his place of birth, where they have a duty to look after him. Or, as it may be in this case, 'she'—she must be interviewed—and who can say what other notorious sins and vices this woman might be guilty of having committed? I must ask— what could have sent her forth, wandering alone and unprotected? She must be examined directly. And sooner rather than later. Is she fit?"

Alarmed at the rector's vehemence and hoping to avoid any further questions that she was not prepared to answer, Astell thought to distract him. She was not proud of the stratagem, but it proved effective. "By the by, Mr. King," she began, hoping that he would not notice her misdirection, "What news of Sir Willoughby Chamberlain? I hope he is feeling well enough that we will see him at the service tomorrow."

Although the Toleration Act had granted some freedom of worship to dissenters, if not to Catholics, it had also reaffirmed the principle that attendance at the divine service on the Lord's day was mandatory. But men like Sir Willoughby, men who had no lawful or reasonable excuse to be absent, paid little mind either to punishment they might suffer by the censures of the church or to the fines they might incur. It need hardly be said that they would not be drawn to the worship service simply to give thanks to the Lord.

"Ahh, Mrs. Astell," said Mr. King, shaking his head solemnly. "The former part of his life has exposed him to many temptations, I fear, but Sir Willoughby has recently made an earnest request that the little black servant who waits upon his wife might with all convenient speed be instructed and made a Christian." The rector's voice was filled with satisfaction. "I hope soon to baptize her."

"A wondrous thing, to be sure," Astell replied. Sir Willoughby Chamberlain's "little black servant" was one of several unfortunates the planter had brought with him from Barbados. Despite Mr. King's hope of saving the girl's immortal soul, it pained Astell to see how easily his attention might be redirected at the mere mention of one of his preoccupations. "I fear I have kept you too long," she said, "I will leave you now to your sermon."

She rose briskly and, before the rector could follow her with any more about the state of Sir Willoughby Chamberlain's religious faith or the whereabouts of Sir Thomas More's house, she was out the door of the study and heading for the stairway.

"Oh, Mrs. Astell, how pleased I am that you have called," said Elizabeth King. And then, as Mary Astell approached, the rector's wife began to frown. "Look at the state of you—has he done nothing to warm you or to make you more comfortable?"

Mrs. King took Astell's damp cloak from her and shook her head in annoyance as they made their way into the small but comfortable parlor where the rector's wife busied herself with the endless sewing and mending that kept her three small children in a presentable state. There was no sign of those children at the moment, and Astell assumed they had been whisked off to some far corner of the house, where they could be neither seen nor heard.

Elizabeth King was much the same age as Mary Astell, making the wife quite some years younger than her husband. She was perpetually worn and harried, and there was an air of sadness that hung about her. Just a few short years earlier, Elizabeth Aris, as she was then, had married the Reverend John Eston, but she lost her much-loved first husband quite unexpectedly when he died soon after their marriage. Necessity had compelled her to take a second husband within the year.

And so she had become the wife of Mr. John King. With his marriage to Elizabeth Eston, the ambitious King acquired not only the Reverend John Eston's widow but also his vacant living. The Reverend Mr. John King had been installed as rector in the parish church of Pertenhall as soon as he married and then, seeing the many advantages to be had closer to the capital, he had transferred to Chelsea after the death of the Reverend Littleton.

Elizabeth King had given birth to a baby within a year of her second marriage, a girl, and the woman had at last found reason to rejoice. She had given the infant the fanciful name of Eulalia, "well-spoken" in Greek (her father, also a clergyman, had been happy to educate his daughter in the classical languages), but the young mother's joy was short-lived. The baby died just a few weeks after her birth. A year later Mrs. King gave birth to Elizabeth and then, a year and a half after that, to Mary, and then, a year and a half later, to John. No more fanciful names. The Reverend Mr. King preferred good English names for his children.

"What may I get you, Mrs. Astell?" asked the rector's wife, in whose lined face a careful observer might read something of her sorrows. She pushed back a few loose strands of hair. Her once-beautiful curls, golden curls she had taken care to arrange just so, were now faded. "And move up closer to the grate, if you please. You look as if you are chilled through."

"I am fine, and I require nothing, Mrs. King. Rest yourself now." As Mary Astell spoke, the rector's wife picked up her needle and thread, a large basket of mending nearby.

"I missed you yesterday," Astell said, "but I am glad to see you are well."

Elizabeth King gave a rueful smile. "The baby had a fretful night, but he is fine, thank the Lord. It is far too early, I know, but he gives every appearance of cutting a tooth."

Astell knew nothing of such things. "I am glad all is well," she said. Astell understood something of Mrs. King's worries for her children, but a tooth, even should it arrive earlier than expected, did not seem to be a cause for fear.

"My dear Mrs. Astell, there is no need for us to talk about such matters—I am sure they are of little interest to you. But how is the young stranger? Mrs. Methuen has been with her all day, I believe, and the Ranelagh coach has stood in front of your door for hours."

Just one of the many things Astell appreciated about Elizabeth King was her directness. The rector's wife would not pretend she had heard nothing of the stranger, nor would she feign disinterest.

"I am on my way there directly. I've just come from Little Chelsea with Mrs. Kettilby, who has gone on ahead of me. Mrs. Methuen asked for her, so I went to fetch her hither. And as we agreed, it seemed best for me to see Mr. King without delay."

Elizabeth King nodded her head. On this topic, too, there was no need for explanation.

"What may I do, Mrs. Astell? How may I be of assistance?" asked Mrs. King. She might be harried and overburdened, left alone with her memories and her children for long stretches while the rector busied himself about the parish with his many important obligations, but she was quick to offer her help when she thought she could be of use. "We have a good stewed hare almost ready for the table. Betty was most annoyed with me—I am afraid I insisted that she follow one of Mrs. Kettilby's recipes, and I sat in the kitchen and read it out to her while she worked! A pint of claret! But with the herbs and onions and anchovy, it smells quite divine." She clapped a hand over her mouth—"divine" was not an adjective that Mr. King approved of applying to such a trivial thing as food.

"Well," Mrs. King continued, "it smells exceedingly good. I will send some to you, along with plenty of bread. I know you prefer not to eat meat—if we are to be honest, Mrs. Astell, you prefer not eat anything much at all—and I know it is too rich a dish for the sickroom, but I will send along some beef broth for your young patient as well. Or would barley-milk be better? And Mrs. Kettilby will surely be in need of some nourishment. I wonder whether she will know I have used her recipe for the hare? And, then, Mrs. Methuen has been in attendance all day . . . Maybe a custard—Betty can make a very good custard, and even if it is too much for the sickroom, I am sure that Sarah will eat it with pleasure. And bread, I know Betty has baked today. Or did I already mention bread?"

Elizabeth King was animated, the tiredness having left her eyes as she considered how she might be of use.

"Thank you," said Mary Astell, touched by the woman's quick generosity. "That would all be most appreciated." She rose slowly to take her leave, once again feeling stiffness in her joints.

Mrs. King rose too, a grave look on her face. "There will be no trouble, I hope?"

"I hope not," Astell replied. "I have seen the archbishop and, now, the rector—they have both impressed upon me the gravity of the situation, which even I could see myself, but neither one has offered me any advice, much less encouragement. No sign at all that either one might stand ready to help the unfortunate girl, should help be needed, nor, for that matter, that they would be willing to offer *me* their assistance should I need it in this most unusual of situations.

"Admonishments, yes, they are generous enough with their warnings and reproofs, but what is to be done now, I ask you? Throw the poor girl out of doors as quick as quick may be? And what ought I have to have done? Leave her lying on the ground in all that rain? Step over her on my way into my own warm and dry home? I sought clarification of the law, and that is what I got from the archbishop at Lambeth. Just that and no more. Nothing from him but warnings." Astell stopped at that. She would not complain about the rector to the rector's wife. But she did not have to.

"Of course not, Mrs. Astell," Elizabeth King replied with a sorrowful shake of her head. "It is all the same with them. 'Charges to the parish.' 'Sins and vices.' 'Black rolls.' Churchwardens and constables. What, I ask you, is a poor person to do? And a poor young woman, in particular? Must she *die* without setting off in search of someplace where she might live?"

Seven

As she hurried along Paradise Row, Mary Astell saw the distinctive figure of Mustapha waiting by the ironwork gate outside her front garden—almost as if he had been expecting her arrival.

"Good day, *Madame* Astell," he said, bowing his head slightly. He had exchanged his dark, woolen coat for one of a deep blue and his red velvet slippers for a pair in the bright yellow color of a Canary finch. Although the rain had stopped, Astell still could not imagine how the man had managed to keep from ruining his footwear—it was only a short distance from one end of the terrace to the other, but mud was everywhere. And yet the velvet shoes were spotless.

"Good day to you, Mr. Mustapha," she replied, still uncertain about the correct form of address.

"Just Mustapha, *madame*," he said, clarifying at least that much for her. "Her Grace has sent me to inquire about your guest. And she has also asked if there is anything she might provide for you or for the comfort of the stranger you are sheltering. We remain, of course, at your service."

Whatever his role in the household of the duchess might be, Mustapha's manner was impeccable. Still, to her surprise, Astell found herself feeling both cautious and deeply suspicious. While she had no reason to doubt the man's sincerity, the duchess of Mazarin, seemed hardly the kind of woman who would offer sympathy, much less charity, without some kind of calculation involved.

Astell had of course seen the duchess on many occasions since each had taken up residence in the terrace on Paradise Row—after all, it was impossible not to be aware of the comings and goings of one's own neighbors—but the two women had never met. Even so, Astell knew far more about Hortense Mancini, duchess of Mazarin, than any mere neighbor should know about another. And what she knew made Astell certain that she wished no closer acquaintance.

Hortense Mancini had been the favorite niece of Jules Mazarin, the Italian cardinal who had become chief minister to Louis XIII, king of France. After the king's death and during the minority of his son and heir, the cardinal had become the *de facto* ruler of the country. He had brought his niece, Hortense, from Rome to the French court when she was just six years old, and the girl had enjoyed a delightful childhood while under her uncle's protection, fêted and petted and admired by all who knew her.

When Hortense was still a few weeks short of her fifteenth birthday, her ambitious uncle married her off to an eager suitor who had been obsessed with the girl since she her arrival at the Mazarin Palace. The husband that the cardinal selected for his niece was a deeply religious man—unfortunately, he soon proved to be as mad as he was devout. When the cardinal died just days after the elaborate festivities celebrating his niece's marriage, her new husband took the Mazarin name, gained complete control of his wife's huge inheritance, and completely lost his mind.

As jealous as he was fanatical, the new *duc de Mazarin* isolated his wife and accused her of every kind of perversion; meanwhile, he was abusive, unhinged, and profligate. At first, his young wife submitted to his bizarre and controlling behavior, and she dutifully gave birth to four children, including a son and heir. But after seven years of marriage and constant torment, the unhappy woman abandoned her husband. Having delivered herself from the madman's clutches, she promptly embarked on an outrageous career of her own.

The runaway wife began her adventures by traveling throughout Europe, indulging in a series of increasingly scandalous love affairs with both women and men. She eventually returned to the French court and charmed everyone there, especially her childhood friend, Louis XIV, who happily settled a generous pension on her. Hortense Mancini then became the mistress of a former suitor, the duke of Savoy, and after his death, she ventured to England, daringly disguised as a cavalier, wearing boots and spurs.

Within months of her arrival in London, Hortense Mancini had become one of King Charles II's many mistresses. She was given an apartment in Whitehall and provided with a handsome income. Even after their *liaison* ended, the king continued to support her lavish life, and she was installed in a fine house next to St. James's Palace, on the Mall and facing the park. There, in the "Little Palace," the duchess and the king met frequently and maintained their friendship despite Hortense's scandalous affair with his sixteen-year-old daughter.

After Charles's death, the new king, his brother James, continued to provide handsomely for the duchess of Mazarin—after all, she was the cousin of his wife, Mary of Modena. When James was deposed, the Protestant king and queen who succeeded him resisted pressure to rid the kingdom of the "Catholic whore," as the duchess of Mazarin had been dubbed by her enemies. William and Mary took up residence in Kensington Palace, and Hortense Mancini followed them, relocating to a townhouse nearby. But after the new monarchs reduced the size of her pension, she was forced to move again, this time to Paradise Row, where she occupied one of the three large apartments on the eastern end of the terrace.

Her reduced circumstances did not mean Hortense Mancini was forced to endure an impoverished life, however. Everyone who was anyone—and many who were nobodies—simply followed her to her new residence in the village of Chelsea. Although the duchess had recently turned fifty—an age by which most women were forced to cede the field to younger beauties—few could rival her loveliness. As the French ambassador described her in a letter to a friend, Hortense Mancini was still a desirable woman: "I never saw anyone who so well defies the power of time and vice to disfigure," he wrote after visiting her in Chelsea one night. "At the age of fifty, she has the satisfaction of thinking, when she looks in her mirror, that she is as lovely as she ever was in her life."

And so Madam Mazarin held court in her home on Paradise Row. Her *salon* was the meeting place of everyone who was illustrious and witty—and of all those who aspired to be thought so. The duchess presided over conversations on a dazzling array of topics, from the new science and poetry to politics and fashion. Composers wrote short operas for her, with the duchess herself sometimes singing a role. Actors staged tragedies and comedies for her, with the duchess—on occasion—performing. And there was always the allure of gambling—the basset-table made its appearance almost every night.

Astell knew all this and more, not because she was an intimate of the duchess of Mazarin but because Hortense Mancini published a detailed account of her many adventures; her *mémoires* had been written in French, but they were quickly translated into English and published not once but twice. Like everyone else in London, Astell read them.

And like everyone else, Astell followed every new development in the endless Mazarin divorce case. Thirty years after his wife had fled from him, Mancini's husband was still trying to force her return. (He had long ago squandered her fortune on his endless legal contest.) Details about the divorce proceedings were everywhere: pamphlets, news-books, gazettes, and broadsheets published titillating accounts of the latest legal maneuvers. More than one of Astell's many correspondents, who found it difficult to keep up with the latest bits and pieces of information, wrote to her, begging for a morsel.

Astell could not deny her interest in the marriage of Hortense Mancini. But for Mary Astell, the attraction was not in the shocking details of the scandal—rather, it was what the terrible mismatch of the couple revealed about the institution of marriage. The cardinal's grand designs and politic schemes, his niece's intelligence, beauty, grace, and wit, the vast estates and glittering wealth, the power and grandeur of the

Mazarin name, even the poor husband's soundness of mind: all lost to the folly of an ill-considered marriage. What remained was, in Astell's view, the "unhappy shipwreck" of Hortense Mancini's life.

The duchess of Mazarin's situation was much to be pitied. To find herself yoked for life to an absolute lord and master, to have her wit and good sense subjected to a tyrant's folly and ignorance, to have her every wish thwarted and her every desire unfilled—these were very great trials indeed. It could not be denied that the duchess was most unfortunate in her husband. But she was not blameless in her marriage.

Though she had been deprived of peace and quiet, and though her husband had squandered her great wealth and vast estates, she ought to have borne all these provocations with grace, fortitude, and patience. No indignity at the hands of her husband could have stained her honor or tarnished her name. No physical torment inflicted on her body by her lord and master could have touched her immortal soul. No despair in this life could have destroyed her hope of salvation in the next. Only she herself could accomplish her eternal ruin, and that she had done. Or so Astell believed.

However much she might disapprove of the conduct of the duchess of Mazarin, Mary Astell could find no fault in the behavior of her man. "Thank you, Mustapha," she said, finding it difficult to articulate the unfamiliar combination of syllables. "We have all that we need, but please convey my gratitude to Her Grace for the kindness." *"Her Grace." She may well be a duchess, but she is not worthy of such respect.*

Mustapha raised his eyebrows quizzically, as though he had heard Astell's thoughts. If she had been the sort of woman who blushed, a faint color might then have been seen on Mary Astell's cheeks. Mustapha, however, seemed not to notice Astell's momentary discomfiture. But as the man inclined his head in farewell and turned toward the opposite end of Paradise Row, Mary Astell was startled by a sudden suspicion that the mystery of the young girl lying ill in her house might be linked to the household of the duchess of Mazarin.

"One question, if you please, Mustapha," she called out. The man stopped and turned back to her.

"Whatever you may require, you have only to ask, Mrs. Astell," he replied.

"I am wondering whether there are any young men in Madam Mazarin's household?" she asked. It was an odd question, seemingly unrelated to the conversation that they had shared, the tall and awkward woman and the smooth and polished man, both of them, in their own ways, outsiders in the world they inhabited.

The impeccably mannered Mustapha could not quite conceal his amusement. "Any young man besides me, do you mean, Mrs. Astell? But perhaps I am no longer quite young enough for you?" H allowed himself a smile before continuing in a more serious vein. "I assume you are not asking about Her Grace's friends and visitors—she receives many guests."

"No, no," Astell assured him. "Are there any men of quality who reside there?"

Mustapha did not ask about why she posed such an unusual question, just smiled before responding. "*Le seigneur de Saint-Évremond* has a home with her ladyship, of course, but then he is no longer young . . . He is in his eighties now . . . The duchess's dearest friend and advocate. He may no longer be young, but you will never find a man of greater quality anywhere."

"What about young men in her service?"

"Am I to understand that you are asking whether Her Grace employs young men in her household, Mrs. Astell? Ah, well, the household is not at all large these days, not as it used to be." With this equivocal answer, Mustapha turned, and headed back toward the Mazarin residence on Paradise Row. Astell watched him go, her suspicions not entirely allayed, before hurrying inside. She was welcomed by the sight of a warm coal fire in the parlor and three of her four comfortable chairs occupied. Lady Ranelagh, Lady Catherine, and Mrs. Methuen sat together, deep in conversation as she entered the room.

Astell removed her outer garments without waiting for Sarah, though she caught a glimpse of the girl hurrying to retrieve cloak, now very damp, from the entry hall and return it to its place by the kitchen fire. It would be nice to have a dry cloak before she had to set out into the weather again.

Astell had parted from Mary Kettilby little more than an hour before, but as the three women seated in the parlor turned to greet her, Astell could see from their somber faces that, in this short time period of time, their concern had deepened. She could also hear the murmur of voices upstairs, so she assumed that Mrs. Kettilby was still with the stranger—the word "stranger" did not seem quite right at this moment, but it was quite impossible to think of the girl as "Lettice de Beauclerk."

"Shall I go up?" she asked, entering the parlor while gesturing to the bedroom above.

"I rather think, my dear, that you ought to sit down and rest yourself here for just a bit. I am sure that Mrs. Kettilby will be down directly," said Lady Catherine. The chair nearest the fire had been left empty for Astell.

Astell looked at the three women and then sank slowly into the armchair. She was not only cold and tired but apprehensive. And she also felt a wave of frustration wash over her. She had work to do, but it was left undone. She needed solitude and quiet for thinking and writing, but she had neither. And now, it seemed, there was something more to be confronted.

"Mrs. Methuen, I think it might be best for you to begin," said Lady Catherine.

Astell looked quickly from Lady Catherine to Lady Ranelagh. There was not even a hint of mischief in Lady Ranelagh's eyes, nor did she seem to be at all interested in catching a glimpse of herself in the looking glass that usually occupied at least part of her attention.

Mrs. Methuen rose from her chair and added a bit of coal to the grate although no more fuel was needed—the fire burned brightly, and even the furthermost corner of the room was quite warm. When the terrace on Paradise was being built, a number of innovations had been incorporated in the construction process, including brick chimneys with flues that drew efficiently, eliminating unpleasant draughts.

After handling the coal, Mrs. Methuen pulled a large linen square out from one of her pockets in order to wipe her fingers. The handkerchiefs she always carried about her person were intended for such ordinary tasks—plain and sturdy, they were quite unlike Lady Ranelagh's tiny embroidered squares, scented and edged with lace, which served only for decorative purposes. But Mrs. Methuen's hands had not been the least bit dirtied, just as the fire had needed no coal. Astell could see that Mrs. Methuen was taking her time, considering how best to begin.

To ease her friend and neighbor into conversation, Astell posed the easiest question first. "Has the girl's fever come down?"

"Yes, I believe so, yes, a bit, but she is not over the worst of it, I fear," replied Mrs. Methuen, adding, "And she is a rather intractable young person." After a pause, the older woman continued. "But it has been very reassuring to have Mrs. Kettilby here. She agrees that the girl's illness is not likely consumption or scrofula, despite the fever. The girl has coughed up no blood, and there is no swelling to be felt in her throat. But a fierce ague, yes, and we will have to keep careful watch to see whether the fits return—she has not been able to tell us whether the fevers come on regularly—she says she does not remember when she first became ill.

"I sent Sarah to fetch my tincture of Jesuit's bark—it is the best medicine for an ague, well, for every kind of fever, really. The patient should have twenty drops in wine or water every four hours, and Mrs. Kettilby has brought with her a useful purge for fever as well, it cools and thins the blood, but the girl will have none of it, I am afraid. I have a plaster, too, made with rue and currants, and I would like to bind her wrists and feet—the plaster draws heat from the head and is most effective, but that too she has rejected, at least for the moment."

Astell could see that her neighbor was troubled by the girl's refusal of these remedies. Mrs. Methuen was regularly called upon to care for worn and harried women, women doubled over with pain and fear, and her services were also frequently needed to treat terrified children who were too young to say just what hurt or where. None of these grateful patients rejected Mrs. Methuen's advice or her medication. Astell felt her heart harden. Who was this girl to dismiss such an experienced and generous healer as Mrs. Methuen, a woman who served all those who needed her out of the goodness of her heart and at her own expense?

"And, then, there is one thing more." Mrs. Methuen spoke these words slowly, looking directly at Mary Astell, watching her carefully. "The girl is gone with child."

Astell stared aghast at Mrs. Methuen. "But that cannot be," she said. "Indeed, that cannot be. Surely you must be mistaken!"

"No, about this I am not mistaken." At Astell's expression of doubt, Mrs. Methuen smiled in spite of herself. "Mrs. Kettilby confirms it, and she is with the girl now, examining her more carefully to see how far along she might be. The girl herself is no help whatsoever."

"But that just cannot be the case," Astell protested. "There is no sign of such a thing—she is very thin, too thin. How can she possibly be carrying a child? She *is* a child."

Mrs. Methuen smiled again. For those who knew how to look, there was every sign of the girl's condition. For all Mary Astell's involvement in the political and religious controversies of the moment, she knew very little about facts of most women's lives—she had not been raised in a house where a baby arrived, without fail, every year, and even now, although she was a passionate advocate *for* women, she had little practical understanding *of* women. Mary Astell spent her day with paper and ink, not in childbearing and child-rearing.

"I am afraid it *can* be the case," said Mrs. Methuen gently. "She is very young, yes, and that is one of the many aspects of her current state that gives me pause, but a a girl her age may be starving, faint with lack of food, and still be breeding, and that, I am afraid, is the state in which our recent arrival now finds herself. The signs of her condition are there, if you know where and how to look."

"Surely she was not aware of her condition?"

"She most certainly *was* aware," said Lady Catherine, for whom the news had not come as a complete surprise. Although unmarried herself, Lady Catherine had spent time at court and knew much more of the ways of the world than her friend. Lady Catherine was acquainted with more than one woman who sought to keep secret the fact that she was carrying a child—a woman did not have to be big-bellied to have a baby, and a woman's clothing, even a dreadful garment like the one that "Lettice de Beauclerk" had been wearing, could be made to cover much.

"I suspected it might be the case last night when I first examined her," Mrs. Methuen said, addressing herself directly to Astell, "but I could not be sure since she did not speak. And, then, it was always possible she did not know her condition—young women are often so ignorant that they cannot tell whether they have conceived or not, and not one in twenty bothers to keep an accurate account of her monthly courses. Mrs. Kettilby is often called at the very last moment in just such situations, when a young woman is suddenly taken by surprise, often with a terrible result. But it was because of my suspicion that I asked you to fetch Mrs. Kettilby, and now the girl herself has confirmed it."

"All the more reason to find her husband, then, and as quickly as possible," said Lady Catherine briskly. "She may still be ill, but there can be no more of her nonsense. She must tell us her name, her proper name, that is, and where she was living before setting out for Chelsea. She must give up her airs and graces so that we can help her on her way, wherever she belongs. We have no more time for any foolishness or impertinence on her part."

Astell sighed with relief. Lady Catherine was just the woman to sort out such difficulties. And once the girl had been sent on her way, quiet would return to Paradise Row. Astell could once again enjoy the smooth unfolding of her days.

"That is as may be," Lady Ranelagh could be heard to remark softly. If she had been asked for her view on the matter, she might have opined that Lettice de Beauclerk would not be so easily sorted.

A large hamper from the rectory arrived just as the women were finishing their conversation, and Mrs. Methuen remained below to see to what Mrs. King had sent. Since her neighbor had proven herself able to get the best out of Sarah, Astell left her to arrange matters. Meanwhile, Lady Ranelagh, Lady Catherine, and Astell joined Mrs. Kettilby in the first-floor bedroom. Astell thought "Lettice de Beauclerk" would be all the more distraught after her talk with the midwife. Instead, the girl was sitting up and looking quite pleased with herself. She was beaming under Mrs. Kettilby's quiet ministrations.

"Now," the girl said, addressing the three women as they entered Astell's bedroom, "you have all heard the good news. My lord will be much pleased, as I am sure that I am carrying a son and heir, and so you must send for him at once, just as I have been asking you to do."

Her tone was imperious, and she looked at the three women who had just entered the room as if their sole duty in life was to assist her. For her part, standing on the other side of the bed, Mary Kettilby looked at Astell and raised her shoulders in a slight shrug. Mrs. Kettilby attended women of all sorts and knew that they could sometimes be taken by strange fancies, but as a discreet midwife, she told no tales. She remained a watchful but silent observer.

Lady Catherine stepped forward, once more drawing herself up to her full height, as if that alone would force the girl before her out of her delusions. Lady Catherine seemed to forget that this tactic had already failed her once.

"Now see here, enough of this," she commanded, looking down her rather long nose to the slight figure propped up in the bed. "We must know at once who you are and whence you have come. You may rest assured that we will do all that is in our power to help you along your way, but you must give up this nonsense immediately. You must tell us your name."

"Nonsense? I have told you before, more than once, that I am Lettice de Beauclerk," the girl replied, her eyes narrowing and a sullen pout replacing the happy glow on her face. Her pronunciation had improved.

She sighed deeply. "I have married a great lord, and I have come here, at his request—"

"Yes, yes, yes," said Lady Catherine, cutting off the young woman—most rudely, it must be said. "We have heard all that. But your name *before* you were married, if you please. And your home—where your father and mother reside, the place where we might find your family."

"None of that matters any longer," said the girl, tossing her head and assuming a pose of great dignity. "My lord has raised me up. And I must be reunited with him."

Astell could see that this would go nowhere. Despite Lady Catherine's formidable presence, there was something about the girl's insistence that suggested she would not be subdued by Lady Catherine's considerable force of mind.

If any situation required Lady Ranelagh's more subtle gifts of persuasion, it was surely this one. The earl of Ranelagh's daughter might be used to having her own way in all things, but so was the earl of Ranelagh's new wife, who had her own distinctive way of achieving her desired ends. And so, she gracefully slipped around the imposing and increasingly outraged figure of Lady Catherine.

The countess was a small woman, slim and quick. As if she were a conjuror, she swept the folds of her skirts in front of the young patient's eyes. And, as if by magic, "Lettice de Beauclerk" turned her attention from the commanding figure of Lady Catherine to the thick, rich fabric being waved before her.

The *manteau* that Lady Ranelagh was wearing was the result of her careful study of *Le Mercure galant*, the most recent issue *extraordinaire* of which had been filled with engravings of the latest in French fashion. The countess had deliberated at some length with her *maîtresse couturière*, a Parisian woman now residing in London, over the particular shade of blue silk to be used in the gown. The two had taken great care with the exact cut and length of the sleeves, and they had meticulously calculated the precise drape and loop of the skirt—all this exacting attention to detail aimed at producing the effect of simplicity and carelessness.

Thick folds of white silk had been softly pleated around the neckline, giving Lady Ranelagh a look of modesty, but as she leaned over the bed, a rather great deal of flawless skin was exposed. Just as she intended. As she eagerly pressed forward, several of her lovely auburn curls fell forward over her shoulder. It was a studied gesture, one that the countess employed to great effect with her many male admirers—but it worked equally well on women, as Lady Ranelagh herself well knew. If she aimed to dazzle, she dazzled. "It sounds as if it were a great romance," the countess sighed, "something like *Oroonoko* or *La Princesse de Clèves . . .* "

Astell once again felt a tendency to snort—she thoroughly disapproved of such nonsense, but she was well aware that the girl's story sounded nothing at all like those popular romances named by Lady Ranelagh, though Astell suspected that their exotic-sound titles would appeal to the girl. But, watching the scene carefully, she saw that "Lettice" was transfixed not by the allure of the countess or by the exotic fictions to which she referred, but by the dress. The patient could not draw her eyes away from the rich fabric that whispered softly as it fell across the bed.

And whether it was the beautiful woman leaning over the bed, the mystery of the foreign-sounding titles, or simply the effect of the shimmering silk, as Astell rather suspected, "Lettice" at last began to talk. Gradually the girl's story—or at least something more of her story— began to take shape.

She vehemently insisted that Lettice was her name, although all four women in the room doubted whether she was telling the complete truth on that score. She would reveal nothing at all of substance about her father or her mother, saying only that she was a "poor orphan," alone in the world. Neither Lady Catherine's imperious commands nor Lady Ranelagh's more subtle appeals could elicit the names of the girl's parents or where they had lived—pressed too hard, she fell back in a faint.

Although she avoided the subject of her parents, she was proud to say that she had attended a boarding school where, according to

"Lettice," she had been well educated in the company of other young gentlewomen and given every advantage. But then, after her father's untimely death, her impoverished mother was forced to provide for her cherished daughter as best she could. Without friends or funds, the widow was eventually compelled to bind her daughter as an apprentice to a milliner in London and then, growing ill herself, died. This part of her story seemed to cause young Lettice some difficulties—it was not so much the loss of her mother as the fact of her indenture that caused her distress. She seemed to think that being trained in a trade was beneath her dignity, and she did not linger on this part of her past.

Lettice offered few details of this part of her life, although it was in the millinery shop where she was apprenticed that she claimed to have been wooed and won by Charles de Beauclerk, a young aristocrat who immediately recognized her inherent worth. The handsome lord had snatched Lettice up as his "treasure" despite her lack of title or money. Having insisted on marrying her, he had then been forced to leave her— with many sighs and much regret, Lettice insisted—but only so that he could share the news of his great good fortune with his parents and make all the arrangements necessary for her introduction to his family. He assured her that his loving parents cared only for his happiness and that she would be welcomed by all who met her.

It was a fanciful story, and as Astell listened while Lady Ranelagh drew out the scanty details from the girl, she reckoned that very little of it was true. Men did sometimes marry for love, a heroic action that made a mighty noise in the world, but what did it amount to in the end? There was no great hope to be found in such reckless action: the man who married for love in a little time found the same reason for another choice. And even if the lover had been violent in the throes of his passion, he was certain to repent, if not sooner, then later. Perhaps that is what "Charles de Beauclerk" had done, rather quickly leaving London and abandoning his new wife.

There was surely less substance than gauzy fantasy in the story Lettice told, and the girl soon fell back onto the bed, the red spots on her pale cheeks flaring into life once more. Whether she had exhausted herself from reliving her unpleasant adventures or was overcome by the effort of weaving an acceptable narrative for herself, she could (or would) say no more.

Lady Catherine was frustrated, clearly believing the girl to be a malingerer. But Astell could see that the girl was ill—of that at least there could be no doubt.

Still, much more needed to be said, but Mrs. Kettilby waved the other three women out of the sickroom. There would be no more questions—or answers—that night.

Eight

Sunday dawned, wet and gray. A chill wind swept down the length of Paradise Row, driving a hard rain against the front windows of the terrace. Mary Astell rose early, as usual, but she soon realized that quiet reflection and meditation were elusive: she could not stop her mind from wandering. Reading was also impossible. She was unable to concentrate on the book in front of her.

She sighed. The evening before, as Lady Ranelagh prepared to take her leave, sweeping up her lace-edged *mouchoir*, her painted fan, her fur-trimmed tippet, her scented gloves, and her sable muff, Lady Catherine had once again broached the subject of sending for Old Bridget, and Astell had signaled her consent with a slight incline of her head. Astell did not want to spend another night in the sickroom, tending to Lettice—to be completely honest with herself, she did not wish to spend any more time than was absolutely necessary with the girl.

The Ranelagh coach had whisked both women off to some party or supper or another—Astell had been too distracted to remember where Lady Ranelagh said they were going. Even Lady Catherine, who usually endured such frivolous events with patience rather than anticipating them with any real pleasure, was looking forward to the evening's social engagement as London had been unusually dull, even for her. After Queen Mary's death two years earlier, the royal household at Kensington had been dispersed and the ladies of the queen's court dismissed. At the same time, the king's annual military campaign kept him away on the continent for months each year, leaving Whitehall quiet and empty. But now that William and his troops had returned from the Netherlands, the capital was awash in festivities, and both Lady Ranelagh and Lady Catherine were fully engaged for the evening.

Soon after they were driven away, Mrs. Kettilby had taken her leave, heading back to her own cottage in Little Chelsea. Kind old Mrs. Methuen, worn out by the day's events, had returned home as well. With their departure, Mary Astell suddenly and unusually felt quite alone.

Although Sarah had been disappointed to see the house empty out, she was thrilled to be able to turn her attention to the hamper that Mrs. King had sent from the rectory, and once Bridget arrived in the Ranelagh coach, the young housemaid and the old nursemaid sat companionably together for a long while in the kitchen, stuffing themselves with stewed hare, custard, and beer while they speculated about the patient upstairs. To her delight, Sarah found that Mrs. King had slipped some marmalade into the basket—made from another of Mrs. Kettilby's many recipes. The girl was particularly fond of marmalade, its inclusion yet another sign of Mrs. King's thoughtfulness.

While Sarah and Bridget had enjoyed their feast and their gossip, Astell ate a bit of bread and some cheese by the fire in the parlor before rising and going up to her study. After closing the door behind her, as if to shut out not only the three other women in the small house but also the cares and worries she had assumed in recent days, she sat down at her desk and looked over the sheets of paper she had partially filled with her crabbed script just two days earlier. She tried to focus her attention on the argument she had been in the midst of making before her life had been disrupted, but it was no use. Words failed her.

But she thought she might be able to concentrate well enough to correct the printed pages that Mr. Wilkin had sent some days earlier, and so she set about altering sentences, changing words, and correcting punctuation. Even though she found it difficult to concentrate, she did not allow herself to stop until the task was complete. With a sigh, she finally turned over the last sheet of paper and put down her pen. As she straightened the stack of proofs, she realized how very tired she was.

Having completed the work to her satisfaction, she felt she might be able to sleep.

Sarah had prepared a pallet in a small alcove of the study for her, and after praying, Astell settled herself there. And yet, despite the day's exertions and her careful preparations for a quiet night, she found that sleep did not come. She could not calm her fears and worries. She tossed and turned fitfully throughout the night, at times listening to Bridget's low voice and Lettice's irritable tones. She could also hear Bridget's footsteps as she paced back and forth, tending to the girl, from which Astell deduced that Lettice's fever had returned. Still, she did not check on them.

And now, although it was still quite early, Astell could hear the old nurse and her young charge once more in the bedroom across the landing from her study, the one speaking patiently and slowly, as if she were addressing a small, petulant child, the other answering petulantly as if she *were* a small child and not a woman who would soon give birth to a child of her own. Astell rose, dressed, and left the house.

There were two services at All Saints on the Lord's day, one early in the morning and one in the afternoon. Astell's habit was to attend both, spending the hours between in private devotion and the remainder of the day in reading and reflection. On this Sunday, after the first service was concluded, Astell hurried home, just as she had on Friday morning. But on this occasion, she was not so much worried about Sarah as concerned about the patient she had left in Bridget's care. As she left her pew, she realized that Mrs. King was not present, and Astell wondered if there were more problems with the teething baby.

Making her way out of the church, Astell was anxious to avoid any private discussion with the rector, who might have more questions about the stranger to whom she had offered shelter. Astell was certain that neither Mrs. Kettilby nor Mrs. Methuen would have revealed anything about the girl's condition to anyone, but she was less sure about Sarah. With the girl's irrepressible love of gossip (and mischief-making), it was hard to know what she might have said to the boy from the rectory who had delivered the wicker basket dispatched by Mrs. King, and with Sarah's uncanny ability to show up where she ought not to be, it was also possible that she had slipped out of the house to have a few words with one of the footmen who attended the Ranelagh coach—she was drawn to them as irresistibly as she was to Mrs. King's marmalade.

Once Astell arrived home, she climbed the stairs to her study. All was quiet—wherever Sarah was and whatever she might be doing, she was out of sight, a blessing for which Astell was grateful. The sickroom was quiet as well, and Astell hoped that Bridget might have a moment of respite from Lettice and her many demands and that the girl was resting comfortably. All this she hoped, but she did not check.

Settling herself behind her desk once more, she took up her small knife in order to mend her quill pen, the nib of which needed trimming and sharpening after the previous night's work. She noticed then that Sarah had swept away the fine blotting powder from the desk, cleared away the scraps of paper on which she had wiped her pen as she worked, and refreshed the little water-pot she used for cleaning her nib while she was writing. Astell appreciated Sarah's efforts. She could be quite useful when she had a mind to be.

Cheered by this sudden realization, Astell looked for a discarded bit of paper—since her desk was neither as large nor as disorganized as the rector's, she quickly found a piece that was suitable for her purpose. She then picked up her pen, dipped the nib into her ink, and began to set down her thoughts. What was to be done? The only way to return to her quiet life of reading and writing was to solve the problem she had found on her doorstep. She must find Lettice's husband, if he existed, but if he did not, or if he could not be found, she must undertake to see that the girl was safely returned to her proper settlement—wherever that might be.

Having thus laid out her challenge, Astell concluded that she would have to locate the milliner to whom the girl had been apprenticed. As her employer, the woman would undoubtedly have the information that Lettice herself had refused to impart, her maiden surname and her parents' names, or at the very least the name of her mother, since it was she who had apprenticed the girl.

The milliner would also be able to help in identifying the girl's rightful place of settlement. Lettice may have been in London long enough to claim legal residence and relief in a parish there, but if she had not, her employer would surely know where the girl had lived before coming to the city. Though none of that would be necessary, Astell supposed, if the woman could confirm the existence of a husband. Even better, the milliner might have some suggestions about the man's identity and, perhaps, where he was to be found.

Astell was hopeful that such information might result in Lettice's reunion with her lost husband—an ideal conclusion, at least for the girl, if not for the man she had presumably married. But failing such a desired end, at least the girl could avoid any disagreeable complications by returning to her legal settlement, either her place of birth or the London parish where she had been working as an apprentice. Astell would not like to see Lettice subjected to the unpleasantness of an examination by the constables and churchwardens of Chelsea, nor would she want to see her forcibly removed from the parish. Not in her condition.

Looking over the notes she had made on the scrap of paper in front of her, Astell was satisfied. She had laid out the dimensions of the problem she faced. She had devised a plan to solve it. She knew the next step to take, and she could take it without having to encounter the girl who lay in a sickbed just across the landing.

Although Mary Astell would not normally undertake a journey to London on the Lord's day, which to her mind was rightly to be observed as a time of prayer and devotion, she could not bear to remain indoors. She must be doing something. An active woman, she knew that a vigorous walk was just what she needed to clear her mind, and so she found herself again preparing to leave her home on Paradise Row. She would pay a visit to her printer, Richard Wilkin, who would be delighted to have her corrected pages. Astell could also count on a warm welcome from Mrs. Wilkin, who managed her husband's business, helped to train and contain his young apprentices, and was always happy to receive guests in her snug rooms above the shop.

Elizabeth Wilkin knew as much about the many men and women of business in the city as Lady Ranelagh did about intrigues at the royal court. Astell felt sure the printer's wife would be able to answer any questions about the millinery trade that might be put to her. Fashion and dress were of little interest to Mary Astell, but Mrs. Wilkin was likely to have a fair bit to say about the trade, the women who engaged in the business, and the young girls who were apprenticed in it. Such information might not move Astell's inquiry ahead, but she thought it best to prepare herself before she sought out Lettice's mistress.

Much as Lady Ranelagh had quickly swept up all her accoutrements the previous evening, Astell gathered her necessaries. Rather than the countess's rich accessories and showy adornments, Astell collected her proof pages and her notes, stowing them carefully in a small leather satchel provided with a sturdy shoulder strap. Her wool cloak, she supposed, was still drying by the kitchen fire.

As she entered the room in search of her garment, she found a disconsolate Sarah sitting alone at the plain wooden table where she had enjoyed the company of Bridget the evening before. The girl was jabbing the point of a knife into the oak.

Seeing her mistress knit her brows and frown, Sarah jumped to her feet, a flustered look on her face. "I am sorry, ma'am, I did not hear you summon me, truly, I did not. I did not know you needed me." She bobbed her head in the gesture of an apology. "I am sorry, Mrs. Astell, but—"

"Enough with the apologies, Sarah. I do not need you. I did not call you." Astell cut the girl off and then immediately repented. Even to herself she sounded particularly sharp. Still gruff but less harsh, she added, "I merely came to get my cloak. As for you, check to see that Bridget has all that she needs." And then, "Make yourself useful for once." As soon as they were spoken, Astell again regretted her words and wished she could recall them—they were unnecessarily cruel.

A look of shock appeared on Sarah's resentful face. "Well, ma'am," she began in a huff, "I must say that is not right. Indeed, it is not right at all. Old Bridget may be happy to do whatever Lady Catherine asks of her, but why should I have to wait upon that Lettuce person . . . Who is she? Nothing. Nobody. Why is she even here?" The girl's tone grew venomous as she grew more emphatic. "*And why am I made to wait upon her?*" she repeated, glaring at Mary Astell, her chin jutting out stubbornly.

"Sarah!" Astell's rebuke was immediate and sharp. "Hold your tongue. It is not for you to decide what you will and will not do in this household. Your behavior is most unseemly." Even as she reprimanded Sarah, Astell realized that the girl's truculence mirrored her own growing hostility to the young stranger lying upstairs—*Who is she? Why is she here? And why am I forced to wait upon her?* Astell was avoiding Lettice and her demands even as she ordered Sarah back to the sickroom.

Sarah was not to be silenced. "And why does *she* get all the attention? All of the fuss over her, all of the fetching and carrying for her . . . All the cleaning up after her. What messes she has made, and I have had the cleaning up of them. Listening to her whinge and complain, putting up with her peevishness and her airs. All on me. And I have had my *usual* chores as well as all this extra work. And you, out and about, toing and froing, while I am always stuck here."

With that, Sarah stabbed at the table viciously. "But whoever thinks about me?" she spit out angrily before rushing from the room.

"Sarah! Sarah, come back at once!" Astell called out. Her anger had evaporated, replaced by remorse. She was sorry for the tone she had used. She had taken some of her own frustration out Sarah, and now that she had fled, Astell began also to have some inkling of what lay behind her outburst.

Before young Sarah's arrival in the house on Paradise Row, she had been under the watchful protection of Lady Catherine Jones, something of a pet project the great lady had undertaken for reasons that were still not altogether clear, not even to the lady herself. The girl seemed little worthy of the care and attention of an earl's daughter—the child had been found wandering the streets of Chelsea one winter's day while the Reverend Littleton was still rector of All Saints. The half-starved girl was unable to give any account of herself or of her situation, much less of her parents. Nor could she offer so much as a surname—she could only identify herself as "Sarah."

Filthy, infested with all manner of vermin, barely clothed and blue with cold, the pitiful thing had been viewed with a mix of titillation and disgust by respectable members of the parish. True, the mystery of the child's sudden appearance had caused a welcome bit of stir among the complacent worshippers at All Saints, but once the first excitement was over, the presence of a poor and needy orphan in their comfortable midst became the source of great concern.

Before pitiful thing could become a burden on the parish, she was disposed of to a local householder who promised to provide clothing, food, and lodging in exchange for her labor. Her new master expected the girl to be thankful and biddable, beholden for the charity she received at his hearth. Instead, she was ungrateful, willful, and rude.

Sarah was soon returned to the churchwardens, who found another willing master eager for cheap labor. But once again she proved to be more trouble than she was worth. And so the unfortunate child passed from one household to another until, having been moved from here to there and with no more willing householders to be found, parish wardens were ready to throw up their hands in despair—or, more practically, they were ready to cart the girl outside the parish boundaries and dump her, relieving themselves of the burden of her care.

It was at this moment of crisis that Lady Catherine Jones intervened. Perhaps to distract herself from her mother's imminent death, perhaps to fulfill a sense of her Christian duty, or perhaps to succeed where so many others had failed, Lady Catherine decided to take on the wayward girl. Whatever the reason, her act was unexpected. While Lady Catherine Jones was a pious woman, she had no particular soft spot for children, and in any case, Sarah was not an appealing child. The girl was by this time clean enough, but she was ill-favored, ill-tempered, and ill-behaved. Still, Lady Catherine had never been one to avoid a challenge—and for whatever reason, she assumed the task of taming the defiant girl.

Sarah had been transferred to Ranelagh, where she was introduced to the requirements of service in a large, well-run household. But she was not tamed. Although she was fed regularly and sufficiently, her appetite was insatiable; she stole any food or drink she could get her hands on, boldly denied her theft (even when caught in the act), and despite repeated discipline, persisted in her thievery. She had also been provided with simple but decent clothing, appropriate to her station, but her garments were in constant need of repair, with rips, tears, and holes seeming to appear on a daily basis, and never mind the dirt and other stains.

She took no pride in her work. As a scullery maid, she failed at the simplest of tasks—she could not scrub a sauce-pan clean, she could not scour a grate or swill a floor, and she could not carry a load without dropping whatever she was supposed to be carrying. She could not fill a bucket without letting it overflow or empty a chamber pot without spilling its contents. She could not be sent to fetch an item without forgetting what it was she had been sent for or bringing back the wrong thing altogether. She was underfoot when she was not needed, nowhere to be found when she was. And the noise was constant. She prattled, she chattered, she blabbed, she whined, she fussed, she complained, she hummed, she howled, she stormed, she stomped, she talked back. She was impertinent, argumentative, and spiteful. She would rather tell a lie than the truth, even if the truth were as plain as the nose on her face.

At last even the old earl of Ranelagh, a man who was pointedly oblivious to his servants (except those who were young and comely), could no longer ignore the girl's unruly presence. He had never been one to take much of an interest in the running of his household, but the illness and death of his wife had sorely disrupted the pleasure-filled routine of his daily life, and the disorderly behavior of the superfluous child threatened to further distract him from his pursuit of the beautiful

Margaret Cecil, whom he hoped to marry. And so Richard Jones, first earl of Ranelagh, surprised his daughter, who had assumed the running his household after her mother's death, by taking a stand. In this experiment, the old earl asserted, his daughter must admit failure. Sarah had to go.

Lady Catherine was never one to accept defeat, but nor would she defy her father. Clever general that she was, she executed a strategic retreat, assuring the earl that the disruptive scullery maid would be removed "as quickly as a new place might be arranged." That bought Lady Catherine some time, and she was right in assuming that her father would find his attentions fully occupied with his soon-to-be bride.

Lady Catherine then rounded her forces upon Sarah with a quick, double-pronged attack—she first scared the wits out of the child by suggesting that the earl was making arrangements to pack her off to the Tothill Fields house of correction where "such as will beg and live idle" were set to hard labor, and then, while the girl was still reeling, Lady Catherine tempted her with the prospect of a quiet home where she would answer only to a single gentlewoman who had few needs—if only Sarah could be persuaded to mend her ways.

Between them, the great general and the little rebel had come to an unspoken truce. Since her arrival in Chelsea, Sarah had spent the better part of three years being moved, nill she, will she, from one unhappy situation to another. She would not acknowledge defeat, not even in this dire moment, but she recognized that she was being given one last chance. And so it was tacitly agreed between the two of them. Lady Catherine had only to convince her dear friend Mary Astell to house the girl, while Sarah, with no other choice left to her, had only to settle herself down.

Lady Catherine then faced a new challenge: how best to maneuver Sarah into Mary Astell's service. She knew that the task would not be easy, but she was undaunted. Sarah's reputation for making mischief was not the problem. Oblivious to most parish gossip, Astell had not paid much attention to Sarah's troubled career in the village. Rather, Astell's own independent nature was the source of Lady Catherine's difficulty, for when it came to her daily needs, which were few, Mary Astell was entirely self-sufficient. Early in her life, servants had been plentiful enough in the Astell home, but after her father's early death, the family's circumstances were much reduced. Of necessity, her widowed mother, her father's unmarried sister, and the young Mary managed all the necessary household chores themselves—there was not even enough money for a washerwoman to help on laundry days.

Astell's mother had baked and roasted and preserved and brewed. Her aunt planted, tended, and harvested vegetables from a small kitchen garden, drying peas, pickling cucumbers, and storing onions and carrots in the hope that they would last through the winter. Mary learned to dust, sweep, scrub, and polish. All three of them lugged heavy basins of clean, hot water up the stairs and carried dirty, cold water back down, they brought in loads of coal and took out heaps of ashes. They had, all three, spent their evenings sewing and mending and darning. Mary's mother and her aunt uttered not a single word of complaint, and though the girl had followed the excellent model of her elders, she had been very bitter at times. But she had learned to do for herself.

And then, even if Astell's self-sufficiency could be overcome, there was still the fact that she had no money. True, she had earned something from the sale of her *Serious Proposal*, but it was very little, and she still relied for support on a small group of wealthy female patrons, Lady Catherine chief among them. Astell had enough upon which to live, but it was just enough to supply her frugal needs, with nothing at all to provide for a servant, even a young and entirely untrained housemaid like Sarah.

Beyond even this, and more important still, Mary Astell guarded her privacy. She did not want or need company. She did not mind living in furnished lodgings; she could quite happily seclude herself in a single room, where no one could, or would, bother her. She was sociable enough when she was in the right frame of mind, but she generally preferred her own company to that of others. She made an exception for her dear friend Lady Catherine, of course, but Lady Catherine was a considerate woman who respected Astell's need for solitude.

And thus a campaign to introduce Sarah into Astell's household would require all of that great lady's not inconsiderable skill and subtlety. To accommodate the girl, Lady Catherine first had to convince Astell to move from her rented room into the small terraced house on Paradise Row. Lady Catherine knew well how to play on the earl of Ranelagh's vanity and ambition in order to accomplish her goals, but the subtle manipulation that was so successful with her father would not work with Mary Astell.

In the end, it was Mary Astell's own practicality that had effected the change: her growing reputation as a writer necessitated a residence where she might receive the number of visitors who sought her out with increasing frequency, while the expansion of her intellectual endeavors meant that a space she could use exclusively as a study had become a necessity. In addition to a second part of her *Proposal*, she was preparing a volume of philosophical letters for publication, and Mr. Wilkin was also encouraging her to undertake a series of political pamphlets—a room that could be dedicated to reading and writing was essential.

The addition of a maidservant was another matter, however, the most difficult part of the change to accomplish, and it had taken some while for Lady Catherine to persuade her dear friend of the merits of such an enlargement of her household. But in the end, as she knew it would be, all had been arranged to Lady Catherine's very great satisfaction, if not entirely to the contentment of the maid or to the comfort of the girl's dubious new mistress.

When Sarah was first introduced to Mary Astell, the girl shrank from the stern figure in front of her. Sarah realized at once that life in the sparsely furnished house with this plainly dressed, unsmiling woman would offer her no luxuries and nothing at all in the way of amusement. However tantalizingly out of reach the pleasures and extravagancies of Ranelagh may have been to her, at least scenes of color, luxury, and beauty were constantly played out before her dazzled eyes.

As for Mary Astell, she was nonplussed when Sarah was presented to her—even the serenely confident Lady Catherine had been a bit flustered on the occasion. The girl had been sour and indifferent, refusing to meet either woman's eye and failing to give any account of herself. She answered the questions she was asked by her new mistress with barely audible monosyllables. Astell had concluded that the girl was rather stupid.

After this inauspicious beginning, the two soon fell into a habit of mutual avoidance. If there was nothing in the person of Mary Astell to encourage the young girl whose job it was to serve her, neither was there anything about Sarah to endear her to her mistress. Astell saw none of the appeal that still made Lady Catherine, who had reason to know better, shake her head and smile at some of Sarah's antics.

Mary Astell's quiet routine on Paradise Row varied little, and she saw no reason why the girl could not adapt to it easily and fulfill the few basic tasks assigned to her. In point of fact, Astell preferred not to bother about the girl at all except to offer her instructions and reprimands, the former to direct her in her work, the latter to comment on its quality. Sarah, meanwhile, was driven mad by the sameness of every day, and amused herself as best she could by her acts of disobedience.

As Mary Astell bundled herself into her still-damp cloak, she could not put Sarah's outburst from her mind. She thought of their uneasy months together: the girl's tantrums and outbursts, her own frustration and criticisms. They could not go on this way, but Astell did not know how best to proceed. Her first inclination was simply to dismiss the girl—she had proved to be of no real use in the household, and little would change in Astell's daily routine without her. Lady Catherine might object, but she knew, better than anyone, how little purpose the girl served, and if Lady Catherine continued to insist that Astell should have at least some help with her housekeeping, then surely a better choice might be made.

But, however appealing that solution might be—and, as Mary Astell was perfectly willing to admit to herself, it was very appealing indeed—

she realized that dismissing Sarah outright might prove to be easier said than done. Could the girl simply be let go? The more Astell considered this possibility, the more it occurred to her that, if she were to dismiss Sarah, she might find herself with not one but *two* young people on her hands, each demanding attention. "Lettice de Beauclerk," if her husband were not to be found, would have to be sent *back* wherever she rightly belonged, while Sarah, if she were to leave Paradise Row, would have to be sent *on* somewhere, but where that might be was not at all clear.

Her shoulders squared, her back straight, and her pace steady and strong, Mary Astell considered her predicament as she crossed the Five Fields, heading for London.

Nine

As she approached the bookshop in St. Paul's Churchyard, Mary Astell wondered briefly whether she should have come to London after all that day. Although Richard Wilkin had frequently urged her to spend a Sabbath-day with his family and to worship with them at his favorite church, Astell had never done so. She had, however, shared a number of companionable meals with the printer and his wife, Elizabeth, and when she felt so inclined, she had also joined the assemblage of like-minded churchmen, lawyers, writers, and book-buyers who gathered in the comfortable parlor above the print shop, where they debated politics and religion well into the evening.

Even as she doubted the value of her trip, Astell did not doubt she would be gladly received by the Wilkins: the Tory printer was a generous, warm-hearted man and an eager host. His wife was likewise generous and warm-hearted, but she had a sounder head for commerce than her husband. Elizabeth Wilkin knew that a hearty welcome and an open hearth could be very good for business.

Indeed, Richard Wilkin's success as a printer and bookseller was due in large part to his wife's knowledge of the trade. "She manages all my affairs for me," he would confide to a visitor to the shop, acknowledging her as his "chief book-seller and cash-keeper." Richard Wilkin, the son of a provincial vicar, was a newcomer to the business, while Elizabeth had grown up in the trade. Her father, Henry Brome, had set up shop under the sign of the Gun at the west end of St. Paul's Churchyard. After his death, his widow had taken over the running of the business.

Elizabeth and her younger brother, Charles, had worked alongside their capable mother, Joanna Brome, who continued as printer and bookseller until her death, after which Charles had inherited his father's business.

Elizabeth Brome, as she was then, remained in the shop, managing the business alongside her brother until she married, after which she helped her new husband into the printing trade. Charles Brome carried on his family's business, still at the sign of the Gun, where he had three presses, nine pressmen, and three apprentices. His sister and brother-in-law, meanwhile, operated just a short distance away, at the sign of the King's Head, one of the many stationers, booksellers, and printing shops crowded together in St. Paul's Churchyard.

Putting aside her doubts, Mary Astell made her way through the deserted streets, hurrying toward Richard Wilkin's shop. The usual hurly-burly of the city was noticeably absent. Sunday was a holiday, and while London's thousands of hard-working apprentices might enjoy a bit of freedom after six long days of toil, there were few amusements to be enjoyed: no card-playing or dicing or gambling of any sort, no cock-fighting, bear-baiting, or horse-racing. No conjurers or jugglers or wrestlers or rope-dancers. Playhouses were dark. Bawdy houses were closed.

Astell turned onto the Strand. The thoroughfare's taverns were also shut up for the day. She passed the Three Tuns at Charing Cross and then, as she headed east, the Castle and the Bell. Clustered together where the Strand met Fleet Street were the Sugar Loaf, the Hercules Pillars, and the Mitre. A bit further along, she passed the King's Head, with a portrait of Henry VIII on its signboard. All were shuttered, dark and deserted. Just past the Bear, she crossed the River Fleet.

As she approached Ludgate, the Belle Sauvage Inn was to her left—Astell remembered having heard a tale about a devil once appearing on stage there during a performance of *Doctor Faustus*. While she very much doubted the accuracy of that story, she did regret not having seen for herself the rhinoceros exhibited there a few years before she arrived in London. After reading an advertisement in the *London Gazette*, Lady

Catherine had insisted on inspecting the great beast for herself, and she still recalled the sight with wonder.

On another day, Astell might have turned onto Warwick Lane and stopped at Child's Coffee-house, a convenient meeting place for the many printers and booksellers clustered around St. Paul's as well as for those who had been forced by the Great Fire to move their premises to Little Britain, a warren of streets just north of St. Botolph's Aldersgate. Although Richard Wilkin was frequently heard to complain that the drinking of coffee gave him a great "stoppage of stomach," he was often to be found at Child's where, as he liked to say, "business and pleasure can be conducted under the same roof." Although Mary Astell had on occasion inquired there for the printer, it need hardly be said that she did not frequent the coffee-house herself, no respectable woman entering such premises.

But since it was the Lord's day, the city's coffee-houses, like its taverns, were closed, and so Astell did not turn aside but entered the precinct of St. Paul's. Work on the new cathedral had been underway since the time of the Great Fire, but even thirty years later, construction of the massive new dome was not complete. The site, usually humming with activity, was eerily quiet, the rising walls of the church looming above her on that gray afternoon.

Richard Wilkin's bookshop, on the south side of the Churchyard, was firmly shut up, as she expected it would be, but she had no sooner rapped sharply with the iron knocker than the door was flung open by Elizabeth Wilkin, red-faced and stabbing at Astell with a menacing finger.

"God-a-mercy!" the printer's wife exclaimed, almost losing her balance as she jerked back in her surprise. "Upon my word, Mrs. Astell, you have given me such a start!"

Astell was just as surprised as Mrs. Wilkin, and she had been forced to step back quickly as the formidable figure of the printer's wife charged out of her door.

At the sight of Mary Astell's shocked face, Elizabeth Wilkin threw back her head and began to laugh heartily. "Truly, Mrs. Astell, I thought you were that young rapscallion of mine who has given me the slip yet again. God-a-mercy, I would not like to think what he has got up to, but he will soon regret his fine adventure, you mark my words."

The Wilkins had no children of their own, but their two apprentices were as cosseted, harangued, nagged, buffeted, and petted as if they had been born to the couple. Just as Elizabeth Wilkin ran the business with a firm hand—"business neglected is business lost" was her motto—she looked straitly to the boys who, slippery as eels, sometimes escaped her tight hold.

"Come in, come in, and do forgive me," said Mrs. Wilkin, ushering in her unexpected guest. "We must do our best to warm you up." As she turned, she began a steady stream of complaint about the season's dreadful "rain and inundations."

The two climbed the stairs, up to the cozy parlor, where Astell's rap on the door had interrupted Richard Wilkin's reading of a sermon to his household. Close to the hearth on a joint stool sat a sleepy adolescent, clearly the poor apprentice who had *not* been fortunate enough to give his master and mistress the slip for a Sunday afternoon fling. On the other side of the hearth sat two equally sleepy housemaids. Entering the room, Mrs. Wilkin drew her monologue about the weather to a close and shooed the two young girls into action while she bustled about, relieving Astell of her cloak and hat and then settling her guest in a comfortable chair drawn close to the grate.

Richard Wilkin was a man of good judgment and sound character some few years older than his wife who was, in turn, several years older than Mary Astell. As a man of business, he dressed soberly but well, taking pride in clothing made from good English manufacture: the wool cloth of his coat and breeches came from Wiltshire, the linen of his shirt from Lancashire, the worsted of his stockings from Nottingham. Like her husband, Elizabeth Wilkin took her choice of clothing seriously; she was well-dressed but not over fine. Her Sunday gown and petticoats were of silk that had been manufactured in Spitalfields. Her lace was from Stony Stratford, her ribbons from Coventry.

Although the family had finished their dinner and the broad oak table had been cleared, Elizabeth Wilkin set about urging food and drink upon her unexpected visitor. Like all successful London tradesmen, Richard Wilkin believed that on the Lord's day his family should eat well, his table an emblem of plenty rather than of extravagance. On this day, the remains of a huge roast beef and an almond pudding were set out on the sideboard. Knowing her visitor's tastes, however, Mrs. Wilkin offered her guest some broth with oatmeal and sage, but Astell declined. She did, however, accept the bread and small beer one of the maidservants set down by her side.

Once they had all settled, members of the family resuming their former places, Richard Wilkin continued in his reading of the sermon. Although Astell was content to listen, her eyes were drawn to the two young servants, once again seated by the fire, their eyelids fluttering and their heads nodding. She tried hard to imagine Sarah sitting so quietly and still, but she could not.

At last, the sermon complete, Mary Astell picked up her satchel and removed the page proofs she had brought with her, handing them over to her delighted printer. "Come, now, my boy," he said, addressing the drowsy apprentice by the fire, who shook himself awake. "We will just take these down to the shop." And then, as if reassuring his guest about his observance of the day, Mr. Wilkin added, "We will just be a moment, you know, setting all in order for the morning."

Once the master and his apprentice had clattered down the narrow staircase, Elizabeth Wilkin turned to her guest. "And now, Mrs. Astell, I am sure you have not come up to London on the Lord's day just to hear us continue our debate about whether we should go to the afternoon service at St. Botolph's or to St. Andrew-by-the-Wardrobe. I argue for Mr. Wren's new church, as you well know—our parish church—but Mr. Wilkin favors St. Botolph's. It remains much dilapidated, but, well, business, you understand."

The couple returned to this topic of debate quite often, carrying on their running argument at great length but without the least acrimony, and Astell could have written a whole tome of pros and contras on the subject. "I am afraid I have no stake in this contest," she said.

"As I well know," said Mrs. Wilkin with a sigh. "But as Mr. Wilkin and I come to no satisfactory conclusion, so we must continue. Since you have not come to help us settle once for ado the game, what has brought you to us?"

Astell took a deep breath, settled herself down in her chair, and began to talk.

"And so," Astell concluded, her tale having been told, "I have come to inquire about the trade. I can think of no one who is so well informed as you. What sort of woman might this milliner be, and what kind of establishment would she have? What kind of girls would she have taken on as apprentices, and what would life have been like there for a girl like Lettice?"

Elizabeth Wilkin had listened carefully while Mary Astell recounted her story, never once interrupting her guest. Now the printer's wife was being asked to call upon her vast knowledge of the city and its guilds, in particular on her experience of women who did their best to operate within that system, and to deliver her opinions, of which she had not a few.

"Well," the printer's wife began, "young men have a thousand ways of improving their fortunes by professions and employment, but as for women . . . " At this she paused a moment to shake her head before continuing. She had little doubt that Mary Astell understood her meaning. From their spot by the fire, the two maidservants were all ears.

"Few livery companies are open to them, Mrs. Astell—as you know, my own dear mother operated my father's printing business for years as a widow, and she ran it quite successfully, as well as ever my father did, but even though she was allowed to continue training his apprentices, she could never be accepted as a member of the Stationers' Company. No, indeed, she could not." Elizabeth Wilkin nodded vigorously, then added a scornful "humph" for good measure. She seemed lost in her memories of the past for just a moment before she continued. "As for millinery," she said, "well, there is no single guild company for the trade, but I have known those who would set up as milliners to purchase membership in other guilds that are open to women, the Clockmakers' Company, for instance, or even the Leathersellers. The Haberdashers would be much better, of course, but that would cost you dearly, given that the company is one of the Great Twelve."

At this, Astell furrowed her brow, but before she could ask a question, Mrs. Wilkin clarified. "The twelve highest-ranked companies. The Haberdashers are eighth in order of precedence, the Leathersellers' Company, fifteenth. The Stationers are forty-seventh, but I am not so sure about the Clockmakers—they are after that, somewhere." By this point the two servants seem to have lost interest in what their mistress had to say, but their attention was soon reawakened.

Elizabeth Wilkin, warming to her task, suddenly thrust forward in her chair, an admonitory finger waving briskly in the air. "At any rate, it costs a girl's parents dear to purchase such an apprenticeship for her—a milliner in good business would never accept a girl without the payment of a considerable premium, and most milliners will only take on a girl who comes from a respectable family. Whatever you might think of her, Mrs. Astell, your Lettice is most likely the daughter of a successful tradesman at the very least or a clergyman or a gentleman of some other sort. But if her parents hope to settle their daughter well, I cannot recommend such a move, no indeed, I cannot."

As Mrs. Wilkin stopped to take a breath, shaking her head decisively, Astell saw her opportunity. "But why not?" she asked the printer's wife. "If all is as you say, if millinery is a well-regulated trade and apprentices come only from respectable families, why do you hesitate?"

"I do not *hesitate*, Mrs. Astell, no, indeed, I do not *hesitate* at all. Do not misapprehend me—of this I am *most certain*. It may be on account of their pride or more likely their misguided hope to improve their daughter's prospects, but most parents who apprentice a daughter to the trade are mightily ignorant about the true state of affairs. Before binding their child in this millinery business, they should know more about the nature of it, they should, indeed," she said, warming to her topic.

"Now, a successful milliner may have a *fine* front in the Exchange where she sells her *fine* wares made of *fine* silk and velvet trimmed with silver and gold, and she may have *fine* profits on every article she deals in, yet she will give but poor, mean wages to any woman she employs.

"And a young girl may be trained to work neatly in all manner of needlework, but she will not be able to earn much after she has served out her apprenticeship—indeed, she will hardly be able to earn enough to cover her board and lodging. Make no mistake, my dear Mrs. Astell, I do not *hesitate* at all—I cannot advise parents to bind a daughter to this business, no I cannot, not if their hope is for her to make her way in this world, for after she has served out her time, she will not be able to make her own living.

"But that is far from the worst of it. No, indeed, not by far. I tell you, Mrs. Astell, the milliner's shop is but the devil's pinfold, and an unscrupulous milliner sets her trap with her innocent apprentices. She instructs them to beg for custom with such amorous looks and affable tones that it seems as if they aim to dispose of themselves rather than the commodities they deal in. 'Fine linens, sir?' 'Gloves and ribbons, sir?' Pah!

"And because of this display, all the young beaux and rakes of the town resort to the milliner's shop, exposing the young creatures there to many terrible temptations. A coxcomb no sooner is master of an estate and a small share of brains than he takes himself off to the shop of a milliner. If he chances to meet an innocent young girl there, he immediately accosts her with all the flattery and all the little raillery he is master of, talks loosely, and thinks himself most witty when he has cracked a stupid jest upon the young creature. It makes no matter whether she be well- or ill-favored, lean or fat, tall or short, he will puff her up and turn her head with his attentions.

"Now, her mistress, even if she may be an honest woman, is obliged to bear the presence of these gallants out of regard to their custom, and she will see to it that her foolish apprentice answers all his rudeness to her with civility and complaisance. And thus the innocent creature is exposed to an intimacy that undermines her virtue and makes his vice attractive—it is but a small step from there to her downfall.

"I am far from charging *all* milliners with the crime of conniving in the ruin of their apprentices, no indeed, I do not charge them all, Mrs. Astell, but my experience leads me to say that many a young creature who is obliged to serve in a millinery shop is utterly undone. Take a survey of all the common women of the town who take their walks between Charing Cross and Fleet Ditch and, I do not doubt, more than half of them will have been trained as milliners—they have been debauched in their place of employment and obliged to throw themselves upon the town for want of bread after they have left their mistress's shop."

As she reached her peroration, the printer's wife rose from her chair. "Whether it is owing to the milliners themselves or to the nature of the business or to whatever cause it is owing, it is not for me to say, but the facts are so clear and the misfortunes attending their apprentices so manifest that it ought to be the last shift a young creature is driven to. These shops are but places for assignations, and the title of 'milliner' is just a polite name for a bawd, a procuress, a wretch who lives upon the spoils of virtue and supports her pride by robbing the innocent of health, fame, and reputation. Milliners promote nothing but vice and live solely by lust."

Her oration having finally reach its conclusion, the worthy woman plumped herself down in her chair again, her two maids and Mary Astell looking on in astonishment.

Mr. Wilkin had lingered below stairs while he heard the increasingly strident voice of his good wife going on at some length, but he quickly reappeared the moment she fell silent. He cheerfully reminded the members of his household and his guest that it was time to depart for the afternoon worship service, and so they gathered themselves to depart, Mary Astell and the two young servants still somewhat dazed.

Neither the printer nor his partner resumed their debate about which church they should attend. Without a word being said either way, Mr. Wilkin shepherded the little group to St. Andrew's, not ceding a point in the long-running debate to his wife, but indicating only that he did not wish to take Mrs. Astell out of her way.

At the end of the service, Astell thanked her hosts, Elizabeth Wilkin insisting that William, their young apprentice, should accompany Mrs. Astell on her walk back to Chelsea. Ordinarily Astell would have rejected this arrangement as a matter of course, but seeing the boy's face light up with the prospect of this outing, even on a gray and desolate day, she accepted the suggestion with good grace and stood by while Mrs. Wilkin delivered a stern lecture to the boy to take care on his journey and to return home promptly.

"Do not dawdle or dally, I am warning you," she said, once again shaking her finger, this time pointing at the boy's nose. Then she smiled, turned to Astell, and spoke so only she could hear: "He is a good boy, Mrs. Astell, and he will watch out for you."

"And I will watch out for him," Astell replied. Then, turning her face west, she began her walk home to Paradise Row, William by her side.

Ten

The boy did not seem to mind that the streets of the great city were empty. He was happy enough with his unexpected release from his mistress's firm grasp. Nor did he seem at all disconcerted by the tall, rigid figure of Mary Astell, with her straight back and her somewhat awkward gait. William was used to the many peculiar characters who frequented the bookshop, and he took Astell's silent presence for granted. At times he rushed ahead of her, and at times he fell back, but he never strayed too far from her side as they headed west.

As for Mary Astell, she was unexpectedly comforted by the boy's presence. She was never one to fear for her safety, God's will be done, but as she made her way through the empty streets of London and then took the path across the open fields to Chelsea, she thought it was not unpleasant, having a companion to accompany her on her journey. The rain had finally stopped, which was a blessing, though it continued very cold. The sky was leaden, more like a winter sky than one usually seen on an October afternoon.

Together they crossed the Five Fields and then the bridge over the Westbourne, walking in a kind of companionable silence. The sun seemed never to have risen that day, and although the day was far from over, it was growing dark by the time they approached Chelsea. Astell was glad when they at last reached the footpath across the grounds of the Hospital and then turned on to Paradise Row.

At the eastern end of the terrace, Hortense Mancini's coach was pulling away from her gate just as Astell and the boy came alongside.

Astell looked in vain for Mustapha, but he could not be seen—though she did catch a brief glimpse of a woman's hand, delicate and very white, pulling a dark drape across one of the glazed windows.

As Astell approached the western end of the row, the front door of her house was flung open, and Sarah launched herself toward the gate, a sour look on her face. As soon as she laid eyes on Astell's traveling companion, however, she stopped in her tracks. Her eyebrows shot up in surprise, her scowl replaced by a broad smile that did much to improve her looks. Still, she had enough sense to appear embarrassed not only by her untoward behavior in rushing out the door but at her slatternly appearance when she did so—she was none too clean, her face smudged and oily, her dress grubby, and her hair untidy.

Her eyes fixed on William, the girl drew herself up, slowed her pace, and did what she could to smooth her skirt. She cleared her throat and then addressed her mistress in a conciliatory tone as they all approached the door.

"Please, ma'am, may I take your cloak?" she asked, then ducked her head and gestured toward the boy, much her own age, who had accompanied Astell. "And about . . . "

Astell waited until they were inside, the door closed firmly, before responding. "Yes, Sarah," she said, her tone, too, much mollified from the sharpness of the morning. "William has accompanied me from Mr. Wilkin's—you may direct him to a place where he can warm himself up and then make sure to offer him something to eat and drink." Turning to the boy, she added, "I trust you know your way back again?"

"Yes, ma'am," William replied warily. Although he could always do with food, he appeared none too eager to spend time alone with Sarah, who was looking at him hungrily, as if she would prefer making a light meal of him rather than of something she might find in the larder. "I have been here before, you know," the boy reminded Astell, "bringing you pages and such from Mr. Wilkin. It is a goodly walk, but I know my way back again." He seemed offended at the suggestion he might not know how to make the return journey to St. Paul's.

"Just be sure you set off before it gets much darker. You may well know the way, but it is best to go as soon as you possibly can. Mrs. Wilkin will be watching for you." Astell turned, then looked back. "And thank you, William, for your trouble."

The boy seemed relieved to be told to take his leave sooner rather than later. He reluctantly followed Sarah out of the front hall and toward the kitchen at the rear of the house, though he kept his cap firmly on his head and looked several times over his shoulder at the front door. Astell was certain he would be on his way just as quickly as he could snatch a bite and swallow.

After removing her hat and her boots, Astell slowly climbed the stairs. She took a deep breath and then, with resolve, turned not toward her study and the quiet retreat it offered but to her bedroom, where Lettice had been installed since her arrival on Friday. Astell opened the door slowly, not sure what she would find.

Bridget was asleep in the chair drawn up to the side of the bed. The room was dark—the old nursemaid had not yet lit a candle, though there was a fire and the room was warm. The girl lay quietly, and Astell leaned over her to see whether she was sleeping.

"It is you," Lettice said crossly, struggling to sit up. "Whatever do you want now?"

Astell pulled back and took a deep breath. Already she felt provoked, but she was determined to get what she needed out of the girl, and so she held her tongue. Instead of the tart reply that sprang to her lips, she swallowed, then asked, "And how are you, my dear?"

"I am not your 'dear,' of that you can be very sure," Lettuce sniffed. "My head hurts, and I fear my fever has returned." She slumped back down, turning her head aside as she did so. "And you will remember I am to be addressed as 'Lady Beauclerk' or 'my lady.' I told you that before. And where have you been? Have you been searching for my husband? Have you found him? Where is he?" She looked eagerly over Astell's shoulder, as if expecting a gallant young lord would rush in to take her in his arms.

But there was no gallant young lord. Astell pulled up a stool and sat down by the girl's side. "I am afraid we have not yet begun the search. We need sufficient information from you if we have any hope of being successful."

The girl looked at Mary Astell in exasperation. "You dare say that you have not yet begun to look for him? What more do you want me to tell you?" she began fretfully. "I have told you all that you need to know—my lord's house must surely be nearby. He said I would find him 'in paradise,' and this is Paradise Row, is it not?" She narrowed her eyes and added, "Although perhaps you would not be familiar with a man of quality, however close by he may live. Where are those other ladies? The two who were here before—they must surely know him. I can hardly expect someone like you to be acquainted with a man of his rank."

Astell looked at the young patient. A few drops of sweat glistened on her forehead, and her hair was once again damp. Her cheeks were also flushed. It seemed as if Mrs. Methuen's fears of a tertian or quartan ague might be justified—the girl's fever, which had abated somewhat the day before, seemed to have returned.

"Lady Ranelagh and Lady Catherine have many obligations and cannot be here every day, so I am afraid you must be content with me," Astell began. "I can assure you it is my very great desire to restore you to your husband. But you have seen for yourself that there are few grand houses here on Paradise Row, and I have lived here long enough to know that there is no young lord such as the man you describe to be found in any of them. Nor do we know of any lord named Charles de Beauclerk—not me, not Lady Ranelagh, not Lady Catherine." This last was not entirely true, but she stated it as a truth nonetheless. The girl remained obstinately silent, looking past Astell toward the grate.

"And so that we may help you find your husband, you must tell us more," Astell continued. "Who else might know him and where he else might he be found? Your mistress in London might well be able to help us in our search." As she spoke these last words, Astell saw the young stranger flinch as if she had been struck. "I do not understand, my dear, not at all," Astell said. "There is no shame . . ."

A mulish expression appeared again on the girl's face. "I told you that I am not your 'dear.' And all that is behind me now, as I have said. Mrs. Rolles would be of no help whatsoever—" Lettice no sooner uttered the name than she clapped her hands over her mouth.

Astell was careful to guard her expression. She did not want the young woman to see how pleased she was at the slip of the tongue. "Ah, yes," she said matter-of-factly, "Mrs. Rolles, so your mistress was named Mrs. Rolles. Very good. And where might she be found?"

Recognizing defeat when faced with it, the girl took a deep breath and replied, quite sensibly Astell thought. "Mrs. Rolles is at the Exchange, of course. Her shop is most exclusive—under the sign of the Golden Fan. Everything there is very fine, of the highest quality—Holland cloth and cambric and lawn and Calico cloth. Mantlets and capes and cloaks of silk and velvet. Hats and hoods and gloves, muffs and tippets and caps . . . And lace and ribbons . . . Every kind of gown can be made up there, as Mrs. Rolles is a perfect connoisseur. She keeps an agent in Paris who sends her news on all latest fashion." The girl sighed, seemingly with longing.

Astell dared not interrupt, though the details of the fabrics and fashions and garments were of no real interest to her—they meant little, in fact, though she had no doubt that they were the very stuff of life to Lady Ranelagh, who would have made a much more receptive audience for the girl's recital.

Astell's silence seemed to prompt the girl to continue. "It was there I met my lord, of course. Mrs. Rolles was very angry, I am sure hoping that one of her daughters would catch his eye, but that was not to be, so much the worse for them. I am the only one he could see, and soon we were wed." She sighed deeply.

While Astell thought it would be easy enough to seek out Mrs. Rolles at the Exchange, she hoped a bit more information might be got, now that "Lettice" had begun to talk. "I can well believe that Mrs. Rolles was very disappointed," she said, "but she may be of help to us now—she must know something of the gentleman who frequented her shop."

Astell was interested in the circumstances of the girl's departure—why and how Lettice had left her apprenticeship and her life in London. Astell could well imagine that the girl's marriage had been reason enough for her dismissal by Mrs. Rolles—if indeed her mistress was aware of the marriage. But Astell thought it best to avoid such questions at the present moment.

Astell also thought it might be important to know something of the girl's origins. Although Lettice might claim to have left "all that" behind her, a return to her family might be necessary if her "great lord" could not be found—if, as seemed more likely, the man had seduced and then abandoned the silly creature. There would be no going back to the milliner, not for a girl in her present condition. And if there were no parents, as she claimed . . . *Well, whatever will become of her then?*

"And your family, Lettice? What can you tell me of your parents?"

The girl frowned, either at the familiarity of Astell's form of address or at the question about her parents, or perhaps at both. "I have told you that already," she said sharply. "My father died, and then my mother."

"But who were your people? Have you no one else, no other family?"

The girl did not immediately reply. She seemed to be thinking about whether to answer at all. Finally, she offered something to Astell by way of response. "My father was a gentleman," she said at last.

"Aye, so was mine," said Mary Astell. "He was a coal merchant in Newcastle." As soon as she said it, Astell knew it was the wrong thing to say. A look of great disgust passed over Lettice's face.

"My father was in trade as well," she said. "Pah!" she added, her nose wrinkling in disgust. "My mother, though—she was very refined, the daughter of a vicar. A true gentlewoman. And she made sure I received the best sort of education, fit for my station—a fine boarding school, we were all young ladies there, and we learned how to comport ourselves well and to dress ourselves well. We had music and dance and drawing lessons."

Astell was only too familiar with the curriculum offered to girls in such places—there were several such schools in Chelsea, advertising themselves as places devoted to the cultivation of the "female arts." Gorges House, Shrewsbury House, Blacklands—places where girls pranced about on stage, paraded themselves at balls, minced their way to church where they could be admired by men who traveled all the way to Chelsea just to see "the young ladies of the schools, whereof there is great store, and very pretty." Places where girls practiced such necessary skills as *japanning*, if you please. Where they were taught to pursue butterflies and trifles, where their natures were spoiled rather than improved, where they were nursed up in ignorance and vanity, where they learned to be proud and petulant, delicate and fantastic, capricious and inconstant.

"And we were taught French, of course." Lettice added this with a faint toss of her head and wave of her hand.

Astell suppressed her exasperation. If the girl's garbled pronunciation of "Beauclerk" were an indication of the what she had been taught in her school, Astell had her view of its worth. She might not speak French herself, but nor, she concluded, did "Lettice," no matter what she might have been "taught."

"But then my father died," the girl said mournfully, "And we were left with nothing! Nothing! I was forced to leave my school. Not long after, my mother grew ill—and in order to provide for me, she sought out advice from my father's business associates! Just imagine—seeking advice from tradesmen! And that's how I was *sold off* to Mrs. Rolles." The girl's disgust was palpable. "Though," she added grudgingly, "I suppose my mother hoped I would come into contact with persons of quality in such an establishment . . . I was in despair at the arrangement, as you might well imagine, but I can see now that it turned out just as my mother planned."

"Let us hope so," replied Astell. The girl seemed to regard the death of her parents as a mere inconvenience and her apprenticeship only as a means to acquire the ultimate end, a husband and marriage.

An uneasy silence fell over the room. Astell looked across to Bridget and saw a glint reflected in the old nursemaid's eye. She wondered how long Bridget had been awake and what she made of the girl's story. Old Bridget had seen a very great deal in her life.

And then, since she had probably extracted the last reliable bit of information to be had from the girl, Astell rose quietly. Nodding to Bridget, she left the room.

Having ascertained from a disconsolate Sarah that young William had headed back to the Wilkins and their shop, Mary Astell thought she would retire to her study, but at that moment, she heard a sharp rap at the door. Although she had not expected to see Lady Catherine that day, the Ranelagh coach had arrived, delivering not only her dear friend but Lady Ranelagh as well.

"We could not wait to hear from you, Mary," said Lady Ranelagh, as if an explanation were necessary for her presence. Although Astell did not see the countess of Ranelagh nearly as often as she saw Lady Catherine, it was not unusual for Lady Ranelagh to accompany Lady Catherine on a visit to Paradise Row. "What news?"

Astell did not think it was necessary to say mention her trip to the city earlier that day—no need to rile Lady Catherine unnecessarily on the subject of her travel. Instead, she focused on her conversation with the girl—although as soon as she began, she found herself almost immediately waylaid by the subject of boarding schools, about which she had many strong views.

". . . not just useless but dangerous!" Astell was indignant. "The preposterous returns on such an investment! If only women were rightly educated, they would obtain a well-informed and discerning mind. Then they would not be imposed on with such tinsel-ware. But when they have been taught to value themselves on nothing but their clothes and to think they are very fine when well accoutered, when they hear others say that it is wisdom enough for them to know how to dress themselves . . . "

Lady Ranelagh and Lady Catherine exchanged glances. When Lady Ranelagh raised her right eyebrow slightly, Lady Catherine pressed her lips firmly together to resist a smile. Once she had regained her self-control, she frowned at Lady Ranelagh, who took a deep, satisfied breath, content that she had been successful in annoying her husband's daughter.

Astell, meanwhile, continued her vehement abuse of the shabby education provided to girls—it was a topic very dear to her, and she could see in the young stranger the ill effects of a system that taught girls that the only subject worthy of their debate was what colors are most agreeable or what dress becomes them best. "There is no reason why women should be content to be ciphers in the world, useless at the best and in a little time a burden and nuisance to all about them. To think that this poor young woman has been taught to value herself on nothing more than the pitiful conquest of some vain, insignificant man—"

"Yes, yes, we quite agree with your principles, as you well know," said Lady Ranelagh, with dismissive wave of her hand. "But what is to be done now, I ask you? The girl may have been utterly ruined, her poor head turned, but what is *to be done*? It seems to me that we must find this husband of hers. She is *his* problem, burden or nuisance or whatever."

"But the pity . . . " began Astell.

"I quite agree," said Lady Catherine, her decisive tone drawing to a close Astell's impassioned speech. "You are right without doubt, Mary, but our problem now, as her ladyship so rightly observes, is not the nonsense to which the girl has been subjected by her unfortunate education but what is to be done with her now. I fear you will have Mr. King or the fearsome Mr. Williams at your door very soon." Mr. Williams enjoyed his role as churchwarden only too well.

"I have at the least found out the name of the woman to whom the girl was apprenticed," said Astell. "A milliner by the name of Rolles, who has a shop in the Royal Exchange. I believe that is where I must go tomorrow. Surely this woman will know something about a young man buzzing around her shop, paying attentions to her apprentice."

"Aaaaah," exclaimed Lady Ranelagh with a great sigh of satisfaction. "This is where you will need me, Mary, you will need me most assuredly."

"Now, Your Ladyship," began Astell, not wishing to impose upon the countess.

"It is just the place for my particular talents, you will see." Looking pointedly at Mary Astell's drab garments and then at her own, she shook her head. "I am afraid this Mrs. Rolles would not have the time of day for you, Mary, indeed she would not. But, now, if I were with you . . . "

The countess smoothed the dark green silk of her skirts, looked down demurely, and then, raising her head, beamed.

Eleven

You know I am right, Mary. You simply cannot not do without me, so there is no point whatsoever in making such a fuss," said Lady Ranelagh, shaking her head as if for emphasis. Since Mary Astell had not uttered a single word, Lady Ranelagh's remark seemed a bit unfair. Nevertheless, Astell thought it just as well to say nothing lest she be rightly accused of making a fuss.

The Ranelagh coach had called for Mary Astell early that morning. In fact, the earl's impressive equipage had been standing outside her gate, ready to sweep her off to the city as soon as she returned from the Monday morning service at All Saints. Inside, the countess had been waiting impatiently, and no sooner was Astell in sight, walking up Paradise Row, than the coach door had swung open, Lady Ranelagh gesturing peremptorily for her to hurry.

The coach wheeled north, skirting the courtyard of the Hospital, and headed toward the king's private road, which would take them all the way to Whitehall. Once they were underway, Lady Ranelagh proved to be in unusually high spirits. Astell listened absentmindedly to the countess's stream of chitter-chatter. The day was bright and crisp—since the sun had not made an appearance for at least a week, the fine weather was a welcome break. Enjoying the cloudless blue sky and her companion, Astell realized, quite suddenly, that she had spent very little time alone with Lady Ranelagh in the ten months or so since Lady Margaret Cecil had married the old earl.

For the first time, Astell directed her full attention to the new countess of Ranelagh, not so much to her words but to her person. Lady Ranelagh seemed to have dressed even more carefully than usual for what she clearly regarded as an adventure. Her auburn hair was dressed with an impressive number of curls loosely piled on the top of her head, the whole arrangement supported by a headdress of what looked to be several layers of elaborately folded and knotted ribbons. A long curl hung down over her left shoulder. No doubt there was a name for this style of coiffure, but Astell was unaware of it.

The countess's dark eyes shone, and her full red lips curled pleasingly as she gossiped on, not noticing her companion's careful observation. While many women of fashion powdered, Lady Ranelagh's complexion was flawless, and on that day, her white cheeks were flushed with the softest of pinks. Astell had come to realize that the countess took care to disguise her keen intelligence behind her mask of beauty, but there was nothing false about this beauty—she did not paint or patch, nor had she any need. She was perfection itself.

And although Astell knew even less about fashion than she did about hair styles, and although she did not ordinarily pay much mind to Lady Ranelagh's elaborate attire, she now saw the care that the countess had taken with her dress. The deep rose silk of her skirts was barely visible beneath the folds of her velvet mantle.

She had not drawn her hood over her head—the hair, Astell supposed—but to further protect herself from the piercing cold, she wore a sable palatine, fastened with silver threads, over her shoulders. Her dimpled chin was nestled into its warmth.

Having studied her traveling companion carefully, Astell predicted that whatever kind of woman Mrs. Rolles might prove to be, she would not be able to resist Lady Ranelagh's charms, not if the countess set out to charm. And, then, one look at the richness of the lady's apparel and the quantity of her many trinkets and ornaments would make clear to any enterprising woman of business that this would be someone who was well worth pleasing.

Leaving the king's road as it entered the city, the Ranelagh coach lumbered along the busy streets that Astell had traveled on foot just the day before. They moved slowly down Pall Mall, the Strand, and the Fleet. The coach then diverged from Astell's route, and instead of continuing on, toward St. Paul's, the driver turned north just before Ludgate, then east at Pater Noster Row, continuing on to Cheapside and Poultry Street before reaching their destination.

The city was alive with the day's hustle and bustle: coaches, carts, and barrows clattered and bumped down the uneven streets, stray dogs and straying apprentices dashing between their wheels and eliciting loud streams of invective from all those whom they startled as they did so. A pall of smoke hung in the air, causing halting beggars and preening gentlemen alike to cough and wheeze. Astell thought that walking was probably a much faster mode of travel through the teeming streets, but there was little chance that Lady Ranelagh would abandon the comfort of her coach, soiling her skirts in the muck and ruining her fine shoes.

At last, however, the Ranelagh coach drew up to the entrance of the Royal Exchange.

The great commercial heart of the city lay between Threadneedle Street and Cornhill. First constructed during the reign of Queen Elizabeth, the Royal Exchange, like so much of the city, had been destroyed by the Great Fire as it had swept relentlessly through the streets. But unlike so many other buildings—St. Paul's, to name only one—the reconstruction of this wondrous emporium had begun almost as soon as the smoke cleared and the embers died. While much of the city still lay in ruins, and while wrangling about what should be rebuilt (and where and how) continued, an expanded Royal Exchange opened for business just three years after the original had burned to the ground.

The main entrance of the Exchange was on Cornhill, through a lofty archway flanked by four columns. Over the portico rose an imposing three-story tower. At each corner of the lower story was a carved griffin bearing a shield displaying the arms of the city. Within the second story was a large clock with four dials that chimed the hour at three, six, nine, and twelve o'clock. Above the clock, in the tower's upper story, was a large bell that rang at noon and again at six of the evening.

The large quadrangle of the new Exchange enclosed an open trading floor lined by a covered colonnade. Around the four sides of this space, merchants from countries far and wide met to share the day's important news as they bought and sold their wares: the French, the Portuguese, the Spanish, and the Italians, Jews and Turks, Russians, the Dutch, and traders from Virginia, Jamaica, and Barbados. In the cellars below the open courtyard were storehouses of silks and spice and furs and sandalwood.

But the attraction for fashionable men and women was not here, in the open-air piazza and its surrounding arcade, but upstairs, in the galleries, where some two hundred exclusive stalls catered to the fancies of the wealthy—to entice them to linger (and to spend), each of these small shops was painted and gilded, wainscoted and glazed, furnished with polished looking glasses and lit by wax candles in silver sconces.

Mary Astell was impressed as Lady Ranelagh made her way through the noisy crowd of rogues, loafers, beggars, cut-purses, orange-women, tumblers, jugglers, and loiterers who jostled one another just outside the Cornhill entrance, spitting, shouting, begging, pleading, swearing, and making a general nuisance of themselves. At the countess of Ranelagh's approach, the unsavory throng parted, and she sailed through, Mary Astell in her wake.

Once inside the Exchange, Astell found her every sense subject to assault: a babel of foreign tongues, a stink of tobacco and pomade, a patchwork of colorful advertisements plastered on every possible surface, a thicket of pointed elbows jostling and jabbing her this way and that. None of this seemed to bother Lady Ranelagh, however. She looked around her with pleasure before making her way across the courtyard. She bent to whisper into the ear of a nondescript little man, listened intently to him as he gestured, then turned to Astell and signed for her to follow.

"Rest assured that there are more discreet entrances, Mary, should you wish to avoid this hubbub," advised the countess. "But I do believe that, in this instance, our more public arrival will stand us in good stead." She pitched her voice quite low, though her words were surprisingly clear under the tumult of shouts and cries.

Astell followed as Lady Ranelagh moved slowly but steadily forward, pointing in the direction of a corner in the upper gallery. They climbed a broad staircase, then passed stall after stall displaying a dazzling array of luxury goods—jeweled snuffboxes, black lace threaded with gold, painted fans, scented leather gloves, gauze caps, delicate Chinese porcelain—all the while heading toward the corner that Lady Ranelagh had indicated.

Astell remained somewhat puzzled by the countess's remark until they approached the booth under the sign of the Golden Fan, an eight-foot frontage in the north-east corner of the Exchange. A dignified woman of some years stood quietly just outside the stall, clearly anticipating the arrival of Lady Ranelagh—news of the countess's intended destination must have preceded them. The woman greeted the countess in a composed way, stepping aside so that her ladyship could enter the premises. And while Mary Astell was quite used to being overlooked whenever she was in the company of Lady Ranelagh, she was not invisible on this occasion. Astell too was greeted by the woman she assumed to be Mrs. Rolles herself.

"Welcome, my lady," she said to the countess. "I am most honored by your visit today."

"Thank you," responded Lady Ranelagh, inclining her head graciously.

"Mrs. Gertrude Rolles, my lady, and I am at your service."

"I do hope so, Mrs. Rolles," replied the countess. "We have most particular needs today." She smiled and, at Mrs. Rolles's invitation, seated herself gracefully on the single upholstered stool within the shop.

Though small, the stall was one of the largest in the Exchange, richly appointed with polished mahogany drawers and cupboards displaying a selection of the items to be found on the premises. From her own position, as she stood near the shop's entrance, Astell could observe the milliner, who was soberly but elegantly dressed. Even Astell could tell that the cut and fit of the gown were superb.

"I hope, my lady, you will find here whatever you might desire, and should you require something that you do not see, we will of course be most happy to search it out for you. My daughters and I are eager to assist you in all your needs," said Mrs. Rolles, gesturing toward two younger women, the very image of their mother. Like their mother, they were carefully but not showily attired. In their demeanor, they were deferential but not obsequious.

"Accompanying me today is my dear friend," said Lady Ranelagh, "Mrs. Mary Astell."

Gertrude Rolles turned quickly to Astell. "Mrs. Mary Astell?" she asked in astonishment. "The *celebrated* Mary Astell? Well, I never. The most esteemed author of *A Serious Proposal*, here in my shop. I am very obliged, Mrs. Astell. You are most welcome."

Lady Ranelagh was not a little surprised at hearing this, being used to receiving all attention herself, but she recovered quickly. Almost nothing could shock her, although she was taken aback at this surprising turn of events.

As was Mary Astell, truth be told. "Well," she began cautiously. "Yes, *that* Mary Astell, to be sure."

Gertrude Rolles smiled warmly, but there was a wry expression on her face as well. "You are surely not surprised that I am gratified to make your acquaintance? We too, we women of the city who work for our bread, we have read and considered your proposal. Did you think we would not, Mrs. Astell? You may not have been thinking of *us* when you wrote, but rest assured that we have been thinking of *you*. While it is true that we do not have the leisure to withdraw from the world and dedicate ourselves to self-reflection and self-improvement, we value what you say about the importance of education nonetheless." As the milliner spoke, her two daughters stared intently at Mary Astell.

"Men may well pen satires about you and enjoy their mockery of you," Mrs. Rolles continued, "but we women of the city congratulate you. We know only too well the indignities women face when they dare to enter into any preserve that men believe to be all their own. I am honored to make your acquaintance."

"Thank you, I am sure," replied Astell, more than a little flustered. She was used to being a silent observer, not one who was observed— she would be the first to admit that she found the raillery to which she was ordinarily subjected much easier to bear than praise from a woman like Mrs. Rolles. And then Astell grew a bit more uncomfortable, recalling her disparagement of the kinds of gewgaws and baubles so proudly displayed on the counters and shelves of the Golden Fan.

The milliner may have been a complete surprise, yet Astell immediately felt her to be a kind of kindred spirit as well. Not because the woman had kind words to say about her work—Mary Astell was not one to be puffed up by such a thing. But she could see that this was a serious, thoughtful woman, not at all the kind of person that Mrs. Wilkin's dire warnings had led her to expect. In fact, Astell suspected that the printer's wife would have much in common with this successful woman of business.

"Oh, I know what you have to say about luxuries like these," Mrs. Rolles said, gesturing to the goods in her stall. "They are 'trifles' and 'tinsel-ware,' if I am not mistaken. And I also have a good idea of what you may have been told about women like me. I have heard it all, you may be sure, and only too frequently. But since mine is a trade in which women have proven themselves to be very successful, such libels are only to be expected." And then, casting another sharp glance at Astell, "Though it is a very great pity indeed if women come to believe such malicious tales about other women."

She continued, still addressing herself to Astell, "I know only too well that some women who call themselves milliners are no better than they should be, although that is surely the case in every trade. But to fit up and stock a shop such as mine requires substantial funds, and no right-thinking woman would risk her investment with any such foolishness as you may have heard tell.

"Millinery is a trade that offers opportunity to a woman who is prepared to work hard. A diligent, sober woman may do well in this business, just as I have done. I am proud to have trained not a few young apprentices in my time—this is a sound business for those who are proficient at their needles, especially if they are naturally neat and of a courteous behavior. No doubt some girls entering this trade have been placed here by their parents in the hope that they will attract a husband, and some foolish girls so placed have been seduced—I myself have seen it happen . . . "

At this Mrs. Rolles sighed before continuing. "But look, here are my daughters. You may rest assured that I would not bring them into this trade if they were compromised in any way. I have an interest not only in maintaining my business but in guarding their reputations as well as my own."

Lady Ranelagh sat quietly during this exchange, not quite sure what it was all about, but she could see that Mary Astell had information she had not shared on their journey together. The countess was far too sharp an observer to interrupt, however. "Just so," she said instead, with a brief glance at Astell. She skillfully turned the conversation in the direction she thought it ought to be headed. "It just so happens that we have come here today to inquire about a young woman who was recently in your employ."

Astell was grateful for the countess's intervention, but she could see that Mrs. Rolles and her daughters seemed a bit perplexed.

"A young woman named Lettice," Astell urged. And then, seeing no recognition in the face of the milliner, she added, "I do not know her surname, but she was, I have been led to believe, indentured to you and only recently left."

Mrs. Rolles furrowed her brow. One of her two daughters, Astell thought it was perhaps the elder, bent toward her mother and whispered something in her ear. A flash of recognition spread across the older woman's face. And then, quite unexpectedly she threw back her head, opened her mouth wide, and gave a hearty laugh. In doing so, she reminded Astell of no one so much as Elizabeth Wilkin, the printer's wife.

"Well, well, well, I know of no *Lettice*, to be sure, but I do know Letty," said Mrs. Rolles. "Ah, Letty, Letty, Letty. Letty Pyke, that is, Mrs. Astell. And, yes, she did take up an apprenticeship with me, though she has been gone for quite some time. I still have *her* copy of her contract, binding her as an apprentice—the foolish girl did not bother to take it with her, though that did not surprise me. A most unfortunate situation, though the girl just would not listen and brought it all on herself. But what business can you possibly have with Letty Pyke?"

Mary Astell narrowed her eyes and pressed her lips tightly together. She *knew* the girl had not been entirely truthful with her name.

It was Lady Ranelagh's turn to laugh now, though she did not throw her head back in the manner of Gertrude Rolles. "Well, Mary, you were quite right," she said as all five women drew more closely together to work out the situation of Letty Pyke.

Mary Astell wasted no words in conveying to Mrs. Rolles the story of how the girl who now called herself Lettice had been discovered in Chelsea just three days earlier, feverish and insensible, and of the rather remarkable tale she had spun when she recovered her senses. Nor did Astell omit the shocking circumstances in which the girl now found herself—carrying a child, searching for a husband who seemed to have vanished, and unlikely to be taken on as a charity case in a parish where she did not belong.

"Tut, tut, tut, it is a very sad story," said Mrs. Rolles, shaking her head. "And a story that could have had a happy ending instead of taking such an unfortunate turn. But I cannot imagine how Letty Pyke ever came to be in Chelsea."

"Why did she leave your employ? And when?" asked Lady Ranelagh.

"And perhaps it might be well to know how she came to be here in the first place," suggested Mary Astell.

"I think that might be where best to begin," agreed Mrs. Rolles. "You see, my late husband dealt in textiles, a member of the Worshipful Company of Mercers, if you please. It was through his trade that he first became acquainted with Letty's father, a wool merchant in Exeter. I did not know the man myself, and after Mr. Rolles's death some years ago, I had no dealings with Robert Pyke.

"In any case, although I assumed my late husband's business as his widow, I was finally able to join the guild in my own right, no longer dealing in woolen cloth but setting myself up as a milliner. It did not come easy, I can tell you, entering the Mercers' Company, nor was it cheap. I have two sons who have continued in the cloth trade, following in their father's line of work, but my daughters will have this business after my death. Though that's not really to the purpose, is it? You did not come here to learn about how Mrs. Gertrude Rolles has made her way in this hard world. Except that it is through this connection that Letty Pyke came to me."

"What connection?" asked Lady Ranelagh.

"Well, my lady, in business as in politics, maintaining relationships can be very important, as I am sure the earl of Ranelagh knows." She nodded her head sagely, causing Lady Ranelagh to wonder for a moment if this woman was somehow privy to Lord Ranelagh's many business arrangements.

As the countess mused, Gertrude Rolles continued in her recital. "While it is true that I never had any contacts with this Robert Pyke myself, one of his fellows, a mercer dealing in wool who had also done some trade with my late husband, contacted me. He wrote to say that Pyke's widow had fallen ill, you see, and that the poor woman was desperate to find a safe harbor for her only child, a daughter. In her time of need, Mrs. Pyke had appealed to her husband's fraternity for help, this merchant remembered my husband, and further inquiries eventually led the dealer to me. He wrote to ask whether some arrangement could be made to send the girl, Robert Pyke's daughter, to me so she could be trained in the millinery business."

"My word," exclaimed Lady Ranelagh. "The woman, that widow, the girl's mother, she did not know you at all! And to propose sending her daughter to you?"

"Well, my lady," said Mrs. Rolles, "the poor woman thought there was much to be said for securing her daughter a place where she would be kept out of harm's way. Mrs. Pyke knew my late husband's reputation, and that was quite enough for her. But to be altogether honest, my lady, she had few other choices—the dealer was very honest when he first broached the topic with me. He was sorry to say that Robert Pyke's widow would not be able to pay the premium I usually receive for taking on an apprentice. Even so, for the sake of the past ties between Mr. Rolles and the girl's father, I agreed."

"Do you know much about the mother? This Mrs. Pyke?" Mary Astell was curious about Letty's mother, wondering whether anything the girl had told her were true.

"Well, Mrs. Astell, judging from the daughter she raised, she must have been a very foolish woman. And, then, reading between the lines of the letters I received from Robert Pyke's old friend and business fellow, I take it that he believed Joanne Pyke had fretted and fussed her husband half to death with all her airs and demands. That is as it may be, I never met her myself, poor woman, but whatever the reason, there was little left to her after Robert Pyke died, and that little was soon gone, with nothing left to secure his daughter's future."

"But why?" asked Lady Ranelagh. "Why ever would you take on such a person as an apprentice? Someone you have never met! I am quite sure that you might have your pick of girls to take into training."

"Well, my lady," Mrs. Rolles conceded, "I have taken on a girl or two in my time, if I do say so, and always for an excellent premium. In the case of Letty Pyke, although there was no money for her training, I was assured that the girl was apt . . . I am sure I still have a letter from her mother somewhere about, telling me how carefully educated the girl had been and how proficient she was in needlework. 'My daughter is eager to learn,' Mrs. Pyke assured me. Be that as it may be, in commerce you never know when you may need a good turn yourself, and what with my sons still working in their father's trade, I was persuaded that there would be little risk in taking on the girl and much good will to be gained by maintaining my late husband's alliances.

"As for the girl herself . . . If she had served out her indenture, her future would have been assured, that much I can say with confidence—the girls I have trained do well, and she could have made her own way in the world by her needle, either setting up for herself or taking a place in someone else's shop, much like my own daughters, working here for me. Yes, she could have earned a very nice living.

"Or, then, the girl might have found a decent husband for herself, her training and skill providing a sufficient marriage portion for some hardworking young guildsman or merchant in need of a wife who would be an asset in his business. This is what some parents hope for their daughters when they place them, and it does come about very happily on many occasions. I should know—I was raised in the cloth business myself. I had a good head for business on my shoulders as well as a knowledge of the trade. Mr. Rolles considered ours a fair bargain when we agreed to marry. But that was not good enough for Letty Pyke, not at all."

"But that, it seems, is exactly what she did, is it not?" asked Lady Ranelagh. "Find a husband who valued her?" While she was interested enough in the story that Mrs. Rolles had to tell, Lady Ranelagh was keen to move on to the chapter about the handsome young gentleman who seemed to have played an important role in Letty's narrative, but who had yet to make his appearance in Gertrude Rolles's tale.

"No, my lady. It most definitely is *not* what she did. I am afraid Letty was unhappy from the very moment she arrived here. She had just lost her mother, and I expected some difficulties with her at the outset, as would be natural, but she did not seem to feel much sorrow about her mother's death, and none at all about her father's. She just could not settle. Her head was filled with nothing but 'froth and emptiness,' as Mrs. Astell has called it."

At this Mrs. Rolle smiled, proud of the reference, though Astell once again felt a trifle uneasy.

"Whatever education that girl may have had," the milliner continued, "some boarding school in Exeter, I do believe, but wherever it was, she learned nothing useful there. Just frippery and folly. She was certainly taught no *philosophy*, Mrs. Astell"—this with another pointed look at Mary Astell—"and that is as may be, but I do not believe any amount of your Mr. Descartes would have served young Letty Pyke well. She could have used a deal more by way of letters and arithmetic, and a healthy dose of common sense would not have come amiss. Some lessons in modesty and decorum would also have done nicely. Such fancies she had! 'But my mother was a gentlewoman,' she would say. 'You must remember, Mrs. Rolles, that my mother was a gentlewoman.' She was too high and mighty, that little miss. Seemed to think it a disgrace that her father had been in trade. Still, she was not stupid, and she might have made something of herself."

"But she decided to leave?" Astell asked, hoping to move the narrative along.

"Decide to leave? Why, she certainly did not *decide* to leave," huffed Gertrude Rolles. The mere suggestion that her apprentice might have willingly chosen to end her training and depart seemed to offend the Exchange woman. The milliner's two daughters, who were still standing silently by her side, looked at their mother with some concern. Her loss of equanimity seemed out of her carefully controlled character.

"That girl did *not* just take *herself* off," Mrs. Rolles scoffed. "Do not believe that at all, although she might claim otherwise. She did not *decide* to leave, she was made to leave. I warned her repeatedly, I did. No, she did not leave of her own accord—I had to send her packing. It could have been disastrous to my reputation, not to mention my business. In the end it was Bridewell for her. Still, it might all have been avoided, I warned her about that rascal, I did—but would she listen? No indeed, she paid me no mind at all, and once I learned the state she was in, she had to go."

No doubt Lady Ranelagh had enjoyed her morning's adventure in the Royal Exchange, but in truth most of the conversation thus far had been rather dull for her—cloth trading and boarding schools and indentures and whatnot. If not for her delightful surroundings in Mrs. Rolles's stall under the sign of the Golden Fan—the rich fabrics, the polished mirrors, the soft glow of the candlelight—she would have been quite bored. But scandal? Bridewell? At last they had arrived at the point.

"Now, Mrs. Rolles, this is exactly why we have come to consult with you," she said, sitting up very straight on her plush seat, directing her enchanting gaze toward the offended milliner. Observing the countess, Mary Astell wondered whether a practical and experienced woman like Gertrude Rolles would fall under her spell. "She claims that she met a young gentleman here. What can you tell us about this man? She says she was discovered here by a young lord who 'lifted her up' and swept her away."

"Took her down, more like, my lady, if I do say so. There is not and never was any young gentleman, much less a lord, not for the likes of Letty Pyke. There was just a clever scoundrel, and not so clever at that, a sly and smirking good-for-nothing. Oh, he was pleasing enough to the eye, I will grant you that, very pretty, he was, but only a fool would confuse him for a gentleman. But he cast a fascination upon her, that he did." Mrs. Rolles shook her head ruefully at Letty's lack of discernment.

Lady Ranelagh sighed and allowed herself to look a bit disappointed at Mrs. Rolles's dismissal of Letty's fantasies. Not that she had believed the young woman, of course, but she would have much preferred a story of aristocratic romance and intrigue to a sordid tale of seduction.

For her part, Gertrude Rolles seemed to regard the expression on the face of the countess as a comment on her judgment. "I encounter a fair number of very fine gentlemen in my line of work, my lady," she insisted, though with a certain tone of sarcasm in her voice. "All those gay, fluttering fops and young beaux and topping sparks of the town, full of blustering nonsense. Men who, as you have observed, Mrs. Astell, 'fancy that a well-adjusted peruke is able to supply their want of brains.' Pah!

These gallants are nothing but time wasters at best, intriguers and schemists at worst, but still they must be served—I cannot afford to turn away their custom.

"Many a shopkeeper will do all she can to cater to these fine young gentlemen of the town. Some will even lay out bait to trap them—you will see young women leaning across the counters of their stalls and casting languishing glances to tempt these fools to purchase all the little toys and trifles they do not need and cannot use. But I would never use any girl, much less my own daughters, in such a disgraceful manner, and any *beau garçon* who thinks to catch one of them in his net soon loses interest."

"But that was not the case with Letty?" asked the countess.

"No, no, indeed not, my lady. That young rascal was always messing about, setting his unhappy snares—he knew better how to catch a woman in his springe than a partridge."

"And she could not be warned?" asked Astell.

"No, indeed, Mrs. Astell, she was much too full of herself for that. And the practiced rascal knew just how to bait the trap, flattering her, filling her head with his nonsense. The fellow was always around, enticing her the moment my back was turned. I warned her, I did indeed, but she would not listen to such a one as me. No, indeed, she was a lost diamond to be plucked from the mud and set in some glittering diadem, or so she believed. 'Oh, he talks so gravely to me,' she would say, 'he would do nothing to betray me, his passion will not suffer him to abuse me.'"

At this point in her narration, Gertrude Rolles abruptly stopped. Her daughters moved close to her, one on each side, as if to support her. All five women were quiet, each contemplating the all too familiar story of a young woman seduced and betrayed. It was an old story, but the tragedy was newly felt.

Twelve

The great bell in the Exchange tower rang, counting out the hour. As the twelfth note sounded, each of the five women was still lost in thought.

The milliner, Gertrude Rolles, appeared regretful. Although she had done only what was necessary, she was now feeling a twinge of sorrow for the trouble that had overtaken the foolish girl in her care. Still, Letty might have avoided all these problems, the milliner reassured herself, if only she had been willing to listen and learn.

For their part, the Exchange woman's two daughters had never liked the young apprentice and had resented her airs and affectations. Every task she failed to complete had become one more bit of work for them to finish. They were happy Letty Pyke was gone, and while they might feel just a bit sorry for her, they were both looking more than a little smug-faced.

Lady Ranelagh was more practiced in hiding her true feelings than the milliner or her daughters. She could manage looking quite distressed even while she was, on the whole, feeling pleased with the day's outing. For her, Letty's adventures were rather like a play. Not a very original play, to be sure, nor a particularly good play, and perhaps not even a play that the countess would have been eager to see, but it was enjoyable nonetheless, at least for the brief while it was acted out on stage for her entertainment.

Mary Astell's feelings were more complicated. She had not taken to Letty Pyke at all—Astell readily admitted this to herself. After her initial sympathy for the girl, Astell had quickly come to feel that she was an annoyance. And now that she knew more of Letty's background, she felt her judgment had been confirmed: the girl was every bit as foolish and willful as she seemed. And yet. *What else, really, could be expected? From her infancy the girl was denied the very wisdom she is now condemned for lacking and nursed up in the very follies for which she is now punished. How could she have acted in any other way since her instructors were froth and emptiness?*

It was Lady Ranelagh who at last broke the silence. "Well, as it now seems, you believe the foolish girl was seduced and then abandoned by her seducer. Am I right, Mrs. Rolles?" she asked.

"Just so, my lady. She might claim that the man married her, but that was all stuff and nonsense. And when it was clear what state she was in, well, she had to go. You know as well as I that a girl in service must be dismissed for such an offence. As for Letty . . . Well, she had already broken the terms of her bond by slipping away with that rascal any time my back was turned, and that alone was reason enough for her dismissal, but then, and what is worse, the wicked girl was clearly committing acts of fornication. I have her bond here somewhere, but I know the terms well enough by heart—they are very clear: 'She shall not absent herself from her said mistress's service day nor night lawfully,' 'She shall not commit fornication'—"

"But the girl does say she married the man," Astell interrupted.

"So she may say, Mrs. Astell," Gertrude Rolles replied sharply. "She made that claim then, too, but marriage is also against the terms of her contract."

And then, since she had been interrupted, and by none other than the celebrated Mary Astell, Mrs. Rolles took care to finish reciting the pertinent article from the indenture: "'She shall not commit fornication *nor contract matrimony within the said term.*' The contract is very plain on this subject, Mrs. Astell—you know as well as I that no woman can serve two masters. It is all right there in her bond, as I say, and she signed her name to it, clear as anything. I can find that contract for you, should you wish to see it for yourself—and the foolish girl left without taking her copy with her, as I have said—but I know the terms well enough by heart.

"And in any case, no matter what she might have claimed about marriage, the wicked scoundrel soon disappeared and could not be found, so who is to say whether she were married or no? Banns were never read out, I know that for a fact, and when she was examined, she could produce neither a license nor any witness to the ceremony. It may have been a Fleet marriage, for all I know, though I hardly think the rascal would have had to go to that much trouble."

"When did you dismiss her?" asked Lady Ranelagh.

"Let me think a minute, my lady," said Mrs. Rolles. It was clear from her puzzled brow that it must have been some time since Letty Pyke had left the milliner.

"Hmm, Mama," said the elder of Mrs. Rolles's two daughters, quietly approaching her mother once again and bending to speak softly in her ear.

"Yes, yes, you are quite right, I remember now," said Mrs. Rolles. "She was gone by about Lammas-Day. Of course, all was done proper on my part. She had no shame to her at all, hiding nothing, flaunting herself and telling the most outrageous lies, blabbing to anyone who would listen that she had been claimed as his 'very own' by that wicked practiser.

"Oh, yes, she was quite happy to make her condition known to all and sundry. She had no shame, none at all. I certainly *would* not have kept her on here, but, you see, once she told everyone she met that she was to have a baby, I *could* not—that would have made me answerable not only for her but for her child. No, no, I could not have that.

"In the end the silly girl found herself hauled before the justices of the peace, and when she was examined, she could produce no proof of her marriage, as I said. They tried to find the father of the child, but no sign of the lying rascal could be found. And to make matters all the worse, the examiners could not make any sense of Letty's rightful parish of settlement. The wardens of St. Bartholomew's certainly did not want the charges to fall to them—she had only come to London in January, just after Epiphany, and signed her bond then, it was clearly dated, so she could make no claim to a settlement here in the parish.

"The wardens thought to send her back to Exeter as quick as lightning before the child was born, or at least that was their intent, though I admit that I did not keep track of her once she left here. I washed my hands of the whole business. In the end she was dispatched to Bridewell, I do know that—but I know nothing about when she was sent there or where she might have been sent *from* there. I would have thought she was long gone home by now."

"So she has been gone from you for over two months?" asked Lady Ranelagh.

"Yes, my lady. And that is the last I knew of Letty Pyke until today—I never expected to hear of her again." After a brief pause, she added, "Truth be told, my lady, I did not want to hear of her ever again. It was a bad situation all the way around."

"What do you know about the young man whom she claims to have married?" asked Mary Astell.

"Well, I never paid much mind to what she had to say about him—it was all nonsense, as anyone with half a brain could see."

"But surely you saw him yourself?"

"Well, of course I did," replied Mrs. Rolles with some exasperation. She had not recovered her dignity after Astell's earlier interruption. "He hung around here a great deal too much, always flitting about like some annoying gnat. Wave him away and he was gone for a second, then back again to trouble you even more. Oh, he put on airs, as bad as Letty herself, I must say, but it was as plain as water what he was."

"What name did he call himself? Or what did Letty say his name was?" Lady Ranelagh asked.

"Well, I never spoke to him except to warn him off, and I am afraid I paid little mind to Letty's blabbing, my lady. As I have already said."

Once again, the milliner's elder daughter leaned close and whispered to her mother. "Speak up, then," said Mrs. Rolles sharply. The Exchange woman seemed to have grown tired of the whole troublesome business. Astell could not blame her.

"My lady," began the milliner's daughter. Her voice was low and well-modulated. She spoke to Lady Ranelagh directly and, with no false modesty, met her gaze. "Letty claimed he was 'Charles de Beauclerk,' but he was most certainly no king's son."

At this the younger of the milliner's two daughters could not hide a smirk. "I saw him one day when he was not fooling about here, pestering Letty," she offered with a note of triumph. "I saw him here in the Exchange, tagging after the duchess of Mazarin. He is no one at all, one of her lackeys, I would guess. Just like one of her lapdogs or monkeys."

The countess of Ranelagh was fulsome in her thanks to Mrs. Rolles and her daughters as she and Mary Astell prepared to leave the premises of the Golden Fan—Lady Ranelagh took the time to praise the shop and its wares before promising to return another day. Mrs. Rolles had regained something of her composure, bowing to her ladyship as she took her leave. Mary Astell added her thanks to those of Lady Ranelagh, and she parted from the milliner with something of their original sympathy restored.

Lady Ranelagh and Mary Astell made their way from the gallery to the broad staircase, down to the teeming courtyard, and then out into the bright, cold day. The coach was waiting where they had left it, one of several lined up just outside the entrance of the Exchange. As soon as Lady Ranelagh settled herself inside, arranging her skirts just so, they set off for Chelsea.

The countess was somewhat cheered by the last part of the conversation with Mrs. Rolles and her two daughters—a few exciting bits of scandal had at last been extracted from the three women. Now, as the coach retraced its earlier route, Lady Ranelagh turned to her companion. "You know," she said, "we might as well go straight this minute to Bridewell, Mary. We will pass right by on our way to Chelsea, I am sure."

"Yes, Your Ladyship, I believe it is just off Fleet Street, toward the river, but I hardly think that it is a fit place for you," Astell replied, thinking of the horrors that were reported about the house of correction and its inmates.

"But who knows what we might discover there if we were to inquire?" asked Lady Ranelagh.

"And who knows what the gossip might be if Lady Ranelagh were known to have stopped at Bridewell, asking politely after a young girl who had been committed there. I hardly think Lord Ranelagh would approve."

"Hmm," said the countess, waving her hand dismissively. "I hardly think what I do is a matter worth his lordship's attention." Considering a moment longer, she added, "Unless *I* were the unfortunate creature who had been committed to Bridewell."

Although Mary Astell was as little shocked at the world's follies as the countess herself, Lady Ranelagh had gone too far. Just as she thought a careful word of reproof might not come amiss, the countess abandoned her frivolity. "I am sorry, Mary, you must forgive me. That poor, poor creature. Hers is such a tired story—it is all too stale, vulgar, and common, is it not? Though I suppose it is all the sadder for that."

"I agree, Your Ladyship. But since Letty Pyke is no longer an inmate of Bridewell but is now resident in my house on Paradise Row, I hardly it worth our while to call there."

"You are right, of course, yet I still believe *something* might be learned there. How did the girl come to be wandering in Chelsea when she had been committed to Bridewell? You must admit that it is a very strange turn of events. But if you would rather not continue our investigation at Bridewell, we might consider going to the Fleet? Perhaps we could find Letty's husband if we knew more about her marriage?"

"If there was anything to be found there, I am sure the justices of the peace would have found it. Not that I am familiar with what goes on in the environs of the Fleet, mind you." She was surprised as she heard one of Mrs. Kettilby's favorite turns of phrase coming out of her own mouth.

"Ahhh, Mary! I think you might be tempted to such an adventure!" crowed Lady Ranelagh.

"Not at all, Your Ladyship. I doubt that the Fleet is any better place for you than Bridewell. We need not stop there either, I think."

"Oh, fiddle faddle! Perhaps not now, I agree, but we must undertake the adventure. We need have no fear, especially if we take Lady Catherine with us. She is more than able to protect us from any danger," said Lady Ranelagh, her irrepressible high spirits returning.

"You may be right about Bridewell," she continued. "I will grant you that, Mary, but, really, how much time and energy could have been spent searching out Letty's 'great lord' by any of her examiners? They were eager to be rid of her, not to help her. I am sure we would be more successful, and if we put our minds to it, we might just find out the very place where that unfortunate girl thought she had been married. Even if this man were putting a sham upon her, there would surely have been witnesses and some kind of license. The foolish girl would never have thought herself married otherwise, would she?"

"But we have no idea if the man really married Letty at all," Astell pointed out. "Her claim could be more of her nonsense. She had no license to show the examiners, and no papers at all by the time she made her way to Chelsea. She might tell us she had been married to her 'great lord,' but she seems to have a very infirm notion of the truth. And, in any case, Mrs. Rolles was not sure about whether there had been a Fleet marriage. She only mentioned it as a possibility."

"Hmm," repeated Lady Ranelagh.

"Now that I have had a moment to reflect, one other curious detail comes to mind, Your Ladyship."

"What is that?"

"Well, you saw the garment that Letty wore when she was discovered. It is nothing like the sober, well-crafted gowns worn by Mrs. Rolles and her daughters. Letty's was a showy thing, and it was far too large for her, even in her current condition. There is no way a businesswoman like Mrs. Rolles would have dressed her apprentice in such a fashion."

"Why, Mary, I am shocked! Look at you—paying attention to Letty's attire!"

"Yes, yes, Your Ladyship," replied Astell. "Mock me if you will. The gown may not be important, but I do wonder where and when she acquired it. Even more interesting is what that one daughter had to say— the younger one, I mean, who seemed a bit sly herself. Did Mrs. Rolles mention her daughters' names, by the by?"

"No, I think not," said Lady Ranelagh.

"Well, no matter. The younger daughter seemed only too happy to have seen the last of Letty Pyke—I thought the older of the two was more sympathetic, or at least she seemed to be. But you are right, I think we should be looking for Letty's seducer."

"It cannot be Charles Beauclerk, Mary, we have been through that," objected Lady Ranelagh.

"No, no, Your Ladyship. It was the older sister who provided that name. The other daughter, the younger one, laughed at the notion—she suggested Letty's 'great lord' was in the service of Madam Mazarin."

"You are quite right—I overlooked that. So you will soon be calling upon the duchess of Mazarin?" The countess laughed. "I am surprised, I will admit it. She is a fascinating creature, but I did not imagine you would want to make her acquaintance."

"Now, now, Your Ladyship . . . "

"Though I am sure she could tell you a very great deal about the institution of marriage, should you decide to make her acquaintance," continued Lady Ranelagh. "That is a subject about which she has a great deal of expertise."

As the Ranelagh coach traveled west on the king's private road, Mary Astell found her mind racing as she considered what ought to be done next. She would certainly have to speak further with Letty, though she was not looking forward to another conversation with the girl. Astell was curious to learn more about her family, her education, her experience as an apprentice, even her clothing, at least to the extent of finding out how the girl had acquired her bedraggled finery.

But even if Letty were willing to talk to her about any of this, Astell realized that it would serve only to satisfy her curiosity. None of this mattered now. Since Letty was in a such a fragile state, the questions posed to her should be purposeful. What mattered was to find the man whom Letty believed to be her husband—and then Astell's responsibility for the stranger she had sheltered would come to an end.

Astell doubted whether she herself was the right person to question Letty about this or any other aspect of her life. Despite the obligation Astell felt to the girl who was now under her roof, Letty rubbed her the wrong way, got right under her skin, and the girl seemed to find Astell's presence to be just as irritating. Nor had Lady Catherine been any more successful when faced by Letty's petulance and obstinacy. Of course, Lady Ranelagh's charms had worked on the girl, as they did on virtually everyone, but Astell was afraid that the banality of Letty's story might cause the countess to lose interest. Maybe a more sympathetic presence might work with the girl—perhaps Mrs. Methuen's quiet, gentle nature might be useful?

As for Lady Ranelagh's suggestions, Astell thought about them more carefully as they traveled back to Chelsea. Although she had dismissed the idea of inquiring at the house of correction, could any good be had by going to Bridewell?

A few men, mainly paupers and unruly apprentices, were confined there for committing minor offenses, but as everyone knew, most of the unfortunates who were committed to Bridewell were women. Bawds and prostitutes, petty thieves and nightwalkers, scolds and beggars, vagrants and wanderers. Masterless women who could give no good account of themselves. Poor women who were charged with incontinent living. And a great number of pregnant women, like Letty, who would not, or could not, name the fathers of their unborn children.

The more Astell considered the subject, the more she doubted that Letty would be willing to reveal much at all about the time that she had spent in Bridewell—even if she were forced to admit that she had been committed there, her pride would never allow her to speak of the experience in a truthful way. She would concoct some fanciful tale or another. And Astell very much doubted that a personal visit to the unsavory prison in order to search out the facts would reveal much of real use when it came to sorting out Letty's problems.

But if there had been a marriage . . . That seemed to Astell a more fruitful avenue to pursue. If a husband could be found, then it would not matter whether Letty had been sent to Bridewell and, if so, how she had managed to leave the prison and make her way to Chelsea. The girl would be his responsibility, no matter whether he was a lord or a lout, and she could be sent on her way.

Gertrude Rolles had been certain that there was no marriage, or at least no regular marriage—no banns published, no public ceremony performed, nothing recorded in the parish register. Nor had Letty been able to produce a special license, with its official stamp, at the time of her examination. Or at least that was what the milliner said. But was it likely that a seducer would have gone to all the trouble of a Fleet marriage for such a willing, if inexperienced, girl as Letty?

"Mary? Mary?"

Mary Astell shook her head and looked at Lady Ranelagh, who was staring at her, a curious expression on her face. "We have arrived," the countess pointed out.

"So we have, Your Ladyship. I have been lost in thought."

The Ranelagh coach had come to a stop just outside Mary Astell's gate on Paradise Row, but Astell had not noticed until Lady Ranelagh spoke.

The countess looked on with concern as Astell was handed out of the coach by a footman. Lady Ranelagh watched as Mary Astell made her way slowly up the walk to her front door without so much as another word or a backward glance.

"Whatever is the matter with her, I wonder," mused the countess, rearranging her skirts more artfully now that she was alone in the coach.

Thirteen

Mary Astell could be a formidable opponent. No less a man than the Reverend Francis Atterbury, a Tory churchman not unfamiliar with disputation, preferred to avoid her whenever he could. "I dread to engage her," he once confessed in a letter addressed to an old friend. The clergyman revealed that he found Mrs. Astell to be "a little offensive and shocking in her expressions," not because she disagreed with his political and religious opinions—which she shared—but because she expressed herself in a forthright manner rather than "insinuating what she means," as a woman "of good breeding" ought to do.

To make matters even more distressing, the poor reverend's painful encounters with Mary Astell took place in his very own home, where she was a frequent dinner guest of his wife. Catherine Atterbury was a sensible woman who found that she had much in common with her distinguished Chelsea neighbor, whose conversation she much enjoyed.

If a man like the Reverend Francis Atterbury were apt to quail when he engaged with Mary Astell, what then could be expected of Mr. John Williams, the churchwarden of All Saints? The unsuspecting man presented himself at the door of the house on Paradise Row on Monday afternoon, arriving shortly after Mary Astell returned from her trip to the Royal Exchange.

The effect of his sudden appearance on the doorstep was unsettling to Sarah—Mr. Williams was one of the church officials who had been only too happy to pass the miserable orphan from one householder to the next, eager to relieve the parish of the burden of her care. Although he did not seem to recognize Sarah on this occasion, she certainly knew who he was.

When Sarah informed the churchwarden that she would see whether her mistress was free to receive him, Mr. Williams chose to ignore her. He pushed his way past the girl as if she did not exist and made for the parlor. He was just ready to settle himself there in one of the comfortably padded chairs placed conveniently before the warm coal fire when Mary Astell appeared in the doorway.

Her unblinking stare stopped the churchwarden's ample backside mid-air, just inches before it could meet the Turkey-work upholstery. Mr. Williams was thereby forced to reverse his downward motion, a maneuver that he was not able to execute with much grace.

"Mrs. Astell, how do you," he began, awkwardly straightening himself up and smoothing his rather rumpled coat.

Astell said nothing, though after a few moments of silence, she did eventually blink.

Taking the flicker of an eyelid as an invitation to continue, Mr. Williams proceeded with rather too much confidence. "I am certain that you know why I have come, Mrs. Astell, quite certain, I dare say."

He managed an oily smile, his thin lips pulled back over his teeth most unpleasantly. And then, still meeting with silence, he repeated himself, as if Mary Astell were somewhat hard of hearing. "I am certain that you know why I have come," he said with increased volume.

"Indeed, I dared not hope for the pleasure of a visit from you, Mr. Williams," Astell replied. The lubricious churchwarden was so pleased with himself that he did not recognize the chill her carefully phrased statement.

Despite her cool formality, Mary Astell was well aware of the reason for Mr. Williams's visit. She had been expecting the arrival of someone from the parish, though she had assumed that her caller would be the rector himself. But, then, she also knew that Mr. King preferred to avoid any kind of unpleasantness and regarded personal confrontation as both unseemly and undignified. Rather than meeting an adversary face to face, he tended to wage only those battles that could be conducted by means of a strongly worded letter or a well-phrased tract. And so, instead of the rector, it was Mr. Williams who now stood before her. As she might have predicted, if she had thought about it more carefully.

John Williams was a pillar of the community, willing, even eager, to take upon himself the weight of many thankless tasks. As churchwarden of All Saints, he oversaw the maintenance and repair of the church building, an obligation that, as a man whose business was supplying bricks and bricklayers for construction projects in the village, he took very seriously indeed.

Before the Reverend Mr. King's arrival in Chelsea, while Dr. Littleton was still rector and devoting himself to his scholarly pursuits, John Williams had also been responsible for managing parish properties and lands, assigning tenants, devising leases, and calculating rents. But once the new rector arrived and discovered his precarious financial situation, Mr. Williams soon found his administration of church holdings was no longer required. Relieved of these duties, Mr. Williams found himself free to devote more time to another burdensome charge, overseeing the settled poor of the parish, a task that gave him no end of satisfaction.

In this capacity, the churchwarden was authorized to assess and collect the poor rates, a duty that he performed with great diligence. He was scrupulous in accounting for the disbursements made to the poor and zealous in finding suitable employment for them. He inquired assiduously into all the particulars of their irregular lives, and, when it was possible, saw to their swift relocation outside the parish.

As he dedicated himself to the faithful discharge of his many parochial responsibilities, Mr. Williams was much to be admired, for the churchwarden of All Saints was not paid for his ceaseless endeavors on behalf of the community. At the same time, however, it must also be acknowledged that Mr. Williams was known to enjoy the not infrequent occasions for eating and drinking that his position offered. He especially looked forward to the congenial suppers that followed the regular auditing of parish accounts. One local wit, observing the churchwarden's uncanny ability "to eat and drink and pay naught," had composed an excellent couplet upon the dutiful Mr. Williams: "when the warden drunken roams, your duty is to see him home."

Unfortunately for all concerned, Mr. John Williams was not now calling upon Mary Astell in regard to her contribution to the refurbishment of the church building, nor had he come to consult with her about the payment of her rates. Nor was he expecting any refreshment, a glass of fine claret, for instance—though the offer might not have come amiss.

No, Mr. Williams had come to see Mary Astell about another matter entirely—as churchwarden, it was his responsibility to deal with poor vagrants who sought refuge in the parish. This he did with ruthless efficiency. And this was the reason for his call: it had been brought to the attention of parish officials that Mary Astell had opened her door to a stranger who had come into the parish.

While Astell's unyielding gaze and upright posture had given Mr. Williams pause, he was not yet at the point where he was ready to admit, like the Reverend Mr. Atterbury, that he feared to engage her. Instead, he stood his ground courageously but uncomfortably, shifting his balance from one foot to the other. He even attempted an ingratiating smile. "Well, Mrs. Astell . . . erm . . . ," he began. "Well, Mrs. Astell, I believe . . . erm . . . a stranger . . . "

"Indeed, Mr. Williams."

He tried clearing his throat. "Ahem." And then "Ahem" again. "Strangers," he began. "Erm . . . strangers . . . a great charge and a great burden . . . defrauding . . . and the rector . . . a stranger . . . erm . . . Mr. King . . . you know, a stranger . . . "

"Indeed," she repeated, furrowing her brow as if she were still not sure what he meant.

At that point, a dam seemed to burst within the unctuous churchwarden, and his words began to flow unimpeded. "Due diligence requires that if a stranger enters a parish, he is to be interviewed at once and sent home to his place of birth!" he exclaimed. Astell said nothing.

"Or *she*!" he continued, hurrying now that the words had come. "*She* must be sent on her way. She cannot be left to be kept at the charges of the parish. She might become a great burden, defrauding the true poor in our midst! And she may well be a notorious and disorderly person, an evil example and encouragement of lewd life! Perhaps she is great with child!"

Astell continued to stare, considering whether she ought to maintain her front, but before she had come to a decision, Mr. Williams discarded his own and hissed a warning: "And if a householder, through her heedless sheltering of a stranger, gives countenance to these sins and vices, well, you may rest assured, Mrs. Mary Astell, that *you* will then be answerable and due for any such an offense."

At that he smoothed his coat again and pushed past her, just as he had pushed his way past Sarah on his way into the parlor. Sarah, meanwhile, had been waiting in the entry hall, just out of sight. She narrowed her eyes and glared at the churchwarden as she opened the front door for him, and he rushed out.

No sooner had Sarah slammed the door behind the departing Mr. John Williams than a querulous voice was heard above, berating the old nursemaid, Bridget, who so patiently attended her.

"There she goes again," said Sarah, affecting a huge sigh but with a self-satisfied look on her face.

Astell, who had joined her in the entry, sighed in response. *What could possibly be the matter now?*

"Whatever you may think, ma'am, that Lettuce is nothing but trouble. Or at least that's the way I see it." Sarah scowled at Mary Astell, no doubt expecting to be reprimanded but challenging her mistress anyway.

Astell sighed again. "Well, Sarah, it seems our guest is not 'Lettice' after all. She is Letty—Letty Pyke when she arrived in London, though her name may be Letty something else if she has married."

Sarah's eyes opened wide. She was surprised that Astell had confided such information to her. She stood up a little straighter. Raising her chin, she asked, "Shall I see to her, ma'am?"

"I will check on her myself, Sarah," Astell replied. And then, as the girl turned to go, she added, "and thank you."

Mary Astell wearily climbed the stairs. She had quite enjoyed the slow, jostling ride to London with Lady Ranelagh, the cool air and bright sun lifting her spirits. She had been cheered by the countess's high spirits and sense of adventure. The visit with Gertrude Rolles had answered some questions and suggested new lines of inquiry. But her encounter with Mr. Williams had left her shaken.

Only three days had gone by, and already there were suspicions about Letty among at least some residents of Chelsea—and once the girl's condition was known rather than suspected, the machinery of the parish would move quickly to expel her.

The full weight of her worries descended on her as she entered the room where Letty Pyke, who now fancied herself Lettice de Beauclerk, was still recovering from her illness. The girl looked very pale, but at least she was sitting upright, propped by cushions at her back. Bridget was sitting quietly by the window, working an intricate embroidered border on a small silk purse, doubtless a gift for Lady Catherine or one of her sisters.

"You have returned, I see," said the girl in the bed. Her tone was less demanding than before, and she kept her head down, refusing to meet Mary Astell's eye.

"Yes, I have, Letty," Astell replied, waiting to see what effect the name would have.

The girl looked up sharply, her gaze then sliding quickly away. And at that moment, whatever force had sustained Letty Pyke in her search for the man she believed to be her husband, whatever resolve had inspired her journey to Chelsea from London or Bridewell or wherever she had come from, pushing her on in spite of her illness, whatever spirit had propelled her, nourished her, whatever strength had overcome her weakness . . . well, whatever that impulse had been, it abandoned her. The proud and petulant "Lettice de Beauclerk" disappeared before Mary Astell's eyes, leaving behind a forlorn figure.

"You have not found him, then?"

"Not yet, Letty. But all is not lost."

"I am afraid it is, Mrs. Astell," Letty said with a great sigh. She was dignified in her acceptance of her loss. "And I suppose Mrs. Rolles had nothing good to say of me."

"Not much," Mary Astell replied, "but nor has she said anything that condemns you—you may have been willful and foolish, but you are not irredeemable.

"So you say now. But what is to become of me?"

"We have not yet given up, Letty. Lady Ranelagh is eager for us to continue our inquiries, and you will find that once Lady Catherine has interested herself on your behalf, she will never cease in her efforts."

"And you?"

"Something led you to my very door. It seems to me that I have been given a charge—rest assured that I will do all I can on your behalf."

"You will find my husband?"

"If he may be found."

"I suppose he may not be my husband."

"I suppose not."

"And if he is not? If he cannot be found?"

"Then you will find that you can have no better friend in this world than Lady Catherine Jones. She will know what is best to be done—you will see."

Letty's momentary courage failed her, and she could not help but wail. "He said I was to be a lady, Mrs. Astell. He said that he would give me everything that I could ever want. He promised I was to have servants and silks and laces, I was to play and dance, with no more cares and no more worries. He seemed a fine young lord to me. After all I had suffered, I was so very happy." As she spoke, a tear rolled down one thin cheek and plopped onto the coverlet. "He said that he would give me everything that I might ever want."

Astell thought that the girl's tantrums were easier to bear than this single tear. "In this world, Letty, I am afraid that 'I want' does not get.

But we will find the truth of it all, if truth is to be found." She would not offer the girl false hopes.

"He was such a pretty gentleman," said Letty softly, almost to herself. "So very agreeable, so well-spoken, so well-carriaged." She wiped her cheek, then added, "He said that he would never betray me, that his passion for me would not suffer him to abuse me—and that is why he resolved to marry me."

"And did he, Letty? Did he marry you?"

"He did, Mrs. Astell, I am a true married woman." Her voice was firm, with a hint of her old haughtiness.

"But not a church marriage, Letty? According to Mrs. Rolles, there was no church marriage."

"No, no church," Letty conceded. "My lord said he could not wait—who would go through all that fuss when we could be married straightaway? And I had no parish home where the banns could be published, now did I? So I stole away from Mrs. Rolles one afternoon, and off we went. In truth, he said it was a grand wedding chapel that catered only to men and women of quality, but it was not very nice, not really. There was a sign marking it out, though—two joined hands, a man's hand clasping a woman's, that was very nice. It was all a very great adventure." Letty sighed.

Astell wondered how any such place could be considered a satisfactory substitute for a church. But Letty's description did suggest a Fleet marriage, just as Mrs. Rolles had supposed. Lady Ranelagh would be eager to see if they could track down the wedding house.

"And a woman—I cannot remember her name—there was a woman who arranged it all, but I was not paying that much attention to her. My thoughts were all on the man who was to be my husband, as you can well imagine. But I do assure you, Mrs. Astell, there was a minister, and all was done very proper."

Looking down at her, Astell thought that it would not have taken much to dupe a young and foolish girl like Letty Pyke. Her marriage had likely been a sham intended to defraud the girl of the one thing of value that she possessed—since her supposed husband had vanished once he had taken her virginity. But Astell could not be certain it was a sham. A marriage, even one performed in the Fleet, required some effort, not to mention expense. And a marriage, even one performed in the Fleet, might still be valid.

"Well, Letty, I will leave you to rest," said Astell, glancing over at Bridget, who quietly nodded to her. "I think Mrs. Methuen might be by sometime tomorrow to check on you."

"Thank you," the girl said, sliding back down into the bed. "She has been very kind."

As she turned to leave the room, Astell realized there were questions she still had not asked—about Bridewell, most notably, and about how Letty had come to leave Bridewell. And, then, the girl's shabby finery. While Astell was curious, these questions were not as critical as the one she asked now. "One more thing," she said. "The young man whom you met, Letty—your 'very great lord.'" She stumbled a bit over the phrase, and Letty grimaced. "Well, I must ask you again, are you certain about his name? He said his name was 'Charles de Beauclerk'—you are sure?"

Letty glanced up sharply. "Well, of course I am, Mrs. Astell. I surely ought to know the name of the man that I married! It was *you* who said there was no such man. *You* knew of no such man, you said. And nor did Lady Ranelagh or Lady Catherine. That's what *you* said." Letty was becoming agitated.

"That is true enough," Astell replied, hoping to calm the unfortunate girl, who was now looking at her suspiciously. "There is no 'Charles *de* Beauclerk'—that is, there is no one who goes by that name in all of Chelsea, and thus no one by that name living here 'in paradise,' either."

"But there is more to it, I can see it now," cried Letty, her cheeks flushing. "Despite what you say, you know my lord and husband, you do!"

Astell looked sorrowfully at the girl lying feverish in the bed. *How quickly the delusion returns. How hard it is for us to let go of the glittering tinsel-ware, even when we know it shines falsely.*

"Calm yourself, I beg you," Astell urged her. "What I have told you is most certainly true. We none of us have heard of a young man who goes by the name of Charles *de* Beauclerk, and certainly there is no great lord by that name, but Charles Beauclerk, yes, there is a man of that name—"

"How could you deceive me?" shrieked Letty as she attempted to rise from the bed.

"Letty, Letty, hush," said Astell, hoping to calm the girl. "I assure you, we have no reason to deceive you. Charles Beauclerk is the natural son of the second king Charles—the king made his son the duke of St. Albans, so he is a very great lord indeed, but not one who would have been hanging around Mrs. Rolles's millinery shop, however exclusive it may be, in order to pay you grand compliments, nor could he have married you, for he is already married—and to a lady of great rank. The duchess of St. Albans has just recently given birth to the duke's son and heir. And the duke himself has been abroad for many months with His Majesty, fighting the Spanish—the army left England last spring and has only just returned from this year's campaign."

Astell was about to remind the girl that the army's return had been widely reported in the *London Gazette*, stopping herself only when she realized that Gertrude Rolles was probably not a subscriber to that journal. While this information had undoubtedly been bruited by the traders at the Exchange, Letty Pyke was unlikely to have been interested in any such news.

"The duke of St. Albans is most assuredly *not* your 'great lord,'" Astell said firmly. "For now, we must hope that we can find the man who chose to present himself to you under a false name, and we must also hope that he has, in fact, married you truly. Right now, that is all we can hope for."

"But what if he is not a lord?" wailed Letty. "What then, Mrs. Astell? What will become of me then?"

What then, Mrs. Astell? What will become of me then? Their conversation had dealt a blow to the girl, that much was clear, but Astell doubted whether, even now, Letty had entirely abandoned all her fancies.

Still, as she headed across the landing to her small study, Mary Astell could not put the girl's question out of her mind. If Letty had tied herself to some worthless jackanapes, that would be unfortunate. But if it were discovered that she was *not* married—well, there was an end to it all, the girl's cake was dough.

Fourteen

Whenever will the coach be ready?" Lady Ranelagh asked with some irritation. She had swept into the parlor where Lady Catherine and Mary Astell were waiting, seated before the brightly burning fire. "I am here at last," she added unnecessarily, since there she was.

Looking at the newly arrived countess, Astell saw that she had dressed as carefully for their outing as she had for the previous day's journey to the Exchange, although her costume was notably different. Instead of the sumptuous fabrics she had worn on their visit to Gertrude Rolles, Lady Ranelagh was now wearing a relatively simple gown of dark wool with woven stripes, over which she had pulled a fine woolen cloak—she had chosen to dress not to impress but to obscure.

Astell was still hesitant about their decision to go to the Fleet, but she had found it impossible to dissuade Lady Ranelagh from making the journey once the subject had been broached. As soon as she heard that Lady Catherine planned to accompany Astell, there was no denying her ladyship. Even a last-minute appeal to the old earl, who had wandered into the small front parlor at Ranelagh, had failed. Richard Jones had no wish to displease his young wife, and he thought it best not to venture an opinion upon the matter. And so Lady Ranelagh had her way.

And now that she had finished changing from her loose, figured-silk *sacque* into what she deemed more appropriate attire for the day's investigation, Lady Ranelagh was eager for them to be underway. "Surely the coach ought to have been brought around by now," she grumbled.

"It usually takes longer for you to prepare yourself to leave than it does for the coach to be readied," said Lady Catherine pointedly. "For once you have been quick—but I am sure it will not be long now." Even as she spoke, the coach could be heard pulling up to the door.

The earl of Ranelagh had begun the construction of his fine house in Chelsea soon after deciding that, as treasurer of the new Hospital, he would have need of an official residence near the royal establishment. To that end, he had secured a crown lease on a seven-acre site near the southeast corner of the Hospital. Then he eagerly set about designing a house that would meet his exacting specifications.

Ranelagh House, as it came to be called, was not large, but it was perfect in all respects—Richard Jones might justly be condemned as a "vain fool," as a man "famed for intrigue," a man "greedy for money" and, in his position as paymaster-general of the army, a man widely suspected of having committed the grossest kind of fraud, peculation, and embezzlement, but it must also be admitted that he was a man with excellent good taste. On seeing the earl of Ranelagh's creation for the first time, one admiring visitor described it as "a perfect cabinet," while another marveled that it was "a little palace."

Built of brick and cornered with stone, the house was set back some distance from the Thames, allowing for a striking river view. On the ground floor, a lovely and well-proportioned entrance hall opened to the great parlor, with five bay windows overlooking the Hospital grounds. This large reception room, running along the back of the house, was flanked by a lesser parlor on one side and a formal dining room on the other. Another small parlor, this one used primarily by Lady Ranelagh, was at the front of the house, just off the entrance hall, while a secluded closet, where Lady Catherine spent much of her day, was tucked into the opposite corner. These light and airy rooms were all wainscoted with Norway oak, the chimneys adorned with carvings, the ceilings covered with decorative plasterwork.

From the entrance hall, a grand staircase led up to the first floor. The symmetry of the ground floor was preserved there, with a wide hall at the top of the stairs leading to Lord Ranelagh's library at the back. To one side was the earl's bedchamber, mirrored on the other by a family dining room. At the front of the house were three private apartments, one belonging to the earl's wife, the other two to his daughters. (Servants' quarters were in the attic—the earl had made sure there would be ample accommodation for the men and women needed to ensure the smooth functioning of his household.)

Richard Jones spared no expense in the fittings and furnishings of his jewel-box of a house. Each room was appointed in the latest grand style but on an intimate scale. Draperies, wall hangings, carpets, furniture, paintings, porcelains, and ornaments were all of the best quality. The earl spent much time in the selection and placement of each item.

As soon as the building of his house was underway, Lord Ranelagh turned his attention to the grounds, a landscape project that occupied almost as much of his attention as his other favorite pastimes, gambling and women (and, it was whispered, young boys). In addition to cunningly designed stables and greenhouses, he laid out Ranelagh's many gardens. Carefully situated walkways had the advantage of opening into those of the Hospital, while borders and beds were dotted with urns and statues and covered seats. Even before the planting was complete, the earl expanded the grounds by adding fifteen acres for orchards and a kitchen garden.

Lady Catherine viewed her father's pet project with skepticism and regarded it as just one more of his many extravagant follies. But, as she had little say in the matter, she wisely chose to say nothing. And the move from St. James's to Chelsea suited her well, since Mary Astell had settled in the village shortly after she began her writing career.

Now that Lady Ranelagh was ready, she was eager to be on her way, and soon, the three women having settled themselves inside, the coach pulled away from the house, heading down the drive and turning onto Wilderness Row, a small lane running north alongside the Hospital to meet the king's road. Once they reached the highway, they headed east, toward the city.

"As you can see, John is driving us today," said Lady Catherine to Lady Ranelagh. "Your Thomas may be a perfectly capable coachman, but I think we will be in need of someone to accompany us into the Fleet, and I prefer a man of John's sober mien and—"

"Substantial figure," laughed the countess. Shortly after her marriage, the new Lady Ranelagh had arranged for Thomas to assume many of John's responsibilities. Tall and slim, the younger man cut an elegant figure in the Ranelagh livery, while John, now well on in years and glad to spend most of his day in the warmth of the stables rather than exposed on a box, still occasionally drove the earl into town on business.

"You may jest all you like, my lady, but I think you will be very glad of his presence once we reach our destination," replied Lady Catherine.

Mary Astell remained silent throughout this brief exchange. She was indifferent to the question of who drove the Ranelagh coach, and she was uncertain what the conditions might be in the Fleet—it was not a part of the city she frequented. But, while Lady Catherine's caution and careful planning were commendable, Astell doubted whether the earl's elderly coachman would be of much use to them. Nor was he likely to be their best guide to the Fleet—for the moment, she said nothing about her own preparations for their day's undertaking.

Earlier that morning, as she left the service at All Saints, Astell had caught up with Elizabeth King, asking her whether she might have use of the boy who ran errands for the rector. Mrs. King had been only too happy to oblige, and Astell had sent him to Elizabeth Wilkin with a note asking if it would be possible for the printer's wife to meet her at the Fleet. If anyone knew London and its workings, it was she.

The Ranelagh carriage soon reached the city, the coachman sweeping around St. James's Park and then onto Pall Mall, where they passed the Ranelaghs' city house. Astell glanced quickly at Lady Catherine—it was the house where her mother had died, but Lady Catherine pretended not to notice it as they drove by. Soon they reached Charing Cross, then the Strand, and well before Astell had quite settled in her mind how to tell Lady Ranelagh and Lady Catherine of her plans, they rumbled across the

Fleet Bridge and turned north onto the street running alongside Fleet Ditch.

The Great Fire of London had razed the tanneries, shambles, tenements, and privies that once crowded together along the banks of the Fleet, clogging the river with offal and filth, turning it into a noisome and stinking sewer. When the city was being rebuilt, a prodigious sum was spent to clear and widen the river. The improved channel, lined with stone and brick, was hopefully renamed the New Canal—sadly, in spite of this optimism, the waterway remained the Fleet Ditch, a common sewer.

The ancient Fleet prison, too, had been destroyed by the fire. Burned to the ground on the third day of the conflagration, it was rebuilt on the same site and, with very few alterations, according to the old plan. The entrance to the four-story brick building was through a narrow passage from the street that ran along the Fleet Ditch.

The prison lay outside the jurisdiction of both the city of London and the church, the area surrounding it governed not by civil law or ecclesiastical authority but by the "rules of the Fleet." The liberties extended from the Fleet Ditch to Old Bailey Street, and from Fleet Lane to the bottom of Ludgate Hill. Within this precinct, packed with alehouses, brandy shops, taverns, coffee-houses, public houses, and gambling cellars, were numerous lodging houses, great and small, where prisoners who could afford to provide sureties for the privilege—and who were also prepared to compensate the warden of the Fleet for his lost fees—could serve their sentences outside the confines of the prison. And within the alehouses, brandy shops, taverns, coffee-houses, public houses, and gambling cellars were the "marrying-houses" of the Fleet.

Those who desired to be married in haste or secrecy (or haste *and* secrecy, as the case may be) would find their needs well met at the White Tower, the Rainbow, the Shepherd and Goat, the Wheatsheaf, the Golden Lion, or the Bishop's Blaze, to name only a few of the places where marriages were performed.

A valid marriage could certainly be had in one of these many establishments—clergymen who plied their trade in the Fleet were eager for business and happy to accommodate those who sought out their services. These obliging men of the cloth were willing to celebrate a marriage without banns having been published, and they were equally prepared to issue special licenses without the necessary tax having been paid. Although such marriages were performed outside the law, they were nonetheless legal and indissoluble.

But the Fleet was notorious not so much for these irregular marriages as for more questionable unions. In a Fleet marriage-house, a penniless adventurer could force himself upon an innocent and unprotected girl who stood to inherit a substantial fortune. A scheming young footman could secure the hand of his titled—and elderly—mistress before her grown children had time to object. A wealthy widow unwilling to lose her jointure could quietly remarry, with no one the wiser, while an enterprising husband could acquire a second (or third or fourth) bride, also with no one the wiser. In defiance of the law forbidding marriage "within the degrees prohibited," a man might wed his deceased wife's sister or an uncle be joined to his brother's daughter. It was even said that two women had been married in a Fleet ceremony.

If a newly married couple wished, they could be provided with a license and their marriage duly entered in the official register—all for a very reasonable price. On the other hand, their marriage might never be recorded—also for a price. The date of any marriage could be adjusted to suit the needs of either party—it could be antedated or even erased after the fact, all for a price. By the stroke of a pen (and the payment of coin), a bastard child might thus be legitimized, and by this means an inconvenient match could later be repudiated. For anyone willing to pay.

In addition to furnishing a parson and a chapel, the proprietor of a successful marriage-house could provide witnesses for the ceremony. The resourceful keeper of the house could supply a ring for those who were unprovided or produce ale and bride cakes for those who wished to celebrate or even hire out a bed for those who were desirous of consummating their union at once. And no matter what the time of day or night, in a wedding-house it was always nine o'clock in the morning, for a marriage was only legal if performed between the hours of eight and twelve of the forenoon.

As the Ranelagh coach pulled up to the arched entryway of the prison, Mary Astell peered out of the window, relieved to see Elizabeth Wilkin waiting for their arrival. With her was a small, rather shabbily clad woman who, despite her threadbare clothing, stood proudly erect, her chin raised as if in defiance. When the coach stopped, Astell opened the door without waiting for the tall footman who was hurrying to perform that service for her. She greeted Mrs. Wilkin and her companion, but before introductions could be made, Lady Ranelagh leaned out and gestured imperiously. "Step in, step in," she said, furrowing her brow and glaring at Astell. The countess was not sure who these women were or why they were waiting for Mary Astell, but she did not want to miss a single word of what was to be said.

The day was once again cold and gray, the skies threatening still more rain. And, then, there was the very great stink, a choking miasma hanging in the air. The two London women were thus more than willing to oblige Lady Ranelagh, and they climbed into the commodious and luxuriously appointed coach. Once inside, the small woman with Mrs. Wilkin took in every particular while appearing not to take notice of anything.

"Lady Ranelagh, may I introduce Mrs. Wilkin," said Astell to the countess. "She is familiar with all of London and is someone who, I believe, will be able to be of help to us. I have asked her if she would be so kind as to meet us here."

"Your Ladyship," said Mrs. Wilkin, with a nod of her head.

For all that she was a pampered darling of the court, Lady Ranelagh took a genuine interest in men and women of all sorts, and although she was not clear about the role Mrs. Wilkin was to play in their day's adventure, she seemed truly delighted to make the acquaintance of the sober citizen who was now seated across from her. "Mrs. Wilkin," she replied warmly.

"Lady Catherine, Mrs. Wilkin," Astell continued. "I believe you have not met."

Lady Catherine was far more concerned with her rank and dignity than Lady Ranelagh, so Astell was less certain of her reaction to the unexpected appearance of Mrs. Wilkin. But since Lady Catherine well knew how important Mr. Wilkin had been to Mary Astell's success, Astell thought that her friend would unbend at least a bit. And she was not disappointed. "I am pleased to meet you at last," Lady Catherine said to the printer's wife with a gracious nod of her head.

"And now," said Elizabeth Wilkin, "may I introduce Mrs. Gower. She is well able to offer her assistance to you, as she spent some years in the Fleet before she was widowed."

The small woman raised her head proudly, as if daring the three visitors to the city to look down on her. But she found no trace of condescension, much less condemnation, on the faces of Lady Ranelagh, Lady Catherine, or Mary Astell. She seemed to relax then, settling just bit more comfortably into the warmth of the coach.

"I hope I may be of some use, my lady," she said, addressing the countess. She glanced quickly at Elizabeth Wilkin, who gave her an encouraging nod. "I do know something of the Fleet and its inhabitants. My late husband, you see, was a prisoner . . . " She paused briefly, looked down to her hands, tightly clasped in her lap, and continued, "It was debt, you see. He was just a poor parson, and he got into debt. And that is how we wound up there.

"I doubt you are aware of this, my lady, and why would you be, but the Fleet used to be one of the king's prisons—those brought before the Court of the Star Chamber were sent there. Poets and playwrights—even bishops, when religion was so unsettled. And Queen Henrietta Maria, too, before the wars. But since the Star Chamber court was abolished by the Long Parliament, the prison has been used for bankrupts and debtors.

'Now, that is neither here nor there, my lady," she continued, with a sad smile. "All this history is of no interest to you, I am sure, but that is why my husband was committed in the Fleet—debt. He was not a bad man, but one who was most unfortunate."

"Humph." Listening to Mrs. Gower, Elizabeth Wilkin could not help herself. Mrs. Gower's husband had not been unfortunate so much as improvident and imprudent, at least as far as the printer's wife was concerned. "A bad man or not, Mrs. Gower, he was the reason *you* were forced into the Fleet as well," she said quite sharply. "His was the crime, but you suffered the consequences along with him."

"Yes, yes, of course, you are correct, Mrs. Wilkin," Mrs. Gower acknowledged. "Like so many clergymen with insufficient livings, the Reverend Gower accrued a very great debt. And without means to pay for his food and lodging, never mind the other fees, he suffered mightily in the prison, while I was left utterly alone and destitute. But Mr. Gower found that he could at least pay his surety and provide us both with food and lodgings in the liberties by performing marriages at a wedding house—and that he did, for some years before he died. He could never manage to discharge his debt, but at least I was able to live there with him. And we could survive—though, to be sure, it was a meager living."

"Oh," breathed Lady Ranelagh, "how dreadful." She reached over to place her hand over Mrs. Gower's. The poor widow looked away quickly, her pride crumbling at the unexpected sympathy.

"Well, my lady," she said, her voice trembling just a little, "he was just another Fleet parson then, scrabbling along with the rest. He performed marriages at the Rainbow Coffee-house, kept by James Lando—it was just at the corner of the Fleet Ditch. And then later for Peter Stymson— he did a good business in his chapel at the Old Red Hand and Mitre."

At this, Lady Ranelagh shuddered slightly. Lady Catherine, however, was made of sterner stuff. As for Mary Astell, she did not wish to hurry the woman, yet she could not see that Mrs. Gower's rehearsal of her personal history was of much help to them. She longed to be underway, to be moving forward in their search. Still, she trusted Elizabeth Wilkin's judgment and sat patiently, watching while the widow fished in her pocket, pulling out a small handbill.

"Here, my lady," said Mrs. Gower, thrusting the tattered piece of paper into Lady Ranelagh's hands.

The countess smoothed it out on her knee, with Lady Catherine and Astell leaning over to see what was on the bill. Below a crudely printed image of a bishop's cross and mitre, they read the advertisement: "At the Old Red Hand and Mitre, three doors from the Fleet and next door to the White Swan, marriages are performed by the Reverend Mr. Henry Gower, lawfully ordained according to the institutions of the Church of England, ready to wait on any person in town or country."

Once the three women had read the bill, Mrs. Gower raised her head, again thrusting her chin out. "Mr. Gower performed a necessary service, my lady. So many men and women, newly arrived in the city, do not have a proper home parish—and then, you see, there are the banns. Seldom are public banns proclaimed without gossip, laughter, and delays without reason. Nowadays few are willing to have their affairs declared to all the world in a public place when they might marry with privacy and without noise.

"There is also the convenience," she continued. "In a marrying-house, nothing at all need be arranged beforehand, and a couple may be married on any day of their choosing, and at any time. And, then, with the new tax, my lady, a proper marriage by banns or license has become so costly. What are humble folk to do?" Mrs. Gower asked, looking steadily at her companions.

"I will say," she added, "that a woman can earn something too, in a marriage shop, especially if she is decent. And it is honest money, you see. Proprietors who keep a wedding chapel must attract custom, and nothing will do quite so well as a respectable woman. 'Sir, will you be pleased to walk in and be married?' she will ask passersby. Of course, Mr. Gower would not hear of that for me, for all that we might have lived better." Chin still raised, she quietly looked at Lady Ranelagh as if challenging her to disapprove.

"How dreadful," said Lady Ranelagh, once more, again reaching out for Mrs. Gower's hand.

"Well, enough of all that," said Mrs. Gower briskly, having delivered what she clearly considered her letters credential. She took back the handbill and folded it along its well-worn creases. "I do know the Fleet, my lady, as you can see, and I do know something of the marriage business. How may I be of assistance?"

At this question, Astell took a deep breath, happy at last that they could begin. "Mrs. Gower," she said, "we are looking to find the record of a marriage we believe to have taken place in the Fleet, in just such a marrying-house as you describe. Will we be able to do that?"

"Mrs. Astell!" the widow exclaimed, looking as if Mary Astell had misunderstood completely the lesson she had just delivered. "There are scores of such places—and you must understand they are not really 'houses' at all, most of them. A small room, an alcove, a cellar, even a corner under the stairs. Any space will serve. You could not possibly search out all the places in the Fleet where marriages are performed—"

"We do know a little more," Astell hastened to add. "We are looking for a marriage-house under the sign of two joined hands. A man's hand and a woman's hand. And the keeper of the house is a woman."

"Well," said Mrs. Gower, "that does help somewhat, though two hands joined is a very popular sign in the marrying business. It is used by Mr. Lilley, for one—his Hand and Pen is near the Fleet Bridge, next door to a china shop. Mr. Burnford's Hand and Pen is just at the foot of Ludgate Hill, next to Noah's Ark, and Mr. Wilson's is also close at hand, right on the banks of the Fleet Ditch. But a woman . . . you must mean Mrs. Ball. She keeps a barber shop close to the prison, but marriages are made there too, under the sign of the Hand and Pen."

Lady Ranelagh looked confused. "The joined hands make sense for a place where marriages are performed, but why 'Hand and Pen,' I wonder?"

"I think the name was formerly used on scriveners' signs, my lady, but it proved to be very popular in the wedding trade."

Astell was less interested in the sign or the name than she was in the information they hoped to find, whatever the marrying-house might be called. "Will there be a record?" she asked the widow.

"The parson enters the names of those he marries in his pocket book—Mr. Gower was very particular, as is right. And the names should then be entered into the register of the house. Unless there is some desire for secrecy, of course."

At that point, the women paused and looked at each other solemnly. Although they had shared no details of Letty's story with Mrs. Gower, the widow guessed that there might be some chicanery at work. For all that she was prepared to defend her husband for performing marriages in the liberties, Mrs. Gower knew that the three women before her would not be proposing an inquiry into a Fleet marriage if something were not amiss.

"I do wish you well, my lady," said Mrs. Gower, sensing that the conversation was at an end. She pulled the threads of her meager cloak around herself a bit more tightly. "And, I pray you, if there is any way I may be of further service—"

"Yes, Mrs. Gower, off we go then," said Mrs. Wilkin briskly. "Mr. Wilkin looks forward to seeing you soon, Mrs. Astell."

"One moment, please," said Lady Ranelagh. She reached out impulsively to the widow. "What about now, Mrs. Gower? How do you manage now? Now that Mr. Gower has died and can no longer provide for you? You cannot be well, indeed, you cannot."

"Thank you, my lady," the widow said, head once again held high. "I am no longer in the Fleet. My sister has taken me in, and I live with her family, not so far from St. Paul's Churchyard. She is a widow too, you see—her husband was a baker, well known to all the printers there, but she could not maintain his business after his death. It was unfortunate— but now we hawk pies, made at a nearby cook's shop, where her husband had once done a good trade. Together we manage well enough."

Astell looked carefully at the printer's wife, who met her gaze straight on, without blinking. Mrs. Wilkin's face betrayed nothing, but Astell could well imagine the difficult life for two widows selling meat pies on the street in order to make a few pennies. It explained how Mrs. Wilkin had come to know Mrs. Gower, the widow of a disgraced clergyman who had once lived in the Fleet.

"And we are very grateful to you, Mrs. Gower," said Lady Ranelagh. "Your assistance has been invaluable to us. Please call on me if you are ever in need. Mrs. Wilkin will be able to direct you. We are in your debt, and I will do my very best to give you any help that you might require."

With that, Mrs. Wilkin and Mrs. Gower left the coach and headed back toward St. Paul's. Mary Astell watched as the two women walked quickly toward Ludgate. It was very cold, and Mrs. Gower's cloak was very thin.

Fifteen

The old coachman shifted his weight uneasily from his right foot to his left and then back again. Driving her ladyship to the Fleet was one thing, but wandering around there was quite another. As for accompanying Lady Ranelagh and her two companions as they traipsed about—well, of that he could not approve. Now he was standing, head down and unhappy, just outside the entrance to the prison with the countess, Lady Catherine, and Mary Astell.

"At least we will not have to travel much farther," said Lady Ranelagh cheerfully as the three women looked about them.

"No, Your Ladyship," said Mary Astell. If they had to extend their search as far as Fleet Bridge or Ludgate, neither was a great distance from where the coach was stopped, although she doubted Lady Catherine would want to venture even that far on foot. But from where they stood, Astell could see two brightly painted signboards bearing the image of a man and a woman's joined hands.

"We could walk across Fleet Ditch, just over there," she said, pointing to a small shop just on the far bank of the river, "but I doubt we will have to cross the ditch, much less go as far as the bridge or Ludgate. If Mrs. Ball operates her marrying-house inside a barber-surgeon's, that should be it. Do you see?"

Just a few doors to the south of the arched entrance to the prison was a long red-and-white pole, topped by a brass bowl. A sign bearing two joined hands hung just to the side. It was quite a bit smaller but still noticeable.

Lady Ranelagh looked a bit disappointed. She had clearly been hoping for more of an adventure, a daring raid into the notorious depths of the Fleet, not just a few short steps down a filthy street. "John," she said rather crossly, "perhaps you might have that tooth looked at while we are here."

The coachman looked horrified at such a suggestion. "Now, now," said Lady Catherine, "no need for that, my lady." And then, squaring her shoulders, she set off in the direction of the shop. "Let us proceed carefully," she warned, as if setting off on a dangerous expedition.

The old coachman reluctantly left his coach in the hands of the footman and trailed along behind the three women. If Lady Catherine had chosen him for his ability to scare off would-be attackers, she could hardly have picked a less fearsome defender. Such was Astell's opinion, at any rate, as she glanced back at John, trudging slowly behind them, grumbling to himself all the while as he followed in their wake.

But he did not have long to complain since they soon reached the door to barber-surgeon's premises. A tout lounging outside stepped forward, but after assessing the small party, he quickly retreated. As Lady Ranelagh extended her hand peremptorily, the grubby boy thrust a handbill advertising the services of the Hand and Pen wedding-house at her. She nodded to him as they ducked inside the barber-surgeon's, the four of them quickly filling the shop.

A rather startled and grizzled man stared at the small group, his mouth hanging open. His surprise turned to apprehension as Lady Catherine stepped forward. "We are looking for Mrs. Ball," she said. Her tone indicated that she would brook no nonsense. She expected an answer, and she expected it promptly.

Before the barber-surgeon could close his mouth, they heard a bold voice coming from behind them. "I am Mrs. Ball."

As they turned, Astell saw a woman who also looked as if she would brook no nonsense. Mrs. Ball was a relatively young woman of middling height. Her eyes were dark, her expression confident, her tone self-assured. She held her ground steadily as Lady Catherine examined her, top to toe. When Lady Catherine had finished her careful scrutiny, Mrs. Ball dropped her gaze and relaxed her posture. She fashioned her lips into a smile, but there was no corresponding warmth in her bright black eyes. "How may I be of assistance?" she asked, a wheedling note now entering her voice.

While the three women and the liveried coachman probably did not look like a wedding party, they still looked like money to Mrs. Ball. Astell could see the calculation in the woman's eyes as she assessed them.

"Thank you for agreeing to see us, Mrs. Ball," said Lady Catherine. Her words were gracious, but her form was still unbending. "We have come here in search of a record—that is to say, the record of a marriage that was performed here, or so we have been led to believe."

"Certainly, my lady," replied Mrs. Ball smoothly, gesturing to a small room that opened off of the barber-surgeon's premises. "Our register is complete, everything here is done proper—all is as it should be."

Lady Catherine had been trying to hold herself in check, but she was incensed at what she regarded as the woman's impudence. "All is as it *should* be, Mrs. Ball? I think not. Whoever thinks to come to a place such as this for a *proper* marriage?"

Mrs. Ball stepped back, the smile fading from her lips. Astell could see that Lady Catherine had offended the woman from whom they sought information. But before she herself could speak, Lady Ranelagh stepped forward and deftly took control of the conversation.

"Now, Mrs. Ball," she began, smiling radiantly. The effect was to soften the marriage broker a bit, but Astell thought it likely that the woman was more susceptible to the prospect of extracting a sum of money from Lady Ranelagh than she was to her charm. The insincere smile had once more appeared on the marriage broker's face.

"I am afraid we have made a bad start, Mrs. Ball," Lady Ranelagh said, shaking her head ruefully. "I apologize for any suggestion that there might be something amiss. We have not come to question your business, which as you say is a necessary one, and one which you no doubt conduct most properly. We are only seeking a bit of information, and we would be very grateful to you if you could oblige." Astell was startled to hear a slightly wheedling tone in Lady Ranelagh's voice as well.

The proprietor of the wedding-house regarded the countess intently. Mrs. Ball clearly did not know *who* the woman before her was, but she could see that the woman who questioned her was *someone*—someone of some consequence. "If I may, my lady, might I ask why, and on whose behalf, you are making these inquiries," Mrs. Ball said at last. "You see, we provide a valuable service for the discerning men and women who come to us—everything is done proper, as I say. I wonder whether you suspect some irregularity. Is there a problem? Has there been some complaint?"

"No, no, Mrs. Ball, I assure you, no one has made a complaint," said Lady Ranelagh. "We are simply in search of information. No, there is most assuredly no problem. No problem at all."

Mrs. Ball eyed the countess, who then added, "We would of course be most eager to offer recompense for your trouble." Now Lady Ranelagh was speaking the language that the proprietor of the marrying-house understood.

"I might well be able to help, my lady, that is, if I knew what you were after, although I must add a note of caution—all those who choose to marry here value the privacy and discretion that we promise them," Mrs. Ball replied, still calculating what she might gain by the transaction.

Astell now stepped forward, although she could tell from Mrs. Ball's expression that the proprietor of the wedding-house regarded her as being just as much a nonentity as the elderly Ranelagh coachman. An almost-invisible attendant, of no account whatsoever.

"We are inquiring after a man who was married here, and nothing more," said Astell.

Mrs. Ball looked at her, pursing her lips as she did. "'A man who was married here, and nothing more,' you say? Hmm. That is rather a lot, I say, but, still, I *may* be able to help."

"We are making inquiries on behalf of a young woman in great distress," Lady Catherine said, having regained control of herself. "She has been separated from her husband and is in the most unfortunate of circumstances. And as I have *just* said, we are searching for the record of her marriage, which we believe was performed here."

"That may well be," snorted Mrs. Ball. "But I fail to see how a marriage document would be of any help at all in such an *unfortunate* situation." The smirk on the woman's face belied her words—it seemed very clear that Mrs. Ball had a very good idea of just the kind of situation that Letty had experienced.

"We are trying to trace her husband—and we have reason to believe that the two were married here," said Lady Catherine, admirably holding her temper in check.

"Aaaaah," said the proprietor of the Hand and Pen. "I begin to see the trouble at last. Your friend has been abandoned, eh?"

"Oh, no, no," said Lady Ranelagh, "that is hardly the case. But it is true that circumstances have separated her from her husband, it *is* most unfortunate, and it is only right to do all we can to reunite them."

"And you have come to me? Am I to understand that you are making inquiries on behalf of a woman who claims to have been married *here*, at my chapel—does she say so? Regardless of what she might have to say, it does not sound as if you are certain. Not certain whether she was married at all, I wonder, or not certain she was married here? And why, pray tell, are you acting as her agents? I must say, I find this all to be very strange." Mrs. Ball paused momentarily and raised her right eyebrow, looking askance at the three women who had sought her out at the Hand and Pen. "Just who is this man, the man she married?" she added.

Lady Ranelagh, Lady Catherine, and Mary Astell looked at one another in consternation.

Mrs. Ball waited, allowing the silence to fill her small shop. "I do wonder," she finally said, "why you seem to think that I could possibly know the whereabouts of your friend's mysterious husband. Why does *she* not know where he has gone? What business it is of mine where he might be—my business is not keeping track of missing husbands. Nor, I take it, have you any idea about *when* this marriage might have taken place—this marriage that you *think* might have been performed here, this marriage between your friend and a man *whose name you do not know*—and who now seems to have disappeared.

"In any case, whatever information you are seeking, *that* is where any inquiry would have to begin: the day this marriage took place. My register is kept by date, you see. If you do not even know whether this pair *might* have been married here, much less when, then I am afraid I can be of no assistance. It would be quite impossible. As it would be impossible anywhere else you might choose to inquire. Even if you did know the name of lucky groom."

The three women looked at one another: Astell, whose desire to track down Letty's husband had raised the possibility of a visit to Mrs. Ball's establishment; Lady Ranelagh, whose desire for adventure had spurred them on; Lady Catherine, whose desire to make sure all went according to plan had guided her. They had hoped to discover the identity of the man Letty married in Mrs. Ball's registry—but they had set forth without the most basic piece of information. The date the supposed marriage had taken place. Nor, Astell realized, was it likely that the girl herself had any firm idea—she had certainly not mentioned any date when Astell questioned her about it.

Mrs. Ball, meanwhile, could hardly suppress a smile of contempt. She might have been able to extract a coin or two from Lady Ranelagh, but this moment of superiority seemed to be payment enough. "If you cannot tell me when this all happened, my lady," she repeated, "Well, I am very sorry, but it will be impossible for me to help you—"

"It must have been a day in March or April," Astell interrupted, thinking back to the story Mrs. Rolles had told. "Or perhaps a day in early May . . . And we know the bride's name. It is not so long ago. Perhaps you might search your registers. You might even remember her. A very young woman, her name is—"

"I am sorry, I am indeed," said Mrs. Ball briskly. "Marriages are performed here every day, many of them every week, and I cannot be expected to remember one young woman who came here to be married months ago. I have my book, and I keep a careful register, all is done proper. But I cannot just let any Tom, Dick, and Harry come here demanding information, I cannot indeed. People come to me not only for convenience but, as I say, for privacy."

Her calculus was now complete: whatever sum she might have gained by answering questions would not be worth the potential trouble that could ensue. "And now," Mrs. Ball continued, "if there is nothing further, I will excuse myself. I have business to attend to."

There was no way to halt her swift retreat. For his part, the grizzle-haired barber-surgeon was no longer standing idly by with his mouth open. His eyes had narrowed suspiciously, his jaw was clenched, and he looked as if he were deciding how best to hurry their departure.

"My lady," whispered John, backing out of the door.

Knowing they had been defeated, the three women also turned to go, Lady Ranelagh leading the way.

"Such barefaced contempt of law and religion," fumed Lady Catherine once they regained the safety of the coach. "And the ill consequences of allowing such marriages as these! Just imagine! How can this practice be permitted to continue?"

"I still think she might have been able to help us," said Lady Ranelagh. "After all, how long could it take for her to have looked through her register? And the very idea that we were acting improperly in our search for information—as if we would act improperly! We would have been content to wait patiently for her to look through however many pages there were—and we would have made the job worth her doing, I dare well say!"

"I am very sorry, Your Ladyship," Astell said. "I have caused all this fuss for nothing. I should have foreseen the problem and realized that this was not an advisable course of action. Doubtless any man who persuaded Letty to marry him in a place like that would have continued his deception there. Even if Mrs. Ball had been more agreeable and we had found the marriage in the register, you can be sure the man would have given his name as 'Charles de Beauclerk.' No one at the Hand and Pen would have raised so much as an eyebrow at such a preposterous name. And, in any case, how would having a name have helped us find him now? This has all been for naught, I am afraid."

"Oh, phoo!" said Lady Ranelagh with a dismissive wave of her hand.

"Lady Ranelagh!" objected Lady Catherine with a scandalous tone.

"Oh, phoo!" the countess repeated. "Now what?"

Now what indeed? As the coach began its return to Chelsea, the three women were silent.

"Perhaps we have started at the wrong end," Astell suggested.

"Whatever do you mean?" Disappointed by the day's adventure, Lady Ranelagh was frustrated. Their journey to the Fleet had not met her expectations. "We have come all this way, and *now* you say it is the wrong place to search?" She was also very cross.

"The city is large, Your Ladyship," Astell said, "and it is filled with many rogues and scoundrels. Even if we had been successful here in the Fleet and were given a name, I realize now that we would still have no idea where to find the man that Letty married. But Chelsea is small— that is where she came to find her husband, and that is where we should be looking."

"Well," began Lady Catherine, "that is where he *told* her he could be found at any rate. All that foolishness about 'paradise.' Really, Mary, why should we take any notice of that?"

"Because that is all we have, my lady," said Astell.

"And it is foolishness, I say." Lady Catherine was quite exasperated. "Even *if* he told her any such thing—and that is a big 'if,' even you must agree—who besides that silly girl would have thought he meant a house-row in Chelsea? Who thinks of a brick terrace when they hear the word 'paradise'? A paradise is a walled garden, as everyone knows, and there are plenty of those in Chelsea. Why, Chelsea is known for its many gardens. The Apothecary Garden and the Great Garden, to be sure— why, there is even a small paradise on the grounds of Ranelagh, as you well know. Why was that girl not looking for a garden or, rather, a house with such a garden? And, I ask you, why Chelsea? Why did the girl think this 'paradise' had to be in Chelsea? The old walled garden at Lambeth—the archbishop has taken to referring to it as a paradise, has he not?"

"All very good points, Lady Catherine," said Lady Ranelagh, nodding thoughtfully. "There is just such a paradise at Hampton Court, a lovely parterre, with fountains, and such a pretty banqueting house set there, a little pleasure palace—"

"And there is the Paradise Room as well, at the end of the Long Gallery," added Lady Catherine, as if that settled the matter.

"But how likely is it that a girl like Letty would know any of that?" Astell objected. "She knows nothing of pleasure gardens or parterres or palaces. She says her 'great lord' told her he lived in Chelsea, in 'paradise,' and she made her way to Paradise Row. That is where we must begin, I do believe."

"I am not at all sure what you mean, Mary," said the countess. She was still irritable.

"I am not altogether sure myself, Your Ladyship," Astell replied. "But having failed in the Fleet, why should we not begin our search for Letty's 'great lord' on Paradise Row? There are not many young gentlemen to be found among my neighbors, nor can I imagine one who would have the audacity to refer to himself as 'Charles de Beauclerk,' but we must start somewhere. And where else are we to begin?"

Lady Ranelagh sighed with satisfaction, her irritation suddenly forgotten. Tallying an inventory of young men—that was a task well suited to her interests. Lady Catherine, meanwhile, shrugged and pursed her lips.

"A kind of census, then," said Lady Ranelagh, "not for the purposes of levying a tax, but for the purposes of numbering the eligible male population. How delightful! The street is not long—we should be able to complete our list before we reach Ranelagh."

"Well, then, let us begin," said Lady Catherine, if a trifle grudgingly. "And I propose we begin at the end nearest the Hospital If we are to be successful, we must proceed in an orderly manner."

Indeed, there were not many houses on Paradise Row, and Astell knew most of their residents, or at least she knew *of* them, even if she did not count all of them among her most intimate friends.

At the east end of the row, closest to the Hospital, was a large brick house that had been constructed by Thomas Hill, the principal mason of the royal institution. "Lady Pelham is living there now," said Mary Astell. "Sir Thomas is a Whig," she added, as if his politics were enough to draw suspicion upon Sir Thomas Pelham's household.

"But there are no grown sons living there, Mary," Lady Catherine pointed out. "There were no sons at all, only two daughters, by the first Lady Pelham, although Sir Thomas now has an heir by the second. But the boy is still quite young, I believe."

"There are actually *two* boys," said Astell, "and another girl. A baby has been born every year since they moved into that house."

"The second Lady Pelham will be quite worn out with breeding," said Lady Ranelagh.

"But no 'young lord' is to be found there," said Lady Catherine. "And Sir Thomas himself must be near fifty, so let us move along. To the terrace itself, Mary. Who is it in the large end-of-terrace house?"

"Madam Hunt, she calls herself," said Astell, again with a note of cool disdain in her voice. "A widow. Her husband was a *Whig* lawyer, and there are no sons. Then there is Lady Wyndham," she continued. "She is newly married." Since everyone knew that Sir Francis Wyndham's father had helped the future Charles II escape to France after the battle of Worcester, Astell entirely approved of his politics, and she had called on Lady Hester Wyndham shortly after her marriage. "Sir Francis does have a grown son from his first marriage, I believe, but he does not live there—and Sir Francis himself is hardly young."

"And then there is the duchess of Mazarin," said Lady Ranelagh.

"Indeed," said Mary Astell. "Her man, Mustapha, says that there are no young gentlemen about the place, but who is to say, when it comes to Madam Mazarin? All manner of men are to be seen coming and going at every hour of the day and night . . ." She paused for a moment, pursing her lips. "At any rate," she continued, "those are the occupants of the three larger apartments at the far end of the terrace—Madam Hunt, the Wyndhams, and Madam Mazarin. Now, in the seven smaller houses, Mr. Upton is next. His wife has just given birth to a daughter."

"Your namesake," said Lady Catherine. "No suspicions there, I trust."

"And no young gentlemen either," said Astell. "Next is Mrs. Pennant," she added briskly. Although Mary Astell was quite pleased about the name Jane Upton had chosen for her newborn daughter, she preferred not to be distracted at the moment.

"Her husband spends a great deal of time at Don Saltero's, I believe," said Lady Catherine, referring to the coffee-house by the river, not far from All Saints. She had long wished she could examine the many curiosities displayed there for herself—her father, who had enjoyed many bowls of punch at Saltero's, often referred to the "ten thousand gimcracks" on view inside. While Lady Catherine did not really believe that the flaming sword of William the Conqueror or the strawberry dish of Elizabeth Tudor were now on view in a Chelsea coffee-house, she would have liked to inspect them on her own. "But Mr. Pennant is near sixty. No 'young lords,' in that house, I need hardly say."

"Mrs. Hill is next," said Astell. The house was currently occupied by Thomas Hill, the mason, and his wife. Now that the Hospital was complete, Astell was not sure whether the couple would continue much longer in Chelsea. But there were no young gentlemen living in the Hill residence.

"And I believe the Reverend Sir William Dawes has just moved into the next house in the row, has he not?" asked Lady Ranelagh. She did not ordinarily concern herself too much with clergymen, but the newly graduated doctor of divinity was noted for both the comeliness of his person and the melody of his voice.

"He is hardly a 'great lord,'" sniffed Lady Catherine. The Reverend Dawes was only a baronet.

"But he is quite young," said Lady Ranelagh, "and quite handsome."

"The father's marriage was something of a scandal, as I recall," said Lady Catherine. "The girl was an orphan, very young, and the two married without her guardian's consent. But, my lady, you cannot seriously be suggesting that Reverend Dawes is Letty's 'great lord' just because he is young and handsome and his father was the subject of scandal—is it likely that such a man would be skulking around a milliner's shop at the Royal Exchange?"

"I doubt that he is Letty's seducer," agreed Astell, "if for no other reason than, handsome or not, he would have been very noticeable in his clerical garb. Or would he have also donned a disguise? Not at all likely, I agree, for the Reverend Dawes is well known for his piety. And he is also a married man—his wife, Frances, is a very accomplished woman, the daughter of Sir Thomas d'Arcy. She lost one baby, poor soul, not long ago, but another is soon to arrive, I believe. The Reverend Dawes is a man bound for the highest dignities in the church, and I doubt that he would jeopardize his career for a dalliance with a milliner's apprentice."

Lady Ranelagh seemed reluctant to abandon the handsome clergyman, and she wondered whether it was worth reminding Mary Astell that men did such foolish things all the time. But she decided against it. Instead, as the coach crossed into Chelsea and approached Wilderness Row, she asked, "Who next, then, Mary?"

"Just three women," said Astell. "Next to Lady Dawes is Mrs. Smith—she first came to Chelsea some years ago with her third husband, although she has been a widow now for many years. She is well into her eighties. Then there is my house, of course, and, at the end-of-terrace is Mrs. Methuen. Not even so much as a manservant in any of our three households, though Mrs. Methuen does have a son, Paul, who is in his twenties, I believe. But he has been in Lisbon for several years, so he cannot possibly be involved."

"Then there is the countess of Radnor's house," said Lady Catherine. Radnor House was the last on Paradise Row, built by John Robartes, earl of Radnor, for his wife, Isabella Laetitia. After the earl's death, his widow had married Charles Cheyne, viscount Newhaven. A noted politician, he was also a great landowner and developer in Chelsea. Lord Cheyne was in possession of the old Chelsea Manor, where the countess of Radnor now spent much of her time, though she still held Radnor House in her own name.

"The place is well kept, but there are no lords living there, great or otherwise," said Astell.

"In her youth she was such a beauty," said Lady Ranelagh with a sigh. "And Lord Robartes—he is said to have been an ill-humored, perverse old man who never let his wife out of his sight. There is a story—you may know it, Lady Catherine—that King James, while he was still duke of York, was completely besotted with her. Out of fear for his wife's virtue, Lord Robartes removed her by force from the court and carried her off—he would not stop until he had taken her as far away as Wales!"

"She is still a very handsome woman," said Lady Catherine.

"Perhaps," said Lady Ranelagh with a slight toss of her head. Enjoying her own youth and beauty, she found it hard to consider a woman well into her sixties anything but old.

That exhausted the dwellings on the north side of Paradise Row. "Across the way, Lady Russell and her husband have just taken up residence in Jephson's house," said Astell. William Jephson, Secretary to the Treasury, had acquired a lease on land to the west of the Hospital at just about the same time Lord Ranelagh had negotiated his own lease in Chelsea. Like the earl, Jephson had quickly started construction on a house; most unfortunately, while the acreage upon which he built extended to the Thames, the frontage was a narrow way right alongside Hospital stable-yard. After Jephson's death, his widow transferred the lease, and now, Edward Russell, First Lord of the Admiralty, had taken up residence there.

"The admiral is doubtless a very great lord," said Lady Catherine, "but he is also a brutal man and quite intemperate." About his suspect financial dealings and misappropriation of funds, as head of the Admiralty, she had nothing to say.

"At the moment he is embroiled in such a political fight that he would hardly have the time for dalliance," said Lady Ranelagh, adding, "and he is not at all a handsome man, nor young."

"He will be raised to the peerage soon," said Lady Catherine. "You may mark my words. They have no children, and Lady Margaret is now past childbearing, so we may dismiss them from our inquiry, I think."

"That leaves only Lord Carbery," said Astell.

"Should we really consider the earl of Carbery? His house is nearer to Ranelagh than to Paradise Row, and it is not yet complete," objected Lady Ranelagh.

"There is a small passage from the house to Paradise Row, and a gate," Astell pointed out.

"And a beautiful garden has already been laid out," said Lady Catherine. She had still not altogether given up the idea that Letty's 'paradise' could be a garden. "He is a wicked man, guilty of every perversion. It has been said that he sold his own Welsh servants into slavery when he was governor of Jamaica!"

"And he is old," said Lady Ranelagh, as if that were his worst depravity. The earl of Carbery was also said to be in search of a wife, his second, Lady Anne, having died just as he had begun construction of his new house.

"The title will go extinct unless he can produce a son," Lady Catherine observed, "but I doubt that he has been hanging out at the Royal Exchange, looking to find a new bride there. His late wife was the daughter of the marquis of Halifax, after all."

"Of course, he will doubtless have manservants about," said Astell.

"As in many of these households," agreed Lady Catherine, "but, as you note, not all."

"If we are no longer looking for a lord but for a servant willing to pass himself off as one, then there is only one place to begin our search," said Lady Ranelagh. "And that is with the duchess of Mazarin's household. Although you seem to have forgotten it, Mary, Mrs. Rolles's daughter said she had seen Letty's seducer in the Exchange, following the duchess. It is all well and good to catalogue the *gentlemen* who live on Paradise Row—if nothing else, it has been a very amusing way to divert ourselves on the drive back to Chelsea, and I am quite over my disappointment about the Fleet—but you must call upon Hortense Mancini, I believe."

"I have not lost sight of that, Your Ladyship," Astell conceded as the coach pulled to a stop before Ranelagh House, "and I dare say you are in the right—the duchess of Mazarin may hold the key to the mystery."

Sixteen

Mary Astell was restless. The house was quiet when she rose, a welcome relief after all the turmoil of recent days. No fretful sounds came from the sickroom, but she was still unable to settle her mind during her daily devotions. Picking up a book, she found that she could not keep her mind focused on the words in front of her. Taking up her pen was equally out of the question.

When it was time to leave for morning prayers at All Saints, she slipped quietly out of the house. She looked forward to the familiar ritual of the worship service, hoping she would find there the calm that eluded her at home. As she hurried down Paradise Row toward the river, she tried to clear her mind of her worries.

But she was to find no peace in the church. She was made uneasy by the shadowy presence of Mr. Williams, the churchwarden. Although he made no attempt to confront her, she caught glimpses of him, darting just out of view, first as she entered the building, then as she spoke briefly to Mrs. King, the rector's wife, and again as she made her way to her pew. During the worship service, she also felt the stares of some of the other parishioners, though no one spoke to her openly of their concerns. When the service was over, she left quickly.

Dark clouds threatened rain as she hurried back to Paradise Row, and a cold wind began to blow just as she arrived home. Sarah greeted her at the door, taking her cloak and hat from her. "That Lettuce is awake," the little maidservant grumbled before she turned to make her way back to the kitchen.

"Thank you, Sarah," said Astell as the girl stomped off. Since Letty seemed to have had a quiet night, Astell considered whether Bridget should be sent home to Ranelagh later in the day. The old nursemaid would never complain but, given her age, Astell thought Bridget might well need her own rest. Letty would still require further care, to be sure, but Mrs. Methuen had seen her the previous day and was encouraged by the progress of the refractory patient. And Mary Kettilby had sent a message to say that she would examine Letty the next time she was in the village, probably on Thursday morning.

So that left Astell considering how best to employ her time. She climbed the stairs and stood for a moment on the landing, struggling with her sense of obligation, before turning to her study and closing the door. She felt as if she should have spoken to Letty, but she told herself that her presence and her questions would only fret the patient. With a sigh, Astell sat down at her desk. After carefully reviewing the notes she had drawn up just days before and with Lady Ranelagh's parting words to her in her mind, Astell decided that there was no way to avoid it—she would have to call upon the duchess of Mazarin.

Mary Astell was not faint of heart, nor was she easily discomfited. Even so, as she sat in her study on that morning, she admitted to feeling a degree of trepidation at the prospect of meeting Madam Mazarin. Given the woman's notoriety, Astell expected to encounter all manner of outrage.

Moreover, to pay such a call—no introduction having been made—was most unbeseeming, and Astell was a woman who carefully stood upon the punctilio. But considering the unusual circumstances that prompted this breach of decorum, Astell concluded she might put aside her sense of propriety on this occasion. And so, resolute, her back held stiff and straight, she once more left her house, and in just a few steps she arrived at Madam Mazarin's residence.

Without pause, Astell passed through the gate and started up the walk. Just as she reached out to grasp the elaborately wrought bronze knocker, the door swung open to reveal Mustapha, standing just inside.

"Mrs. Astell," he said, welcoming her with a brief nod. "Her Grace has been looking forward to making your acquaintance. Follow me, if you please." He turned quietly, then gestured toward the parlor, from whence came the low murmur of voices.

Astell was confounded as she entered the room: nothing was as she expected it to be. Rather than being fitted out for ostentatious display, the duchess of Mazarin's reception room was arranged for comfort. Unlike the grand public rooms at Ranelagh, it had not been newly appointed with the most fashionable (and expensive) of furnishings. However magnificent they may once have been, the upholstery and hangings were noticeably faded—but for all that, each well-worn piece of furniture, each distinctive, if odd, ornament, each slightly threadbare cushion and cover reflected a singular taste, the arrangement not just pleasing to the eye but welcoming to the visitor. And while the shabby elegance of the duchess of Mazarin's parlor was as far from the spare simplicity of her own as it was from the stylish splendor of Ranelagh, Mary Astell felt surprisingly at her ease.

She had also expected her senses to be assaulted by the sight, sounds, and smells of Hortense Mancini's fabled menagerie. Astell was not unfamiliar with dogs—the earl of Ranelagh kept a variety of hunting dogs, of course, and Lady Ranelagh had two or three pampered little lapdogs (indeed, it was hardly possible to call upon anyone in London these days without encountering an annoying number of such beasts). But, although Astell was prepared to be indignant, no lapdogs, monkeys, squirrels, or other such noisome creatures laid siege to her skirts.

Instead, and much to her surprise, she was confronted not by dogs or even monkeys but by three flamboyantly colored parrots—none of Mary Astell's many friends and acquaintances kept even one of these exotic birds. While she had observed them in paintings, she had never before seen a living bird. Astell's eyes darted from one to the next. Much to her chagrin, she realized she was gaping in wonderment.

In the corner farthest from the doorway, the largest of the three was enclosed in a silver metalwork cage. The parrot's head was scarlet and its throat a fiery orange, while its wings were a deep blue, the sweeping red tail feathers tipped with the same dramatic color. The bird snapped at the bars of its cage with a huge black beak.

In the corner opposite was a second cage, this one topped by a gilded cupola. Perched inside was a parrot much smaller than the first, perhaps a foot in length. Its plumage was a yellowish-green, though there were a few bright red feathers dancing on the crown of its head.

But the most spectacular of the three, at least in Astell's estimation, was just inside the parlor door. On a tall pedestal placed alongside a Delftware cage stood a large, pale green parrot with a brilliant blue forehead and crown. The creature peered intently at her, cocking its head to one side. Astell found both the parrot's direct gaze and its strange yellow eyes quite unsettling.

"Ah, I must warn you, Mrs. Astell, Pretty stands ever upon her guard," said the duchess of Mazarin. She had risen from her chair as Astell entered the room and had watched in some amusement as her guest stared at the birds. Now the duchess approached and smiled. "Pretty seems eager to meet you—and that is most unusual for her. She can be aloof, you see, and even very haughty, so you should feel honored by her welcome."

Nor was Hortense Mancini what Astell expected, at least not at first glance. Just as she had supposed the interior of Hortense Mancini's home would reveal scenes of riot and debauchery, she had assumed the duchess's person would reflect the excess and abandon of her life. And yet the woman did not appear in the guise of the wanton libertine. She might still *be* such a woman, of course, but there was no hint of dissipation in face or figure.

She was tall, at least as tall as Lady Catherine, but she was slim and bore herself with none of that lady's monumental stateliness. Although she was no longer young, the duchess moved with the ease of youth, her gestures quick and natural rather than studied and formal. Astell had heard that Hortense Mancini affected an air of languor and world-weariness, but of that she saw no sign.

Even Madam Mazarin's most vicious detractors did not deny her beauty—Mary Astell, who did not countenance idle talk, petty gossip, or tittle-tattle, had nevertheless heard a great deal about the duchess's unsurpassed loveliness. Although Astell suspected that the woman's beauty had caused her as much harm as it had brought her good, she could not deny it. The dark and abundant hair may have been streaked with silvery threads, but these few gray hairs were the only signs of age. The duchess of Mazarin's complexion was creamy, her face unlined, her cheeks tinged with a delicate pink. Her dark eyes were striking, neither blue nor gray nor quite black, and as she fastened these remarkable eyes upon her visitor, Astell found it hard to look away.

"We have just been talking about you, Mrs. Astell, and hoping you would soon call upon us," the duchess began, breaking the spell cast by her dark eyes. "Well," she added, "to be clear, Pretty and I have not been discussing this possibility, Pretty has not expressed her views on the likelihood of such a visit to me, but *le seigneur de Saint-Évremond* and I—"

"*Mais non, mais non,*" said a very old man who was sitting quietly by the fire. With her attention drawn first to the birds and then to the woman, Astell had not noticed him. He was well made, his face bright and intelligent, his eyes blue, keen, and full of fire. Rather than a fashionably curled wig, he was wearing a black skull cap over his white hair.

"Mrs. Astell, Charles de Marguetel de Saint-Denis, *le seigneur de Saint-Évremond,*" said the duchess.

"Your Lordship," Astell said, acknowledging the introduction.

The man inclined his head, offering her a bemused smile. He then rose from his comfortable chair. Despite his age, he stood tall and erect. "*Je vous laisse maintenant, ma chére amie,*" he said to the duchess and then, to Astell, "*Madame Astell.*"

"*Hélas!*" the duchess cried as the old man headed for the door, but when he turned toward her and raised an expressive eyebrow, she laughed. "*Eh bien, eh bien, au revoir,*" she added, stretching out both hands in a gesture of conciliation.

And then, as he left the room, she turned to Mary Astell and said, with a shrug. "I am sure Mustapha has already called for the sedan—Mustapha knows my dear friend's quirks so well, you see." Shaking her head, she continued, "I am afraid that his lordship is of the opinion that you intend to berate me, Mrs. Astell, or possibly that you will accuse me of the most abominable crimes, and he simply cannot bear it." The duchess was smiling, but Astell could not quite read her expression.

"Surely so distinguished a gentleman would not judge me guilty of such a crime against good manners," Astell replied. In the face of Hortense Mancini's ease and gaiety, Astell felt stiff and heavy.

"And such a brave soldier as well! To think that he retreats from the battlefield without engaging, leaving me quite defenseless!" The duchess of Mazarin laughed, but the laughter did not reach her eyes. "The truth is, Mrs. Astell, despite his many years in London, he has never bothered to learn the language. Oh, he can speak a few words when he must, but he rarely feels any need to express himself in English when he is at court or among friends. He would be no match at all for your facility and subtlety—he would hardly be able to defend himself, much less me, against so sharp a wit as yours, or so at least he says. I doubt that is the case, but even so he has decided it is much wiser to cede the field."

Hortense Mancini carefully observed the effect of her words on her guest. For her part, Mary Astell again felt the deficiencies of her own education. But whatever the real reason for Saint-Évremond's departure, Astell thought that the duchess of Mazarin would be more than able to defend herself in any battle of wits.

"As for me," said the duchess, "I am most happy to receive you, Mrs. Astell. Nanon, please call for some tea." She spoke to a pleasant-looking, plump woman in a dove-gray dress who had just entered the room.

"My dear companion," the duchess explained as Nanon turned and left without a word. "She has been with me through it all, from the very beginning."

"Indeed, Your Grace," replied Astell. The small, silent woman in the understated gown bore no resemblance to the Nanon who had featured so comically in Hortense Mancini's memoirs—a rather hapless and accident-prone figure who took part in her mistress's daring escape from her husband and who was a witness to the runaway wife's increasingly scandalous romps.

"You seem ill at ease," said the duchess as Astell settled herself gingerly in the chair by the fire. "You are most welcome, I assure you. I have long wished for the pleasure of meeting the celebrated Mrs. Astell, though I do have cause to wonder at your temerity—to risk your honor by visiting the great Italian whore! Such bravery! Such daring!"

"Your Grace!" Astell began, shocked at the duchess's impropriety. "I beg of you—"

"Oh, let us not beat about the bush, my dear Mrs. Astell. You are far too honest to play such games, and I am far too old. I know your reputation, as you know mine. We shall speak truths to one another here. I am not surprised that I have been believed to be such a one as I have been painted."

"Indeed, madam, you painted the picture yourself—by your own account, you have been a rover."

"Ah, now we begin, I see! A 'rover'! Alas, it is too true, and even if I myself had not acknowledged it to be true, everyone would no doubt have claimed it to be the case. But, yes, Mrs. Astell—I have indeed painted myself as an errant wanderer. An adventuress! And yet, you know, I was brought up to be a queen . . . " The duchess of Mazarin paused briefly and then shrugged. "I know that a woman's glory lies in her not giving rise to gossip—but one cannot always choose the kind of life one wishes to lead, I am afraid."

"You were given every advantage in life, Your Grace."

"I was taught to sing, to dance, to play the guitar, and to speak French. These wondrous advantages did not stand me in much good stead, Mrs. Astell." The duchess of Mazarin shook her head playfully.

"You were also blessed with great wealth."

"Ah, yes. And yet all this wealth served only to purchase a madman as my lord and master. I was the unhappiest wife in Christendom."

"The matrimonial yoke may be grievous, Your Grace, but it is a wife's duty to bear it nonetheless."

"Is it also her duty to suffer without complaint?"

"A woman who meets with a disagreeable temper in her husband may find herself as unhappy as anything in the world can make her," Astell conceded, "but she must nevertheless be content with her lot and make the best of it."

"We are in accord in this, Mrs. Astell: a disagreeable temper is surely to be borne. But I ask you, must a wife bear a husband's madness and cruelty? If I were not afraid of boring you, I could tell you quite another story—of a husband guilty of a thousand acts of brutality and violence inflicted on his wife simply for the pleasure of tormenting her, of a lord and master whose malice dreamed up infinite tortures to impose upon every single member of his suffering household, of a man determined to destroy all those whom it was his duty to cherish and protect. If a wife is bound to such a man—what then, I ask?"

"Such is the institution of marriage, Your Grace. When she marries, a woman gives her husband an authority she cannot recall however he misapply it. She puts her fortune and person entirely in his power, and no matter how difficult her life may be, neither law nor custom affords her redress—it is not lawful for her to will or desire anything but what her husband approves and allows."

"Must she entirely submit to a tyrant, Mrs. Astell? If, as Mr. Locke has said, all men are born free as they are born rational, why must we accept that all women are born slaves? Women too are endowed with reason—why then must a woman surrender to the imperious dictates of a man's blind will and wild imagination just because he has the name of 'husband'? Pho! Any fool who can keep himself clean and make a bow believes himself worthy of that title.

"As for me, I suffered for as long as I could at the hands of a man who was vicious and brutal—a man I did not choose but who had been chosen for me, a man I married out of obedience to the wishes of my family, and a husband to whom I was a dutiful wife.

"But in the end, Mrs. Astell, I preferred my reason to all my riches—my deliverance cost me all those riches that have made so much noise in the world, but liberty can never be too dear bought by one who is delivered from tyranny. In making that grievous choice, I was divested of everything I owed to fortune—but I could never be robbed of what nature bestowed upon me. My condition now is not unhappy."

The rapid exchange of words stopped as suddenly as it had begun. As she faced the duchess of Mazarin, Astell felt an unfamiliar perturbation of mind. Hortense Mancini's questions had not provoked in Astell any outward sign of agitation, or at least she hoped not, but she could not deny the challenge they posed to her own settled views of marriage. The duchess seemed to sense, even if she could not see, Astell's discomfiture, and to take no small degree of satisfaction in it. She pursed her lips as if to hide her amusement.

"Is it a drawn match, Mrs. Astell?" she asked. "We have each won a trick or two, but I fear neither of us has won the game."

"I am afraid I do not play at cards, Your Grace."

"Of course not, Mrs. Astell. If I remember correctly, you have opined that all such pastimes are 'pitiful diversions,' mere 'idle amusements' serving only to 'distract our thoughts and waste our precious time.' Well, well, then, since you have not come to waste your precious time much less to distract yourself with the pleasure of my company, I suppose we must turn our attention to more serious matters."

Before Astell had time to respond to Hortense Mancini's raillery, Nanon entered the room, followed by a servant pushing an ebony tea table mounted on a wheeled platform. Once the table was in position and the servant had hurried away, the duchess of Mazarin opened a gilt canister and, using its thimble-shaped lid, measured out a small quantity of tea leaves, placing them into a tiny silver pot. She sat back while Nanon dispensed a stream of hot water from a somewhat larger silver pot, wetting the tea so it could steep. After a minute or two, the duchess herself then poured the fragrant, pale green liquid into two porcelain bowls.

While she ordinarily declined refreshment, Astell accepted the cup without a word. Although tea was costly, its preparation requiring a great deal of show, the drink's medicinal benefits were manifold. While neither Mary Kettilby nor Elizabeth Methuen had the means to include tea among their treatments, those who did not find the cost prohibitive found the beverage to be very useful in the cure of headache, colds, catarrh, shortness of breath, and sluggishness of the stomach. It was also helpful in strengthening the memory.

But Mary Astell doubted whether the duchess of Mazarin served tea because of its medicinal properties. From the moment that Charles II's Portuguese queen had popularized the drink at court, the taking of tea had been a mark of wealth and fashion. Lady Ranelagh, who professed to find the ceremony of its preparation and consumption very tiresome, nevertheless served tea to her guests with great éclat.

"I suppose you have come about the girl," said Hortense Mancini, settling into her chair. "She is another wanderer, if I am not mistaken? But, forgive me—I should not jest at the expense of such a poor and unfortunate one as she, should I, Mrs. Astell? I trust Mustapha has been of service, and you have only to advise me if you have any other need we might be able to fulfill."

"He has been very helpful, Your Grace." As she spoke, Astell could not help looking past the duchess to a huge oil painting on the wall just behind her. In the center was Hortense Mancini, her figure draped in loose robes that exposed one bare breast—the portrait was clearly intended to represent the duchess of Mazarin, however improbably, in the guise of the virgin goddess Diana. She lay recumbent in the center of the painting, a quiver of arrows at her feet.

A long spear rested loosely in the crook of her right arm. With the other hand, the robed duchess gestured toward a brown and white hound, a small, dark-skinned boy dressed as a page sitting astride the great beast. A second boy, attired like the first, gripped the leash of another dog, while a third little boy held aloft a horn. But it was the youth who stood behind the duchess who drew Astell's attention.

With a shock, Astell realized that it was Mustapha—a younger version of the man, to be sure, but clearly Mustapha nonetheless. Like the three smaller boys, he was also gazing at the duchess. Standing by a large fountain, he was filling a vessel with water for her. Perched alongside of him was a red parrot—the very same bird that now sat in a cage in the far corner of the parlor. In the painting, the young Mustapha was fitted with a broad silver collar, the very same collar the man wore now. In fact, as Astell drew in her breath sharply, she realized that all four of the Africans in the portrait were wearing silver collars—and that the two dogs bore identical collars about their necks.

"Ahh, I see that you have recognized Mustapha," said the duchess, who was studying Astell all the while Astell was studying the painting. "Very good, Mrs. Astell. It is now many years since he was painted—he has been with me almost as long as Nanon." At that, she smiled at the quiet woman in gray who had taken a place by the fire. "Mustapha was only five or six years old when the duke of Savoy presented him to me— the poor, unfortunate child had been rescued from pirates just off the coast of North Africa—"

"*Presented him to you?* The boy was given to you as a *gift*, Your Grace? He is a your possession? Do you mean to say he is your *slave*?" Astell was aghast.

Hortense Mancini regarded her in amusement. "He is no more my slave than Nanon, I can assure you, Mrs. Astell. Mustapha and Nanon are my only family now—we three have been through a great deal together." She paused briefly before adding, "He is certainly no more my *slave* than the young African now at Ranelagh is a slave. 'England is too pure an air for slaves to breathe in,' *n'est-ce pas?*—is not that what is said? But, then, I may be mistaken. Perhaps, much like Sir Willoughby Chamberlain, the earl of Ranelagh and his family take pride in such possessions, and if so, I beg your pardon."

While Astell had thus far maintained her composure during her verbal contest with the duchess of Mazarin, she could no longer conceal her agitation. That such a woman, a woman of her reputation, should suggest such a terrible thing! The imputation had not merely startled her, it had come as a blow.

"Are you quite well, Mrs. Astell?" The duchess of Mazarin assumed a look of concern, but her guise of solicitude was betrayed by her glittering dark eyes. She knew that Astell was wounded. And she seemed to take pleasure in having delivered the blow. "Some more tea, perhaps, to calm you—or shall I call for Mustapha to accompany you home?" she asked.

With a deep breath, Astell replied calmly. "It is nothing, Your Grace." And yet it was not nothing. In truth she had never once thought about the African who had been a member of the earl's household for as long as she had known Lady Catherine.

Struggling to recover her equanimity, Astell now recalled the large portrait proudly displayed in the grand parlor at Ranelagh—of a younger Lady Catherine and her sister, Lady Frances. A small black boy, dressed as a page, knelt at the side of the two sisters, offering them a garland of flowers. The child's gaze was fixed intently on the two richly dressed women who paid him no mind but stared coolly out of the canvas at the viewer.

The boy in the Ranelagh painting was as familiar a presence to her as Old Bridget—indeed, like Mustapha, the boy had grown into a young man since the portrait of Lady Catherine and her sister had been painted—and yet Astell realized she had no idea who the African boy was. In all the years of their friendship, she had never heard Lady Catherine refer to him by name. Astell also realized that she had no idea how he had entered the Ranelagh household in the first place or what his role there was now. Beyond fetching and carrying for Lady Catherine and her sister, his only function seemed to be as an exotic presence during grand occasions when he was colorfully attired in Turkish dress and stationed near the staircase.

Astell felt a flush of shame and saw a corresponding flash of triumph on the face of Hortense Mancini. Accustomed as Mary Astell was to attacks on her words and her person, she recognized something new in the subtle insinuations of the duchess of Mazarin. Hortense Mancini was neither challenging Mary Astell's political views, nor was she mocking Astell's appearance. She was probing Astell's heart

Seventeen

As the duchess of Mazarin offered her guest a sly smile and more tea, Mary Astell attempted to regain her composure. She remained deeply unsettled, however, and not just by the way she had overlooked the presence of the young black man who had been living in the Ranelagh household for so many years. At the same moment and with devastating effect, she also recognized that her disregard for him extended to those for whom she professed her greatest regard.

Her settled views about the institution of marriage, for example—the very certainties that she had even now propounded to Hortense Mancini—they had been entirely worked out in the quiet and isolation of her study. While Mary Astell acknowledged the ill effects of marriage *on* women and did not hesitate to prescribe the appropriate behavior in marriage *for* women, she had neither sought out nor considered the opinions, much less the experiences, *of* women. Indeed, as she now realized with something of a shock, she had concerned herself not at all with the cruel subjection so many women experienced after they married.

In her defense, Mary Astell might have argued that her struggle to establish herself in London had left her little time for anything but her own survival. And she might also have noted that her cultivation of well-disposed patrons and like-minded supporters had, of necessity, drawn her attention from anyone but those whose intellectual pursuits matched her own. Although she knew that women suffered in marriage, she counted few married women among her circle of acquaintances, and she had little interest in the intimate details of their private lives.

It was one thing to hear a sad tale from a woman like Hortense Mancini, a woman whose own scandalous behavior gave Astell little cause for pity. But as she now realized, she had never spoken with the few married women of her acquaintance about their experiences as wives. She knew that Mrs. Methuen had been deserted by her husband, but Astell had never considered the painful abandonment her neighbor had endured. As to how Mrs. Methuen had managed to survive this personal catastrophe, deprived of her fortune, her place in society, and her home—Astell had never bothered to inquire. What might Mrs. Methuen have to say about the institution of marriage if Astell had cared to ask?

And the rector's wife? While Mary Astell was aware of Elizabeth King's abiding sorrow, she had never spoken with the unhappy woman about her experiences. Her remarriage seemed to be the source of her heartache—was Mrs. King still mourning her first husband, who had died only a few months after their marriage? What circumstances had compelled her, a young, grief-stricken widow, to join herself so soon to her dead husband's successor?

And Lady Ranelagh, newly married to the old earl—what pain, even despair, might be hidden behind the former Margaret Cecil's guise of gaiety and frivolity?

Have I said too much and asked too little?

Astell's thoughts then turned, as they must, to Letty Pyke who, even now, lay ill, alone and abandoned, soon to give birth to a child. A young woman—no, a *girl*—for whom Astell felt little sympathy and a great deal of resentment. A girl Astell easily dismissed as foolish and affected, a girl whose supposed marriage Astell had decided was the inevitable result of ill education and ignorant delusion. A girl Astell had chosen to ignore that very morning.

"She is recovering well, I trust," said the duchess, as if privy to Astell's thoughts. The duchess of Mazarin's calculating smile had been replaced by an appearance of concern. "I refer of course to the young stranger you are sheltering. Mustapha informs me that she is receiving excellent care. What a great deal of activity, in and out, to and fro! Have you called upon me now for some further assistance?"

Still struggling to overcome her perturbation of mind, Mary Astell reminded herself of the reason for her visit. "We have all that we need, thank you, Your Grace, nor will I impose upon your time much longer. The girl was unexpectedly overcome while on her way to meet her husband—but, in truth, I begin to think she has been most cruelly imposed upon by this husband."

"Ahh, well, Mrs. Astell, have not all wives been most cruelly imposed upon by their husbands? In one way or another? But we have said enough upon this subject already, have we not?"

"Indeed, Your Grace. In spite of my doubts, I am hopeful of reuniting this unfortunate wife with her husband. To that end, I have been making inquiries on her behalf, attempting to locate the man for whom she has been searching."

"How very intriguing, Mrs. Astell. But I fail to see why that should that be such a difficult task or why it should involve me. You can be very sure that there are no stray husbands to be found here!" Hortense Mancini laughed somewhat bitterly before continuing. "Surely this wife must know where her husband is to be found since, as you say, she was on her way to meet him. And as the village of Chelsea is quite small and your own acquaintance is very large, I fail to see how finding him can pose any difficulty for a woman of your undoubted perspicacity. Though perhaps the man does not wish to be found, eh?"

"Indeed, Your Grace, you may be correct. I begin to suspect there is at least some confusion, if not deceit—which has led to my suspicion that the girl has been badly treated."

"That may well be the case, but I still do not see how this is a matter for my concern. Or how I may be of assistance to you, though you can be sure I stand ready to help." The duchess of Mazarin sipped her tea, staring intently over her cup, waiting for Mary Astell to continue.

Finding herself at something of a loss for words, Astell began again. "I have some reason to suspect that the man she believes to be her husband may not *be* her husband—to be plain, Your Grace, I begin to fear that the unfortunate girl has been seduced and abandoned. And I have also begun to wonder whether this man might not be a member of your household—"

"My household?"

"Indeed, it is a delicate question, Your Grace, and one I hesitate to pose, so I do beg pardon, but . . . to be plain, could you have in your employ such a man? That is, a young and clever man, a man about whom you may perhaps have some concern? One who might be so unfeeling as to seduce and betray a foolish girl? One who is bold enough to present himself as someone he is not?"

"You have piqued my interest with this delicious story, Mrs. Astell. And although you did not ask for my opinion, I will nevertheless assert that very few men, if given the chance, would hesitate to take advantage of a foolish young girl. But, then, I suppose you have not come to seek the wisdom of my experience." The duchess of Mazarin smiled, though without joy.

"Be that as it may be," she continued, "I fear that my days of having a grand establishment are now long past, and even if that were not the case, I hardly think that you would presume to inquire into the staffing of my modest household. But these are most unusual circumstances, are they not? And so I can assure you that there is no such young man in my service—no young man at all, in fact, only an old manservant and a little page boy, neither of whom is clever enough to seduce a woman, foolish or otherwise."

"Perhaps a coachman or a footman, Your Grace?" Astell had no wish to persist, but having ventured this far—and remembering the words of Gertrude Rolles's daughter—she nevertheless persisted. *What were her words? "I saw in him the Exchange,"* she had said, *"tagging after the duchess of Mazarin . . . One of her lackeys or followers. Just like one of her lapdogs or monkeys." Those were her very words.*

"Ahh, not these days, I am very sorry to say. Where do you think I could accommodate such a crowd, here on Paradise Row—and with no stable-yard or coach-house? No, Mrs. Astell, I am sorry to say that I no longer keep a coachman or footmen or a groom of my own. For such luxuries, I am indebted to a dear friend, a favorite of the king, who is kind enough to provide me with a coach, horses, and the necessary equipage, but the coachman and the footmen are members of his household, not mine. They are at my command but not, alas, in my service. And an old acquaintance or two, remembering the happy times we shared in the past, will on occasion supply me with a manservant when I am in need. But we are few in this house. I am afraid that you will not find any misplaced husbands here."

With that, the duchess of Mazarin rose and nodded to Nanon. "Now I must bid you good day, Mrs. Astell. I am pleased to have made your acquaintance at long last. Do call again. You are welcome any time."

"Thank you for seeing me, Your Grace. I am most grateful," Astell replied, still unsettled by the encounter.

As Hortense Mancini turned toward the door of the parlor, a cacophony of screeches and shrieks erupted. The large red parrot spread its wings and screamed a loud, harsh *raa-aar*, the green bird opposite answering with a rapid series of shrill cries. Startled, Astell drew her breath in sharply.

For her part, Hortense Mancini ignored the two squalling birds, but she paused just at the door of the parlor to stroke the head of the blue and green parrot that still perched outside her cage. "Pretty," she said to the bird, "Pretty, please bid our guest farewell."

"*Au revoir*," said Pretty obediently, fixing her yellow eyes on Astell. "*Au revoir, au revoir*, farewell."

"I bid you good day, Mrs. Astell," said Hortense Mancini as she left the room. Astell failed to offer her thanks to the duchess for her time. Instead she stood there silently, staring in fascination at the bird, bobbing up and down expectantly on her perch. Suddenly feeling rather foolish, Astell found herself responding to Pretty with a muttered "goodbye."

Nanon struggled to suppress her laughter as she followed the duchess of Mazarin's visitor out of the parlor.

Stepping out of Madam Mazarin's house and turning toward her own, Mary Astell considered whether she could entirely take the woman at her word. The duchess of Mazarin might well deny the presence of a double-dealing young manservant in her household for her own perverse reasons—or for no reason at all, aside from sheer perversity. But, then, Astell acknowledged to herself, the unscrupulous rogue who had pursued Letty might very well have been one of those servants on loan to the duchess, one whose only connection to Paradise Row was his occasional employment there.

And even if Hortense Mancini's claims of ignorance were to be believed, there was always the stream of visitors and curiosity seekers who made their way from London to her door, one of whom might well be attended by a guileful manservant or an intriguing footman. How easy it would be for such a ruffler to seduce a love-struck girl and then to concoct a story about being a great lord who lived on Paradise Row. And was the daughter of Gertrude Rolles even to be believed when she offered her opinion about the man she had seen following the duchess of Mazarin? She herself seemed a little sly.

Astell had no sooner concluded that finding Letty's missing husband was likely impossible than she faced another, though not unexpected, vexation. Just as she approached her front garden, Sarah threw open the door and came bounding out.

"He is here again, ma'am, and this time he has brought the others with him!" she hissed.

Astell was just about to reprimand her ungovernable maidservant when she realized that the girl was not disobedient but distraught. Her face was pale, her eyes full of fear.

"Who is here, Sarah?"

"That Mr. Williams has come again! And he has two others with him! They have come for that Lettuce, and maybe, Mrs. Astell, maybe they have come for you too!" As she spoke, Sarah kept turning her head to look over her shoulder, as if sure that she was being pursued.

"Now, Sarah, I assure you that there is no need for any of that." Astell meant to calm the girl, but she could feel a tremor in her own voice as she spoke. "Take yourself off upstairs, and see to it that Letty is not disturbed."

Despite her fear, Sarah stopped short and glared at her mistress with a look that was equal parts doubt, disgust, and ill humor. "Oh, to be sure, Mrs. Astell, I understand, *she* is not be disturbed no matter what—but I will make sure she keeps quiet too!" With that, Sarah produced a dramatic sigh, turned, and stomped back inside. Astell could hear her thumping up the stairs.

Astell sighed too. As she entered her parlor, she saw that the churchwarden had once again made himself quite at home, warming his ample backside at her grate. With him were Joseph Budgett, whom she recognized as a member of the vestry, and the parish constable, Richard Jones.

"Mr. Williams," she said, entering the room.

"Mrs. Astell," the churchwarden replied as he turned toward her.

The two faced off like duelists, each taking careful measure of their opposite.

"What a surprise, to see you again so soon. I trust you have come on important business?"

"Most assuredly, Mrs. Astell." On this occasion, the churchwarden offered her no ingratiating smile, nor was there any anxious smoothing of his rumpled coat. Instead, bolstered by the comforting presence of his two companions, he faced his adversary boldly.

"Mr. Budgett, Mr. Jones," she said, acknowledging the other men. The vestryman looked uneasy, as if he wished to be anywhere at that moment but in Mary Astell's parlor, while the parish constable's eyes were bright with excitement.

"Ahem," the oily churchwarden began, clearing his throat and puffing out his meager chest. He spoke solemnly. There was no stumbling or lack of words on this occasion. "We have come here in order to examine the immigrant, Mrs. Astell. She has come into this parish, unknown and haphazard. We must be on our guard lest we be imposed upon by rogues, idlers, and vagrant persons. To begin, we must have her particulars—her name, her parish of settlement, her reason for coming into Chelsea. Perhaps she has employment in the parish? What can you tell us?"

"Is there something amiss, Mr. Williams?"

"By all accounts, madam, the woman you harbor is a stranger—and we are already overpressed with the burden of the poor. It is our duty to ensure that she will not be chargeable to the parish."

'By all accounts?' Who has been talking to him?

Uncertain as to what the churchwarden might have heard (and from whom he had heard it), Astell replied carefully. "Hmm. I understand, Mr. Williams, but I do not see any cause for complaint or any reason for fear. In any case, if an examination is necessary, surely that is to be made before a justice of the peace. Or have I been misled?"

Mr. Budgett seemed relieved. "Just so, Mrs. Astell, just so," he said, turning to the churchwarden. "I told you that the examination must be taken by a justice of peace." The vestryman seemed eager to be gone, but his two companions were made of sterner stuff.

"There is no great urgency, surely," Astell continued, attempting to take advantage of the moment. "The unfortunate woman has just arrived in the parish, Mr. Williams, as you must know since you are so very well informed. It has only been a matter of a few days—and even if it were to be determined that she has no ties here in Chelsea, you have no cause for concern. I believe that she could only claim a settlement after forty days? Is this not the case, or have I been ill advised?

"And while you have forgotten to ask about her condition, Mr. Williams," she added, "I will tell you that she is very ill, not at all fit to be interviewed. I hardly imagine that a worthy man like you would expect to interrogate her in her sickbed. Even in your official capacity."

Astell hoped that her imperfect knowledge of the settlement act was correct, at least as far as she had ventured to go. Elizabeth Tenison's concise tutorial on provisions of the law had proved far more useful than Archbishop Tenison's fulminations on sin and vice.

Mr. Williams's greasy face grew red, and his eyes narrowed as he confronted Mary Astell. For a moment she feared he would fall into an apoplectic fit. "Pah . . . pah . . . phah . . . ," he sputtered, emitting great puffs of air and an alarming amount of spittle.

Recognizing his leader's momentary incapacity, Mr. Jones, the parish constable, pushed forward. "May I remind you, *madam*, it is our *sworn duty* to ensure that *this person* is not some disreputable *vagrant*—an infectious *drain* upon the parish." His emphatic diction was quite alarming.

"Mr. Jones, the unfortunate woman fell ill on her way—"

"Just *so*, Mrs. Astell, just *so*. On her way *where*, I ask you? Wherever she may *claim* her settled place, she does not belong *here*, and if she is *allowed* to stay, she will be *guilty* of *defrauding* the true poor and needy of *our* parish—and the *charges* for her maintenance will be *imposed* upon us all!"

Now we have come to it—that is the worry. No word of pity or charity. Only fear for 'the charges.'

"And I need *hardly* to remind you, Mrs. Astell," the man continued, only too happy to remind her, "harboring a *vagrant* is itself a *chargeable* offense. You have *knowingly* received a *vagrant* into *your* residence. Unless you are prepared to *expel her* at once, you *hinder* the execution of justice, *for which offense* you yourself will have to answer."

Having summed up the situation to his satisfaction, Mr. Jones took a gratified breath and grew silent. While he was delivering these emphatic warnings to Mary Astell, Mr. Williams had regained some measure of composure, the unbecoming beet red of his face fading into blotches of vermilion on his otherwise pasty complexion.

"You will need have no further cause for concern, Mrs. Astell," the churchwarden added with an unctuous smile, smoothing the sleeves of his rumpled coat. "Once she has been examined, she can be sent on her way. But for now, we bid you good day."

•

Having put off the three visitors from the parish, Mary Astell wearily climbed the stairs, preparing herself for another encounter. She could avoid the girl no longer. In spite of all her exertions, Astell had made little progress in finding the man who seemed to have seduced and abandoned Letty Pyke, and she was now reconciled to the view that the impudent rogue would not be found. As she had come to fear, Letty would be sent out of the parish—the visit from Mr. Williams had served to make that very clear. Nor would the girl be able to return to London, where she had established no claim to a settlement. The unfortunate Letty might be able to return to Exeter, though it was hard to see just how she could make her way there, in her current condition.

Astell met Sarah on the landing. "Have they gone, then?" the girl whispered.

"Yes, for the moment," Astell replied, looking past her toward Letty.

"You can be sure they will be back, ma'am," Sarah said. She crept quietly out of the room and down the stairs without her usual bumping and thumping. Astell entered the room and stood by the side of the bed, looking down at Letty. For the moment, the girl seemed chastened.

"Whatever shall I do?" she wailed.

"We will not worry about that for the moment," Astell replied, all the while knowing that she herself was worrying a very great deal.

"And I suppose you have not found my lord and husband," Letty said. A bit of her former haughty tone had crept back into her voice.

"No, I have not, and I fear he is not be found," Astell replied. It was better to be honest with her.

"Whatever shall I do?" the girl wailed again, a bit more loudly this time. There was something practiced in her tone, something theatric, even exaggerated. She wiped at a tear on her cheek and fell back onto the pillow.

'Whatever shall I do?' That is the very question, is it not? What is now to be done?

Astell summoned up her patience. If she could not be entirely sympathetic, she could at the very least strive for calm and self-control.

"I am not sure, Letty," Astell replied at last. "I fear you will face many difficulties." She would not mislead Letty about what ahead.

Reason and truth are firm and immutable. She who bottoms on them is on sure ground.

"What do you mean?" asked Letty, a querulous tone returning to her voice. "Since you have been unable to find my husband, I will just have to stay here until you can do so."

"I doubt whether that will be possible," said Astell. "Our recent visitors were here to determine your reason for immigrating—this is not your parish of settlement, you see, and I little doubt but that you will be removed. You will not be able to stay."

"But I am here now!"

"That is as may be, Letty, but you were not born here, married here, or employed here. The ratepayers of Chelsea have no wish to feed you, clothe you, or shelter you. You can be sure that you will be sent off as soon as they deem you are well enough to be examined, which is probably sooner than you might think."

"Well, then, I suppose I will have to go back to Mrs. Rolles."

"Nor will that be possible, I fear. You have broken your indenture."

"She will not be so mean!"

"There is no meanness about it. You must realize that no employer would—or could—afford to take you back, not in your condition."

The girl regarded Astell with a measure of contempt before she slid back down into the bed. "I suppose, then, that you had better find my husband."

Eighteen

Mary Kettilby shook her head as she entered the room. "Even now she refuses to understand how serious her situation is. Mind you, I have seen this kind of willful obstinacy before, so it is nothing new to me, yet I fear what the future holds for her."

"But will they really remove her? A woman in her condition?"

Mrs. Kettilby settled herself in one of the chairs in Mary Astell's parlor. She looked at her friend with disbelief. "Must you ask? They will remove her without a doubt, and they will do so sooner rather than later. Now in the case of a child, such as Sarah was, well, she could be bound out so that the parish did not bear her charges—and you know how well that played out. If it had not been for Lady Catherine taking her in, who knows what would have become of her? But a pregnant stranger? A woman with no husband to be found? You may rest assured that Letty Pyke will be sent on her way as quickly as possible so that neither she nor her child will be chargeable to the parish." The midwife paused for a moment before adding, "I have seen this happen many times."

She turned back to the glowing coals in the grate before rising briskly from her chair. Astell, meanwhile, was so focused on Letty's predicament that she failed to take note of Mrs. Kettilby's reference to Sarah. Even after taking the girl into her home, Mary Astell knew very little about the girl's experiences in the parish. She had never thought to ask.

"And now," the midwife announced, rising to her feet, "I really must be on my way. George will have my further orders ready for me upon my return—that boy allows me no time for rest." Mrs. Kettilby smiled at the thought of her young taskmaster. "As for the girl," she continued, "for now she is doing well enough. Mind you, she is obstinate and willful, but then most women in her condition can be troublesome and changeable. I will call again the next time I am nearby."

As she spoke, the midwife was busy gathering up her various bags, purses, and pouches. "By my reckoning, she will give birth right before Christmas, so there is some time yet. But I fear they will never allow her to stop here."

The fine weather continued. It was unseasonably cold, but with no rain or wind to contend with, Mary Astell enjoyed her short walk to Ranelagh House. Seated now in Lady Ranelagh's small front parlor, she stared at the wood fire burning brightly in the grate.

"So she thinks that she will be allowed to stay right where she is?" asked Lady Catherine. "Well, I am afraid that young woman has another think coming." Lady Catherine was in her most self-righteous temper.

"I have advised her that she will be removed, but I fear she pays little mind to anything I might say," Astell replied.

"We shall see about that."

"For a short while it seemed as if she had given up her delusions, but she has returned to them and clings even more strongly—and since I am no great lady, she disregards all that I have to say. She has her own notions of what is due to her, and I have not been able to disabuse her." Astell sounded weary. "After I told her she would be removed from the parish, she said that she would return to Mrs. Rolles, although that is also quite out of the question. Knowing she would not be welcome there, however, seemed only to relieve her."

Lady Ranelagh was staring thoughtfully into the fire, her complexion safely protected behind an embroidered fire screen. "I had occasion to speak about her to Lord Ranelagh last evening," the young countess began. Lady Catherine looked at her in some disbelief.

Lady Ranelagh frowned at her husband's daughter before continuing. "*No*," she said pointedly to Lady Catherine, "his lordship was not the least interested in Letty Pyke, or at least he was not interested once he learned that she was not a great beauty. And when he was informed about her condition, he grew quite agitated, insisting that you should not even think about bringing *another* pet project into this household." She gazed intently at Lady Catherine to gauge the effect of her words. "He was adamant," she added.

Hoping to avoid any further discussion of Sarah's fractious career at Ranelagh, Lady Catherine changed the subject. "The foolish girl has thrown away her prospects with the milliner, that is clear enough. If there were no child coming, I suppose that another place might yet be found for her—a young woman with good needlework skills will always be employable."

"Given what Lady Ranelagh and I discovered at the Exchange, I doubt whether Letty acquired much in the way of skill with a needle," Astell replied. "And even if she had, Mrs. Wilkin claims that it is very difficult for even the most proficient needlewoman to earn enough to support herself—though naturally the milliner offers quite a different story. But which of those two women is nearer the truth makes no difference because no one would take on a girl in Letty's condition, even if she were a marvel with her needle and thread."

"Precisely," said Lady Catherine. "And she might also have gone into service—" At this suggestion, Lady Ranelagh looked as if she would interrupt, but before she could do so, Lady Catherine hastened to add, "I know, I know, my lady, she regards herself too highly for any such thing, but she would have little choice in the matter. Her airs and pretensions would mean nothing to the justices—with no other employment, she could be bound to compulsory service."

Here Lady Catherine paused. If she had succeeded in solving the problem of Sarah—and Lady Catherine considered her solution to the problem of Sarah to be altogether successful—she regretted not being able to test her mettle with the question of what to do with Letty Pyke. What a challenge that would pose for a lady of her great skill and determination! But after a moment of further reflection, she was forced to admit that it might have been a challenge beyond even her own unsurpassed abilities. And so it was best to acknowledge the impossible situation and to move on. "The quickest and surest remedy for the parish will be her removal," Lady Catherine said with finality.

Lady Ranelagh was aghast. "Driving her out of the town? What, I pray, is she to do then? In her condition? Sent away without food or shelter—when she has been so ill? Either she will lie down and die at once, or she will just come right back into the parish and be found squatting in the church porch!"

"Little fear of that," said Lady Catherine. "Mr. King made plans to have it gated and railed as soon as he found that poor widow living there with her five starving children."

"If only Letty's parents had taken more care with her education," Astell said, returning to her old theme. "To introduce a child into the world and then fail to provide her with the means to defend herself from temptation! If only Letty had been rightly educated, she would have been able to see through those artifices that were used to ensnare and deceive her."

"Really, Mary, we are far beyond all that now," said Lady Catherine.

"But ignorance has laid the foundation of vice."

"That may very well be true, Mary, a point you have made on many occasions." Lady Catherine knew her friend's preoccupations and hoped to avoid yet another detour down that well-trod path. "But, as you must admit, no education will cure Letty's present afflictions. No, I fear that removal is the likeliest outcome for her, and even if she were able to make her way back to London, she would likely face the same response—no parish would willingly bear the charges. If she were examined by the justices there, I suppose she might be sent back to Bridewell or to Tothill Fields. Or she could be ordered back to her place of settlement . . . But who can say? It is foolish for us to speculate since we can hardly be expected to know the details of such a process."

"What about the child? What will happen to the child?" asked Lady Ranelagh. "Surely no parish would desert an innocent child?"

Lady Catherine answered only by pursing her lips and raising her eyebrows. The countess of Ranelagh might wonder about the fate of poor bastard children, but she herself had a fairly good idea.

"Despite what Lord Ranelagh may say, I am in a position to offer her relief," insisted Lady Ranelagh. "And you, Lady Catherine, you who are so well known for your acts of charity—between us, surely, we could do something."

"I am not sure you *are* in such a position, my lady," said Lady Catherine. "I doubt whether his lordship would like to see his wife involved in such matters. Who knows what rumors might arise if it were to be discovered that an unmarried girl and her bastard child were taken in by the countess of Ranelagh? As for me, I have been a party to some few arrangements in the past made by Mr. Sancroft. His Grace provided for several unfortunate young women who had been similarly abused. But I only helped to fund his charitable acts—I certainly did not involve myself personally in the arrangements, nor would I presume to do so. It is quite out of the question."

Lady Ranelagh's sympathy for the unsympathetic Letty Pyke was much to be admired, but as a woman only too familiar with the way of the world, she ought to know that there were conventions to be observed. Such were Lady Catherine's opinions at any rate.

But the new countess of Ranelagh, who did indeed know the way of the world, was not willing to allow Lady Catherine the last word. "The way we live now, Lady Catherine, *the way we live now*," she said angrily, shaking her head. "If *I* were to take a lover and bear him a child, as long as I was the pattern of discretion, all would be well. Even my lord and husband would be happy enough to look the other way—lest I remark his own indiscretions! But a woman like Letty—then it is all 'sin' and 'vice' and 'fornication.' Such hypocrisy!"

The countess of Ranelagh's unexpected outburst seemed to shock her as much as it did her companions. Thereafter the three women sat in an uncomfortable silence. Lady Ranelagh glared at Lady Catherine, her face flushed, red patches suffusing cheeks that were usually so delicately pink.

Lady Catherine, averting her eyes, was also red-faced and silent, well aware as she was of her dissolute father's many liaisons and of her elder sister's well-known *amours* at court.

As for Mary Astell, she sat still, her heart racing. Lady Ranelagh's outburst was most unbecoming, and although she was not incorrect in her observations, she was rash in her judgment. And to fall out with Lady Catherine . . .

At that instant, a sober footman entered the small front parlor and approached Lady Ranelagh, bending low in order to speak a few discrete words to her. Her eyes opened wide, and she looked with alarm at Mary Astell before she responded to him. "Show her in, by all means," she said.

"But, Your Ladyship—" the solemn footman began, objecting to her order.

"Show her in at once." Lady Ranelagh was firm, and the footman turned to obey.

"Mary, my dear, I am afraid—" Lady Ranelagh began, as the parlor door slammed open as Sarah, unkempt and short of breath, burst into the room.

The girl did not spare a glance for either Lady Ranelagh or Lady Catherine. As she met the astonished gaze of her mistress, Sarah paused dramatically, spread her arms wide, and declared, "She is gone, ma'am. That Lettuce has just taken herself off! Now, before you blame me, I was not spying on her, not at all, I was only showing Mrs. Methuen up, that is all I was doing, and she was gone! Lettuce, I mean, *she* was gone! No sign of her anywhere—and her nasty old gown, the one you had *me* brush and press, is gone with her. That Lettuce has run clean off, Mrs. Astell."

The three women in the parlor at Ranelagh, so recently at odds, were at once united in astonishment.

Thursday, December 17, 1696

A dreadful frost had fallen early in the month of November, followed by fierce storms and widespread flooding. During the first week of December, the unrelenting rain had turned to snow.

In London, measures undertaken by the Commission on the Coinage had stalled, and the continued shortage of coins made even the simplest of transactions difficult.

While a plot against the king had been discovered before an attempt on His Majesty's life could be made, fears of Jacobite conspiracies persisted. Despite the swirl of rumor and gossip, the king's birthday was celebrated with great thanksgiving, the joyful entertainment concluding with illuminations and bonfires.

The Reverend Sir William Dawes had preached a sermon at the palace of Whitehall, taking as his text a verse from the book of Job: "He disappointeth the devices of the crafty so that their hands cannot perform their enterprise." The king was delighted with the sermon, which was quickly published by special command. It seemed certain that the young prelate would soon be appointed as the new royal chaplain.

In Chelsea, on the property where the house of Sir John Danvers had so recently been pulled down, three new houses were being put up. And the Reverend Francis Atterbury was fined yet again for his failure to keep the river wall opposite his residence in good repair.

Mrs. Kettilby successfully delivered a pair of twins, a boy and a girl, whose baptism was performed at All Saints. That same week, the infant granddaughter of the countess of Radnor was buried in the churchyard.

The November issue of the *Mercure galant* included a letter wickedly satirizing women's fashion—the piece ridiculed the luxurious clothing, stylish coiffures, and "odd" ornaments that were popular at Versailles and predicted that they would soon be all the rage among Englishwomen who aped the fashions of the French court. This distressing bit of humor absorbed the attention of Lady Ranelagh and her favorite *maîtresse couturière* for several days.

Lady Catherine continued to busy herself with her many good works in the parish. She had also begun the daunting process of sorting through her grandmother's letters and papers. A worthy woman of long life and great renown, Katherine Jones, viscountess Ranelagh, had numbered poets, scientists, politicians, and philosophers among her numerous illustrious correspondents.

As Lady Catherine set about the task of sorting and ordering this rich archive, her grandmother's most important legacy, she began to consider whether something ought to be done with the three books of physic Lady Ranelagh had compiled. After some thought on the matter, she concluded that Mary Astell's odd friend, the midwife, might be interested in her grandmother's useful receipts for treating the painful breasts of nursing mothers—an ointment to be applied as needed and a properly prepared cerecloth for binding.

As for Mary Astell, she had settled once again into her quiet routine of prayer, meditation, reading, and reflection.

But on many nights, long after Sarah had thumped her way up the stairs to her bed under the eaves, Astell lay awake, remembering what had transpired during those few disturbing days in October.

On her frequent trips to the city, as she crossed frozen fields and made her way through crowded and muddy streets, Astell wondered what had become of Letty Pyke. The unfortunate girl's time of delivery was rapidly approaching.

And on many occasions, just as Astell's thoughts turned to Letty Pyke, they returned to the duchess of Mazarin. Despite the rain and snow, Hortense Mancini was regularly to be seen on Paradise Row, her coach heading toward London or returning late at night from the city. Mary Astell had no wish to call a second time upon the duchess of Mazarin, but she did harbor a secret desire, one she would not even share with her dearest friend, Lady Catherine—Astell wished that she could see the parrots again.

As she wrote each day in her small study, Mary Astell found the creatures springing unbidden to her mind: "Women have been bred up in idleness their education neglected by imprudent parents who have taught them perhaps to repeat their catechism and say their prayers with as little understanding as a parrot," she wrote. And again: "We make use of words without joining any ideas to them, prating away like parrots who can pronounce words though without the use of reason and without understanding anything by them."

And so the weeks passed. Astell asked about the African boy who had been painted kneeling at the feet of Lady Catherine and her sister. She learned that he was called Demetrius. Astell also discovered, much to her chagrin, that he had been presented as a gift to Lady Frances by an admirer—a sugar planter who had brought the boy with him when he returned to England from the West Indies.

Astell had not yet completed the second part of her *Serious Proposal*, though she promised Mr. Wilkin that he would have it early in the new year. She had begun to think seriously about the women whom she had neglected, those women like Mrs. Rolles who could never be afforded the luxury of withdrawing from the world in order to spend their time in reading and reflection. Astell was determined now to remedy her earlier failing by reassuring these female readers that they too were capable of improving their minds: "An ingenious woman is no prodigy to be stared at, for you have it *in your power* to inform the world that you can, *every one of you*, be such a woman."

But as she sat in her study on that cold December afternoon, she put aside her paper, pen, and ink so that she could turn her attention to a new project that had increasingly occupied her mind: the establishment of a charity-school for girls. A school that would be organized and established by women, funded by women, administered by women, and staffed by women. A school that would meet the needs of girls whose families were otherwise unable to provide for them. A school where girls could be taught to read, write, spell, and cast accounts. A school where girls might be taught to make something of themselves.

Nineteen

The silence in the small house on Paradise Row was broken by a commotion at the front door, followed by Sarah's caterwauling and the hushing sound of someone trying unsuccessfully to calm her.

Mary Astell rose quickly from her desk, but before she could reach the landing, she heard the girl clattering her way up the stairs, howling as she climbed.

Astell sighed. *Now what?*

As soon as Sarah caught sight of Astell's stern face, her mouth snapped shut. As silence fell, Astell looked over the girl's shoulder and saw William, Mr. Wilkin's young apprentice, standing at the bottom of the stairs, shifting uneasily from one foot to the other. "Mrs. Astell," he cried as he looked up, clearly relieved to see her. "If you please, ma'am, Mrs. Wilkin asks that you come at once, without delay."

Brushing past Sarah, who stood frozen on the step where she had stopped, Mary Astell made her way down to the boy. She had never before received such a peremptory summons from the printer or his wife, and she could only assume that Mr. Wilkin had come to some desperate harm. *What could possibly be amiss?*

"I will come post-haste, William, but whatever is the matter? Has your master taken ill? Has there been an accident?"

"No, no, no, ma'am. But Mrs. Wilkin is in a state—some woman arrived at the shop this morning, asking after you, and when she had spoken a few words to my mistress, well, Mrs. Wilkin hurried her right up to the parlor, and then after a bit there was such a fuss and commotion—they both came back down to the shop, and Mrs. Wilkin took up her pen to write a note to you, then she threw it down and told me to come and fetch you as quick as could be. She said I was to tell you it was about that girl—"

"A girl? What girl?" But Astell knew at once the source of Mrs. Wilkin's consternation. "Does she mean Letty Pyke? Has your mistress received some word of Letty Pyke?"

"That may be for all I know, Mrs. Astell, but she did not tell *me* who she was talking about. I know only what I have told you and no more. But Mrs. Wilkin and that other woman are both in a ruffle, that is the very truth, so can you hurry please?"

William had no further need to urge Mary Astell to make haste. While he spoke, she was already making ready for her departure. As she turned to gather what she would need for the journey, she found Sarah at hand with her cloak, hat, and boots. "Thank you," she said and then turned back to William. "I will be with you in a trice, and then let us be on our way."

An icy rain was pelting down, and it was miserably cold. The snow that had fallen a few days earlier still lay on the ground, now lumpy and filthy with the passage of many feet. As soon as they stepped out of the front door and turned toward the city, Mary Astell noticed that the apprentice was already soaked through, his face white with cold. Stopping short, she asked the boy, "Will you stay behind and warm yourself?"

William pressed his lips together and shook his head, determined to accompany her on the trip into town, but Astell was concerned for his well-being. "I will make sure Mrs. Wilkin knows that you stayed behind to warm yourself at my insistence," she said to him. "It will be quite all right for you to linger here a little while."

"No, ma'am, I will be fine."

At that very moment, they were overtaken by the Mazarin coach, just pulling to a stop in front of Hortense Mancini's door. A tall footman, resplendent in his livery, jumped down and stood at the ready. As he helped the duchess descend, she waved gaily to Mary Astell. "Ah, we meet again, Mrs. Astell." And then, sensing Astell's agitation, "Is anything amiss?"

Astell shook her head. She had no wish to explain herself to the likes of Hortense Mancini. "An urgent summons into the city, Your Grace, that is all."

"'An urgent summons.' That is 'all'? What nonsense is this, *Madame* Astell? Mustapha!" As the duchess called out his name, the man himself emerged from the coach, elegantly attired as was his wont. "Mustapha will accompany you and your young companion," she said to Astell. And then, addressing Mustapha, the duchess added, "Mrs. Astell has business of some pressing importance in the city and, as the coach is just at hand, we can ensure her safe and swift journey."

"No need, Your Grace," Astell began. Uncertain of what exactly lay ahead but certain that Letty Pyke was somehow in trouble, Astell had no wish to involve Madam Mazarin. And no desire to be indebted to her.

But the duchess of Mazarin had already issued her instructions to Mustapha, who in turn conveyed them to the coachman. William was grinning with delight at the thought of a journey to town by means of such an impressive conveyance. With Mustapha's hand at her elbow and the elegant footman waiting patiently for her, Astell found herself moving forward. Before she was quite able to account for her actions, she had mounted the footboard and was inside the coach, Mustapha tucking a thick sable robe around her as she sank into the seat.

"With them, boy, or up here with me?" the coachman asked William. After a quick look at Mary Astell, ill at ease among the rich trappings of the duchess of Mazarin's coach, the young apprentice scrambled up onto the box despite the cold. Mustapha gave the signal to be off as he swung inside and onto the seat across from Astell. The coach moved smoothly away from Hortense Mancini's door.

"The boy will direct him," said Mustapha, in answer to Astell's unspoken question. She had indicated to no one her destination. Mustapha adjusted the curtain over the glass windows in the door, sat back in his seat, and settled himself. He did not quiz her. He made no small-talk. He demanded no confidences. And yet the silence between them was easy.

In contrast to the worn elegance of her residence on Paradise Row, Hortense Mancini's coach was bright and stylish. The fashionable new *berline* was smaller and more maneuverable than the massive Ranelagh coach—while Lady Catherine would undoubtedly have judged it to be lacking in solid and substantial dignity, it was quicker and lighter, its ride much smoother. The *berline* was also sumptuously appointed, its interior lined with a deep blue velvet that matched the livery of the coachman and footmen. Heavy curtains of the same velvet were sprinkled lavishly with stars drawn from the Mazarin coat of arms and worked in gold thread. The generous benefactor who provided this coach for the duchess had spared no expense.

Although the way to town was muddy and rutted from all of the rain and snow, they made good time. They soon left the king's road and were rumbling along the Strand, thence to Fleet Street. The city traffic seemed to part for the duchess's coach, with its gilt window frames, glossy varnish, and coat of arms prominently displayed. They were soon in St. Paul's Churchyard, pulling up to the Wilkins' print shop.

As the footman opened the door for Astell to step out, William clambered down from his perch on the box with the coachman. He reached Astell's side just as Elizabeth Wilkin rushed out the door of the shop. On her heels was the last person Mary Astell ever expected to see in the company of the printer's wife: Gertrude Rolles, the milliner from the Royal Exchange.

"I can see now why you have made such good time," Mrs. Wilkin sniffed, looking askance at the rich and showy coach before adding, "Pray, come up at once."

Before Astell had time to reply, Mrs. Wilkin turned, putting her arm around the Exchange woman, the two bending their heads together in close confidence as they entered the shop under the sign of the King's

Head. "And you," the printer's wife suddenly added, suddenly rounding on the young apprentice, "off with you now."

William, surrounded by a few rowdy apprentices envious of his ride atop the coach, caught Mary Astell's eye, gave a wicked grin, and shrugged. After a final celebratory clap on the shoulder from one of his fellows, he ducked inside the shop, searching for Mr. Wilkin.

Having paused to watch the boy enjoy his momentary pleasure, Astell discovered that the two women had left her standing alone in the street. As she hastened to join them, Mrs. Wilkin called to her. "Mrs. Astell, make haste, if you please!" There was excitement in her voice, but also something else—a note of fear, perhaps, or of dread.

Before following them, Astell turned again toward the coach. Now that she had reached her destination, she assumed Mustapha would return to Paradise Row, but he leaned out of the window, signaling that he would be waiting for her to conclude her business. Rather than engage in a public debate, Astell turned and entered the shop.

Quickly climbing up to the parlor, she saw that, despite Mrs. Wilkin's earlier disdain for milliners, the two women were thick as peas in a pod. They were seated comfortably before the fire, quite as if they were old and intimate friends enjoying a bit of a gossip on a winter's afternoon.

"Now, then—" the printer's wife began, glancing apprehensively as Mary Astell joined them.

"Pray tell me, what news?" Astell cut right to the point. "The boy could offer no details, but I gather there has been some word of Letty Pyke—is she here? Or has she made her way back to you, Mrs. Rolles? I have heard nothing myself in all this time. It has been nearly two months since she disappeared." She looked from Mrs. Wilkin to Mrs. Rolles, waiting expectantly.

After a nod from Mrs. Wilkin, the milliner turned to Mary Astell and began. "Well, now," she said slowly, "it was not long after you and her ladyship paid your visit to me that Letty Pyke turned up again—"

"But that was weeks ago!" Astell could not hide her surprise. "Why did you not send for me at once?"

"Well, I suppose I could have sent you word, Mrs. Astell—but I saw no reason for doing so, and to be fair, you left me with no means of getting news to you even if I *had* thought to do so. I ask you, just how was I to know where to send for you? Did you think to tell me where you were living? When I finally decided you *should* be informed, the only way I could think of to find you was to look in your book, for surely your bookseller would know how to reach you. And there it was, 'R. Wilkin, at the King's Head in St. Paul's Churchyard.' So that is what I did, and that is why I am here now."

"And very ingenious of you too, it was," said Mrs. Wilkin, consoling her new friend. The two women nodded in unison, in complete agreement about the Exchange woman's undeniable cleverness.

Her ingenuity established, Mrs. Rolles continued. "In any case, Mrs. Astell, I had no reason to think Letty Pyke had left you without you knowing all about it, and as I have just said, I had no way of knowing you might be worried about her. I will remind you that when you paid me a visit, you were asking only about a husband and a marriage—why would I have any reason to send for you just because Letty Pyke was back in London?

"And once she was back, I had every reason for *not* involving you or her ladyship. Perhaps it was wrong of me, and if so I do beg your pardon, but hear me out now, I pray you, and then judge for yourself." Mrs. Rolles had a reproachful look on her face. Mary Astell held her tongue, waiting for the milliner to continue.

"Now then, Mrs. Astell," Mrs. Rolles said, a hint of indignation in her voice. "In a word—and I must speak frankly—the sight of Letty made it clear to me what had happened between the day she was committed to Bridewell and the day she turned up on your doorstep. Just as soon as I saw her or, rather, as soon as I laid my eyes on that bit of trumpery she was wearing, I could tell well enough how Letty Pyke had managed to get herself out of that place. How she had come to leave Bridewell, I mean—that was something about which you and her ladyship had questions, if you recall.

"You see, Mrs. Astell, and I speak frankly now, there are some women in this city whose business is to trade in young girls—country girls just arrived in the city who are looking to find work, poor girls whose parents are willing to sell off their daughters for a bit of easy money, and foolish girls like Letty who have gotten themselves into one sort of trouble or another . . . That is just the way it is, Mrs. Astell, though there is no reason for a woman such as yourself to know these things. But, as I say, there are dishonest women who are always on the lookout for fresh wares with which to stock their notorious houses.

"And such women are especially eager to buy the freedom of likely girls who have been sent to Bridewell—why, Bridewell is a great emporium for these women, and they can shop there for good merchandise at their ease. A little coin slipped quietly to the right jailer, and any girl they want is theirs, no questions asked. They can carry their purchase away with them at once! Now, excuse me for my frankness, but this, you must understand, is how Letty Pyke came to be out of Bridewell so soon after she was committed—but that girl leapt right out of the frying-pan and into the fire.

"As I say, that gaudy gown she was wearing told me all that I needed to know. I could see at once that Mrs. Wisebourne, a notorious old bawd, must have bought Letty's freedom. She is known to frequent Bridewell, looking for new girls. Once she has them in hand, she clothes them in showy attire, dresses them up with paint and patches, and pretends to everyone that she is a mantua-maker and that her brothel house is a millinery shop! No one believes her, for her real business is known to all, but so it is. Now I ask you, is it any wonder why honest women of my trade are subject to suspicion?" Mrs. Rolles glanced with some lingering resentment at Mrs. Wilkin, who mollified her new friend with a quick squeeze of her hand.

Mary Astell looked at both women with shock and confusion. "I can hardly take this in, Mrs. Rolles. But if your suspicion is correct, I wonder what such a woman would have wanted with Letty Pyke. The girl is no great beauty, after all—and in her condition?"

"Youth is all the beauty that is required, Mrs. Astell. Again, and I speak plainly, this Mrs. Wisebourne is well known in the business for selling a girl's maidenhead to the highest bidder. Of course, the old bawd knows all the tricks for mending and repairing a girl's virginity, so she is able to sell this same 'maidenhead' over and over again. A girl of Letty's youth is a profitable investment for Mrs. Wisebourne."

"But surely Letty would never go willingly with such a woman?"

"Oh, Mrs. Astell," Mrs. Rolles said, shaking her head sadly, "she likely had no choice in the matter. If Mrs. Wisebourne pays the right price to the right man, the unfortunate girl will belong to her, like it or not, and off the girl will go, whether she wants to or not. But Letty may not have known any better. 'Mother Whybourne,' as she is also pleased to call herself, is practiced in her trade, and she knows how to allay a girl's suspicions. The old bawd carries her prayer book with her into the prison, claiming she is a pious woman who aims to save the poor souls who have been committed there. As 'Mother Whybourne,' she offers sympathy and assistance to the foolish girls who have been committed to Bridewell. It is all lies, of course, and the woman is a terrible fraud, but there you are. It is likely that Letty went with the woman willingly enough.

"Of course, it may also be that Letty Pyke had her own tricks to play. No woman who runs her business as sharply as Mrs. Wisebourne does would bother to take on a girl who was already breeding, not when there are so many other likely girls to choose from. Why, a woman as well practiced as Mrs. Wisebourne is spoiled for choice these days! Who can say exactly how it all played out? When Letty turned up again, I asked her about it—she clapped her mouth shut and would not say a word, but I knew the truth of it all, I tell you, as soon as I saw that dress.

"Now one thing will be of great interest to you, Mrs. Astell, given your previous inquiries. Mrs. Wisebourne's premises are on Drury Lane, near the theater—those who are known to frequent her fine house are all men of quality, courtiers and clerics among them. Why, even some of those zealous moralists who belong to the Society for the Reformation of Manners have been known to sample the pleasures on offer at Mrs. Wisebourne's house. And among all the rest, Charles Beauclerk, duke of St. Albans, is well known as a frequent and a welcome guest. Perhaps it was there, at the bordel, that Letty Pyke got it into her head she was 'Lettice de Beauclerk,' wife of a fine young lord. Who can say the truth of it? She might even have met him there . . . " Mrs. Rolles stopped, raising her eyebrows as she let this bit of speculation linger in the air.

Mary Astell, that woman of words, was for once at a loss for words. She stared blankly at Mrs. Rolles and Mrs. Wilkin, who was still nodding her head vigorously as the milliner told her tale.

"Now, I trust, you can see why I would never have sent word to Lady Ranelagh when Letty Pyke returned to London," said Gertrude Rolles. "Even if I imagined her to have any further interest in the girl, I would have known not to involve her ladyship. Nor could any good have come from further entangling you, Mrs. Astell. A woman on her own needs to be doubly careful of her reputation."

Astell recovered her thoughts and her tongue. "Your discretion is commendable, Mrs. Rolles, and you are undoubtedly correct, especially in your concern for Lady Ranelagh. I should never have questioned your judgment. But you *have* sent for me now."

"Yes, Mrs. Astell, though Mrs. Wilkin and I have been in some doubt as to whether we should—"

"But you have, and so I ask you again, what has happened? If Letty returned to you all those weeks ago, what has changed? Why do you send for me now?" Astell appreciated the caution of the two women, but the length of Mrs. Rolles's story was testing the limits of her self-control.

As if sensing Mary Astell's impatience, Mrs. Wilkin reached out and placed her hand on Mary Astell's. "Remember, Mrs. Astell, that we judge amiss when our judgment is hasty," she cautioned.

Astell looked from one woman to the other. They exchanged worried glances before Mrs. Rolles again took up her story. "Now, as I said, Letty showed up not long after you and her ladyship were at the Exchange. She could never make her way inside, of course—dressed as she was, like a common strumpet, and all dirty and bedraggled besides. The entrance was barred to her. But she waited for me outside, she did, and once she made herself known, I had to shoo her off in no uncertain terms."

And then, when it looked as if Astell would object, Mrs. Rolles added, "I am not heartless, Mrs. Astell. I sent her on her way with a little money in her pocket and a bit of a wrap so she could keep herself warm—which, I will say, was more than she had when she turned up at the Exchange."

The milliner spoke pointedly, casting a meaningful look at Mrs. Wilkin, who was once more nodding in agreement. The two had clearly concluded that Astell's treatment of the girl had been unduly harsh, that Astell had sent Letty on her away with nothing. Mary Astell had said very little to the printer's wife about Letty after the girl left Chelsea, so neither of the London women knew the circumstances of Letty's disappearance. But defending herself against a charge of negligence was not Astell's concern at the moment.

In any case, Mrs. Rolles had resumed her narrative. "And then, Mrs. Astell, there was quite a tussle—for a while Letty was back and forth between the parish of St. Michael Cornhill and the parish of St. Bartholomew-by-the-Exchange. Now St. Michael's, that is my church, but of course they wanted nothing to do with her since she had not been long in the parish to begin with and was no longer living there at all. And St. Bartholomew's also refused her since she had never resided in the parish—she had only been employed there but not for long at that. Neither one wanted to be burdened with an unmarried girl, soon to give birth.

"It was the same push and pull as before, right after she left my employ, and just as before, she would no doubt have come to the attention of the justices of the peace soon enough, and I am sure that they would have sent her right back to Bridewell, but . . . "

At this point, Mrs. Rolles stopped, and she hesitated, as if unable to continue. "There, there," said Mrs. Wilkin softly, seeing her new companion so overcome with emotion. Mrs. Rolles took out a fine lawn handkerchief to daub at her eyes while Mrs. Wilkin took over the story for her. "But before the churchwardens in either parish could decide what to do with the girl, aside from making sure she was not chargeable to their ratepayers, she was gone again. And all seemed well for a time— the problem of Letty Pyke had once more solved itself."

Just as Mary Astell thought she would be unable to control her irritation for one more minute, Mrs. Rolles blurted out where all of this background, detail, and explanation had been heading. "But she gave birth in Sweeting's Alley, near the Exchange, the last night in November, all alone and in secret. And then, Mrs. Astell, she killed the babe and left the little body lying in a gutter, blood everywhere. The poor infant was discovered the next day, covered up in a bit of the wrap I had given Letty. And that Letty—well, she was found and arrested straightaway, everyone knew it was she who had done it. She was taken off to Newgate until she could be tried at the Old Bailey sessions. And she was found guilty, Mrs. Astell, condemned to death for the murdering of her own child."

Twenty

When Mary Astell asked to be driven to Newgate, Mustapha did not challenge her, frown at her, or argue with her. Nor did he furrow his brow in consternation or raise his eyebrows in astonishment. In fact, without so much as a word, he spoke briefly to the coachman and then slipped inside the *berline* as it left the churchyard and wheeled back down Ludgate Street, turning north onto Warwick Lane. The Ranelagh coach could never have managed the narrow, rutted passage, but before Astell had time to register this, the duchess of Mazarin's sleek *berline* made a sharp left turn and quickly drew to a stop on Newgate Street, just short of the tall brick buildings that stretched along the south side of the street.

She had not realized that the prison was so close to Mr. Wilkin's bookshop—even Lady Catherine could have managed the short walk, though doubtless she would never have been persuaded to venture that short distance on foot, much less to visit a prison. Having been handed out of the coach once more by the liveried footman, Mary Astell stood some way from the arched gate that spanned the street. Three female figures—she thought they were intended to represent Justice, Mercy, and Truth—stood guard over the portcullis, each one oddly imprisoned within her own stone niche.

Newgate was one of the principal gates built into the old medieval wall surrounding the city of London, but from the start, the gatehouse had also been used as a prison. (King John was particularly fond of Newgate "for the safe-keeping" of his many prisoners.) The original structure had been repaired many times over the centuries before it was destroyed by the Great Fire. The prison was deemed so essential that its immediate reconstruction had been funded by a generous government subsidy, and it reopened just five short years after the fire.

But that was long before Mary Astell's arrival in the city.

Now, as she stood on the street outside Newgate, she could not help but note its grand façade, in the Italian style, about which there had been such a public outcry when it was rebuilt. As a prison, it was still "a dismal failure," as the anonymous writer of a recent broadsheet avowed. In an opinion shared by many, he claimed that the building had been designed "rather for ornament than use," the structure "of more cost and beauty than was necessary"—the "sumptuousness" of the building's "outside" served only to aggravate "the misery of the poor wretches within.

"You will be in need of this, *madame*." As he spoke, Mustapha put a fat pouch into Astell's hand. Although coins were in short supply everywhere in the city and beyond, his bag was heavy with them. As she attempted to return it to him, he put her off. "Trust me, Mrs. Astell," he said, "you will need all this and more. The girl will not survive without someone paying her garnish—she will have to have money for a mattress, a blanket, even for bread to eat, and if she has been ironed, her fetters will only be loosed after a payment for easement."

He smiled ruefully, adding, after a brief pause, "The vicissitudes of her life have taught the duchess of Mazarin a few very useful lessons, the chiefest of which is that ready money is the only sure remedy for many of life's pains."

Although Astell could hardly agree with the wisdom of Hortense Mancini's observation, she acknowledged Mustapha's great kindness. Her hand trembled as she tucked the pouch into her pocket.

"Just continue down the street," he advised. "The keeper's house is there, on the right, just before you reach the gate, but it is best not to ask for Mr. Fell. Avoid him if you can. The entrance to the prison is directly across from his door. The girl will have been brought there, and with no money, she is likely there still. You will have to pay for any information, but for the right price, you should be able to learn where she is, and you ought to be able to see her. You will doubtless be met by the turnkey—but I suggest that you have no dealings with Mr. Robinson either, if you can help it. Insist on seeing the ordinary." Mustapha spoke calmly, as if conveying the most commonplace of directions. "Of course, Mr. Smith is also keenly interested in turning a profit, but he is at least a clergyman."

"*The Ordinary's Accounts* are his invention? They are the work of a *clergyman*?" The pamphlets, purportedly recording the criminal offenses and dying words of condemned "malefactors" just before they were executed at Tyburn, were published after every hanging day and sold thousands of copies. Astell had often seen them in the hands of eager readers, but she had believed them to be works of fiction, not the crass handiwork of a man of the cloth.

"A perquisite of his office as chaplain of Newgate," said Mustapha.

Astell closed her eyes and sighed. While they made great show of warning eager readers about the horrible wages of sin, the *Accounts* were snapped up for their gruesome stories rather than their moral teaching—the cheap publication competed with the even cheaper broadsheets that reported on sensational crimes and their ghastly punishments. Astell could hardly pass through the city without having one or the other waved in her face or thrust into her hands, but she had not realized that a priest—*a man of God*—made money on the misery of those whose souls were in his charge.

"I am indebted to you for all your kindness, Mustapha. Please express my gratitude to Her Grace, as well—I am perfectly able to manage from here, and so I bid you farewell."

"Nonsense, Mrs. Astell. You will find us waiting here when you have concluded your business."

She nodded in agreement, thankful for his presence. Then, squaring her shoulders, she studied the sprawling prison that stretched along Newgate Street. She walked slowly forward.

The stench was worse the farther she went, as if the looming brick walls concentrated the noxious stew of filth and disease. An open sewer ran across the street in front of her. She was also assaulted by a hellish noise—roaring, swearing, shrieking, and clamor. She saw a low doorway on her left, just this side of the gate, which seemed to be the entrance Mustapha had described. Taking a deep breath, she passed through the door and stepped down into a dark, cramped space. Before her eyes could adjust to the dim light, a large figure suddenly appeared, rattling a bunch of keys in his hands, a small, slatternly woman at his side.

"Look here, Doll—if I am not mistaken, we shall have a hot supper tonight and a quartern of brandy to keep us warm," the man bawled to his companion while rubbing his hands together vigorously. "Call the cellar-man at once, I say! This fine lady looks as if she has brought the blunt, and we will have our share before it is all over with, mark me." And then, leering as if he were already drunk, the man turned his gaze to Mary Astell. "Welcome to the lodge, welcome, I say!"

"Madam," Astell said, addressing the woman rather than the shadowy male figure. The woman might be dirty and unkempt, but she did not look drunk—or, at least, she did not look quite as drunk as the keeper appeared to be. "I wish to speak to Mr. Smith."

"Aye, and so do I, now that's the truth of it," the little woman cackled. She slapped her knees with glee, almost overcome with hilarity.

"Off with you," the man bellowed, giving Doll, if that was her name, a great cuff that sent her crashing to the filthy stone floor. She quickly crawled out of reach before scrambling to her feet and dashing out the door.

"Madam," the man said, mimicking Astell's demeanor and tone, "a worthy lady like you must have come here on business of some import." He dropped the impersonation then, adding, "So speak plainly—I do not have all day."

"I will speak with Mr. Smith," she repeated.

"Then I suppose you will not speak," he said, "for he is a busy man and cannot come just because it may please you."

Astell wondered if one of Mustapha's coins might secure a different answer, but she thought it advisable not to produce the plump bag that he had given her. She fumbled a bit in her pocket, at last withdrawing a small silver penny, perfect and unclipped.

The turnkey staggered and squinted as she held out the coin. "Very nice it is, ma'am, but of what use is a penny to me when my brandy will cost me four pence?"

She thought that he had consumed quite enough brandy already, but instead of the sharp retort she longed to deliver, she quietly pulled two more coins out of the bag concealed in her pocket. "I trust that this will do," she said, calculating that it would be enough. He did not seem like a man who would refuse any sum, particularly not when the coins were right before his eyes.

"Tomorrow, around this time," he growled, lurching toward her—or, rather, toward the pennies. He grabbed them and turned on his heel, disappearing back into the gloom.

Astell stood there, in the filth and stink of the lodge, momentarily in doubt about what had transpired. But as she turned to leave, she found the woman, Doll, waiting for her on the street, just outside the door. The woman sidled up to Astell. "Mayhap I can be of use, madam," she said, cringing as if she expected another blow. "I know most of what goes on in here, I do, and what I do not know, I can find out."

Astell did a careful calculation and then reached once more into Mustapha's bag, pulling out a glittering sixpence. Another perfect coin, newly minted, with an engraved and milled edge.

Doll's bleary eyes grew large, but she made no move to reach for the coin. She stood as if transfixed while Astell considered what to ask. "I am seeking a girl," she began, "just found guilty."

"Aye, there's lots come here, looking for a girl!" Doll guffawed, once more delighted by her own wit, then continued in a more sober fashion. "Well, what's this girl done then, eh? There's women a-plenty in here, some coiners, some debtors, some pickpockets, and any number of housebreakers, thieves, shoplifters, and such-like. Even a woman who has stolen some sheep—six ewes and six wethers, she stole, but not a single ram!" At this, Doll doubled over, laughing uproariously.

"She has been condemned to death," said Astell.

"Ahh, clipping coins," said Doll, shaking her head knowingly.

"No, not for clipping coins," said Astell.

"There are a few women here found guilty of that, waiting for the hangman," replied Doll, as if she had not heard Astell.

"She did not clip coins," repeated Astell. "She was found guilty of the murder of her child."

Doll's eyes filled with loathing, and she spat onto the foul street where they were standing. "A filthy and unnatural act it is, and I will gladly see her hang for it."

"But is she here? Have you seen her?"

"Aye, I know who you mean, she's here, and I've seen her too, I have. All filled with woe, she is, as well she should be, crying and complaining and lamenting her fate—she should have thought about that before she killed her poor innocent babe, I say."

"But how does she fare? When I last saw her, she was very ill, and she has just recently given birth, so she is probably quite weak as well."

Doll looked at Astell as if she were crazed, then softened a bit. Astell thought to press home her point, hoping she might gain an advantage with Doll. "The girl is just a child herself," Astell urged, "and she was all alone in her time of travail without even so much as a friend to assist her."

"And where were you then, I wonder?" Doll asked. "When this poor, sick girl was all in trouble and alone, I mean. Where were you? A friend like you is not much use to her now, are you?"

The woman was right, Astell reflected. *Where was I? Could I have prevented this tragedy?*

But Doll did not wait for an answer. "She should by rights still be here, in the lodge, since she's not paid her garnishment. Mr. Robinson is not at all happy, I can tell you, since he did not get his two-and-sixpence from her before she was moved. It was Mr. Fell took her right on up to the hold for condemned women, quick as could be. She looks like to die before she's hanged—he wanted her out of the way, I suppose. At least he had that fine gown off her, so he's got something for his trouble, but Mr. Robinson, now, he got nothing at all, and that's the truth."

"The keeper took her gown?" Astell was aghast.

"Oh, that's nothing," Doll replied, waving her hand airily. "She's still got her petticoat and her stays. Of course, now, if she was up for it, she could easily earn enough here to keep herself warm and well supplied with food and drink and *still* make sure Mr. Robinson got his, if you know what I mean, but as it is . . . "

Doll's explanation trailed off, but she shot a crafty glance in Mary Astell's direction and then, clearly thinking about the bright coin in Astell's palm, she continued her recitation. "Plenty of women are happy to earn what they can how they can while they are here, and even if they are just waiting for the hangman, it's still worth their while to make themselves more comfortable. And then there's always a chance—a woman can plead her belly and, who knows, she may just get lucky. A Newgate baby will earn her a delay in her execution." Doll winked and nodded.

"Now, in the hold where the girl is," she said, rattling along, "there's a wooden barracks on the wall so she's not on a stone floor, but there's no fireplace and she's got no blanket. In this cold, she's like to freeze to death before she's hanged, that's the truth of it. She's got nothing at all, ma'am, no food and nothing to drink. No candle either, and it's a dark and dismal place." At this point, the woman stopped, looking pointedly at Astell. "And she is still ironed."

"Can you assist her at all? Can you provide any of what she might need? A blanket at least, and something for her to eat. And can you tell she has friends who will be doing their best on her behalf?

"A murderer, ma'am? And not just a murderer, but one who's killed her own sweet infant? Are you asking me to do that for such a one as she is? A woman who's done what she's done?" Doll opened her eyes wide and assumed a look of virtue.

"I am," said Astell.

"Well, I suppose could see to her, ma'am," Doll responded.

She looked at Astell for a few moments before adding, "I am a good ward-woman, I am. I do what I can. I could get her what she needs, I could. It'll cost, but anything can be got for the rhino."

Seeing Astell's perplexed expression, Doll added, "The ready, ma'am, the ready, the blunt, the rhino, the *money*." She rolled her eyes in exasperation. Astell held out the shiny sixpence.

"Will this suffice?"

"It's a start," said Doll, reaching for the coin.

"I must know what you can provide," said Astell, withdrawing the money from Doll's grasp. Astell had learned from her encounter with Mr. Robinson.

"I cannot promise to ease her fetters—only Mr. Robinson can do that—but I can get her a blanket and a bit of bread."

"Can you also let her know that someone has been here, asking after her?"

"That too, ma'am." As she spoke, Doll glanced uneasily at the doorway of the lodge, perhaps wary that the turnkey would emerge. Seeing no one, she added, "I can do that, I can. Shall I tell her who was here asking after her?"

"Tell her Mrs. Astell has been here. And tell her I will return tomorrow. Mr. Robinson has said that I will be able to speak to the Reverend Mr. Smith tomorrow. Will he keep his word?"

"Not like, ma'am, but then, who knows? Perhaps. If he thinks there's more to be had from you, perhaps."

"I want to speak to the girl. If Mr. Robinson is not to be trusted, where will I be able to find Mr. Smith?"

"Oh, that. Now, you won't have need of Mr. Smith to see the girl. Just the rhino. Mr. Robinson will be more than happy to arrange all that for you." At that she winked and nodded again, clearly confident that Astell had been schooled. "Mr. Robinson will be happy to oblige you about that," she repeated, "and he is always here. He can bring her down to the gigger in no time." And then she clarified her meaning. "There's a hallway right next to the lodge—prisoners are brought down there, and they speak to their guests through a grate in the door. Mr. Smith has nothing to do with any of that. You will have no need of him. Now, it will cost you—one-and-six a day—but you can see her, no doubt about it. Mr. Robinson will be happy to oblige, no doubt at all."

While she delivered these assurances, Doll looked over Mary Astell's shoulder, clearly worried that the drunken turnkey would emerge from the lodge at any moment. Astell thought she had extracted as much from the woman as she could. She doubted whether the ward-woman would keep her word, but without Doll's help, Letty would receive nothing. And so, before Doll could dash away, Astell placed the coin into her grubby hand. The woman gave a sharp nod, scuttling quickly down Newgate Street before she disappeared.

Astell watched her go and then followed, eager to escape from the smells and sounds of the prisoners. Just beyond the lodge, she passed a large door—she realized that this must open into the hall where she would be able to speak with Letty. She could also see a few stone steps leading down into what looked like a cellar below the hall—the bellowing, cursing, carousing, and roaring that filled her ears seemed to emanate from this cellar, doubtless the tap-room where Mr. Robinson enjoyed his brandy.

As she hurried by, she saw another stone stairway, this one leading up—it was here that Doll seemed to have disappeared. Perhaps the woman would be as good as her word, even now carrying relief to the poor girl who was imprisoned in a hold for the condemned.

Astell's voice shook with anger and revulsion. "It is a nursery of crime and vice. A seminary of degeneracy. A tomb for the living. The very emblem of hell itself."

They were traveling back to Chelsea. The Mazarin coach had been waiting for Astell right where it had stopped on the approach to the prison. As she emerged from the gloomy complex and made her way back down the street, she had been met by the liveried footman and handed into the *berline*. Rather than attempting to squeeze through the narrow street that led through the gate and onto Holborn, the coachman turned the coach in a neat maneuver and retreated down Newgate Street and then Warwick Lane, emerging on Ludgate, thence to Fleet Street and the Strand.

"I am sorry you have had to experience the horrors of Newgate, Mrs. Astell," said Mustapha.

"I am indebted to you, sir. I would not have fared half so well without your knowledge of the way things must be done there."

Although Astell did not expect personal confidences from Mustapha, they were approaching a degree of intimacy that she had not anticipated. While he had not asked about her visit with Mrs. Wilkin nor questioned her when she asked to be taken to Newgate, he seemed to be well aware of the reason for her urgent meeting with the printer's wife and her trip to the prison. She had had little time to reflect upon the day's events, but she could not help but wonder how it was that Mustapha knew so much about the way business was conducted in that dreadful place.

Not for the first time in their brief acquaintance, he seemed to read her thoughts. "I have traveled far and wide on Her Grace's business," he said. "We have faced more than a few disagreeable situations over the years." He paused before continuing. "The duchess of Mazarin is a remarkable woman," he said before falling silent, as if that was all that needed to be said on the subject.

By the time they approached Charing Cross, Astell had resolved upon her course of action. "If you please, Mustapha, once we are approaching the village, I will ask to be put down just at Franklin's Lane. I need to go on to Little Chelsea, and that will be a convenient place to part ways."

"Her Grace would not thank us for leaving you in such a spot, Mrs. Astell," said Mustapha. "We will see you to the end of your journey." He signaled to the coachman with a sharp rap, then slid open a small door and issued a few words to the driver, who leaned back from his perch to receive his new instructions.

"There," said Mustapha, settling himself back into his seat. "We will take the road from Knightsbridge."

"I fear it is out of your way," Astell objected, "and I have already taken up too much of your time."

"There is no need for you to be at all concerned," he replied. "Her Grace would have us do no less."

Twenty-One

The arrival of Hortense Mancini's elegant coach in Little Chelsea caused a flurry of excitement among a handful of small boys as it drew to a halt before Mrs. Kettilby's cottage. Despite the cold, the boys seemed to have been enjoying themselves, kicking at the melting snow and stamping in puddles of half-frozen mud. George, the midwife's capable assistant, separated himself from the ragged, boisterous group as Mary Astell emerged from the *berline*, its door emblazoned with the Mazarin crest. He assumed a dignified pose, saluted the footman as he handed Astell out, and then ushered her toward the little house.

"Mrs. Kettilby has just now returned from a very hard delivery," he informed her, "but she will be pleased that you have called."

As they reached the door of Mrs. Kettilby's cottage, Astell turned back to the highway. The coach had already performed a well-executed reversal and was pulling away. She wondered whether the coachman would find Church Lane passable after all the snow and rain, or whether he would be forced to go as far as Blacklands in order to return to Paradise Row. But she set aside her concern about the conditions of the roadway as soon as Mrs. Kettilby opened her door.

"Mrs. Astell, do come in—how good it is to see you here," said the midwife.

It was warm in the cottage. Astell was pleased to see a glowing fire in the grate and a plentiful supply of coal in the box. Mrs. Kettilby helped her remove her cloak while George bustled about, pulling a chair closer to the warmth. Astell sank down into it gratefully—despite the luxury of the coach, she was chilled through and, she realized, very tired. She also thought the stench of the prison clung to her garments.

"What is it?" asked Mary Kettilby, gesturing for the boy to bring some refreshment for their guest. George looked longingly at the fragrant kettle of pea soup simmering over the fire but, knowing Mary Astell's preferences, he cut a few thick slices of bread—Mrs. Kettilby's loaf was extremely good—and set them on a small plate on a low table he positioned carefully by Astell's side.

"And a little of the elderberry water, I think," said Mrs. Kettilby, observing her friend's weary expression. "It is a very wholesome cordial, Mrs. Astell, and it will help to restore your strength and spirits."

"Thank you," Astell said with a deep sigh.

"And now, I think, you had best leave us for a little while, George. You will come back later, of course," said Mrs. Kettilby, "for I will want your opinion on that soup."

Even before the midwife had finished speaking, her young assistant, displaying both his excellent judgment and his sense of discretion, was in retreat. He nodded sharply to both women, quietly shutting the door of the cottage as he left them. Mrs. Kettilby sat down next to her friend.

"I am afraid I have come about Letty Pyke," said Astell, without any further prompting. "A few hours ago, I received an urgent message— from Mrs. Wilkin, of all people—summoning me to the city. The boy who delivered it knew nothing, other than suggesting it had something to do with Letty Pyke, so I was off as quick as could be, hurrying to town to see whatever was the matter. I was not certain how Mrs. Wilkin had become involved with Letty, but I expected to see the girl herself, and I thought perhaps she might be preparing to give birth. But that was not the case—instead, the news was very grim."

Astell paused, staring into the fire for a moment. Mrs. Kettilby sat quietly, waiting for Astell to continue. "I found Mrs. Rolles with Mrs. Wilkin—if you recall, she was the milliner to whom Letty had been apprenticed—it was she who had seen Letty. According to what Mrs. Rolles had to say, the girl had somehow made her way back to London and turned up at the Exchange, expecting her former mistress to take her in. Of course, Letty was sorely disappointed on that score—Mrs. Rolles refused to have anything to do with her. And given the trouble Letty was in, Mrs. Rolles is not to be blamed."

After another deep sigh, Astell continued. "In any event, the girl seems to have tarried for a while in the neighborhood, but she found no welcome anywhere. And then, without any shelter or support, she was gone again, no one knows where." As Mary Kettilby urged a bit of the cordial on her guest, Astell sipped it gratefully. "Not that anyone was bothered by Letty's disappearance. Quite the opposite. As far as Mrs. Rolles was concerned, that was the end of the matter."

"When was all this? And how was Letty's health?"

"I am not altogether sure just when the girl turned up, but I gather it was not long after she left us. Likely she went straight back to the city, but that is only a guess. Nor did Mrs. Rolles have anything to say about her condition, only that the girl was dirty and cold. But that was not why Mrs. Wilkin summoned me this morning—all that was weeks ago. The reason she sent for me today is far worse, I am afraid." Astell shuddered. "You see, wherever Letty disappeared to after she finally left Mrs. Rolles, she must have gone back yet again, or at least tried to—she was alone in the neighborhood of the Exchange when she gave birth, right on the street, it seems. The infant was found lying in a gutter the next day. Dead. And Letty was discovered close by. That was at the end of the month. Last month, I mean. The end of November."

Mary Kettilby did not seem at all shocked by the story Astell related. Her face was filled with pity rather than disgust or anger. "Probably died of cold, the poor little thing. And Letty? Is she now being looked after properly? Do you want me to attend to her?"

"But that is the thing, you see—the infant did not die a natural death, or so it seems," said Astell. "According to the story Mrs. Rolles told, Letty abandoned the child, but only after she—the baby was a girl—had died. And it seems the infant did not die from exposure—her body was discovered the next morning, lying in a pool of blood. After Letty was located, she was examined and charged with murder—she has already faced a judge and been found guilty of the crime. Her trial was a few days ago—at the last sessions. She is being held in Newgate now, waiting to be hanged."

"A quantity of blood, you say? And not the mother's blood, but the infant's blood? Most unusual," said Mrs. Kettilby. "In such a situation, with a girl who has no experience in such things, I could well imagine her new-born infant dying from exposure or from simple ignorance . . . Letty knows nothing of childbirth and delivery—so much could have gone wrong. And the child may have come before its time—I would not have been surprised if the baby were still-borne.

"But blood? And that blood belonging to the baby? Now, I have known more than one distracted woman who has been driven by circumstance to extreme measures, abandoning her child and leaving it to die, or even smothering her baby. But violent acts are something else again. When Letty was here, she was pleased to be with child, even proud of herself . . . though I could well imagine that the intervening weeks might have deprived her of all her fancies and delusions. And she was not well when she ran away, not at all . . . Still, a deliberate act of murder seems unlikely, and a violent murder even more so. We shall have to see, Mrs. Astell."

Mary Astell sighed with relief. She had hoped to persuade Mrs. Kettilby to make the journey to Newgate with her the next day, but persuasion would not be necessary.

"Mind you, there may be little to be done now," said the midwife matter-of-factly. "If Mr. King were inclined to intervene and offer some assistance, well, there might be some kind of an appeal made on the girl's behalf. The rector is known to have powerful friends, but I wonder . . . Could he be persuaded to help a poor and friendless girl like Letty? Humph. Well, we shall see soon enough."

After a few moments of silence, Mrs. Kettilby asked one more question. "What about the archbishop?" The midwife was familiar with Mary Astell's habit of looking to Lambeth for advice. "He has influence with the king, and His Majesty has granted a free pardon to those who have been found guilty of the worst of crimes."

"Humph." Astell echoed Mrs. Kettilby's expression of disgust. "I have no doubt of His Majesty's great mercy, but I am not sure of the archbishop's. I will certainly seek counsel from Mrs. Tenison about the matter—I am sure of her sympathy at least. She will know whether any appeal to the archbishop would be worthwhile."

"Humph." Mrs. Kettilby looked skeptically at her friend.

"I have little doubt that the archbishop is fully occupied with other matters," Astell continued. "After much discussion, Parliament has finally passed a series of new taxes to support this 'just and necessary war.'" In her indignation, Astell momentarily forgot Letty. "Eight years of war . . . and still no end in sight. And then there is yet more legislation to remedy the ill state of the coin." As she spoke, Astell realized she still had Mustapha's purse in her pocket, its weight hardly reduced by the few coins she had drawn from it.

"Well," said Mrs. Kettilby, shaking her head. "Mrs. Tenison will know whether the archbishop might be persuaded to appeal to His Majesty. Your interest on the girl's behalf ought to count for something." Despite her words, the midwife did not look hopeful. "Still, I am perplexed by what happened here. The girl's wretched condition should have earned her some sympathy at her trial: so very young, seduced and then abandoned, alone and friendless. It is a pitiful story, even in these times! Mind you, being unmarried and a vagrant no doubt counted against her but, that said, a girl like Letty is not often condemned at trial—not if she declares her innocence and certainly not without good evidence. We will have to see, Mrs. Astell, we will just have to see."

"What kind of evidence?" asked Astell.

"Well now, according to the statute, a woman who gives birth to a bastard child is condemned as 'lewd and unnatural.' The law assumes that such a woman will kill her child in order to avoid shame and escape punishment. But it must first be proved that the child was born alive and not stillborn. Now, if Letty's baby was lying in a pool of blood, that may have been all the proof of murder that was needed. There could well be other reasons for the blood, mind you—but until we know what may have been said in her defense, we cannot be sure."

Mary Astell was startled not only by Mrs. Kettilby's knowledge of the law but also by the assurance with which she spoke about it.

With hardly a pause, Mrs. Kettilby proceeded with her disquisition. "That same statute makes it clear that concealment is critical to a determination that a crime has been committed—if a woman has concealed her pregnancy and the child's birth, she is always suspected of murder if her child is found dead, but concealment is not conclusive evidence of her guilt. It is another matter, however, if the woman has concealed the *death* of her child. Now that act is considered to be decisive—if she has concealed the death of her infant, she is then presumed to be guilty of the child's death unless she can offer good evidence to the contrary. A witness, even one, who can say the child was born dead, for example.

"In Letty's case, we know that she did not conceal her pregnancy in any way, and if what you heard from Mrs. Rolles is to be believed, nor did she make any effort to conceal the death of the infant. She did not bury it secretly or hide the body, and the absence of concealment is usually taken as a sign of an accidental death. But, then, the girl was alone when she gave birth, and that is always a danger for a mother when her child is found dead."

Suddenly aware that Astell had not asked a question or made a comment, Mrs. Kettilby guessed the reason for her silence. "While all this is no doubt terrible for you to have to think about, I fear that these are the issues to be considered in such cases. I wish I was not quite so familiar with the law, but situations like Letty's are not unknown to me, more's the pity. Babies die, and their mothers always come under suspicion. Even so, though the law presumes their guilt, there is always a reluctance to condemn them for murder. Some reason or another for a verdict of 'not guilty' is often discovered. I fear there must be more to Letty's story, Mrs. Astell. Something more, indeed."

Mrs. Kettilby, usually not one for many words, had at last reached the conclusion of her lengthy speech.

The two women decided they would travel to London early the next day, agreeing to set out right after the morning service at All Saints. Mary Astell wondered whether it would be advisable for her to stop at the rectory on her way home, but as it was already growing late, they agreed that perhaps it would be best to appeal to the Reverend Mr. King after they had had a chance to talk to Letty—assuming, of course, that they would be able to see her.

By the time they concluded their plans, it was already quite dark. The driving rain had melted much of the snow that remained on the ground, but the half-frozen pools and puddles made the path treacherous.

"Georgie," Mrs. Kettilby called out as she opened the door of her small cottage. The great volume of the little woman's voice once again startled Mary Astell. Turning toward Astell, Mrs. Kettilby explained. "The boy will see you home. And I will hear no objections, so there's an end of the matter. This is no weather for traveling alone."

Mary Astell said nothing—it was on the tip of her tongue to remark that Mary Kettilby traveled alone in every sort of weather and at all hours of the day and night. But before she could speak, the boy appeared out of the gloom holding a torch that suddenly sparked into life. He seemed to know exactly what was required of him. Without a word of direction from Mrs. Kettilby, he gestured toward Astell, and the two set out together on the trip to Greater Chelsea. "Come right back, my boy," Mrs. Kettilby called after them. "There will be a bowl of soup for you waiting here."

They made their journey in silence, and again Astell found herself glad for the company and especially thankful for the torch that illumined their way. Despite the terrible weather, they managed to cover the distance fairly quickly, but by the time they arrived in the village, making their way past the rectory and then the church, they were both thoroughly drenched, and Astell was relieved when they finally left the path along the river and veered onto Paradise Row. Just as they approached the Apothecary Garden, she thought she could see a dark shape just outside her gate. By the time they reached Mrs. Methuen's house, the shape materialized as the Ranelagh coach.

Sarah jerked open the door before they were halfway up the front walk. "I have been worrying and watching for you, ma'am," she said, eyeing the boy who had accompanied Astell.

"Thank you, Sarah," Astell murmured. Before she could say more, Lady Catherine emerged from the parlor, shaking her head in exasperation. But seeing Astell's young companion, she regained her composure, and rather than protestations or remonstrances, she helped Astell remove her hat and mantle quietly.

"I am surprised but pleased to find you here," Astell said.

"That woman sent a message to Ranelagh right after you took off in her coach," said Lady Catherine. She sounded as if she would like to say more, but again she restrained herself.

"I did not have any time to send you word myself," Astell replied. She felt somewhat guilty because, truth be told, she had not thought about sending Sarah to Ranelagh with word of her plans. And then, before continuing, she paused to look at George, who was standing uneasily just inside the door—Sarah was glaring at him, and he seemed anxious about the effect of his dripping coat and muddy boots on the gleaming floorboards. "Come in, boy, come in," she urged him. "We will warm you up before you leave."

"No thank you, Mrs. Astell," George said. "Now that you are safely home, I will be off. I intend to be back in Little Chelsea before Mrs. Kettilby starts to worry." He said nothing about the hearty soup that awaited him, though Astell suspected that the prospect of a warm meal contributed to his determination to be on his homeward journey.

Lady Catherine reached into her pocket and pressed a coin into the boy's hand. He smiled broadly and nodded his thanks. Not for the first time, Mary Astell regretted her inability to offer such gratuities—while her own wants and needs were few, she would have liked to be able to make a small gift for services like those George had performed. Seeing the boy's happy face, she considered whether Madam Mazarin might not be correct, after all, in her views about the usefulness of a little ready money.

Opening the door, George turned back briefly. "Mrs. Kettilby is called out in all kinds of weather," he said, "and she never utters a word of complaint. The least I can do is follow her example." And with that, the cheerful boy was out the door, on his way back to Little Chelsea.

Lady Catherine looked as if she might have liked to snort a "humph" as a rejoinder, but such an unseemly response was hardly worthy of a lady of her very great dignity. As she and Mary Astell turned to withdraw into the parlor, she added, as if the intervening exchange with young George had not occurred, "And later, that man of hers, the duchess of Mazarin's man, I mean, stopped by with further news. Newgate! Mary Astell, I must protest! Newgate! And all on account of that worthless girl!"

Tired as she was with the day's events, Mary Astell took careful note of her friend's reaction, calculating that Lady Catherine's evident distress could be used to advantage. Astell was fairly certain that when she made clear her intention to return to the prison the next day, accompanied by Mrs. Kettilby, Lady Catherine would feel it incumbent upon herself to make one of their party. But, however high-minded Lady Catherine might be, Astell knew that under no circumstances should a woman of her birth and breeding subject herself to such a grim mission. Even worse, if Lady Catherine insisted on being a part of this venture, then Lady Ranelagh would not be denied.

Now it should be noted that, while Lady Catherine took great pride in her knowledge of the way of the world, the world about which she was so expert was extremely limited. As the daughter of an earl, she had even less experience than Mary Astell of the harsh and brutal lives endured by the vast majority of women. While her many acts of charity were undeniable, it must also be said that they were performed at Lady Catherine's own considerable discretion. Her beneficence was carefully directed only to those whom she judged to be *worthy* of her assistance. The case of young Sarah may have tested Lady Catherine's faith in her own judgment, but if so, she had kept those doubts and misgivings to herself. In the meantime, she remained firm in her insistence that the objects of her charity could not possibly be blamed for their lamentable state.

The events of the last few days, however, suggested to Mary Astell that women who were neither virtuous nor blameless might also need help. She had also begun to see that otherwise honest women might be forced by circumstance into all kinds of depravity. Some women were weak, others were foolish, and more than a few were ignorant. Women could be lazy, rude, greedy, or stupidly unashamed. They could be cold and hard, deceitful and cunning, cruel and thoughtless, even vile and contemptible. And these women, women who might be imperfect, unworthy, and utterly unsympathetic—these women, too, were needful. And however much she may once have ignored them, Mary Astell could ignore them no longer.

This much I have learned. I, who thought myself in a position to instruct other women—I closed my eyes to all of this. But my eyes have been opened now.

Twenty-Two

Hawkers, ever eager for trade, were out in great numbers all along Fleet Street. There had been a severe frost during the night, but the rain held off, and a pale sun was doing its best to shine.

As Mary Astell hoped but hardly dared to expect, Lady Catherine had been persuaded not to undertake the journey to Newgate prison. After carefully considering Astell's suggestion that a call upon the Reverend Mr. King might prove to be helpful, that dignified lady, with her usual great good sense, saw the advantage in a division of labor, particularly when it was a task so suited to her unique set of skills. If anyone could persuade the busy clergyman to leave off his epistolary debate about the site of Sir Thomas More's manor and deploy his persuasive skills on behalf of one of her ladyship's very special cases, it would be Lady Catherine Jones herself.

So it was that Mary Astell had risen from her pew at the conclusion of the service that morning and watched with some interest as her dearest friend armed herself for her encounter with the rector of All Saints. For the briefest of moments, Astell felt a twinge of sympathy for the clergyman. But only for a moment. While Lady Catherine bore down upon her unsuspecting prey, her commanding gaze arresting him in the act of wishing his departing parishioners well, Mary Astell set aside her pity for the Reverend Mr. King and slipped out of the church with Mary Kettilby. The two women set off together, heading into the city. Without the constant downpour that had made travel so difficult over the past weeks, they made good time and crossed the Fleet Bridge well before midday.

Just before they reached Ludgate, they turned north onto Old Bailey. As they approached the Sessions House, a ragged boy rushed toward them and thrust a news-sheet into Astell's hand, loudly demanding payment as he did so. Before she could return the unwanted paper and shoo him away, she caught sight of the bold title at the top of the single sheet:

A MONSTER IN NATURE:
Being a Full and True Account of One
Letty Pyke, a Murderous Mother.

Fumbling in her pocket for one of Mustapha's coins, Astell pulled out a halfpenny and handed it to the importunate boy, who grabbed it and was on his way, eager to find more readers attracted by his wares. Mrs. Kettilby peered over Astell's shoulder as they scanned the half broadsheet, covered by screaming lines set in large type:

No Natural Mother, But a Monster:
The Full Account
Of a Most Barbarous and Bloody Murder,
and the True Relation of the Trial
at the Sessions of Oyer and Terminer,
Held for the City of London,
County of Middlesex,
which began in the Old Bailey
on Wednesday, the 9th of December 1696,
as particularly of Letty Pyke,
who secretly delivered herself of a female bastard
and afterwards, to hide her shame and lust,
most unnaturally murdered
the fruit of her own womb
that the world might not see

the seed of her shame;
Tried on Wednesday last, the 16th of December,
being found guilty of willful murder
and condemned to death.

Without a word, Mary Astell turned the sheet over. On the reverse were two badly inked columns of type. "Is there any useful information at all, I wonder?" she asked.

"This will hardly have been written by someone knowledgeable about the hazards of childbirth," said Mrs. Kettilby, "but at least it appears to be the work of a man who was in court and not the usual fantastical tripe." As it promised, the news-sheet's account of Letty's "barbarous and bloody" crime seemed to have been drawn from the proceedings of her trial.

Still looking over Astell's shoulder, the midwife read aloud the first paragraph: "'Letty Pyke, vagrant, indicted for the murder of her female infant bastard in the parish of St. Bartholomew-by-the-Exchange on the night of the 30th of November 1696.' Well, that seems clear enough, and the charge conforms to what you heard from Mrs. Rolles."

Mary Astell looked somber as she nodded slowly in agreement. Mrs. Kettilby continued her reading. "'When the Statute of King James was read to her, the prisoner declared that she had a husband and that the child was no bastard, which claim she could not prove.' You see, Mrs. Astell, the court refers to the law I mentioned yesterday—the act 'to prevent the destroying and murdering of bastard children.' Though if this account is correct, the girl has still not given up her claim to be married."

"I feared that she would not let go of that fancy," Astell replied, "despite the fact that we could discover nothing to confirm it. I have come to believe that the girl ran away from us because she was unable to face the possibility that she had been misled about her 'great lord'—or, rather, she could not bring herself to accept the fact that she had been deceived and did not want to be reminded of her folly by our questions."

"Still," said Mrs. Kettilby, "it is a great pity she had no proof of her marriage, even if it was all a sham played upon her—the statute is concerned only with the death of those infants born to unmarried mothers. If she had some kind of evidence that she was the victim of a vile seducer, even if it was clear that the marriage was a fraud, it might have gone better for her."

Astell sighed. "Will you read out the rest?" she asked, handing the sheet to her friend. "I would rather hear it from you than read it for myself."

Mrs. Kettilby observed Astell carefully, wondering whether she could discern any sign of faintness. But Astell appeared strong and resolute. "We are very close to the Sessions House," the midwife said. "Surely the court is done sitting, and we will be able to find a place there, in the yard, where we can read this away from all the hustle and bustle of the street."

Passing through the arched entry in the brick wall, they discovered a crowd of litigants and witnesses in the yard, waiting to be called. Clearly the session was not yet concluded, but since all those who were waiting were fully occupied with their own business, the two women were able to find a quiet spot, out of the way and next to the wall, where they could peruse their paper in relative privacy.

"Let me see," said Mrs. Kettilby, her finger running down the column until she found her place. "Ah, here:

> The prisoner declared that the child came before its time and that she called out for help, but no one heard her cries.

> It appeared upon her trial that the prisoner had brought forth the infant in secret and then made away with the child, leaving it alongside Sweeting's Alley, lying in a pool of blood.

> The evidence deposed that the body of the infant was found in a gutter outside of the Swan Tavern early on the morning of the 1st of December by Mr. John White. The witness declared that he, being in an upper room of his premises, looked out of his window and saw the body in the gutter and covered with blood.

The witness declared that thought it to be a dead dog at first, but when he took the body out of the blood, he saw it was a baby, wrapped up in an old cloth. It was proved that the prisoner owned the infant to be hers, as she confessed in the presence of several credible witnesses.

The prisoner would not give any account why she so disposed of the child, and none, she said, was present at the labor.

The infant's body was searched, but no mark of violence could be discovered.

The prisoner said that the child bled to death on its own, but she could prove nothing. She, being searched by the midwives, had little to say for herself, being a very ignorant and silly girl.

Then the statute was read to her: *Except such mother can prove that the child was born dead by one witness at least, then she shall be accounted guilty*, which she could not prove, so she was found guilty of willful murder.

"A terrible story," Mary Astell concluded, once Mrs. Kettilby had finished reading.

"It is," the midwife agreed. "But there is more sound information and less titillating detail in this account than is usually to be found in this kind of thing." She quickly folded up the paper and thrust it into one of her several bags. "Shall we go?" she asked.

The two left the relative seclusion of the Sessions House yard and, back on the street, continued on Old Bailey until they reached Newgate. Approaching from the west, Astell looked up to see that there were four stone niches above the arch on this side of the gate. As on the eastern façade, each was occupied by a carved female figure. "Libertas" was engraved below one of the sculptures. Before Astell could determine what three virtues the other figures were meant to represent, they had passed through the gate, heading deeper into the prison.

Now somewhat familiar with the doors, rooms, passages, and stairways of Newgate, Astell approached the lodge without hesitation. She glanced at Mrs. Kettilby, close by her side, and saw that the midwife seemed not the least discomposed by the smells or the sounds swirling around them.

As soon as Astell passed through the low doorway, the turnkey emerged from the gloom, just as he had the day before. This morning, however, he was alone. Astell experienced a twinge of regret that Doll was not by his side. No matter how disreputable the woman might be, Astell realized that she had hoped to encounter her again.

"Oh, ho, look here!" the man bellowed to no one in particular. Without Doll to support him, he was even more unsteady on his feet. "Back again, eh? I hope you will not be so stingy in giving today, ma'am—you do your friend no favors, indeed, you do not. No time or place to be spare-handed, I say!"

"Mr. Robinson," Astell said, acknowledging him with a slight nod.

"And no mewling for Mr. Smith today, I pray you. In any case, you have come before your time, so he is not yet arrived, but even if he were around, he would not be able to help you—I am the only man here who can see to your needs. What use is a clergyman to you in a place like this?"

At this the turnkey erupted in laughter. Like Doll, he was delighted by his own wit. Stopped short by a fit of coughing, he hawked up a lump of phlegm, spit it onto the stone floor, and wiped his mouth on his sleeve before continuing. "Now, may I ask," he wheezed, "what is it that you require? Ready cash is all that *I* require." Struggling to catch his breath, he held Astell's gaze as steadily as he could, given his considerable state of inebriation.

"We wish to see a young woman who is imprisoned here," said Astell. She had the fee that Doll had named ready in her hand so that she would not have to fumble in her pocket, but she planned to produce no coin until the turnkey had met her terms.

Mr. Robinson focused a bleary eye on her and gave a wide smile. It was most unsettling. "A service I can readily perform, ma'am," he said, with an effort at a deep bow. Nearly upset by the attempt, he righted himself and added, "The fee is modest—just two shillings."

Astell pulled a shilling from her pocket, then slowly extracted the sixpence. "This, I believe, is the usual sum required for you to bring a prisoner to speak with friends."

"Oh, is it now?" he asked, his dark eyes glinting with anger—or, perhaps, with desire for the bright silver coins. "If you are so sure of the way my business is conducted, then you must also know that is the fee for a *single* visitor. Two shillings for the both of you is a kindness, madam."

Astell held his gaze and added nothing to the two coins in her palm. He exhaled dramatically, an action that seemed as if it would precipitate another paroxysm of coughing. "As you are a lady," he said, catching his breath. "I will bring her to you—" With that he gave a vague gesture, which Astell interpreted to mean that he would meet them in the hall she had seen on her last visit.

"I have not given you her name," Astell said.

"Oh, I know well enough who it is you have come for," he replied. He began to cough again, but even as he struggled through the fit, he stuck his hand out for the coins. Astell sighed and, in an act of faith, handed them to him. Wiping his mouth on his sleeve, the turnkey disappeared.

The low-ceilinged hall where the two women waited was empty—filthy, but empty. They stood silently by a massive wooden door that had been fitted with an iron grate. This, presumably, was the gigger, through which the unfortunate prisoner would be able to speak to them.

"It is the blood, Mrs. Astell. And no visible wound on the infant. I begin to see what has happened," said Mrs. Kettilby, the low sound of her voice breaking through the din of the drinking-room in the cellar just below them. "Mind you, I am not sure, but I begin to suspect."

Astell had no time to reply before they could hear the sound of footsteps in the passageway behind the door. And then, suddenly, Letty was there, before them, her small, pinched face pressed up against the grate.

"Mrs. Astell, Mrs. Kettilby," she cried out as she peered through the framework of bars. She burst into tears. Her eyes were already red and puffy. There had been many tears.

"Hush now, hush," murmured Mrs. Kettilby, her voice at once calm and consoling. While the midwife soothed her, the girl clung desperately to the grill.

As she stood by, Astell noted with relief that, for whatever reason, Letty had been loosed from her fetters.

"Whatever shall I do?" the girl wailed. "What shall I do? You must help me." Her voice was muffled by the thick walls and the heavy wooden door.

"You must compose yourself, Letty," said Mary Astell. Even as she addressed the girl, she knew her words sounded sharper than she intended. With an effort, she spoke more gently. "We may not have much time, so we must use the time we have wisely. Mrs. Kettilby has questions for you. If we are to help—if any help is at all possible—you must answer, and you must answer truthfully and fully. Do you understand?"

The girl sniffed and rubbed her nose and eyes with a grimy fist. While it was difficult to see her clearly through the grate, she did have a tattered bit of blanket clutched around her shoulders. Doll had done at least that much for her, and Astell silently offered her thanks to the ward-woman—a slattern she might be, but she had kept her word.

Doll seemed also to be correct in her claim that the keeper, Mr. Fell, had relieved Letty of her gown—the girl was wearing only a pair of stays and her petticoats over her shift. Despite the grate that obscured her view and her own rather limited knowledge of fashion, Mary Astell could tell that these were of superior quality, undoubtedly supplied to her apprentice by Mrs. Rolles and worth far more than the tawdry garment Letty had been wearing. It was cold comfort to know that the keeper had mistaken trumpery for finery, but Astell took that comfort nonetheless.

"Now then, Letty," Mrs. Kettilby began briskly but not unkindly, "we have read the record of your trial, so we need not inquire about the proceedings. What I ask you now will help me understand what has happened. If there is any remedy for your situation, we must know everything. Do you understand?"

"Yes, ma'am."

"Now, to begin, you told the court that you came into your labor unexpectedly. When I examined you at Mrs. Astell's, we calculated that the child was not like to come much before the end of December, did we not?"

"Perhaps about Christmas-tide, you said." Letty's attention was drawn by the quiet efficiency of the midwife.

"I may have misjudged the time of your necessity—first babies are notoriously unpredictable, and a young woman breeding for the first time often misses the signs. But I think it may well be, as you told the court, that the child came before it was expected. It is to be regretted that I did not examine the infant's body for myself. But there is nothing to be done about that now."

"No, ma'am," said the girl.

"Although it was not yet your time, had you made any provision for the birth?"

The girl began to sob. "What could I do when no one would help me?" she cried. "After I left Mrs. Astell's, I went directly back to Mrs. Rolles, but she would have nothing at all to do with me. She refused me outright—her daughters mocked me to my face! When she would not have me back, I was worried from place to place and jeered at . . . No one cared about me at all, everyone was just anxious to be rid of me. Not a bit of kindness in a single soul. And yet I did not want to stray too far from the Exchange, because my lord and husband might come looking for me . . . "

"Hush, now," said Mrs. Kettilby. "We have no time for that."

"But I was meant to be a lady," the girl whimpered.

Looking at Letty now, and hearing her return to her tired refrain, Mary Astell expected her own feelings of frustration to come rushing back, but they did not. Instead, she felt a profound sorrow.

Twenty-Three

The two women began their journey back to Chelsea at once. As they approached Newgate, Mary Astell glanced up at the representations of Justice, Mercy, and Truth, each carved figure isolated and imprisoned in her own niche just over the archway. After she had passed under the portcullis, Astell turned her head to see the four female sculptures on the Holborn side of the gate.

"Liberty," she said. Her voice showed no emotion, but as she gazed at Mrs. Kettilby, Astell pursed her lips and raised her eyebrows.

"And the other three are Peace, Plenty, and Concord," replied Mrs. Kettilby, who had not bothered to look.

The two women retraced their steps, making their way back down Old Bailey, this time without stopping in the yard of the Sessions House. They turned west on Ludgate Street and crossed the stone bridge over the Fleet river. Walking silently and briskly, they passed through Temple Bar, where Fleet Street met the Strand. No half-clothed allegorical figures were perched atop this stone gate—when it was rebuilt after the Great Fire, Christopher Wren had decided to pay tribute to the Stuart monarchs, and so James I and his wife, Queen Anne, posed regally on one side of the gate. On the other, Charles I and his son, Charles II, stared off into the distance, ignoring passersby.

The two women were jostled and pressed as they made way through the city. "I wish we could have done more for her," Astell said at last.

"Yes," Mrs. Kettilby agreed, nimbly sidestepping a foul pile of horse dung steaming in the cold air. While they walked, she patted two or three of the pouches and bags slung about her person. "I had hoped to be able to provide the girl with oil of St. John's wort and a supply of linen napkins—the oil for her abdomen, the napkins for her purgations. And I brought some cloths to bind her breasts. After giving birth, she should have been bathed with a decoction of chervil, though I know that such a treatment is quite of out the question in her present circumstance. Mind you, if she had been under the care of a good midwife, all of this and more would have been provided for her. And she should have been given nourishing broths to restore her strength—"

"You have thought of everything," said Astell, only now aware of all that the midwife had carried with her.

"Everything, that is, except how I could actually supply her with what I had brought," Mary Kettilby, replied, speaking matter-of-factly. "It was quite clear that there were not enough coins in your purse to ensure she would get what we had brought." She stopped suddenly, nearly run down by a pair of heedless apprentices following too closely behind her.

"Make no mistake about it, Mrs. Astell," she said, "Letty is still in a fragile state. Oh, she has survived her travail well enough—many women suffer a terrible loss of blood immediately after the delivery and feel such bitter pains in their belly that it seems as if they will give birth again! And if the secundines are not expelled, they will corrupt—a midwife must make haste to drive forth the after-birth, or convulsions and fevers will soon be followed by death.

"The girl gave birth two weeks ago—no, more than two weeks ago, almost three—the fevers would have come on by now if the after-birth had not been fully cast out. Still, she should have been kept warm—cold is not good for her womb . . . " The midwife shook her head. "She has managed to survive the hazards of childbirth, Mrs. Astell, but I am afraid that no treatment I can offer her will be of any use in her current situation."

After this exchange, the two women continued down the Strand together, dodging busy tradesmen, bawling street criers, peacocking gentlemen, heedless ruffians, and gawking visitors to the city, trailed by sly and persistent beggars looking to take advantage of their gullibility. When they reached Charing Cross, they veered left, following King Street as they passed Whitehall and then the abbey. At the Gate House, they turned west, heading away from the river, onto Tuthill and then St. James Street, finally reaching the footway that would take them back to Chelsea.

"I think I know what has happened," Mrs. Kettilby said to the women who were assembled in Mary Astell's parlor. The midwife sat close to the grate so she could warm herself. No rain had fallen during their walk home from the city, but it continued bitterly cold. The weak sun had never fully broken through the day's gloom, and by the time Astell and Mrs. Kettilby were making their way back to Chelsea, it had disappeared entirely. While Mrs. Kettilby was never deterred by rain, snow, wind, or freezing temperatures, setting off to care for women in childbirth no matter the hour or the weather, she was not too proud to admit that she was thoroughly chilled. She had gladly taken a seat near the fire at Astell's urging.

For her part, Lady Catherine had directed Mary Astell to a second chair drawn up to the warm coal fire, and once that great lady had achieved her goal, she placed herself in Astell's usual seat. Mrs. Methuen perched rather self-consciously in the fourth of the comfortably padded chairs in Astell's parlor, the one usually reserved for Lady Ranelagh, who had insisted that Mrs. Methuen take her own accustomed place while she herself gracefully sank onto a low stool in the very center of the room, her skirts fanned out around her. She made a charming picture, of which fact she was quite well aware.

"That girl was entirely unprepared for childbirth," said Mrs. Kettilby, speaking to no one in particular. "A practiced midwife would have given her draughts of sage ale to prepare her womb, and when it was near her time to be delivered, she should have had warm baths and an ointment made of ground almonds and butter for her secret parts. She should have soaked herself every day for six weeks before her lying in—"

Although none of this was to the point, the four women nonetheless listened attentively as Mrs. Kettilby spoke. Usually so calm and practical, the midwife was visibly agitated. "A woman should be well prepared for the time of her necessity," she continued, "and all things provided that should cause her to be easily delivered—and of course, even before her labor began, divine assistance should have been invoked: 'for in him we live and move and have our being, for we are also his offspring.'"

As if suddenly aware of the silence in the room, Mrs. Kettilby looked around her and shook her head. "This is not a matter of professional pride," she asserted with dignity, "but rather of simple human decency. To abandon any woman in her time of great need—and in Letty's case, hardly a woman, but a girl . . . Well, it is a frightful thing for any woman to face childbirth alone, and doubly so when she is ignorant and entirely unprepared." As a midwife, Mary Kettilby had assisted many women as they faced the terrible prospect of labor and delivery, but of the four women in the parlor that day, only Mrs. Methuen had given birth.

"Well," Mrs. Kettilby said, "enough of that. In spite of her ignorance and despite the cruelty of all of those who knew her condition but chose to do nothing for her, the girl survived. And I believe her infant might well have survived too . . . "

"Then she did no harm to the infant?" asked Mrs. Methuen. "I could not believe her guilty of such a terrible crime."

"I am almost certain she did not," said Mrs. Kettilby. "It is the blood, you see. Many unfortunate women suffer a fatal hemorrhage in their time of delivery, especially if the birth is not natural and the child's head does not come first. Now, there was a pool of blood where Letty gave birth— the witnesses agree upon that, and the girl confirms it—but it was *not* her blood. The blood came not from the mother but from the infant."

"But I thought there was no sign of violence on the poor creature," said Lady Ranelagh.

"If the account of the court proceedings is accurate, that is correct, Your Ladyship," replied Mrs. Kettilby. "No injury was discovered on the child's body when it was examined, and if a wound of any sort had been found, I am sure that it would have been noted." After a brief pause, she added, "Such horrible details help to sell scandal sheets."

"Did she fail to bind the navel-string?" asked Mrs. Methuen. "Is that the source of the blood?" In addition to having given birth herself, Mrs. Methuen had also attended a fair number of women in childbirth.

"You are not far from the purpose, Mrs. Methuen," said Mrs. Kettilby, "although I have my doubts whether Letty cut the navel-string at all—she certainly made no mention of doing so when we spoke to her. I hardly think she would have known she was *supposed* to do such a thing, and even if she did, I doubt she had a knife or string with her.

"Still, even if she had no idea that it was necessary, all would have been well—the navel-string need not be cut and tied at once. The mother gives both vital and natural blood to the child by the navel, and if a newborn child be weak, a midwife may well refrain from cutting the string right away—the blood that comes into the child's body by the navel will refresh a baby newly brought forth from the womb. I have known many children, even those that seem to be born dead, to recover by this means."

"Then what *was* the source of the blood?" asked Lady Ranelagh. While Mrs. Kettilby had been speaking, the countess had busied herself in rearranging the folds of her skirts. She had been attentive enough to Mrs. Kettilby's remarks, but Mary Astell could tell that she was also growing somewhat impatient.

"Just so," said Mrs. Kettilby. "That is the question, Your Ladyship. Now if Letty had cut the navel-string but failed to tie it, that could well account for the blood, if not for the death of the child. But those who examined the body of the infant would surely have seen this and made note of it if that were the case. No, I think what happened is something unusual, but not unknown. I have only seen it happen once, mind you, and that was when I was a still a girl, assisting my mother, God rest her soul.

"So it was many years ago now, but I well remember the case of a young woman under my mother's care. She had just given birth to her first child, a boy, and my mother was busily tending to the woman after her travail—it had been an easy and uneventful birth, but my mother kept her wits about her nonetheless, and a good thing, too. Shortly after the birth, she noticed that the infant, who had been born loud and lusty, was become cold and pale, and although he had already been swaddled, she unwrapped him and saw that he was soaked in blood. She confirmed that the navel-string had been tightly bound and that the ligature had not come loose—the blood was flowing from a rupture in one of the veins in the navel-string, close to the umbilicus.

"For all of her very great experience as a midwife, my mother almost lost this infant, for he would surely have died from loss of blood, but calling on all her skill, she was at last able to save him. First, she caught seven or eight drops of the blood from the navel-string and gave it to the child by mouth to refresh him, and then she applied a little powder of bole armoniac—"

Suddenly interrupted by the sound of choking from just outside the parlor door, the midwife stopped abruptly, mid-sentence. Astell thought it probable that Sarah had positioned herself there in order to listen in on the conversation, her suspicion now borne out by the muffled coughing.

"Sarah," Astell said, watching while the girl slid reluctantly into the room. Sarah clearly anticipated a reprimand, and Astell could see the girl's eyes filling with resentment. Before Sarah could cause any further disruption, Astell surprised not only the maidservant but herself. "You bore a great responsibility for Letty when she was here," Astell said. "You are entitled to know what misfortunes have overtaken her."

Her eyes wary, Sarah stood uncomfortably inside the door. For once she was quiet, and she managed to remain still, without fidgeting, twitching, or squirming.

Mrs. Kettilby smiled at the girl before continuing. "Well," the midwife said, resuming her narrative, "you do not need all the details of the treatment my mother administered, but thanks to her careful attendance and great skill, the poor babe lived, though it was some time before he thrived. And this, I feel sure, is the cause of the death of Letty's infant—a rupture in one of the veins of the navel-string. It would account for the pool of blood in which the infant was found, but no wound would be discovered upon the body. A complication such as this is rare, so uncommon that I have never encountered it since, for which I am very thankful, but if Letty had only been under the care of a midwife—"

"Not just any midwife," said Mrs. Methuen, interrupting Mrs. Kettilby. "I say you are too modest by half."

Mrs. Kettilby flushed uncomfortably. She was not one for praise. "If Letty had been attended by a competent midwife," she continued, "the child might well have been saved—but even in the unfortunate case of the infant's death, no one would have thought the mother guilty of any crime."

A great silence fell. Even Sarah held her tongue. At last, Lady Catherine roused herself. "I am afraid we will find no assistance from Mr. King," she said. "While you were in the city, I made sure to speak to this *worthy* divine, as we agreed I would. He made time to hear me out, but as for his willingness to offer any assistance? Well, it seems that he has come to a particularly critical moment in his research on the location of Sir Thomas More's house, and he finds himself in the midst of composing a very sternly worded letter to some upstart, newly entered into the field, who dares to posit an altogether unacceptable theory. And so the rector—this worthy *man of God*—is very sorry, but he is unable to take up any new cause for want of time."

At this it was Lady Ranelagh, not Sarah, who began to snicker. As for the maidservant, she looked shocked, her eyes opening wide as she sought out Astell's. A glance from Lady Catherine silenced the countess, who smothered her laughter.

"I beg your pardon," Lady Ranelagh said, regaining her composure. "I know that this is no cause for amusement. But I despair of men and their follies! Such weighty matters! Such worthy goals! How dare they? How can they look away from such terrible injustice? Whatever can be done for the poor girl, I wonder, for something must surely be done."

Lady Ranelagh's outrage was sincere, her concern for Letty, genuine. "Perhaps his lordship might be persuaded to use his influence. Or, if not his lordship, then we might appeal to—"

Now it was Lady Catherine's turn to scoff. "I am quite sure that Lord Ranelagh is fully occupied with follies of his own, Your Ladyship. And may I remind you, as well, that any too *public* involvement with such a scandal might compromise you—the earl of Ranelagh may be an indiscreet man, but he expects the utmost discretion from his wife. Your caution and discernment are required."

Lady Ranelagh might toss her head and cry "Fie," but Astell was certain that the countess would heed the warning, however sharply it had been worded. Lady Catherine was keenly aware of her father's reputation for recklessness and duplicity, but she knew only too well that scandal did little harm to a man's reputation. Lady Ranelagh was not without her own follies, and if she hoped to continue her pleasant way of life, she must be made to realize that circumspection was required.

Even as she watched Lady Ranelagh acknowledge the truth of the counsel she had received, Astell was unsettled by Lady Catherine's own indiscretion. That she would refer to her father at all here, in the presence of Mrs. Kettilby, Mrs. Methuen, and Sarah . . . Much less to acknowledge his imprudent conduct. Well, it was a measure of Lady Catherine's discomposure. Though she might hide it with mockery, Lady Catherine Jones, daughter of the earl of Ranelagh, had clearly been disappointed in the failure of the Reverend Mr. King to come to her assistance—or, more likely, she had been disappointed in her powers of persuasion.

"What, then, is to be done?" Mrs. Methuen's gentle repetition of Lady Ranelagh's question returned them to the moment before Lady Catherine's uncomfortable revelation.

Mrs. Kettilby, having delivered her assessment of what had happened on the night Letty had given birth, sat back in her chair before the coal fire. She would be wanting to get back home soon, Astell realized, back to her small cottage and the many women who relied on her care and experience. Standing just inside the parlor door, Sarah remained upright, still, and silent. Lady Ranelagh reached out and adjusted an errant fold of her heavy silk skirt.

"I suppose there is no reason for me to go to Lambeth," said Astell.

In one more unexpected response, Lady Catherine turned suddenly toward her friend, her eyebrows shooting up in surprise. "*No reason for you to go to Lambeth?* I thought I would never hear you say such a thing, Mary Astell—you are always off to Lambeth straightaway, no matter what anyone else might think or say. You announce your intention, and then go you do."

"But my old friend is no longer there," said Astell. She smiled warmly, remembering that Lady Catherine had spoken those very words to her not long ago.

"No, my dear, no, he is not, and he has not been there for some while." Lady Catherine was much mollified, and there appeared to be a tear in her eye.

"I doubt that His Grace will be of any more use than Mr. King," said Lady Ranelagh. Still a bit subdued after Lady Catherine's sharp words, the countess refrained from her usual exuberant mockery of the archbishop of Canterbury.

"A trip to Lambeth would serve no purpose," said Astell. "But I will write to Mrs. Tenison. She was very kind when I was there, seeking the archbishop's opinion about Letty's situation when the girl first arrived in Chelsea. Mrs. Tenison might be a useful advocate—and doubtless she will be able to offer us advice. If anyone were in a position to assist us—and be willing to assist us—it will be Mrs. Tenison."

"Very wise," said Lady Catherine. "Far better to consult this sensible woman than to trudge up to Lambeth and cool your heels for who knows how long in the hope that His Grace will deign to see you."

"I agree," said Lady Ranelagh, rising gracefully, her skirts falling into perfect place around her. She cast a quick glance into the looking-grass and seemed pleased with what she saw there.

Mrs. Methuen rose slowly from her chair. "Time for me to go, I do believe. Do not hesitate to call on me, Mrs. Astell—let me know if I can assist you in any way." She looked about her to make sure she had not left a stray handkerchief.

At that moment, a sharp rap was heard at the door. Sarah jumped to attention and quickly went out into the small entry hall. A short, excited exchange was heard, and just as Sarah returned, Mrs. Kettilby got up from her warm spot by the grate. "This will be a message from George, if I am not mistaken," she said.

"Indeed, ma'am, you are not wrong," said Sarah. She handed the midwife a bit of paper, somewhat crumpled. Mrs. Kettilby smiled as she recognized the scrawl, read the note quickly, and said briskly, "As I thought. I must be off, Mrs. Astell. I am needed—and very lucky it is that I am here, since I am called to Church Lane, just across from the rectory. Not far to travel at all. A young woman carrying her first child."

As Mrs. Kettilby spoke, Sarah handed her a leather bag, small but well filled. "The boy brought it, ma'am," Sarah explained.

"I will be right there," said Mrs. Kettilby, obviously speaking to the child in the entry hall. "One of George's brothers," she explained to Astell before hurrying out. "He is not so apt with his letters as George, but he has a quick mind, and he is very reliable." And then, turning again to the boy, "Look now, I am on my way. Off you go, and let George know that all is well—and make sure you warm yourself and eat once you are there."

With the newly delivered bag in her hand, the midwife took up the various pouches and pockets she had carried with her into the city and was out the door, striding down Paradise Row. Sarah handed Mrs. Methuen her cloak, saw to Lady Catherine's hood and fur muff, and assisted the countess of Ranelagh in gathering up her many and varied accoutrements and accessories.

And then they were all gone. "I will bring you some refreshment, ma'am," said Sarah, leaving Mary Astell suddenly alone.

Twenty-Four

Mary Astell's hair was arranged even more severely than usual. Not a single strand escaped from the linen coif she preferred to wear despite Lady Ranelagh's persistent but gentle raillery about its outmoded style—there was no occasion for such good-humored teasing.

Astell's plain, dark attire seemed plainer and darker than ever. Her back straighter and more unyielding, her expression more somber. She had slept very little. She emerged from her study only to attend morning prayers at All Saints.

She slipped into her pew as the service began and listened intently as the Reverend Mr. King read the opening passage from scripture: ". . . turn unto the Lord your God, for he is gracious and merciful, slow to anger, and of great kindness . . ."

She kneeled, joining with other members of the congregation as they repeated the words of the confession: "Almighty and most merciful Father, we have erred and strayed from thy ways like lost sheep. We have followed too much the devices and desires of our own hearts . . ."

Still kneeling, she heard the rector intone the absolution: "Almighty God, the Father of our Lord Jesus Christ, who desireth not the death of a sinner, but rather that he may turn from his wickedness and live."

She repeated the words of the Lord's Prayer, listened to the reading of the Psalms, heard lessons from the Old and New Testaments, recited the Apostle's Creed, kneeled during the collects for peace and grace, and prayed for the health of King's Majesty. But she did not linger after the last "amen" was said.

When she arrived home, Mary Astell returned to her study, closing the door behind her. She took no food or drink. She gave no orders to Sarah, nor did she issue any corrections and reprimands. Indeed, Astell seemed hardly aware of the girl's presence.

For her part, Sarah was strangely quiet. She did not grumble or stamp or bang. No doors were slammed, no pottery shattered on the scullery floor. She crept silently about the empty rooms, sweeping grates where no fires were laid and polishing the already gleaming wainscot.

When she completed these tasks, Sarah slipped off to Mrs. Methuen's house, where Mary Astell's neighbor was preparing various unguents and powders that she would use to ease the suffering of many of the residents of Chelsea. Sarah was eager to learn, and Mrs. Methuen found her surprisingly adept. Sarah was also very grateful for the meal supplied by a woman who understood the appetite of a growing girl.

If Astell noticed Sarah's absence, she made no sign.

After a great deal of thought, Mary Astell finally picked up her pen and wrote to Mrs. Tenison. Astell had taken to heart Lady Catherine's tender words, repeated so often in the last few years: "Your old friend is not there. Your old friend is no longer there." At last she acknowledged the truth: *My old friend is no longer there.* William Sancroft, her first benefactor and friend, was no longer archbishop of Canterbury, no longer in Lambeth, no longer alive.

And she acknowledged another truth as well. A visit to the current archbishop of Canterbury, the Most Reverend and Right Honorable Thomas Tenison, would be of no use. Perhaps if she were to consult with him about the letter of the law, he would be ready and eager to advance an opinion, but he would have nothing to say if asked about the *spirit* of the law. A weary Christ on the road to Galilee might have time for the Samaritan woman, but the current archbishop of Canterbury was too busy for such dealings.

And so Mary Astell now turned to his wife. Mrs. Anne Tenison would not only lend a sympathetic ear, but she was well situated to assess the current state of affairs—if *any* remedy for poor Letty Pyke were possible, if an appeal to His Majesty could be made, Mrs. Tenison would know how best to proceed.

Just as Astell was finishing her long missive to the archbishop's wife, Lady Catherine arrived. While Lady Catherine could do nothing more for Letty Pyke, she would do what she could for her dearest friend. After a quick assessment of the situation on Paradise Row, she took matters into her own hands, dispatching a boy from Ranelagh to Lambeth with the letter for Mrs. Tenison.

Lady Catherine then helped her friend with one further, more delicate task—the return of Mustapha's purse, now significantly lighter than when he pressed it upon Mary Astell outside Newgate prison. A second letter was thus composed, this one expressing Astell's deepest gratitude, and a second messenger was then dispatched, this one to the residence of the duchess of Mazarin.

Whether Lady Catherine was so busy about the messengers and messages that she did not think to inquire about the contents of the bag or whether she could sense Astell's reticence on the subject, she let the matter rest. As for Mary Astell, she had no wish to deceive her friend, but she had said very little about *how* the money had come into her possession, much less *why*. She thought it unwise to enumerate her expenditures at Newgate, and she also believed she could best honor Mustapha's generosity by keeping the matter between themselves—if Lady Catherine knew just how much had been spent, she would insist on repaying the man herself. And so both women, wisely, decided to remain silent.

With these few tasks completed, Lady Catherine was satisfied that all was as well as it could be on Paradise Row. It must not be thought that she had failed to note Sarah's absence, however. Lady Catherine was far too keen an observer not to have noticed that the girl seemed to have taken advantage of the moment to play the truant. Resolving to look further into this matter, Lady Catherine went home to Ranelagh. As for Mary Astell? Her letters dispatched and her friend returned home, she was left with nothing further to do. She remained in her study, sitting at her desk.

The next day, after returning from the morning service at All Saints, Mary Astell found herself unable to concentrate on the private devotions that usually occupied her on the Lord's day. Nor did she have the attention needed for reading or writing. She found herself straightening papers that did not need arranging and dressing a quill that did not require sharpening. Once that unnecessary business was completed, she decided to walk. She refused to give in to silent brooding or useless moping. The day was chill and the air misty as she headed across the court of the Hospital toward Chelsea Common, but she did not feel the cold.

On Monday morning, Mary Astell received a reply from Mrs. Tenison, a small packet sent from Lambeth. As Astell unbound the string, a single sheet of letter paper fell out of the wrapping and on to her desk.

"My dear Mrs. Astell," the archbishop's wife began, "I fear it is with His Grace as you suspect. The House still sits, and my lord is much occupied with the bill of attainder for all those involved in the late assassination plot. Debate continues with great acrimony, and there is no end in sight. When he can spare a moment from this dreadful business, my lord continues to be wondrous intent on various schemes to reform the coin."

All of this was expected, but Astell was surprised by the next line. "In light of your recent experience at Newgate," Mrs. Tenison continued, "you will be interested to hear that a report from the Committee upon the Abuses of Prisons is due to be presented to Parliament. Whatever reforms may be recommended therein, you may be sure that they will have no effect whatsoever on the unfortunate souls condemned to suffer in such places. According to several of my informants (and yes, my dear Mrs. Astell, although Mrs. Stubbs and I rarely venture far from the comforts of the parlor here at Lambeth, we still manage to hear a very great deal), when witnesses were examined by the committee, they were quite happy to admit that they had obtained their offices by bribery—and they were equally happy to admit that if their cases were ever to be laid before Parliament, they would be in the company of the very men who had been compensated so very well!"

"Humph," said Mary Astell before turning over Mrs. Tenison's letter.

"Thus the world rolls merrily along, my dear Mrs. Astell," wrote the archbishop's wife. "I enclose herein the most recent *Proceedings*—it has just been printed. Mrs. Stubbs was delighted to leave our cozy retreat and make a trip in to the city to make inquiries on your behalf, and she was able to acquire an early copy from the bookseller in Warwick Lane. We have read the account of Letty Pyke's case, but it offers no details of which you are unaware."

Astell turned to the parcel lying on her desk. Inside the brown wrapping was a slim pamphlet, just six cheaply printed pages: *Proceedings on the King's Commission on the Peace, and Oyer and Terminer, and Gaol-Delivery of Newgate, Held in the Old Bailey.* She turned it over and read the summary at the end: "The trials being over, the court gave judgment as follows. Received sentence of death, 23. Burnt in the hand, 33. For His Majesty's service, 14. To be whipped, 2. To be whipped and stand in the pillory, 4."

Opening the pamphlet, Astell saw that each page was filled with brief accounts of the trials of the men and women who had appeared at the December sessions in Old Bailey. *Theft, theft, theft, theft, theft. Burglary. Killing. Violent theft. Coining offences, coining offences, coining offences, coining offenses.*

And there it was, on the third page: "Letty Pyke, vagrant, was indicted for murdering her female bastard-child on the 30th November last, disposing of its body in a gutter; upon the magistrate's inquest, she admitted the child was hers. It appeared upon the trial that she gave birth alone and at night, abandoning the infant in a pool of blood. The prisoner alleged that she did not harm the child, but said that she had come before her time. As she had little else to say, the jury having considered the matter found her guilty of murder."

"Oh, Letty," Astell whispered, before once again picking up Mrs. Tenison's letter.

"I can find no one who is able to tell me for certain when those who were sentenced to death are to be hanged," the archbishop's wife wrote. "I fear it may be soon, though surely there will be no executions during this holy season—I pray no hangings will take place between Christmas-Day and Epiphany. But Mrs. Stubbs informs me that Mr. Baldwin, the bookseller, assures her they will take place before the end of the month, a claim which I can hardly credit but that I fear may be too true, as he is someone whose livelihood depends in part upon knowing such things. Indeed, my lord says Parliament will sit until the 24th and then adjourn only until Tuesday next.

"Of course, as you note, His Majesty is sometimes moved to issue a warrant of reprieve for those who have been condemned, but however much I might share your feelings, I regret to say that I do not think His Grace, the archbishop, could be persuaded to petition on the poor girl's behalf. He has lately taken a resolution to intervene no further on behalf of those whom he believes to be unworthy of such mercy. Despite all your powers of persuasion, my dear Mrs. Astell, I fear even you will find no remedy here."

Astell drew a deep sigh. It was no worse than she expected, but it was some minutes before she could take up the letter and read the postscript.

"By the by," Mrs. Tenison had added, as if to soften the blow of her letter, "my lord has informed me that the bishop of Salisbury is to preach before His Majesty at Whitehall on Christmas Day, no doubt because of his zealous promotion of the bill of attainder against those who plotted against the king. He was the Reverend Mr. Tillotson's man, if you recall, and my lord says there is always something of the buffoon about him."

"Humph," said Astell once more. As Mrs. Tenison knew, Gilbert Burnet, bishop of Salisbury, was to be numbered among Mary Astell's many critics. He had loudly condemned the educational institution for women Astell had described in her *Serious Proposal*, claiming that the "religious retirement" she advocated would "be reputed a nunnery" and denouncing it (and her) as "preparing a way for popish orders." But not long after lodging this criticism, the bishop offered his own suggestion for a school for women: "something very like a monastery" would offer a "glorious design," he wrote, quite pleased with his bold ingenuity. Whether the archbishop of Canterbury thought Burnet a buffoon or not seemed hardly to matter at this point, though Astell appreciated Mrs. Tenison's kind intentions in offering the tidbit.

On Tuesday morning, Mary Astell finally left her study. She had to act. The very least she could do was go back to Newgate to see if she might learn something of Letty's condition. She told no one of her plan, fearing that Lady Catherine would insist on accompanying her in the Ranelagh coach—Astell did not consider it any wiser for her friend to be seen frequenting the insalubrious environs of the prison than it was for Lady Ranelagh. And although Astell would have appreciated the company of Mrs. Kettilby on her journey, she decided not to turn to her for support. She did not want the midwife to take time away from the many women who depended upon her.

Truth be told, Astell considered hers to be a fool's errand. Having returned Mustapha's bag of coins, she was far from having the fee Mr. Robinson would demand for an interview the prisoner, and she was not looking forward to the ridicule he would heap upon her. Nonetheless, to Newgate she would go, hoping that she might hear something of Letty. The turnkey would likely have nothing to do with her, but Astell thought that, if she could find the woman called Doll, well, perhaps the ward-woman would be willing to tell what she knew. And perhaps Doll could even be persuaded to take a message to the prisoner.

As she passed the duchess of Mazarin's house, Mary Astell thought again of the brilliantly plumed parrots, and for a moment, the pleasant memory almost caused her to smile. But then she recalled the grim purpose of her journey. She had no time for such distractions.

Accordingly, rather than smiling, she pressed her lips tightly together, lowering her head against the freezing rain, and turned toward the city.

She followed the familiar route: across the broad court of the Hospital to the small stone bridge over the Westbourne and then along the track through the Five Fields to the grounds of Arlington House in St. James's Park. From St. James's Street to Charing Cross, the Strand, Fleet Street, and Ludgate, landmarks from her many travels on business. Then on to a less familiar route: north on Old Bailey Street, past the Sessions House, and through Newgate to the prison, places she had never thought to visit before the last few terrible days. The streets along her route were crowded, but she was intent on reaching her destination, distracted by nothing and no one.

After passing through Newgate, she approached the lodge with some trepidation, wondering in what state Mr. Robinson might be found. She ducked her head, stepping down into the low, dark room, steeling her resolve for the encounter. But the turnkey did not appear. She had a moment of uncertainty and waited, expecting him to emerge from the gloom. *Where is the man?*

The sounds of cursing and carousing that emanated from the drinking-room seemed louder than ever, and as she backed out of the lodge, Astell thought she could hear Mr. Robinson's swearing above the cacophony. She approached the steps that led down into the cellar, a place she dared not enter. Suddenly the turnkey himself emerged. Although it was not quite midday, he was already roaring drunk, his face sweaty, his eyes bleary. He stumbled up the few steps, nearly falling to his knees as he reached the last one.

"Brandy, ma'am, I have plenty of brandy today, no thanks at all to you and your parsimony," he bawled, waving his arm cheerily. Flecks of spittle flew. "Your disdainful looks and niggardly ways were of no use to your friend, were they? No use at all. What a shame it is to show yourself so pinching in necessary benevolences! Pah!" He carried an earthenware drinking cup—held on to it with some difficulty, in fact—and raised it to his lips, nearly missing his mouth.

He gulped noisily, a stream of liquid trickling down his chin and falling on to his chest. "Aaaah." He emitted a sigh of pleasure, smacking his lips before renewing his tirade. "What kind of friend are you, I wonder? Not everyone is so penny-pinching and hard-fisted as you, thank the Lord! As if that was any way to ease the sufferings of a friend. Why bother to come here if there is no generosity in you?"

He belched loudly, then adopted the same mincing tone he had used with her at their previous encounter. "And what, I pray, may I do for you now, madam? I am at your service." With this he attempted a bow, nearly falling on his face.

"I have come once more to see your prisoner," said Astell stiffly.

"You have come too late, madam, too late indeed. She no longer has need of such a thing as you."

Astell blenched. "She has not been hanged yet, has she?"

"Have you not heard the news, madam? What kind of friend are you, I ask? She has been delivered from her sufferings, *madam*," he replied, still affecting the mannered voice.

"She has died, then?" Astell forced out the question, hardly daring to ask.

"What in God's name do you mean, madam?" he roared. "Have you no sense at all? Do you not take my meaning?" He seemed to grow angry, but perhaps he was just drunk and irritated. "She is no longer here. She has gone. She has been delivered. I can be no clearer, madam, and her release is no thanks to you, I might add. And now, I bid you *adieu* and farewell. I return to my brandy."

Astell was stunned by his revelation. Stunned and confused. But the turnkey executed another unsteady bow, this one ending in a turn, and he tumbled back down the steps into the tap-room. His fall was broken by several disreputable revelers who loudly cheered his return to their midst as they disappeared into the depths of the cellar.

Astell stood for a moment, uncertain what to do. And then she felt a gentle tug on her cloak. Hardly knowing what to expect, she turned to see Doll. The ward-woman jerked her head toward Newgate and hurried off, turning every few steps to make sure that Astell was following her.

Doll slipped into the postern on the left side of the gate, just below the carved figure of Mercy. Or was she Truth? The stench of the prison was so concentrated here that Astell could barely draw a breath. She wondered what it would be like to stand there during hot weather. Doll, however, seemed unaffected.

"I never thought to see you again," the little woman whispered. "Why have you come back?"

"Why would I not return?" asked Mary Astell, still confused by the turn of events. "I have come for news about Letty Pyke. What has happened to her?"

"I was sure it was all your doing," said Doll. She was still whispering, and she looked around her as if she feared the turnkey would deliver another smart blow.

"What was my doing? I know nothing about what has become of her, nothing but what little Mr. Robinson would say."

"Oh, him," said Doll, waving her hand dismissively. For a moment, Astell was afraid that the woman, who was also a bit unsteady on her feet, would upset herself and fall back down the steps that led up to the postern. She too seemed to have consumed a fair amount of strong spirits, perhaps brandy but, it would seem, not nearly as great a quantity as the turnkey.

Astell persisted. She found herself whispering too, just as Doll had been. "Is it true that she is gone? That Letty Pyke is no longer in the prison? Where has she been taken?"

"And here is me, thinking it was all your doing," the woman repeated. "You could have beat me down with a feather, truly, because she didn't seem the kind, and I never would've expected it. But a friend in high places is better than a penny in your purse, I always say." Doll nodded sagely, inviting Astell's agreement.

"What did you think was my doing, please? What has happened to her? Speak plainly, I beg of you."

"She's *gone*, ma'am, I don't know how much more plain I can be, and I thought you had your hand in it. She's bailed. Yesterday, it was—all of a sudden that fine coach wheeled in here, scattering everyone every which way, why I was nearly run down, I tell you. That same coach as you came in just the other day. Now, I didn't see inside last time, but since I was almost run over when it came back yesterday—I was that close—I could see *her* inside, such a fine lady, she was. And then that fellow was with her, all sure of himself . . . The same one who brought you here the other day. He is such a one, I dare say, that black man, so well turned out . . . He sprang right out of that coach and was demanding Mr. Fell—no one would do for him but the keeper himself, and Mr. Robinson was mightily offended at that . . .

"But that strange fellow, he went straight in to the keeper's house, and then after a bit out he came again, waved to the coachman, hopped back into the coach, and off they went, back wherever they came from. And she was bailed, quick as that—your girl, that is, your friend. I hear she's to be transported—whether or no that's the case, that's what I hear. Off to Virginia, or to Barbados, or to one of those places, God help her. I imagine she'll be sold off there quick as lightning, but at least she won't be hanged at Tyburn. You can be sure a deal of money has been spent on fixing all this up, that's for certain. And for all that he had nothing to do with it, Mr. Robinson's got plenty of rhino out of the deal, so he'll keep a still tongue in his head. He's been in drink ever since."

Doll stopped suddenly, having come to the end of her tale. But then, as if needled by her conscience, she added, "He can be very generous, can Mr. Robinson, that's the God's truth, and to be honest, I've had a drink or two today myself. But it's the season, you know, and a drink or two is most cheerful. It's very welcome in all this cold." She assumed a look of virtue, or what passed for virtue with such a woman in such a place.

And with that, the ward-woman slipped away, leaving Mary Astell standing quite alone in the postern.

Twenty-Five

As Doll disappeared into the maze of the prison, Mary Astell realized that, while her troubles over Letty Pyke were not quite done, they were coming to an end. Now, to reach that long-desired conclusion, she would have to make one final call.

As she made her way steadily from the city to Chelsea, Astell thought about the encounter that lay ahead. If the price for information at Newgate was dear, she wondered what sum Hortense Mancini might exact for revealing what role she had played in arranging Letty's reprieve. A woman like the duchess of Mazarin would have no need for a few silver coins, but she would want something.

Still, Mary Astell would do what she must. If Letty Pyke had indeed been saved from hanging, it had been the duchess of Mazarin's doing. And so, with her usual determination, Astell did not tarry on her journey back to Paradise Row. She did not hesitate as she crossed the Five Fields. She did not stop to see whether Sarah was anywhere to be found, nor did she made a detour to Ranelagh so that she could consult with Lady Catherine. Thus she soon found herself turning up the walk that led to Hortense Mancini's front door.

She hoped that she would encounter Mustapha, that she would be able to ask him about what had happened, but she was disappointed to see no sign of him. Instead, a rather elderly man greeted her at the door with exquisite politeness. The buttons of his livery strained across his portly figure—he was decidedly not one of the tall, elegant footmen who attended the Mazarin coach. Astell decided he must be one of the few long-time servants that still served in Hortense Mancini's household.

The manservant ushered her into the parlor. As she entered and much to her surprise, Mary Astell found herself relaxing into the room's warm embrace. The sensation was unusual, but not unwelcome—she rarely felt entirely at her ease anywhere aside from her own study. Settling into the agreeable room, she felt like a ship that had reached a calm harbor after a long and dangerous voyage. She struggled to remain on her guard.

Nothing could be greater than the contrast between the horrors of Newgate prison and the faded elegance of Hortense Mancini's parlor. Quite improbably, Astell found herself wondering what the canny Doll would make of the duchess of Mazarin—or, for that matter, what the duchess of Mazarin would make of the ward-woman.

And, then, as if such fantastical thoughts were not distracting enough, there were the birds. The parrots greeted her arrival with an impressive volume of shrieks and squawks—the parlor may have been warm and inviting, but it was not silent. While Astell studied the room's colorful inhabitants, her head swiveling from one end of the room to the other, the three parrots stared at her, their heads bobbing in unison.

So intent was she on the birds that she did not hear the footsteps of the duchess of Mazarin as she entered the room.

"Ah, *Madame* Astell, what an unexpected pleasure," said Hortense Mancini. "We are honored to welcome you here once again. I am afraid that Saint-Évremond has just gone—he will be disappointed to have missed you." She sank gracefully into the chair opposite Mary Astell, examining her guest with some amusement before turning to her companion. "Nanon, will you arrange for some tea?"

Astell had been so focused on the elegant figure of Hortense Mancini that she had not seen her silent attendant. Nanon withdrew at once from the room, leaving the duchess of Mazarin alone with her caller.

"That is not at all necessary, Your Grace," Mary Astell said.

"The tea is certainly not necessary—on this point, if no other, we are in absolute agreement, *Madame* Astell," Hortense Mancini replied, "but it is very pleasant nonetheless. And, I must say, all the more enjoyable for being superfluous."

As she spoke, the duchess of Mazarin watched her guest struggle to draw her eyes from the brilliantly plumed parrots and their antics. "Nor are *they* among life's necessities," the duchess added slyly, "but they are quite amusing, *n'est-ce pas?*"

"They are most impressive, Your Grace, but I am afraid I have not come for such diversion." Astell could hear a note of stiff constraint in her voice and regretted it as she saw the glint of humor in the duchess of Mazarin's eye.

"Of *course* not, *Madame* Astell, of course you have not come to be diverted. I would never accuse you of such frivolity."

Astell pressed her lips together sternly. "I have come to confirm what I have learned just now, though I can hardly credit the truth of the tale I have been told," she began.

"Oh, *hélas!* Whatever dreadful rumors are whispered about me now, I wonder?" Hortense Mancini smiled with delight and then learned closer to her guest. "I am far too old for scandal, surely, *madame—nous vivons ici une vie très calme*, do we not?"

Ill at ease, Mary Astell did not know quite how to reply. The woman seemed not only to read her very thoughts but to find them highly amusing as well. And, then, it also seemed to Astell—though she could not be certain—that Hortense Mancini spoke with a more pronounced accent and a greater sprinkling of French phrases than she had on the occasion of their previous encounter, that she was performing for the occasion, that she relished her performance, in fact, and that she was diverting herself at Astell's expense.

Nanon's return signaled the entrance of the tea table and all its paraphernalia. "Ah," sighed the duchess of Mazarin. "*Merci*, Nanon."

While Madam Mancini gave her full attention to the elaborate process of tea-making, Astell found her attention returning to the parrots. The green and blue bird, the one named Pretty, was becoming particularly animated. After an impressive number of shrill cries and deafening screeches, she glared at Astell with suspicion before retreating into her cage, turning her back on the room and its occupants.

"There," sighed the duchess, who had paid no attention to the birds. She sank back into her chair, holding a porcelain bowl to her lips and sipping the fragrant tea. "And now, Mrs. Astell, what is it you have been told? I almost fear to ask." She shuddered dramatically, then laughed merrily. "I trust you have not come here again in search of young gentlemen!" She eyed Astell over her bowl of tea. Hortense Mancini's gaze was as calculating as Doll's.

Astell refused to be drawn. "I have just returned from Newgate, Your Grace," Astell began, "I hoped learn something of the young girl about whom I spoke to you on the occasion of my last call—the foolish young girl who had come to Paradise Row in search of her husband. But instead of finding her there, I discovered that *you* were there yesterday, or so at least I was told. I can hardly credit this tale, but if what has been reported to me is true, then it seems you have somehow managed to save the girl's life. I need hardly say that my informant at the prison may not be entirely creditable, but I have reason to believe her."

"Oh," said the duchess of Mazarin, waving her hand airily, much as both the Newgate turnkey and the ward-woman had done earlier that day. But since Hortense Mancini was comfortably seated in her parlor, and since she had not consumed a great quantity of brandy, the action did not unbalance her. At the same time, her gesture managed to be both eloquent and elegant, not at all dismissive or contemptuous. "Yet the girl was not in prison simply for being foolish, now was she, Mrs. Astell?"

"No, Your Grace, as we both well know. She was accused of the most horrible of crimes, and while I do not believe her to have committed the offense for which she was condemned, I acknowledge that she was guilty in the eyes of the law. Guilty or no, she suffered a great deal for her folly, and if you have saved her life, that is nothing to discount."

Hortense Mancini's dark eyes were steady as she studied her guest. After a few moments of silence, she spoke. "Whoever he was, the man who seduced her and abandoned her, he accomplished her ruin, did he not? Did he marry her, I wonder? Probably not, but, then, who can say? Well, that is all in the past, and perhaps all will go smoothly now for her." She shrugged and then continued. "In any case, I have not done so very much, *Madame* Astell. I may be terribly old now and no longer quite *à la mode*, but I can still rely on the devotion of a few dear friends . . . If she knows the right strings to pull, a woman—even an old woman—can accomplish almost anything. A little tug here, a gentle twitch there, and it is done."

"A young woman's life is a very great deal, Your Grace. I will not ask why you have intervened or how you have managed it, but I would like to know what will become of the girl now—I could find out very little at Newgate, only that she was no longer there, that she had been reprieved, and that she was to be transported."

For a time, the duchess of Mazarin was silent. She rearranged the tea things upon the cart, then refilled her small bowl and took another slow sip. Astell watched her carefully. If the duchess of Mazarin chose to amuse herself at Astell's expense, toying with her as the price for information, she could expect more jests.

But Hortense Mancini seemed to drop her pose, at least for the moment. Still looking at the tea table, she said, "Yes, the girl has been reprieved, and I believe that she is now on her way to a ship that is soon to set sail—for the West Indies, I take it, for Jamaica, that is, or perhaps Barbados. It makes no difference, really."

"The ship's destination may make no difference, Your Grace, that is true, but the girl will not hang. She will live. That is quite a difference. But, I pray you, will she be sold there?"

Startled, the duchess of Mazarin looked up. "Really, *madame*, I wonder who might have suggested such a thing to you! What kind of question is that? 'Will she be *sold* there?' *Mon dieu!* She was properly reprieved—a warrant was signed, and the departure fee for her release from the prison was paid—paid and then some, I might add. I can also assure you that her passage to the West Indies has been paid. No shipowner will have a claim against her for the cost of her transportation. There will be no need for her to be 'sold,' as you choose to phrase it. And she has even been provided with a small stake to be given to her upon her arrival—some care has been taken to arrange all this on her behalf.

"If she survives the passage, she will not starve, or at least she will not starve for a lack of money. She will have enough upon which to live for at least a while. She may find a willing husband in the colony, though who knows whether that would make her or mar her?" Hortense Mancini poked again at the delicate objects on the tea table for a few moments before adding, "Let us hope that experience has taught her something, *Madame* Astell—perhaps she will take this opportunity to make something of herself."

"Let us hope so, Your Grace. But you underestimate yourself—your act of generosity is to be commended. You had no reason at all to interest yourself in the girl or in what might become of her."

"Oh, phoo," replied the duchess of Mazarin, once more waving her hand, this time as if to ward off Astell's words. "I protest, *Madame* Astell! To charge me with such crimes! Kindness? Generosity? Disinterest? I proclaim myself to be innocent of all such charges! The whole enterprise has been very amusing, far more entertaining than any play I have seen recently . . . It has been even more diverting than a successful night at the basset-table. I have not had such an adventure for many years now."

Hortense Mancini sighed dramatically before continuing. "And we must admit the possibility that the girl will not survive the rigors of the voyage or the perils of the wilderness, so who knows?" As she looked at Astell, she raised her right eyebrow, once again assuming a mocking tone. "Besides, Mustapha has taken a keen interest in you and your affairs. He would have made my life a complete misery if I had done nothing—"

"You have saved a life, Your Grace."

"And you, Mrs. Astell? Have *you* not saved a life?"

"No, Your Grace. I am afraid that I have saved no one. Despite my efforts, I was of no real help to the girl, and I cannot even say that I acted out of a generous heart. I sowed sparingly rather than bountifully. The little that I did for her was done grudgingly, of necessity—I was never a cheerful giver."

At this, Pretty looked over her shoulder and let out a triumphant squawk. Mary Astell was startled by the parrot's interruption, but she was more surprised by her admission—to Hortense Mancini, of all people.

Nevertheless, Astell was determined to continue. "I have begun to see that there is much about life I did not know." She paused, realizing that there was something more. "And I have also been forced to acknowledge that there is much that I still need to learn—I who presumed to teach others. That realization has been painful . . . but, then, that which causes us pain does us good—"

"Very commendable, I am sure," said the duchess of Mazarin, "but I cannot agree. The salutary effects of pain and suffering have been much overrated. Are you never angry, *Madame* Astell? Do you never rage at the cruelty and folly of it all? Are you never full of fury and despair? Surely mute acceptance is not the only remedy you can suggest for the pain?"

"We are only free when we are in control of our passions, Your Grace."

"Hmm" was Hortense Mancini's only reply. She sat silently for a while, sipping her tea and considering Astell's response. And then, lifting her eyes to look at her guest, she smiled a truly genuine smile.

"You are a very good woman, Mrs. Astell," she said at last.

And then, shaking her head, she sighed. "What a pity."

Tuesday, February 2, 1697

On Christmas Day, the Right Reverend Gilbert Burnet, bishop of Salisbury, had the honor of preaching before His Majesty at the palace of Whitehall. After the lengthy sermon, the king and members of the court received the sacrament from the bishop's hand.

Five days later, fourteen Newgate prisoners who had been tried and convicted at the Old Bailey during the December sessions were hanged at Tyburn, ten of them for coining offenses, the other four for theft.

Early in January, Charles Beauclerk, duke of St. Albans, paid a visit to the court at Versailles. The *London Gazette* published a lengthy account of his warm reception by the French king and noted that, immediately upon the duke's return, he was expected to wait upon His Majesty at Kensington.

In Parliament, the Commons passed a bill to prohibit the wearing of all wrought silks from the East Indies, the importation of which had caused great harm to English silk weavers and their trade. The Committee upon the Abuses of Prisons presented its report to members, who quickly resolved that the extortions and ill practices described therein were scandalous and illegal. The vexed question of how such extortions and ill practices should be corrected was left unanswered.

The Lords, meanwhile, finally passed the act of attainder against Sir John Fenwick for his part in the late assassination plot, and the king had quickly signed the warrant for his execution. Despite the desperate efforts of the conspirator's wife and friends to save his life, he was beheaded on Tower Hill.

At about this same time, news of the death of the countess of Radnor spread rapidly through the capital. In Chelsea, however, these reports were greeted with some degree of skepticism since the vigorous old woman was still regularly to be seen in her pew at All Saints.

The Reverend Mr. King continued to be occupied with matters of great import, for the precise location of Sir Thomas More's manor house was still hotly contested. Consequently, the rector paid little heed to rumors of the death of his distinguished parishioner, nor did he have any time whatsoever to consider a mystery that was much discussed in other parts of the village.

The mystery originated with a report of the loss of a silver pendulum watch in a tortoise-shell case—this valuable item was said to have been left in a hackney coach by a gentleman traveling from Chelsea to the city. The incident was particularly intriguing because the gentleman who reported the loss preferred to remain anonymous. The unidentified man placed a notice in the *Gazette*, promising that if the watch were brought to one Mr. Knight, goldsmith, under the sign of the Flower-de-Luce on Russell Street, no questions would be asked, and the bearer would be assured of all expenses and a guinea reward.

While this curious tale might be of no interest to the rector of All Saints, it had been taken up by the countess of Ranelagh, who was bored almost to tears by recent issues of the *Mercure galant*, where the pages had been filled by an on-going dispute carried on by two eminent gentlemen-scholars over the correct interpretation of a certain passage in *The Aeneid*. Without the diversion of the magazine's usual delectable morsels of gossip, scandal, and fashion, Lady Ranelagh amused herself instead by concocting many delightful stories about the mysterious gentlemen, the missing watch, and the circumstances of its loss, each version more fantastical than the one that had gone before.

Lady Catherine disapproved of such idle speculation, frowning at the amount of time Lady Ranelagh wasted upon this kind of frivolous nonsense. Even so, that distinguished lady found that she could not refrain from herself contributing an odd detail—or two—to embellish the tales, much to Lady Ranelagh's amusement. Despite their best efforts, however, the mystery of the silver watch in the tortoise-shell case was never solved.

As for Mary Astell, she completed the work she had promised to deliver to Mr. Wilkin. As the month of January drew to an end, the printer had begun to set *A Serious Proposal to the Ladies, Part II: Wherein a Method Is Offered for the Improvement of Their Minds* into type.

Candlemas dawned clear and sunny but exceedingly cold. If old proverbs were to be believed, a Candlemas day that was "fair and bright" meant winter would "have another fight." Despite the worrisome thought that the terrible cold might yet last for some weeks, Mary Astell decided to take advantage of a break in the persistent frost and snow to go into the city, where she spent a pleasant afternoon with Mrs. Wilkin in the snug parlor above the bookshop in St. Paul's Churchyard.

Although she had not intended to do so (Astell was not a woman prone to confidences), she found herself revealing her plan to found a charity school for girls in Chelsea, a project that Mrs. Wilkin heartily endorsed. Indeed, so delighted was she with Mary Astell's ambition that the printer's wife agreed to attend the Candlemas service at Mr. Wilkin's preferred church, St. Botolph's, without a word of protest.

As Mary Astell crossed the stone bridge over the Westbourne on her return to Chelsea, she found herself thinking not about her charity school nor about her visit with Mr. Wilkin and his family (much less about the mysterious gentleman who had lost a silver watch), but about Letty Pyke.

Before setting out for the city, Astell had received a message from the duchess of Mazarin with some news—after a delay of several weeks, Letty had sailed at last. She was one of a number of reprieved felons on board the *Elizabeth*, bound not for the West Indies, after all, but for the colony of Virginia. In her note to Astell, Hortense Mancini explained the reason for the delay—merchants from Jamaica, meeting with the newly appointed Lords of Trade and Foreign Plantations, had refused to accept the ship's load of Newgate felons pardoned for transportation because, they claimed, "persons of bad character are not wanted in Jamaica." Nor were these "jail-birds" wanted in the colony of Virginia, the duchess had written, but to Virginia they had been sent, Letty among them.

Astell was not certain how long the voyage to Virginia would take. While she now knew at least something of what conditions were like for prisoners in Newgate, she wondered whether Letty's confinement in the last few weeks, when the prisoners' destination was still uncertain, would have been any better. Would the girl be healthy enough to survive the perilous journey? And if she did survive, what would she endure in the colony once she arrived? What would become of her? Astell could not imagine, and she asked herself whether it might not be better, after all, if the unfortunate girl did not survive the sea voyage.

Such were the thoughts that occupied Mary Astell during the last part of her return trip to Chelsea. Despite these worries, she walked quickly, her energy never flagging, and she was soon approaching the small house on Paradise Row. She was just turning onto the front walk when Sarah flung open the door, her eyes as wide as they had been several months earlier, when Letty Pyke had first been found lying in a crumpled heap just outside the gate.

"Oh, Mrs. Astell," Sarah said. Despite her evident excitement, she did not shriek or yowl. Her unaccustomed restraint demonstrated something of the transformation in her behavior during the last few weeks, the result of Mrs. Methuen's continued influence upon her. The girl was no longer consumed by discontent and driven by rebellion. Astell had begun to think that something might be made of her yet.

"Whatever can be the matter now?" asked Astell, as she entered the hall. She might once have asked this question with more than a trace of annoyance in her voice. Now, however, she was able to address the girl without vexation.

"Such a wonder, ma'am," the girl replied. "You will just have to see for yourself—you will be amazed!" With that, Sarah headed back to the kitchen, but before she disappeared, she turned and nodded toward the staircase. "I have put her up there, ma'am, in your study. I thought it would be the most congenial place for you both, and she seemed to take to the idea at once."

Filled with trepidation, Mary Astell slowly mounted the stairs, worried about what new problem might await her. She slowly pushed open the door to her study.

The parrot was not large, nor was it flamboyantly colored—at first glance, in fact, the creature seemed rather demure, with a charcoal-colored back and wings and a soft, silvery underside. The scalloped feathers on its head and neck were edged in white, the beak black. But then, as the bird turned on its perch, Astell caught the brilliant flash of a crimson tail.

A small, handwritten card was attached to the birdcage next to the tiered stand on which the parrot perched. "I have been informed by Mustapha that her name is Prudence," wrote the duchess of Mazarin. "She has just arrived from Africa, and he assures me that this is the most intelligent of all the several species of parrots."

The ash-colored bird watched with great interest as Astell read the note. "Prudence," Astell whispered. In reply, the parrot bobbed her head and clicked her tongue.

"Well, Prudence," Astell replied, reaching out slowly with her right index finger. She gently stroked the soft feathers on the side of the bird's head.

And then Mary Astell smiled.

Maps

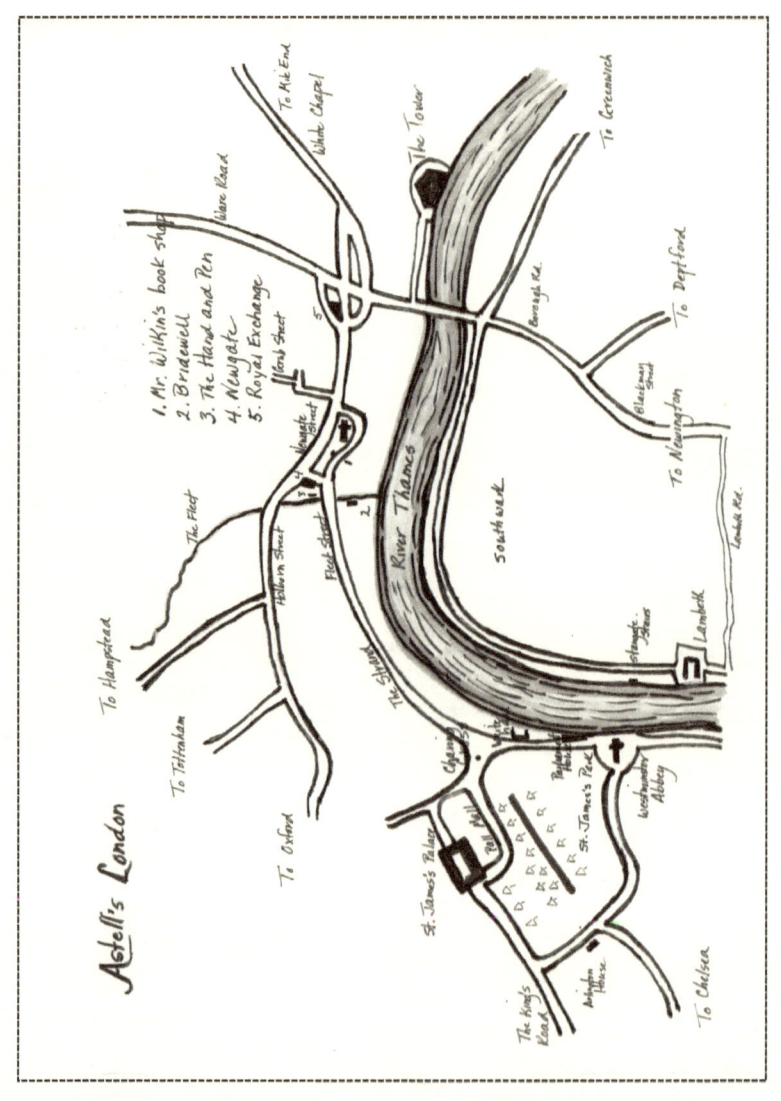

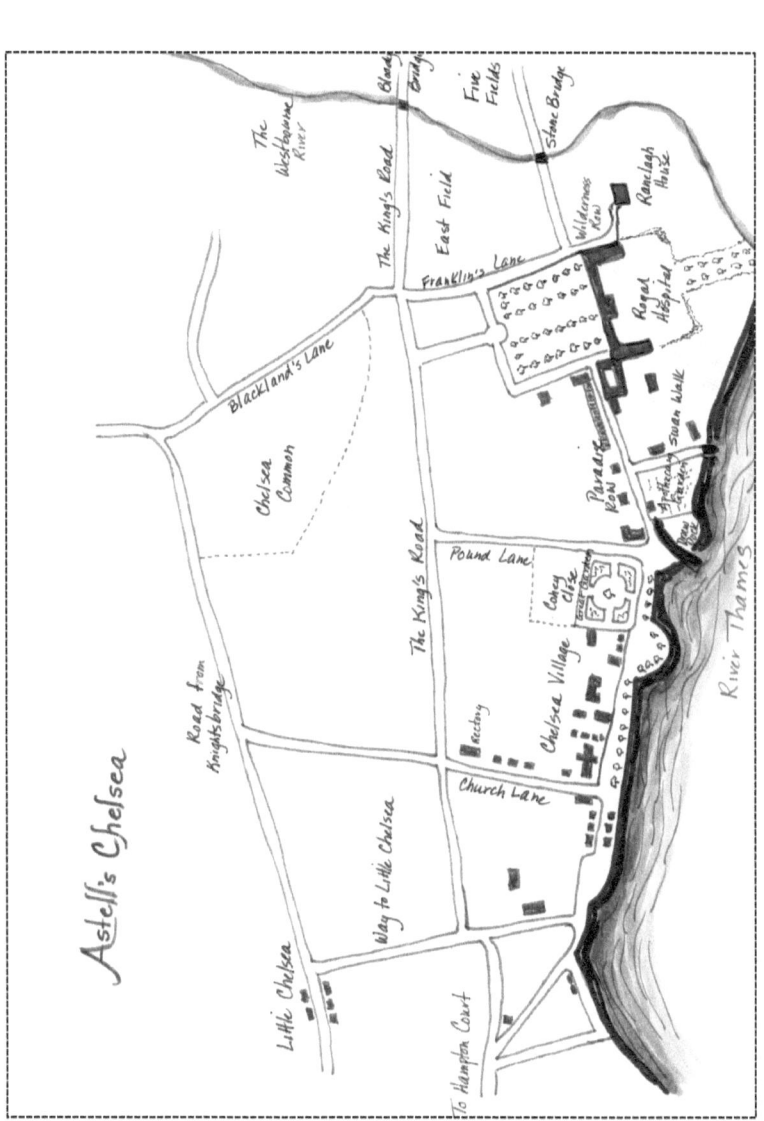

Astell's Chelsea

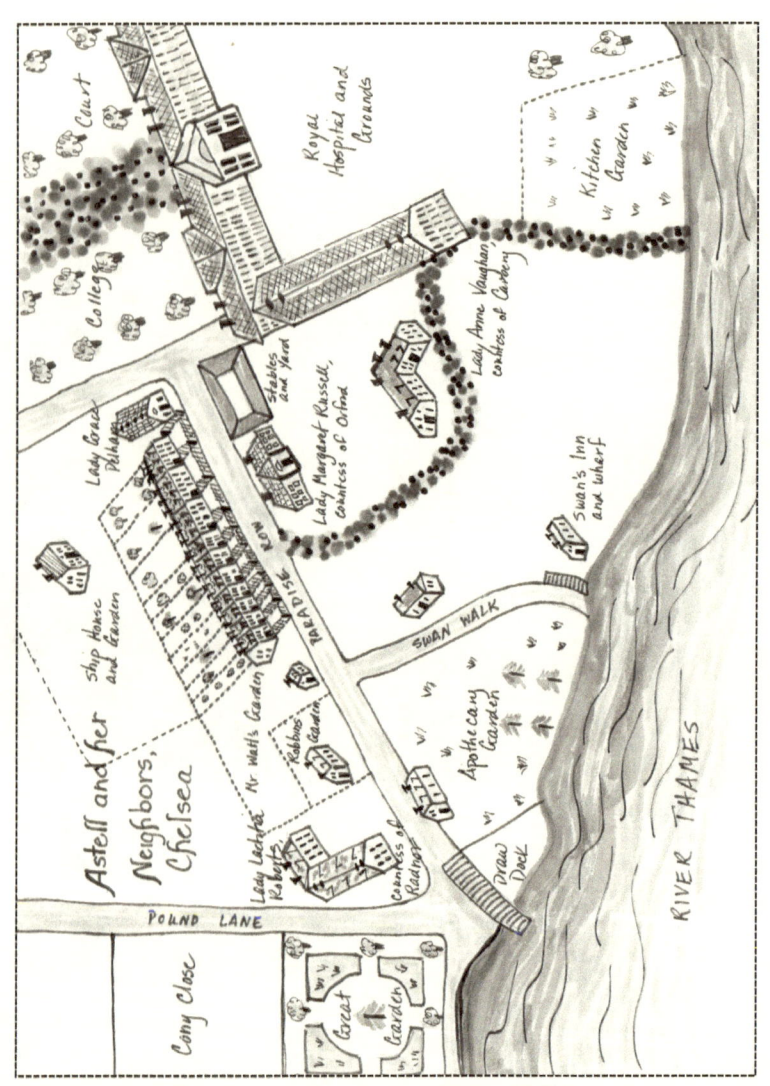

Astell and her Neighbors, Chelsea

Cony Close

POUND LANE

Court

College

Lady Gerard Palace

Ship House and Garden

Lady Lechere Rabutz

Countess of Radnor

PARADISE ROW

Mr Watt's Garden

Rabbos Garden

Stables and Yard

Lady Margaret Russell, Countess of Oxford

Lady Anne Vaughan, Countess of Carbery

Royal Hospital and Grounds

Kitchen Garden

SWAN WALK

Apothecary Garden

Draw Dock

Swan's Inn and Wharf

RIVER THAMES

Great Garden

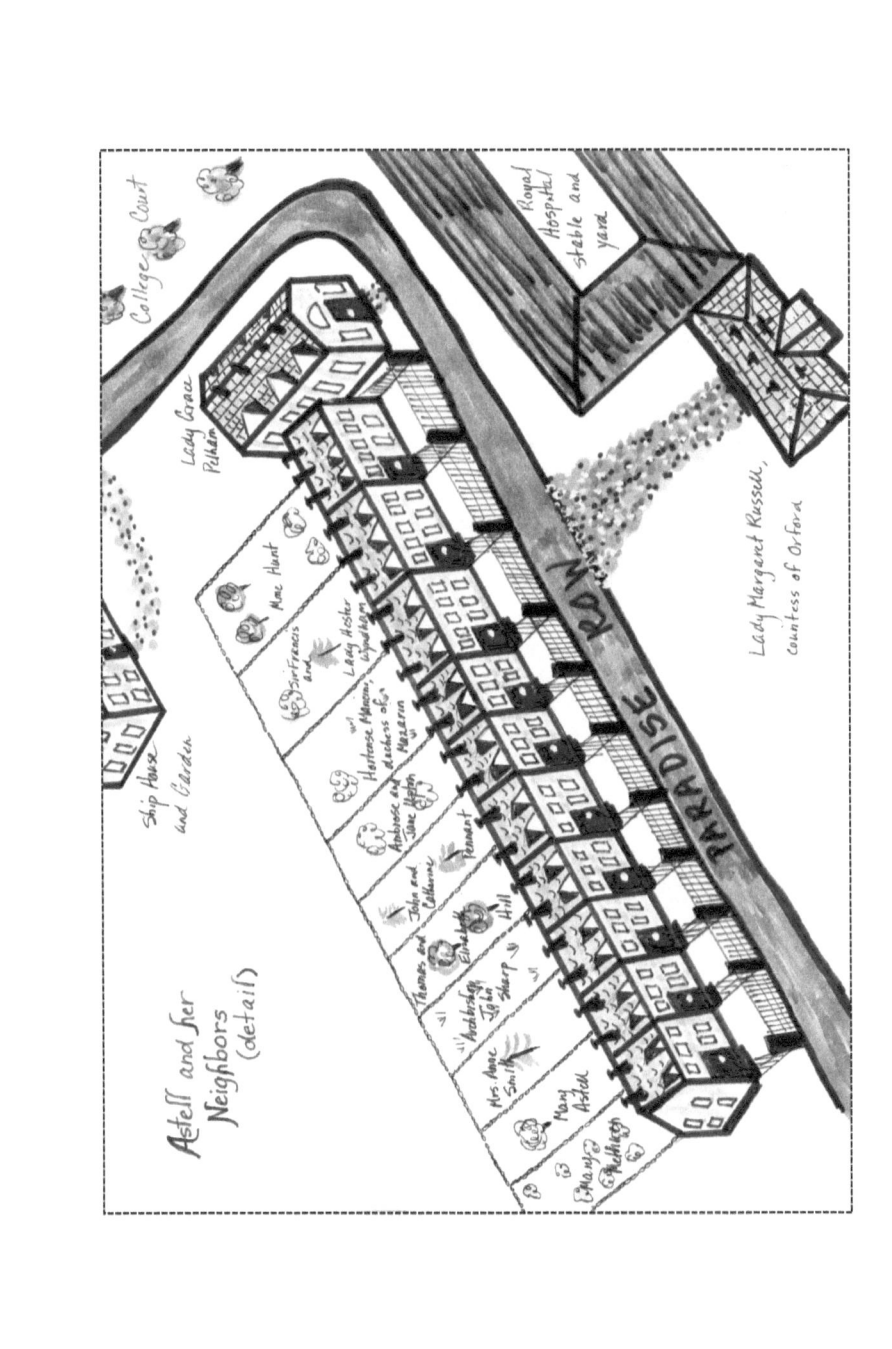

Astell and her Neighbors (detail)

College Court

Ship House and Garden

Lady Grace Pitkin

Mme Hunt

Sir Francis and Lady Astley-Cooper

Hortense Mancini, duchess of Mazarin

Ambrose and Jane Hyslop

Pennant

John and Catherine

Thomas and Elizabeth Hill

workhouse Job Sharp

Mrs Mme Smith

Mary Astell

Edward Brethrow

PARADISE ROW

Royal Hospital stable and yard

Lady Margaret Russell, Countess of Orford

www.ingramcontent.com/pod-product-compliance
Lightning Source LLC
Chambersburg PA
CBHW031546240626
47153CB00002B/397